JUSTICE IS FOR THE LONELY

JUSTICE
IS FOR THE LONELY

A Kristen Kerry Novel

STEVE CLARK

RORKE PUBLISHING

Rorke Publishing
101 Park Avenue, Suite 210
Oklahoma City, Oklahoma 73102

ISBN-13: 978-0-9903700-2-4
LCCN: 2015901417

Typeset by Sophie Chi

Printed in the United States of America

"But when the blast of war blows in our ears, then imitate the action of the tiger . . ."

—King Henry V, *Henry V*, William Shakespeare

ACKNOWLEDGMENTS

I OWE MUCH TO MANY for plowing through early and rough versions of Kristen's story, including Mort Welch, Steve Peterson, Kari Hoss, Terry Feix, Laura Johnson, and my daughter Kira. Former DA Wes Lane was particularly helpful with criminal procedure. Dave Hoof helped streamline this story. Carey, Brie, and Nyssa typed hundreds of versions without much complaint. Literary agent Scott Mortensen gave me great beatdowns.

My Texas brothers and sisters in the law will recognize that this adventure was plotted before citizens of that state lost many of their common law rights, but I elected to pretend that didn't happen. In a small way perhaps *Layne* demonstrates how much of the Sixth Amendment was surrendered.

Finally my wife, Jane, had to read every version over many years and provide constant encouragement. I pray she doesn't go blind before Kristen's story continues.

CHAPTER 1

Dallas
Saturday, February 9

SITTING IN CASWELL'S PORSCHE, Kristen knew that if she invited him inside, she would be inviting a contest, a competition, whether she extracted useful information from him or he got her clothes off. It was a contest she had no desire to enter. She couldn't stand the guy, would rather have a lobster crawl over her skin than him touch her.. And unfortunately waterboarding him was probably illegal.

Oh, what the hell. "Coffee?"

Whatever further boredom or boorish behavior she'd have to endure would be better than suffering through yet another "date." Dinner had been a washout, nothing accomplished, other than learning far more about him than she wanted to know. Maybe she could still pry some nugget out of him and have something to report to her boss without getting mauled.

She knew Tony Caswell thought the evening teemed with romantic possibilities. She let him think that, since this was part fishing expedition, part spy mission. That it was ordered by her client, Hospital Casualty, and boss, Pete McGee, made it only more disgusting.

"Find out what Stern's got planned. Is he going to hose us on Layne? Use Caswell, that annoying pup associate of his. He'll blab just to impress you. Then we'll know how to play our cards."

Nice try, McGee, she thought as she extricated herself from Tony's Porsche. Try as she might, she didn't get Tony to even talk about *Layne,* and what he did blather didn't impress her. She pretended to ignore the thinly veiled sexual innuendos and acted interested in his stories of past relationships, which all sounded like they were about the same woman, if they weren't completely made up.

Tony followed her to the front door with the enthusiasm of a stallion trotting to his breeding post. She already wondered if she had made a big mistake. But no way would she lose this competition. A draw maybe, but no defeat.

In fact, the Yellowstone volcano exploding and destroying North America was more likely over the next hour than getting it on with Caswell. But she'd already suffered a lunch and a drink after work with him and not learned squat. If she uncovered more nothing tonight, she'd have to stomach a fourth encounter. He'd certainly expect some form of gratification by then.

Sleeping with Tony sounded about as exciting as getting a Pap smear. No, a Pap would be better. No need to see her GYN the next morning. She just wished she'd tried harder to pay for her half of dinner.

"I've got a 15K early tomorrow," she said as she opened the door, hoping he'd get the hint.

Tony followed her in, his gait unsteady and his head bobbing about, reminding her of a bird dog sniffing up her rear.

Kristen forced a smile as she flicked on lights. "Cappuccino?"

"Rather have brandy, love."

The toff English accent had lost its cuteness long ago. It might have worked better if he used it all the time. At least it wouldn't sound quite so phony.

"Sorry, I don't have any."

"Got whiskey? Pour it in my coffee."

The last thing Tony needed was more to drink.

As she headed for the kitchen, Tony checked out the first floor, scanning books and curling his nose, as if allergic to literature.

"Dickens. Trollope? You read this crap?" he called out in a voice unnecessarily loud, the accent now forgotten.

Crap? Dickens? She loved Dickens. *Bleak House* reminded her of some of her cases—modern versions of *Jarndyce v. Jarndyce*. She wondered if being obnoxious was his way of acting like some bad-boy seducer. It wasn't working. If possible, things had deteriorated since dinner. She was having trouble finding anything positive about the man. *He doesn't smell bad* was the only thing she could come up with.

Apparently bored with her library, he strolled to the kitchen. He tried to make some small talk as the coffee finished brewing—about trading in his Porsche for a newer model—while his eyes wandered over her clothes. The invitation inside had revved him up several more RPMs. She poured an ounce of Glenfiddich into his mug. He grabbed it from her, quaffing the brew like Pepsi. He made an exaggerated "Ah!" sound, exhaling booze breath. She withdrew her mental comment that he didn't smell bad.

It just keeps getting better and better.

She had planned on sitting at the kitchen table, but Tony beelined back to the living room, tossed his coat on a chair, and plopped on the couch. He didn't look like he wanted to discuss symbolism in Victorian fiction.

Kristen sipped and followed him. She leaned against the mantle, trying to act pleasantly curious. She needed to find out more about the patient, the unfortunate Brook Layne. The longer the comatose plaintiff survived, the bigger the risk to their clients. Vegetables are expensive to keep. "Do you guys have a good estimate how much longer Layne might live?"

Tony's slow-moving eyes made their way to the general vicinity of her face. "You are so beautiful. I could live a long time in bed next to you."

Her face started to reveal a look of total disgust, but she managed to keep it blank. *"Find out what Stern's firm is going to do . . . whatever it takes,"* Pete had said. Unfortunately he hadn't added, "Within reason." Even Pete would have to admit that three hours with Tony Caswell pushed the boundary of *reasonable.*

She tried again. "Does Stern want to hire joint experts with us? Maybe a cardiologist? Or a heart surgeon?" She set her coffee cup on the mantle.

He patted the empty space on the couch. "Sit. And we'll talk."

Kristen stared at Tony, as if seeing him for the first time. He wasn't bad looking, though he was too short for her. His hair was already receding, but his thick beard, shaved moderately close, was an attempt to look like a *GQ* model.

"I've sat all night."

He plunked his mug on the coffee table and, surprisingly limber, he rocketed up and sauntered to the fireplace. The way his shoulders rolled reminded Kristen of a bad Cary Grant impersonation.

He moved to within inches of her. Even in flats she was looking at the top of his head. His right hand crept around her, as if he thought she wouldn't notice. The left remained in his pocket.

Ambition and pride had carried her here. She wanted on *Layne* badly enough to follow orders. Victory would cement her career. She might someday be the female Joe Jamail or Racehorse Haynes—the greatest lawyers in Texas history. A blown knee had ended her first dream of becoming an All-American small forward, but you didn't need knees to be a great lawyer.

Sensing his fingers snaking up her back, she changed her mind. Partnership be damned. McGee had no right to pimp her. When Pete *suggested* she see Caswell, she should have said "No." Scratch that. She should have said, "Hell no." But she hadn't even uttered a polite "No thanks"—let alone resigned. Quitting would've taken guts.

Gutless wonder!

She bit her lip and looked off toward the curtains, trying to withstand the hand on her back.

Maybe she shouldn't be so hard on herself. Justice meant as much as ambition. Maybe more. She liked the two nurses who had cared for Pain Layne during his short stay in Adventist Hospital. They didn't deserve to take the fall or lose their jobs over the medical disaster that was obviously the doctor's fault. Caswell's client had put Layne in a permanent coma. If she had to listen to Tony's exploits for a few hours, to make sure Stern didn't double-cross the nurses, so be it.

Tony's clammy palm clamped her neck. His deformed claw of a left hand fumbled with the buttons on her blouse.

She looked around, trying to tune out the insanity. Think of the greater good. Think of England. Think of . . . anything.

The townhouse had been a good buy before the market got really hot. She'd leveraged herself into it after paying off her law school loans. The flax-colored walls should have more yellow. She remembered painting alone on Christmas Day. All alone. The Delacroix print drew her attention. Happy kids playing in a Paris fountain. She bought it because her shrink had one in the waiting room, and Kristen found it soothing.

His fingers tried to massage the tension in her neck, tension put there by those very fingers.

Her psychiatrist had said, *"Take chances. Get out of your shell. And remember NMNS."* *Not Mary, Not Shit.* The problem with taking a chance tonight was she didn't like Caswell. She couldn't take him seriously—not his stories of world travels, nor his clumsy seduction. And when she'd asked other women about him, what she'd heard hadn't been good. *Creep* and *weirdo* were the kindest descriptions.

NMNS. Right! NMNS meant she didn't have to tolerate this. She blinked as if coming out of a hypnotic therapy session and looked down. Her blouse was open. She checked out her bare abdomen. Not bad considering she billed two thousand hours a year and helped coach a kids' basketball team. Tomorrow she would run a 15K two minutes off her pace in college. But she had little social life, so maybe her accomplishments weren't so impressive. *Oops.* She'd slipped into a negative thought. *Wake up!*

"No."

He shushed her, like she'd violated "time out" rules.

The last button popped loose.

She twisted, trying to spin out of his grip.

Staring at the engineering complexity of her bra, Caswell held on to her neck tighter with his good arm. She was surprised at his strength. His right arm probably compensated for a shitty left.

He got two fingers entangled with the clasp.

Kristen managed to push his hand away and pulled her shirt together.

He kept his iron grip on her neck.

"Tony, please stop. Nothing is going to happen between us."

"You just came on to me to spy?" He smirked. "Trick me into giving away the firm's secrets? You would've given Stern a go, but he's married?"

Before she could conjure a reply, he ripped her dainty bra open.

She froze. Stunned.

He jerked her close, his mouth smothering hers. He tasted of coffee and booze. Mostly booze. Tony cupped her bare breast.

That did it. She wedged a palm against his chest and pushed. Hard.

"Tony, please go. Now."

He snickered, retreated, and glanced around for his jacket. "Whatever you say, babe."

Kristen clutched her shirt together and managed to draw in a breath, relieved he was leaving. *Hail Mary.* Her bra was ruined, useless now. It had been a rare expensive purchase made the day after her first victory in trial. She wondered if she could bill the client for it.

Suddenly, Caswell turned and stepped toward her, wrapping his right arm around her neck again, moving fast, too fast for her dull senses to react, levering her over his hip, and flipping her onto the carpet.

She landed hard on her butt, stunned. *Holy Mary and Joseph.* A lawyer at a firm supposedly working with her on the same case was bent on raping her.

Before she could get up, he was straddling her, on her, unzipping his slacks.

For that instant she lay paralyzed in disbelief, unable to move. He opened his pants and pulled his half-erect penis out of his briefs, thrusting it at her.

"Come on, doll. Suck it. You know you want it." The accent was back.

Kristen stared for a second at his dong, dangling in her face. They all looked ridiculous, but this one more so, maybe because she had such a bird's-eye view. He must have forgotten his Viagra, or the alcohol prevented it from going to full staff. She smelled cologne, and realized he must have splashed it on his crotch, just for this occasion. Like that would help.

He scooted closer. His ass rested on her belly, his dick inches away.

Although he had managed to pin her to the floor, he missed her arms. With a rush of adrenaline, she shoved him off. He fell backward, still holding his pathetic penis.

His head had bounced off the Chippendale coffee table, knocking over and breaking a mug, splashing coffee.

She quickly got to her feet.

His face flamed red. He managed to stand, snapping his wiener back into his briefs, but not bothering to pull his pants up.

"*Bitch!*" he screamed. His right arm flailed out behind his ear threateningly.

Was he going to hit her? When she'd left New Jersey, she'd sworn nobody would strike her again. If she let it happen, all that therapy would've been wasted.

He hesitated a second, and she used his mistake against him.

She jammed her thumb and fingers into his sternal notch. Special forces all over the world used the technique to disable an enemy. It could have undesirable effects, so she pulled up a bit, not wanting him throwing up on her carpet.

He crumpled backward onto the table again. Snorting and struggling for air, his hands clutched his throat.

She exhaled heavily, both out of fear and relief, thinking the fight over. Surely he'd leave after she basically humiliated him. Take his lumps and go. She waited a moment, expecting him to get up and concede failure.

Instead, he grabbed the biggest hunk of broken ceramic and threw it at her. "Whore!"

Still basketball quick, she dodged. The missile grazed her ear and stung. *Asshole.*

In disbelief she watched him get up, tug his pants to his waist, and advance toward her, his teeth locked, his jaw offset, making fists. She could run, and considered it, but decided the next woman Caswell assaulted might not have a second-degree tae kwon do black belt and Krav Maga training. He needed an attitude adjustment.

She retreated a few feet, gaining space and time to kick off her shoes. She balanced herself, assumed her stance, and blasted the heel of her hand at his throat, just missing a square-on blow that could have crushed his larynx. The shriek that emanated from her had to be heard a block away.

Her next move quickly followed, and she planted a foot in his crotch a moment later. She felt a nasty crunch, and he doubled over. She had been trained to break his nose next, and he was in the perfect position. Use her knee while holding the back of his head—but she stopped herself, unsure why. Maybe she didn't want blood spraying everywhere.

He toppled over into a fetal position, wailing.

She stood over him, daring him to get up. Hoping he would.

"Want some more? Come on, short stuff. I'm not even warmed up yet. Thought you could *rape* me? Bad idea."

His face scrunched, his eyes disappearing. After another minute of retching and squalling, Caswell wiped his nose and crawled toward the door, glancing back, looking terrified she might follow.

She buttoned up. The altar girl in her wondered whether she should help him. Call an ambulance? Would he pass out in her place? Have a cardiac arrest? *Please don't.* She'd rather be stretched naked on the rack than perform CPR on Caswell.

She trailed him for a second. It looked like he was breathing, but his bright red face scared her. She felt awful, even though the guy deserved it. In her entire life, she'd never hurt anyone, except by accident in the gym.

Before she could decide what to do, he managed to grip the doorknob and pull himself up with his good arm. He turned his back to her, struggled to zip his pants, and then staggered out, barely able to place one foot in front of the other.

He said something that sounded threatening, but Kristen couldn't pick it up through his warbling. She locked the door behind him.

CHAPTER 2

TONY CASWELL SOMEHOW REACHED his car, bent at the waist and gasping, fearing each step would be his last. This posture helped keep the jewels from being jostled. Kristen's blood-chilling martial arts scream echoed in his head, only matched by reverberations of his wail. He leaned against the Targa door, trying to breathe.

His normal hand fumbled inside his pants for the key. Even this small movement reinforced the agony. He wasn't sure he should—or could—drive, but didn't want to collapse in the street.

He caught his reflection in the window glass. His face looked purple, and it frightened him. *Am I going to fucking die in front of this whore's house?*

He realized the blow to his crotch may have hit the vagus, the cranial nerve that wandered all the way to the gut. It was sensitive enough that bowels, lungs—everything—could shut down.

The courtyard around Kristen's townhouse swirled.

He had to get a grip.

Breathe.

After a minute, Tony opened the door and tried to sit in his Porsche without his balls touching the seat. That proved impossible.

The pain shot from his groin into his belly. He feared he might throw up all over the beautiful leather, so he faced his head out the window.

His throat threatened to close. The spit he tried to swallow stayed mostly in his mouth. While his good hand held up his smashed balls, his bad one searched around his Adam's apple. The worst pain seemed left of dead on. He probably wouldn't die. Probably. Some air reached his lungs, but the distress made him retch. He coughed out something disgusting, but somehow managed to start the car with his left claw.

As he often did when he had to use his left arm, he cursed his parents, who were in Jakarta chasing oil deals when Tony was born, leaving the delivery in the hands of an incompetent Indonesian obstetrician. Erb's Palsy they called it, meaning the shoulder got stuck in delivery. Pulling his head out of the birth canal had ripped nerves from his spine. He hid his atrophied hand when he could, and blamed his greedy parents, who were too busy to fly to Australia for a real doctor.

More retching carried a disgusting mix of booze, gastric juice, and coffee. He spat fearing he could aspirate crap into his lungs. A pulmonary arrest outside a hospital would be fatal. Even if he didn't quit breathing, he could get a nasty form of pneumonia. With his luck it would be resistant staph and he'd die of sepsis next week. At this point, it was almost something to look forward to.

After a few more breaths of dry Texas winter air, his brain cleared enough to weigh his options. Crawl back to Kristen's door and beg for help? More likely she'd hammer him again just because he'd seen her tits. Or find an emergency room? Methodist Hospital wasn't far, but they would ask questions. Lots of questions.

The truth could eventually get him charged with attempted rape. She had said, *"No."* And he sure didn't want to complain about getting beat up by a girl. If that got out, he'd be a laughingstock for years.

The ER would call the police, regardless of the story he invented. Even if he claimed to have been mugged in some random parking lot, the cops might press him for details—where he'd been, whom he'd been with. A hospital sounded like a bad idea.

He could drive home, ice his nuts, and hope tomorrow would bring some relief, if she hadn't already called the police and they'd showed up at his door. Her torn bra and the scratch on her ear might be enough to get him arrested or at least questioned. Again not good for the rep.

One more alternative. His sister, a nurse at Texas Medical Center. She might have a drug stash. She lived way up the Central Tollway, north of the LBJ. It would take half an hour, but she'd be with him, if things got worse.

Jennifer was the only reason he stayed in Texas. Whenever her brother got knocked down, she was there to pick him up. His mom was out chasing gigolos in exotic lands. Dad had returned to Britain after churning money in Houston. England had been the low point of Tony's life. Boys at Harrow, sons of earls and MPs, had teased him without mercy about his hand and ineptitude at sports. More than one had pulled his pants down and bent him over. College in Houston was better only because he knew nobody and kept to himself.

He managed to hit the number for Jennifer on his phone. Voice mail. More crap burbled up into his throat, scaring him. He wasn't able to choke out a message. He could drive there anyway, but if she wasn't home it would be a waste of time.

The downstairs lights went off in Kristen's townhouse. She was going to bed while he flirted with death. The thought of hiring some gangbangers to rape her in a parking garage floated by. Squeezing off a clip from the Beretta he kept in the glove box sounded like fun, right through her living room window. But he would be suspect number one, since he'd flapped about his hot date to everyone in the firm. *Too bad.*

He tapped the gear paddle into drive, still unsure what to do, where to go. Sometime between blows he'd figured out she was just using him to get info—she'd likely been told by Pete McGee to go out with him.

Polite rejection wouldn't have been surprising. She had every incentive to string him along, but why go raving nuts over a little tit-grabbing? "Little" certainly applied to the bitch. An A cup for sure, though she had nice erect nips. She had looked like a crazy Amazon warrior, all buff and topless. The image and the sound that replayed in his head caused a shiver along his spine.

He decided to head home. Call it a temporary setback. Two hundred bucks down the drain. He'd taken the bitch to the Mansion on Turtle Creek, had bragged to the guys at the firm about his anticipated conquest. And it had been quite a boast, since nobody he knew had had any luck with the standoffish, loner Kristen Kerry. Assuaging a twinge of guilt, he assured himself the lonely girl would've been disappointed if he hadn't tried *something*.

At his firm, Tony only got trash nobody wanted to do. Kristen had already made partner at McGee's. She tried cases on her own. She was a rising star. But Caswell figured she had sucked her way to success and was too stupid to appreciate his sophistication. Tony doubted she'd even been to Paris, let alone lived on the Left Bank. Still, if things had sparked, it would've been a coup to have Kristen next to him in the bars frequented by lawyers after work.

He loosed a half smile. Had Tony seduced Kristen, the joke would have been on her. Although he was the senior assigned associate on the case, Tony had no idea about Stern's plans on *Layne*. Stern treated him like a dog begging for scraps, blocking his partnership.

Caswell had noticed Stern eyeballing Kristen at the first *Layne* hearing, licking his chops. That overdressed redneck thought getting laid was as important as winning the case. If Stern nailed Kristen, Tony would be humiliated. Glancing at his deformed hand, he wished he were Stern—tall, rugged, and confident.

He coughed up coffee and stomach acid he'd already aspirated. Crap, his chest hurt. Like somebody had performed an esophagus exam with barbed wire. Maybe he should get to a hospital.

Tony pushed the car faster. He tried to concentrate on something other than his distress. Perhaps *Layne* offered the opportunity to hammer both Stern and Kristen without risk to him. A crushing loss would take the shine off their careers. Feed inside information to the plaintiff's lawyer? Or he could even conduct his own investigation into the disastrous night Brook Layne spent at Adventist Hospital. Dr. Galway's story made no sense, although obviously Kristen's nurses were guilty. They had put Layne in a coma by their negligence. But he had practiced law long enough to know not to believe your own client.

He made it another mile when the burn in his balls worsened. He hadn't thought that possible. His bladder demanded relief. Tony pulled behind a dark Safeway. Unable to get out—at least not quickly—he rotated in the driver's seat and eased the zipper down on his slacks. His crotch screamed. He aimed just outside the doorframe. The first squirt felt like a red-hot nail driven up his urethra. To his horror, piss streamed a dull red.

Shit. I could lose my testicles.

Caswell hacked another blob of gunk, zipped up, swiveled back in, slammed the car door, and tapped the shifter. Despite the torment in his crotch—or maybe because of it—he jammed the accelerator and sped for Methodist.

He'd read every Raymond Chandler and Agatha Christie story. The perfect murder long intrigued him. He often thought he would've made a great detective, strolling the streets of 1930s L.A. or the villages of Devon.

Every criminal makes a stupid mistake. One stupid mistake that gets him caught.

But Tony was smart.

CHAPTER 3

Huntsville, Texas
Thursday, March 28

THE NEXT PRISONER'S FILE described an ugly crime. A young professional woman had been sexually assaulted, and then kidnapped in a bungled effort at extorting a ransom from her husband. Photos showed the victim's bruises and a bite mark on her left breast. Bad, but not as bad as it could have been, since the woman escaped within a day.

Diana Stern had seen far worse in the year she'd spent on the Texas Pardons and Paroles Board. She had wanted university regents, but the governor thought that appointment should go to a public school grad. She vacillated. Everyone deserved a second chance, but she knew this guy needed to be kept in prison. It all worked in the abstract, but Diana wouldn't want to spot Leonard Marrs on the street.

The door opened, and she closed the file. The other panel member looked up as she did, watching two burly guards usher in a prisoner clad in dungarees hanging off his shoulders, a size too big. He would have looked like every other one, except he walked erect, not slumped like most convicts. He was short, but to Diana most men looked short, compared to her husband's six-three frame.

Marrs carried an odd confidence where humility and pitiful remorse were expected. His nose and chin were small, his skin smooth.

With a fresh haircut and no sideburns, the man was almost pretty.

According to the file, Marrs came up for review two years ago and received a positive recommendation from the interviewing commissioner. Then the victim appeared at the meeting of the entire panel, weeks after the interview.

She described her pain, and how a knife at her throat felt. Marrs's bid for parole had tanked. His sixteen-year sentence after a plea bargain continued, a sentence Diana thought light as she read on. The woman probably hadn't wanted to relive the experience in front of a jury. Who could blame her?

Parole commissioners, usually ex-cops assigned to help the appointees with the process, lent insight on criminals. Diana didn't particularly like the commissioner next to her. A former Houston detective in his sixties, he wanted to keep prisons packed. She let him launch the usual questions to the prisoner while she tried to size up this strange man carrying the name of the God of War.

The prisoner handled the questions well. After all, he'd been through the process before. After a few minutes she asked Marrs, in her Texas aristocracy drawl, what he would do if paroled.

Marrs smiled. "I have a job lined up with my half brother. He's a food broker. I took accounting classes in college and—"

The commissioner cut him off. "Why did you commit such a crime? A man with your intelligence?"

Diana was annoyed, wanting to hear more about the prisoner's plans, not the usual plaintive confession, already boring after a year.

"My unstable home—"

"Are you blaming your parents?" The commissioner wrinkled his capillary-lined nose in obvious derision.

Geez, Diana thought. *He can barely get a word out.*

"No." Marrs swallowed hard. "It was entirely my responsibility. I'll never forgive myself, but I'm anxious to find a useful place in society."

Diana decided to jump back in. "How can we be sure you're no longer a threat to women?"

"I'll continue treatment."

"You have a place to live?"

"My half brother has a rental house I can live in."

"And you'll be making deliveries for him?"

"I have a spotless driving record."

The old man snorted and rolled his eyes. Diana thought it *was* a goofy response under the circumstances, but perhaps simply spontaneous. And the commissioner's attitude made her more sympathetic to the prisoner.

"You realize parole would require close supervision?" Diana asked, hopeful for an appropriate answer.

"I understand. And it should."

* * *

Back in her 1930s old-money Highland Park mansion, Diana decided she was actually getting better at separating the reprobates from those who should be given another shot. The short man with the pretty face impressed her with his sincerity and had undoubtedly suffered greatly in prison. The commissioner would fuss, but give in, and eventually the entire panel would go along.

Still, the victim's statement made her shudder.

She could assuage her guilt by getting Marrs assigned to Lyndon Zelner, the hardest parole officer in Dallas. Word had it, he could make murderers cry. Not that he ever came across any, since Texas executed them before they could dream of a parole board hearing.

She lay on the couch half-watching a Lifetime movie and nursing a beer. Whether it was her third or fourth didn't really matter, and neither did the movie. They were both only placeholders for the main event.

After interviewing dozens of parole candidates, flying from Huntsville to Dallas, and then driving the short distance home from

Love Field, Diana needed beer. She had loved beer from the first taste in high school and had won beer-chugging contests in college. One of the traits her husband once found delightful, but now sneered at.

When she'd gotten home, Diana had turned on the TV and seen Michael standing in front of a score of microphones for the six o'clock news.

Oh yeah. The Layne press conference.

So she waited and wondered when he'd make it home.

The case was a mangled mess of lawyers and defendants, and she could barely keep the facts straight, but it was in the news enough to help. It started simply enough—the Channel Seven sports anchor had gone in for elective heart surgery and was now a vegetable. The nurses blamed the doctors, the doctors blamed the nurses, all of them fending off the patient's attorney, and so a soap opera was born. And her husband, the illustrious Michael Stern, was in the middle of it, helping write the script.

She saw Rusty, her Irish setter, raise his head, then heard the back door from the pool open. She glanced at the clock. 9:45. Early for Michael.

Rusty bounded off to the kitchen to greet his master, and a minute later Michael was pouring himself a drink, ignoring her.

"You looked good on TV," she said, trying to sound sincere, trying to make the rest of the evening bearable.

At first, he didn't say anything. He walked next to the couch, and stared at the stupid movie.

"Thanks." He sipped his drink. Scotch and ice. "They're replaying it on the late news."

"Great. You only snarled at Pete McGee once on the six version."

"The man's a greedy, hypocrite. Worse than Bragg."

She started to argue about McGee, whose wife worked with her on the symphony board, whose little sister she had competed with on swim teams as a kid, but instead took the last swig of her beer. "I need a scorecard—which one is Bragg?"

"The scumbag for the broccoli."

Translation: *The lawyer for the victim.*

It wasn't hard for Diana to understand why Michael was known in the local legal community as the Prince of Darkness—though everyone else thought it was because he was better at hustling clients and had brass balls in the courtroom. She knew the real reason—he could be ruthless.

"So who's that woman?" she asked, trying to sound both curious and a little naive. It wouldn't work. She had been onto him a long time ago, and he knew it.

Again, he didn't answer right away. Instead, he loosened his already-loosened tie.

She waited.

"I don't know. She works for McGee."

I don't know. What a howler. He probably knew her dog's name. Diana looked away with the slightest smirk, kind of hoping he saw it. If he did, he didn't say anything.

She had spotted his expression when the woman in her early thirties stepped up to the microphones to answer a reporter's question that the two big-shot attorneys didn't want to—or couldn't—answer. She towered over her boss, McGee, and spoke with a calm, confident voice—a voice that kind of became the "wow" moment of the whole event. She'd swatted away the seemingly tough question like a hanging curveball, and now the reporter could only stammer a follow-up asking the woman's name.

"Kristen Kerry," she answered.

As well as she knew Michael's lustful look, Diana also couldn't help but notice the man in the background. A man she knew, but couldn't quite place his name. Not that she had asked when he'd "escorted" her into a storage room and lifted her little black dress up to have his way with her at the company Christmas party. If pressed, she might have come up with "Tommy."

"Who was that other guy?" she asked, playing half-dumb. "The one just behind you."

"Tony? I introduced you at the Christmas party."

And—*boom*—there it was. She remembered.

Tony Caswell. A new associate at Michael's firm. If she'd had a sixth margarita that night, it might have all been erased—the name, the frantic humping that was more like uncontested rape, the whole evening. But, no, she somehow retained enough to create a few guilty nightmares of the man with the withered arm pounding her like a desperate schoolboy.

What struck Diana as odd about Tony Caswell at the press conference was not the lustful look he had as Kristen Kerry fielded reporters' questions, but the murderous one. His eyes bore into the back of her head as if he were trying to make it explode. He looked like some potential mass murderer, eyeing his first victim.

"Where's Sarah?" Michael asked, looking like he wanted to go away.

"Spending the night with Becca, supposedly to study for midterms."

Diana was trying to be more lenient with Sarah, but they both knew Michael was better at balancing discipline and tolerance. Diana and Sarah often ended up at odds, with Sarah back-talking and walking off. It didn't help that their only child was so into sports—especially boring ones like soccer and softball. Diana should be proud, yet found herself perplexed. Why bunt? Just hit the stupid ball.

"Well, I think I'll take a shower," Michael said, heading toward the back stairs.

"Pretty weak excuse for a press conference—an amended answer?" Diana knew enough about law to know paperwork was usually meaningless. "Couldn't you have said something interesting? Like—*We admit we screwed up.*"

Michael turned back, rolling his eyes. "The guy was that station's sportscaster. We have to do all we can to fight the publicity everybody's giving the case."

Diana smirked. Michael would use any excuse to get his handsome mug on TV. He'd probably watch the rerun upstairs in his bedroom. There was a time when he might have invited her to join him in the shower. But that was another life, a few mistresses ago.

She'd often tried to pinpoint the time when things changed, and the best she could come up with was ten years ago at the country club dance when Diana had spent most of the night throwing up in the bathroom. When she finally found her husband getting drunk with a surgeon friend, the doctor hazily listened to her symptoms, poked around through her flimsy dress— practically feeling her up—and pronounced she needed to stop drinking.

When things didn't get better, instead of calling an ambulance, Michael called a cab and sent her home, alone, where her appendix later burst. The infection led to an abscess, which another quack didn't drain properly, and a second surgery that would leave Sarah an only child. Yeah, things went pretty much to hell after that.

Diana switched channels and stared at the TV, running part of the news conference again, wondering how long it would take her husband to make a pass at the tall, poised attorney at McGee's firm. Diana reluctantly gave her husband credit—the woman was classy— thick brunette hair pulled back, darling cheeks, and obviously fit, early thirties.

But Diana almost felt sorry for her. She would be the scapegoat if the case went to shit. McGee would throw her to hungry, muddy hogs to keep his clients. If she fell for her husband, she would get burned but good. Michael used women and tossed them away like crushed empty beer cans at a frat party. *Kristen Kerry.* Diana told herself to remember the name. That poor *chica* would soon get torn to shreds.

CHAPTER 4

Dallas
Tuesday, April 8

KRISTEN KNEW TODAY MIGHT be her last at Wright McGee. She was scheduled for a debriefing with both Pete McGee and Tammy Robberson, the adjuster for Hospital Casualty, Adventist's insurer. Robberson had been assigned to the Layne case.

Sitting at her desk she noticed her fingertips were white, but her heart raced faster as the meeting time approached. She had the credentials for another good job, but would anybody hire a crazy woman who beat a handicapped man half to death? Who might still be charged with felony assault?

Her doctor had invented an acronym. NMNS—Not Mary, Not Shit. It meant she was no Virgin Mary, but not a failure. Because she wasn't. But the saying wasn't helping her anxiety. Today, she felt like a failure. It was something that would have been easy for most women, stringing the guy along, teasing information out of him. She had to remind herself that he attacked *her*. Many women would have been raped that night. But she still felt guilty. She could've used a ninjutsu hold and ushered Caswell out the door without hurting him, but instead she'd expended anger from events fifteen years ago on a little guy with one good arm.

Six years. She had advanced at Wright McGee to partner quickly, skipping over other young associates. McGee appreciated her work and seemed to like her from the beginning. He called her a natural and sent her on bigger and better assignments. Trials on her own. Wins.

For weeks she had dodged questions about her spy mission. Today Pete would want to know all she had learned about Stern's plan. Would Stern blame the hospital's nurses or Layne for waiting too long to come to the hospital? Or God, for giving Layne a lousy heart? Was there any chance of cooperation between defendants? She sure didn't know and would have to confess her ignorance soon. Very soon.

The suspense was killing her. She got up, headed down the hall, and walked into Jenny Norton's office just as the associate had taken a huge bite of cinnamon roll. "Hey," Kristen said, plunking down in a chair.

"Morning," Jenny tried to say. She broke off a hunk of pastry and pushed it across the desk. Jenny was a forty-year-old former nurse, four years out of law school. She wore heels to work, promptly took them off, and went barefoot all day. Her hair sported spikes like a girl in a street gang.

Kristen snagged the pastry, mostly out of politeness. She didn't feel hungry.

"I'm giving you *Layne*." Kristen fixed her gaze on Jenny's coffee mug, which was decorated with a redhead screaming, *I'm a bitch in the morning*. "There's a meeting in five minutes with Pete and Tammy." Kristen doubted she had the authority to reassign the case, but was willing to give it a whirl.

"Huh?"

"I want out. You and Pete can handle it."

"I don't understand. You wanted *Layne* so bad." She blinked several times. "You were dynamite at the press conference. You've done the paper discovery."

Kristen put the chunk of roll down. "I have to stay away from Caswell."

Jen stared for a painful moment. "Don't tell me you slept with the little turd."

She pictured Caswell's slimy mouth, his fingernails digging into her neck. "Worse. He tried to rape me."

Jen got up, padded around her desk, and took Kristen's hand. "Are you okay?"

"I'm fine." Kristen smiled appreciation at Jen's concern. "But he may not be. I hit him in the throat. Then I took out his balls. I didn't hold back and I could have. I should have. After it was over, I almost called 911, but he crawled out. I heard he's missed a lot of work. He didn't say a word at the press conference and walks like he's got a corncob up his ass."

"Shit."

Kristen shook her head, trying to knock the memory from her brain. "I froze when he pawed me. I was stupid. My attention drifted away. He probably thought I wanted to. Then I told him *no*, but he kept on. I exploded. You know,"—she paused—"my anger issues."

Jen blinked, but to Kristen's relief, didn't lecture about her temper. "Doesn't sound misplaced—this time."

"I'm afraid he would've shot me at the press conference, if there hadn't been so many witnesses." She reached into her jacket pocket, retrieved the latest mysterious note, and handed it to Jen. "I've gotten four of these since our big date."

Jen studied the piece of plain copy paper with the letters *You're dead* pasted on it, likely cut out from a magazine. "Holy crap," Jen said. "Have you shown this to the cops?"

"If I do something, he could still press charges. My word against his, and he's got real injuries to back up his story." She pointed at the note. "He'd be too smart to leave fingerprints."

Jen crossed her arms. "He likely won't file charges now. But be careful. He's got a major problem."

"Seems to live in a fantasy world. One minute he's a super sleuth, another he's a world traveler." Kristen sighed. "If I get real sick, like in the next two minutes, can you make the meeting and take the depo tomorrow?"

"After all you've done for me? I wouldn't have lasted a month without you." Jen sat down again. "Let's see if I got the picture. Layne shows up, two weeks after heart valve surgery; routine lab work shows slow clotting from too much warfarin. Takes the drug for the valve to work."

Kristen nodded. "Yes. Blood's too thin. Layne's light-headed, nauseous, so the ER cuts his meds back and gets him admitted. Seen later by his cardiologist—Galway, Caswell's client—around eleven. Galway thinks he's stable, orders an echo and CT for the next morning. Dumbass could've gotten it done immediately, but wanted to go home." She took a bite of the roll.

Jen made a note and finished the story. "Plaintiff's theory is Layne had a slow-developing cardiac tamponade, with blood filling the sac and compressing his heart during the night. It should have been spotted by the nurses and Galway called so he could draw the blood off."

Kristen swallowed. "Yes, and for all the money the plaintiff wants, it's not that complicated. You got three players, plus Galway. A cute nurse named Robbie, worked a twelve-hour shift, six to six. Layne codes an hour after her replacement, a nurse named Nancy, comes in. The director of nursing—your old boss, Casey—was doing her monthly shift as floor super. Helps with the code. I've met our people. They're okay and don't deserve to take the fall."

"And Pain Layne, former Cowboy All Pro, is in a coma."

"We've got possible defenses. Sudden arrhythmia is one." Kristen smiled. "And we can blame Caswell and Stern's client. We can even pin it on the poor patient."

Jen, the former nurse, asked, "How could he have an arrhythmia that nobody noticed, when he was on a cardiac floor being monitored?"

"We think his wife unhooked him so he could shower."

Jen laughed. "Seriously?" She shook her head. "Good story."

"And in addition to what it costs to warehouse him, Bragg claims Layne was going to make millions when his TV show went national."

There was a rustle and jingling from behind Kristen, and suddenly Tammy stormed in, pointing a long red nail.

"I wondered why I never got a report about Caswell, then I find out you put him in the fucking hospital," Tammy screeched.

Panic rendered Kristen speechless. Although Adventist Hospital was the named defendant, Tammy was the real client. If they lost, Tammy's insurance company would pay the tab—so she had the right to dish out orders, assign or fire lawyers, and she wasn't shy about doing it.

Tammy stepped nearer, her nail coming dangerously close. "I know what goes on at every hospital and law office in town. Caswell was at St. Paul's in February. Could hardly swallow and was pissing blood. Emergency surgery barely saved his balls. They thought about a fucking trach until his swelling went down." Tammy drew a breath. "You were with him that night. Either you beat him up or he got mugged on the way home."

She didn't wait for a reply. When Tammy was excited, her high-pitched wail reminded Kristen of a puppy weaned from its mother.

"I have Pete assign you this case, ask you to use a little charm on a nice-looking guy, find out what he knows, and you beat the shit out of him?"

"He got out of line."

The button popped open on Tammy's stylish tweed jacket, revealing a jelly roll under her silk blouse and plastic boobs that wouldn't wiggle in a hurricane. "Jesus, sugar britches, you never been on a date? You can't tell a guy *no*, without putting him in the hospital? A poor bastard with one good arm?"

"He wouldn't take *no* for an answer."

Tammy scrutinized Kristen. "Are you a dyke?"

Kristen could feel the anger coming on, rising up alarmingly fast.

She closed her eyes, clenched her teeth, and shook her head.

"Then what's your problem?"

Kristen's vision clouded. Instead of Jen's office, she saw grotesque visions from her frequent nightmares. Ugly dwarfs chasing her. Her trying to fight off hundreds of them.

She barely heard Jen jumping to her defense. "Caswell's a creep. Harassed an eighteen-year-old runner at Klein Patton. Eighteen!"

Tammy pointed again at Kristen. "Your assignment was to find out whether they're going to double-cross us on *Layne*. Whether you fucked him was your business. Don't you understand Stern's firm is as much an enemy as that goddamn Bragg and his comatose client?"

Kristen turned her attention back to Tammy, resigned to taking a beating. "I guess I'm not very good at spying. Maybe you ought to put Jen—"

"I got lots of smart lawyers begging for work, but not many with great hair and gorgeous long legs. Even if you are short on tits."

Speechless, Kristen white-knuckled the arms of her chair.

Tammy blew a breath of exasperation. "It may be just as well. I heard Stern's last girlfriend quit his firm and threatened to sue for discrimination. Let's quit wasting time with the underling."

Kristen's gut knotted again.

"Now that he's on the prowl again, you're just the ticket, Kristen."

"You're not telling me—"

"Are you a virgin? At thirty-something?"

Kristen felt her face redden. Maybe it was time to go back to giving kids basketball lessons. It was all she could do not to stand up and tell Tammy to march her fat ass and fake boobs out.

"Girlie, all I'm telling you to do is keep him panting. String him along. This is a big opportunity. Biggest malpractice case ever in Texas. When we shaft the philandering bastard, you'll be the toast of Dallas."

The morning was going from bad to calamity. Instead of seeing Tony zWhile she absorbed Tammy's orders, her boss and partner, Pete

McGee, strolled into Jen's office. The man, the father figure, who'd promised Kristen six years before that they were all family, stood there in his three-piece suit, conservative as always, his hair cut like Caesar's in a Hollywood epic, a *Father Knows Best* expression on his face. He took a sip from a coffee cup.

"Tammy's plan is a home run," McGee said. "Stern's probably planning on blaming the nurses, leaving the big hospital with all the liability, and walking his dirty doctor."

Everyone nodded, as if he were a sage expressing great depth and insight, not caring if he had just said the moon was made of cheese and they should all take a bite.

Pete took another sip. "You know I don't care for Joe Bragg."

Jen smirked. "Don't like fat blowhards in Italian suits?"

"And I *detest* Michael Stern. He represents everything wrong with our profession. If anybody but Stern was defending the doctor, we'd be allies. This case has generated so much publicity, it cries out for a joint defense, hospital and doc working together."

Kristen nodded dully.

Pete exhaled slowly. "This time, Bragg's client isn't some Medicaid bum who wandered into our ER looking for drugs. He's got a former superstar on a feeding tube. This'll blow up on somebody. I don't want it to be us."

"Pete . . ." Kristen hesitated a second. "I got zilch out of Caswell."

Tammy rolled her eyes.

Pete didn't seem to notice. "I heard Stern hates that kid. Rumor has it he came on to Diana. Stern wouldn't share strategy with an associate on the way out. Might have fed you the wrong dope to trick us. Good thing it went nowhere."

Kristen guessed her job was safe for now. She had wasted a lot of time on anxiety, nightmares, and second-guessing. Caswell had almost lost his nards for nothing. And she had just gotten chewed out by a silicon floozy, who called her a dyke. All to be swept under the rug by the suave Pete McGee. Lovely. Just lovely.

Pete continued, "Stern'll see this case as a chance to glorify his greasy reputation and screw me at the same time."

"Sleazeball," Jen muttered.

"Kristen, if you can bait Stern into a unified defense—you know, sudden cardiac death nobody could've prevented, nobody did anything wrong—we can double-cross *him*. Tell the jury that the more evidence we hear, the more obvious it is Stern's client put Layne in a coma. Stern gets creamed and winds up chasing ambulances."

Jen mouthed to Kristen, *Sorry.*

Pete held up a palm. "I'm not asking you to do anything unethical or immoral. I put you on this because you're bright and not afraid of work. There's nobody in the firm I trust more."

So much for the happy *we're all family* horseshit Kristen had been fed when she signed on. She was beginning to suspect that Pete, who taught Sunday school at a Methodist church, was just as crooked as he claimed Stern was—only McGee was more subtle. She was getting the job because she was attractive enough to entice Stern. The implicit orders were obvious. Get Stern undressed and unaware.

She looked around for a spare legal pad on Jen's desk, so she could scribble her resignation.

But a second later, her competitiveness took charge.

Maybe she could tough her way through this, the way she'd slogged through everything else—or could figure out a way to get the job done without following their sick little game plan.

She recited to herself. NMNS. *Not Mary, Not Shit.* The girl who walked to a park every day in Philly to play street basketball with boys would not back down.

Tammy caught her eye. "Don't look so sad. He's damn good looking."

Kristen looked away. *Give me a fucking break.* She wouldn't care if he looked like a better-hung version of Michelangelo's *David*. She had the urge to tell Tammy that she should sleep with Stern herself, but guessed the guy had better taste and would turn her down even if she begged like a spaniel.

Pete raised his forefinger. "Distract him. If Stern's paying attention to you, we can sell him out when he's least expecting it. But be subtle. We don't want him getting suspicious and cutting a secret deal with the plaintiff."

"Right." Kristen tried to sound enthusiastic.

"And one more thing," McGee said, back to sounding fatherly. "Stern has no conscience. I'm not just saying that. It's literally true. He's capable of anything."

CHAPTER 5

O N THE THIRD HOLE AT Dallas Golf and Country Club, Michael Stern pulled out his Callaway driver, then wiped sweat from his right hand with a towel. Even before noon, the temperature flamed toward ninety, rivaling the humidity, with the oppressive combination compounded by the completely still air. The only sliver of hope from the weather's persecution was the presence of low black clouds building in the west that might electrocute them with lightning or deliver concussions by hurling baseball-sized hail.

Stern pointed down the course. "Sharp dogleg right, but reachable with a perfect shot."

Bob Russell, a bull-necked former college wrestler and claims manager for Standard Physicians Mutual—one of Stern's best clients—dabbed his forehead. His shirt clung to his powerful, sweaty torso as if he'd just stepped out of the shower. He jammed his tee and ball into the manicured turf between the blue markers, like he was stabbing the grass. "I guess rich guys like your father-in-law designed it to hook the suckers."

The jab about his rich wife conjured a fleeting image of the first time Diana had taken him to play at The Cage. She had been so gorgeous, and he had felt intimidated by the wealth surrounding him. Sometimes he would trade all the last few years' philandering and boozing for those first months with his wife. But it was too late now.

It wouldn't hurt to drop some pocket change to Russell. He couldn't stand the guy, but he was a paying client and his company insured Dr. Galway. The Layne case promised to be very profitable.

Stern watched Russell drive a straight shot 200 yards across the perfect Bermuda grass to the dogleg.

Losing at anything was abhorrent to the Prince of Darkness, who grew up on the bad side of a refinery town. People expected you to lose there, and he preferred not to do what was expected. With a high ball and cut, he could clear the trees and reach the green. Trees didn't get very tall in Texas, but these were high enough and close to the green. He'd done it before, but landing short in the woods would mean the round was over.

"Who's takin' Betty Layne's depo tomorrow? Caswell?"

Stern knew Russell was intentionally interrupting his concentration, but acted like it didn't matter. "I am."

"Why not send Tony? He's cheaper."

Stern forced a smile. He billed at twice the rate as Tony. Whenever he won a case for Russell, the guy complained about the bill, instead of being happy with fifteen wins in a row. "Caswell got in a bar fight. Can't talk very well. And I think this is big enough to justify my time."

"Who's covering for McGee?"

"Kristen Kerry."

Russell smirked. "You'll enjoy that. Want to double the bet?"

Stern planted his tee, more determined to go for the green.

"You lose and you buy dinner and drinks," Russell added.

That changed things. Stern wanted to catch Sarah's game. She'd be thrilled, since he'd told her that morning he might not make it. He could spring for cones for the whole team afterward. Diana wouldn't show, since there were convicts to free and parties to plan.

Maybe he was getting old, but he enjoyed Sarah's games more now than carousing, especially if the alternative was an irritating client. Even odder, he felt some affection, even gratitude, for Diana, because she'd given him Sarah. And that appreciation meant he sometimes found her attractive again, as long as he didn't have to hear about galas and paroles. Not that his feelings generated a response from his wife. But he tried not to think about it, since it only reminded him how much he wanted a son—a son she couldn't give him.

He scrunched his brow at Russell, who was waiting for a reply. In Russell's world, it was either man up and take the bet, or wussy out. Like any good hustler, Stern sounded uncertain.

"Well . . . okay."

Stern aimed at the trees, and pounded his driver with a lovely *twang*. The ball soared and cleared the tallest oak by a foot.

He smiled at Russell.

Nobody beats the Prince.

* * *

Kristen opened the door to the court reporter's office in One Main Place, the agreed-to neutral field for the first Layne deposition. She'd taken one call too many before leaving and was late. If Caswell showed, at least there'd be no time for fake civility. She'd just have to watch her back during the breaks. If Stern appeared instead, her new undercover assignment started. Or was it supposed to be *under the covers*?

The receptionist directed her to a conference room. She hurried in, spotting Joe Bragg, the Laynes' lawyer, sitting with his client nearest the door. He looked like a portly doorman in his double-breasted suit. Almost as wide as he was tall, Bragg lumbered up out of his chair. He spoke with a baritone's timbre.

"Hi, Kristen."

Contrary to Tammy's take-no-prisoners attitude, Kristen kept relations with opposing lawyers civil.

"Hi, Joe."

As the other lawyer rotated in his chair, she realized the broad-shouldered man couldn't be Caswell, but was Stern. Their eyes met and lingered, his the color of burnished steel.

He stood, rising well above Kristen's near five-ten frame. "Nice to see you again."

They shook, and Kristen smiled politely. There were pros and cons. His eyes were magnetic, his voice easy to listen to, and she liked a pair of good hands. And his hair was salted gray with darling waves on the sides, like a little boy's. The tan, in her opinion, was a little much. He'd better have an annual skin exam. He had the build of a former athlete, who'd softened just enough for it to be noticed. Overall, Tammy was right. He was damn fine.

Kristen turned and introduced herself to Betty Layne. Her grip clamped Kristen's hand with strength that suggested she, too, played football. Her ski-jump nose had probably been cute when she cheered Layne in college. She carried an odd birthmark on her forehead, but still, the woman was attractive in a rough way.

Kristen poured herself coffee and sat next to Stern, across the table from Bragg and his witness. The court reporter sat at the end, a vague presence who would be ignored unless something went off the tracks.

After Betty took the oath, Stern wasted little time jumping on her. "Didn't you know heart-valve surgery could have complications?"

Complications, Kristen thought. As if going to the hospital or having a disease made the disaster Layne's fault.

Betty groped in her purse and pulled out a pack of Winstons.

Bragg shook his head.

She jammed the cigarettes back. "My husband didn't have a *complication*."

"You knew abnormal clotting could happen after the valve surgery?"

"Yeah. We were told to watch for the symptoms. For a *complication*. That's why we went back to the hospital."

Before Stern could fire another question tinged with righteous indignation, Betty Layne blurted, "The hospital records are a lie."

Bragg paled. Tension electrified the room.

Kristen and Stern looked at each other. Even if Bragg was going to claim a fabricated hospital record, he couldn't have wanted his plaintiff to divulge it at this point.

Betty softened her tone slightly. "He did shower, but I hooked him right back up."

Kristen couldn't believe it, though she did her best to not look amazed.

Before Stern could go in for the kill, Betty Layne added, "I can prove it."

The room went silent. Only the sound of the air conditioning was noticeable.

As if making sure she had everyone's attention, Betty waited a moment. "I kept notes that night. Galway never saw my husband. And the nurses hardly bothered to pop in all night."

Even the court reporter looked shocked, but kept tapping her keyboard.

Betty Layne scrounged through her purse and pulled out a dog-eared spiral notebook. "Look here."

Kristen hardened her voice. "Joe, I requested in initial discovery all relevant documents. I even asked if you contended the record had been altered."

"Yeah, Joe," Stern added. "I want a recess to look this over."

Obviously embarrassed for apparently withholding evidence, Bragg reddened. "Take what time you need."

Kristen got the impression this was the first he heard of it, too. Or he was a great actor.

Bragg slid the notebook across the table to the defense lawyers. His client and the court reporter stepped out of the room.

Stern flipped through the pages. "This is a typical Bragg stunt." He slid it toward her. "This happy horseshit was probably created yesterday in Bragg's office."

"I assume she's going to testify she wrote all this at the hospital the night Pain went south," Kristen said.

"Of course."

As she adjusted her position in the chair, her skirt rode up a little and Stern's gaze followed the hemline. She didn't bother to tug it down. Let him spy a little leg.

"The hospital records document a late-night examination by your client and show my nurses took vitals every hour."

"Let me guess, Betty babe says Layne was sick as a dog all night and nobody did squat."

Kristen strained to read Betty Layne's handwriting. "She's made an entry every thirty minutes on his condition and who'd been in to see him. Even noted the person who picked up his breakfast selection and the time." She flipped the page. "Wrote his pulse and blood pressure off the monitor. The woman may have married a dumb jock, but she's not stupid."

"You need more cynicism."

"I've got more than you can imagine," Kristen said, without looking up. "We could suspend her testimony and get a document expert to analyze this."

"Not likely anyone can tell when it was written. But if it's legit, you and Pete got a problem. My doc didn't stand around all night with his head up his ass while a TV star went south. He assumed your nurses were watching his patient. If these notes are half-right, he's guilty of assuming wrong."

"If the notes are correct, why didn't your client do *something* when he was there at eleven? What was he there for? To scope out the new trainees?"

Stern stared at her, seeming surprised she argued. Kristen met his glare without blinking.

Stern got up and left the room without a word.

Kristen took a deep breath.

She wondered if Pete and Tammy had overestimated her appeal. Was her "assignment" already over? She had to watch it, or she could push Stern toward a deal with Bragg.

Oh, to hell with all of them. Just defend your nurses.

CHAPTER 6

Huntsville, Texas
Thursday, April 17

LEONARD MARRS WAS LED INTO the little room inside
Huntsville maximum security prison and sat across from Sowak,
his lawyer. The troll was a mess, possibly incapable of withstanding the
heat. Apparently the ACLU-mandated air conditioning wasn't capable
of keeping up with it either.

"Mr. Marrs," Sowak said, making only the briefest of glances at his
client before doing a double take. "What happened to your face?"

"Freddie Lee Lance is what happened."

"Who's that?"

"A big black guy who has a thing for rapists." He smiled a little, but
it hurt.

"What kind of thing?"

"Well, some creep molested his baby sister on her way to school,
and so he thinks we all like jailbait."

The fat slob breathed heavily and sweated some more before
returning his attention to the file folder.

Marrs didn't really need a lawyer, but his half brother Jimmy
thought he did. And Jimmy was helping him out with a job and a place
to stay, so he was stuck with a heavy, wet, jiggly man who smelled like
whatever he'd had for lunch. Today, it was mostly onions.

"You're not going to retaliate, are you?" Sowak suddenly asked.

Marrs blinked. "No. The guy's the size of a bear." In reality, he was planning to tweak Freddie when his parole came down—mention to the monster on his way out that the first thing he was gonna do was look up his little sis for some one-on-one time. Marrs had no intention of doing any such thing, but it would torment Freddie to no end. And since parole for Freddie, the cop-shooter, was about as likely as Bigfoot getting his own Vegas lounge act, Marrs could savor it for years to come.

Sowak picked up the file folder and began fanning himself. The fat fuck was going to expire right in front of him.

"So what do you think?" Marrs asked, hoping to get the guy's mind off the stifling hell before he keeled over. "Do my chances look good?"

"Hard to say," Sowak said, his cheeks brushed with red. "It could go either way."

Well, shit, I know that. Marrs hoped his rough life growing up would be of some help. If being abandoned by his dad, his meth-addicted mom going in and out of prison, and being raised by his decent but distracted Aunt Cindy didn't mean anything, then he didn't know what the point was. He went to college, for Christ's sake. Didn't quite graduate, but going meant *something*.

He had kept his nose clean—or at least never got caught—until that mixer when the coed came on to him and they snuck off to an empty room. He ejaculated the moment she touched his penis, which made her laugh and point, and made him lose it. It was the night he discovered hitting a woman was more exciting than having sex. He agreed to leave school in lieu of charges being pressed, so it never went on his record, but it started a chain of events that did.

"Do you think the stockbroker will be there?" Marrs asked, trying again.

"Who?"

Marrs sighed, half-wishing the heatstroke would kick in. "The victim. The woman I . . . who testified against me."

"I don't know. They don't announce who will show. It's not like court." The giant piece of blubber looked almost thoughtful. "There won't be any surprise witnesses, will there?"

"No," Marrs said, shaking his head and doing a pretty good acting job. No one knew about the teenage runaway hitchhiker in New Mexico, who fell for his good looks and charm. He left her in a shallow grave somewhere in the desert. She wouldn't be turning up. But if the broker performed like she did last time, the whole board might be bawling by the time she was done talking.

He still thought she was hot.

That woman who interviewed him, Diana Stern, wasn't as hot as the broker, but not bad. Not bad at all. And she seemed to really have feelings for Leonard Marrs. Liked his story. Believed him.

"I heard through the grapevine that if this comes down, they've already assigned your PO."

That was promising. If they were considering parole officers, then it sounded like a done deal.

"The guy's a hard-nose." Sowak stopped fanning himself long enough to open the folder and check something. "Zelner."

Marrs's heart sank a little. He'd heard of the guy—a neo-Nazi who'd be just as happy sending your ass back to prison as having a steak dinner. Maybe he was one of those by-the-book law-and-order guys, or figured sending parolees back to the slammer was easier than doing his job. Either way, it didn't matter. He could make it work. He'd fooled the law a dozen times before. He could do it a dozen more.

"Anything else?" Marrs asked.

"Nope," the lawyer said, the fanning action making a return. "We're just waiting for them to call me."

Marrs hadn't slept, thinking about how the drama would play out. If it went his way, he'd have to thank Diana Stern in person.

CHAPTER 7

Dallas
Wednesday, May 7

WELCOMING HIS CLIENT INTO his office, Michael Stern gestured Dr. Gary Galway toward the chair nearest the snarling stuffed black bear that Stern had shot in Alaska.

The cardiologist clanked his cup and saucer down on the edge of Stern's desk and then sat. "I've got the catheter lab booked at nine."

Ever the cynic, Stern wondered how many of those patients really needed dye run through their coronary arteries. As long as Galway signed off on it, the insurance companies didn't ask. "This won't take long. Betty Layne's depo—"

"Is bullshit." Galway clenched a fist, color rising on his neck. "Saying I never showed. Lying. For all I knew, he had the flu. If I ordered expensive tests for everybody a little short of breath, they'd kick me out of every hospital in town."

Stern liked Galway's passion, even if he didn't like Galway. "But he wasn't just anybody. He had a new heart valve."

Galway sputtered. "That's what that Bragg asshole said on TV."

Although only forty, Galway's cheeks were flabby, and creasing. But he looked good enough to give them a chance. Stern knew many jurors decided a medical case on whether they would want the defendant as their doctor. Galway would do. Barely.

Stern waited several moments to let the tension dissolve. "I know. That's why I've drafted a possible script for your depo, but no tellin' what crazy Bragg'll do." Stern tossed the stack to Galway.

Galway picked up the outline. "Who defended Adventist at the wife's deposition?"

"McGee sent his new partner, Kristen Kerry."

"I saw her at the press conference. Looks great. Got much experience?"

"No, but she's not dumb."

"Why isn't McGee doing this case himself? What's up with that? Their top lawyer isn't handling it?"

Stern smiled. "Pete sent her to encourage a joint defense. To sucker me into eyeing her, then screw us. I'll string 'em along, but we can hose them anytime, right up to closing argument. After all, if Layne was going south like Betty said, why the hell didn't the nurses call anybody? Were you supposed to sleep in the guy's room?"

Stern paused to let that sink in, then added, "Or a jury could decide it was Betty's fault for unhooking his monitor so he could shower."

"This case could bankrupt me," Galway said, "and I've heard Tammy what's-her-name, that hospital adjuster, can't be trusted." He seemed to ponder things a moment. "I could demand Standard settle for my policy limits. Not my cash. Why do I want to sit at the courthouse for two weeks when I could be making money?"

Stern shuddered at the thought of the case dissolving so soon. It would kill the publicity. And Kristen intrigued him. He wondered if she'd sleep with him to encourage the joint-defense/double-cross plot Pete McGee had obviously cooked up.

"Gary, you don't want a five million payment on your record. You're only forty. You may want privileges at another hospital someday. That big a settlement would be a problem." Stern let that warning be absorbed. "We ain't drawing to an inside straight. We've got a fat ol' hospital—"

"The nurses testify after me. They could torch me, and I'm stuck."

"If Pete's told Kristen to cozy up to me, we'll be fine." Stern decided he'd better hedge himself from a future legal malpractice claim. Nailing Kristen wouldn't be worth getting sued by Galway, if things went to shit.

"You sure?"

"You could stuff assets offshore, just to be safe. Pay off your house. Creditors can't take it, no matter how big it is." Stern shrugged to signal this was standard advice. "Bragg says Layne deteriorated all night. Who was watching him?"

Galway stood. "Guess there's no reason to panic."

Stern felt relieved. He got up and saw Galway out, then stopped in his longtime paralegal's office.

"Janet, sweetie, you still have a buddy at Wright McGee?"

"Yeah, Sheila and I took paralegal classes together."

Michael pretended to think about this. "See what you can find out about Kristen. You know, subtly."

"You going to get in trouble again?"

"Nah. Just curious."

"You want to know who she sees or has seen?" Janet asked.

"You got it."

"Want me to find out if she's a moaner or a yeller?"

Stern laughed as he returned to his office, then turned back. "Also, track down Ted Ettinger."

Janet picked up the phone, and he went back to his desk.

After a minute, Janet buzzed him. "On three. Make it quick. He's going into surgery."

Stern punched the blinking light. "Ted, I'm gonna have to draft you to be my expert witness." Stern heard techs chatting in the background.

"Okay. But you should know Galway's squirrely."

"Drugs or drinking problems?"

"Don't think so, but the guy's wound tight as your ass during a prostate exam. Wife spends every dime he makes."

"Plaintiff's lawyer wants to retire. Your rates would skyrocket."

Ettinger sighed. "I'll help, but it won't be easy. He should've ordered an immediate echocardiogram, and stuck around. Everybody in town knows it."

"You'll think of something. Also, what's the prognosis on a veg like ol' Layne?"

"They can live twenty years, if they don't get an infection."

"Ouch. That would get expensive. May need to hire a hit man." Stern chuckled to indicate he was kidding. "I'll send you the records."

As Stern hung up, Tony Caswell sauntered in and planted himself on Stern's leather couch on the end farthest from the bear, as if afraid it would spring to life. It could still fall on him.

"Yes?" Michael asked.

Stern noticed the guy didn't look nearly as fit as when he started at the firm. He might yet run Caswell off from overwork.

Caswell thumbed green suspenders. With his yellow tie he reminded Stern of a parrot or a weird frog species. "I'm feeling better. What do you want me to cover in *Layne*?"

Nothing sounded wrong with Caswell's voice. Stern pinched the bridge of his nose. "You flaked out before the answer was due. I didn't see you for a week."

Caswell coughed. "I got hit in the throat. I could've died."

Stern waited for more excuses, heard nothing, and wondered what really happened during his alleged bar brawl. Caswell wasn't saying.

"Well, if it's all right with you, I'll keep it." Stern let him feel the sarcasm.

"Jackson said I *had* to be on the file with you."

"I don't care if he told you to jack off *twice* a day. Standard isn't Jackson's client."

Caswell showed more nerve than Stern expected, hopping up and coming toward the desk. "Jackson thinks you're going to fuck up the case, chasing Pete McGee's darling new partner. You need somebody to keep an eye on you."

Stern resisted jumping up and removing Caswell's throat. "If I needed help, my thirteen-year-old kid would be more useful than you. And you can tell Jackson that as long as I've got an office in this firm, you'll never see a courtroom."

Looking as if he'd just been slapped, Caswell slunk toward Stern's door. "Don't waste your time with McGee's babe lawyer. She's frigid."

"She rejected you? That tells me she's got class."

Caswell glowered and slammed the door on his way out.

Stern wondered why Jackson, his senior partner, didn't realize Caswell would only hang around long enough to steal clients and sneak out in the night toting files. Caswell had spun a tale to Jackson about his dad being on the board of a big hospital chain. Stern guessed the story was nonsense. The firm hadn't seen any new cases from that supposed connection. On top of that, Stern had noticed the pecker-snot bird-dogging Diana at the last Christmas party, not that anybody could get his wife interested in anything but hoods and soirees.

Well, at least he had played Kristen perfectly at Betty's depo, letting her think he wasn't enthralled, walking away and making her think he might cut a deal with Bragg. Initial disinterest always made the woman want him more. He had gotten laid more by accident than Caswell had by trying.

If the gimp had made a pass at Kristen, she probably hadn't spared Caswell's pride. He chuckled at the image of Caswell getting the brush-off. Probably much harder than a mere brush. Maybe she'd told him her men had to have two arms. How sad.

Stern would have to let word of his coming conquest seep back to the preppy little snot. Maybe it would make him cry.

CHAPTER 8

EXHAUSTED AND HUNGRY, Kristen slammed her front door. She'd juggled calls and demands on a dozen files, but still felt unprepared for the depos coming in *Layne*. Late in the day, she'd been asked to substitute coach the AAU club girls' basketball team she helped with, because the head guy was sick. Ordinarily being around those fourteen-year-old girls and calling the shots was a joy. But this time, it had been less than joyful.

Kristen's nose picked up on the aroma of Alfredo sauce, and her stomach seemed to jump for joy. It led her into the kitchen, where her little sister, Tina, was sneaking a taste from the pan. Tina had the same thick hair and Mediterranean skin as her big sister, and stood an inch taller. Despite being both confused and delighted last week to see Tina standing on the front porch, announcing she had finally left Santa Fe and her mediocre artist/abusive boyfriend, Will, Kristen wanted nothing more than a hot bath and a P. D. James mystery tonight. After a bit of dinner, of course.

Tina put her spoon on the countertop. "Does the world end tonight?"

"I'm just tired. Got a bad call and lost."

"Temper again?"

Kristen shook her head, not eager to recite the story. "We were tied with eight seconds left. Our ball. This baby ref in tight shorts, barely out of high school, called a stupid, touchy foul. He'd slurped and winked at me the whole game."

"Was he cute?"

"Christ, give me a break. He was embarrassing me in front of the girls."

Tina shrugged. "You could've played along, to win. I would've."

Her little sister was making the evening worse, as she usually did. As a refugee from drug dealers, strip club owners, and bad-boy boyfriends, Tina had an edge to her that got tiring, fast.

"It wasn't just a bogus call, more like he was getting even with me for ignoring him. Then he called a fucking technical when I complained."

Tina shook her head. "You probably yelled, called him a dumbshit, then said what you really thought."

"He was a jerk. What would you have done? Blown him during a timeout?"

Tina grinned and wiggled her eyebrows. "Maybe."

Rather than scream, Kristen turned and gritted her teeth.

"Krissy, you should go back to therapy."

Kristen clamped her palms over her ears. The last thing she needed was advice from her loopy little sister. "Don't go there, Tina."

Tina put up her hands in surrender. "Sorry! I made a Spinello recipe from the old country. And brownies."

Kristen smiled at the mention of their grandmother's surname and sat on an ice cream store chair in the kitchen and untied her sneakers. Peeling off her sweaty socks cooled her hot feet. She could also feel her temper cooling down as well.

"Pete said you could temp while Cindy, at the front desk, goes on maternity leave. You could probably stay on part time while you take classes."

Tina cocked her head. "I'll think about it."

What the hell is there to think about? Kristen thought. *How many stitches was it going to take? An easy office gig and college, versus bare-knuckle brawls. Some choice.*

As she tried to gather enough patience not to argue, the phone rang. Kristen grabbed it before Tina could. "Hello?"

"Kristen, is Tina there?"

"Missing your punching bag?"

A pause before, "Let me talk to her."

Kristen watched Tina shake her head, relieved she didn't want to talk to Will. "I don't think so."

"Kristen—"

"You know what shrinks say? Guys who hit girls got tiny peckers."

Tina paled and dashed toward Kristen, grabbing for the phone. Kristen whirled around and slammed it down. She felt much better about the evening now.

"Krissy, you shouldn't have said that."

"You're thinking about going back."

Tina reddened and looked away.

"If you even *call* that bastard, find another place to live."

Tina stormed closer. "I may not have a degree, but I'm not a walking volcano."

Kristen stepped eyelash to brow with her little sister. After all she'd done for Tina, Kristen wanted to slap her, but realized that was how Will handled his mouthy girlfriend. Kristen summoned every reserve of willpower, turned away, grabbed a cold one out of the fridge, and headed upstairs, hoping her pill stash was full.

* * *

Three days later, Kristen sat in the reception area of Jackson, Stern and Randolph, wondering how Stern would greet her. The black eye wouldn't help. Makeup hadn't covered it very well. Someday she'd learn to stay out of the paint in a men's basketball league. After getting pummeled, she had shaken off all chivalrous offers for help from the guys and kept playing. Never show weakness.

A thin, late-forties woman in a stylish gabardine suit entered the reception area, sized her up, then announced, "I'm Janet Wharton, Michael's assistant." Gold-frame glasses hung from a matching neck chain. Her eyes bugged out a little, but her posture was perfect, like a marine's. "Please follow me."

Kristen trailed her down a corridor lined with English hunt prints and brass lamps, into a conference room dominated by a mammoth round table, cut from a single tree.

"Mr. Stern will be just a minute." Wharton left without another word, treating her like a copier salesman.

She stared out the window. The jammed freeways and glass buildings made her miss Philly, with its ethnic neighborhoods dating to other centuries, soft pretzels, and steak sandwiches. There, people didn't expect to drive everywhere and park four feet from the front door. Philadelphia had four seasons, while Texas was only warm and hot. With the exhaust from thousands of vehicles outside, it would soon be an insufferable hundred degrees. Inside Stern's suite, the AC blasted cold air. Kristen kept her jacket on. *Texas.*

Stern sauntered in, barely greeting her, not even coming around the table to shake hands. A white shirt and gold cuff links showed off his tan. "Now that we've heard Betty's story, got any ideas?" He sat.

Kristen followed suit and decided to take the offensive. "You could recruit some young stud to seduce her. Get her interested in something besides her case. Rumor has it you hired a prostitute to bust up a family whose kid died."

"Stories get embellished."

"What about some *lost* morphine records?"

"You're cruel."

She stared, not sure whether he was kidding or flirting.

"Course, if we need to stretch a little to defend this case, I'd be useful," he said.

"*We?*"

"*We* is why I wanted to visit. You don't trust me, and I sure as hell don't trust Pete McGee or that claims psycho, Tammy Robberson. I'm not stupid. I can guess why you're here and not Pete."

Kristen decided to play her role straight, use the explanation she had ready. "He can't stand you."

"And it's mutual." Stern made a church steeple with his fingers. "This case is potentially enormous. Before we start guessing when one of us is going to shaft the other, let's cooperate. Bragg wants to retire to the Caribbean. What can we do to diminish the settlement value of this mess?"

Kristen looked down at her notes, buying time.

Stern continued, "If somebody wants to bail later, we promise to give fair warning."

She looked up. "Why didn't Galway get an echocardiogram when he was there at eleven?"

Stern shrugged. "Galway didn't know poor ol' Layne was bleeding, and neither did your nurses." He paused. "At least, according to their notes."

"*Hurst's Cardiology* says these patients can mask symptoms. They can roll along okay clinically, even if their lab work's off, and fool everybody."

"Bragg's expert will say that's more reason to watch them," Stern said.

"Why don't we settle? I'm sure I could get Adventist to chip in to help you."

"Help *me* settle? Your people have the problem. They were there all night."

"Doing what your guy ordered."

For a minute they stared at each other. Kristen kept her expression stony.

Stern raised his palms, as if asking for a truce. "Kristen, no case I'm in is hopeless. Plus, you'll learn something from me if we stick together. You've got lots of potential."

"Potential?"

"To be a great lawyer. I know you're smart." He smiled and pointed at his eye. "And tough."

Embarrassed, she said, "Basketball," then focused on the small wrinkles around his eyes. If he wasn't totally full of himself, he would be nearly irresistible.

"I didn't get to be the Prince of Darkness by getting my ass kicked."

"Then I'm sure we can come to an arrangement." She paused. "Keep that creep Caswell off the case."

"Same with McGee. From now on, just us together."

He stood and stretched his hand toward her.

She gripped it and looked into his gorgeous blue eyes.

"Okay, deal."

* * *

Arriving home that night, Kristen spotted a Chevy with a *Land of Enchantment* tag and a bug-splattered windshield. She got out of her car and opened the front door, and was met with the sound of people upstairs reaching orgasmic bliss. Slamming the door stopped the grunting.

A minute later and sporting a sheepish grin, a T-shirt, and panties, Tina nonchalantly ambled down the stairs. Will followed, buttoning his jeans under his beer belly, his ponytail bouncing behind him.

"Hi, Krissy. Been a long time," Will said.

Kristen felt her cheeks flush. She hissed at her sister, "I want him out of here."

"Kristen, we've had a long talk. Will's—"

"Promised, absolutely promised to quit hitting you?" Kristen took a step toward him. How she wished that her mother had shown some spine. "Get out, Will."

Tina stepped in front of Will, shielding him. "Let's cool off and talk!"

"There's nothing to talk about." Kristen darted around her sister, getting in Will's face.

Will sprayed spit as he blabbered, "Your little sister was lap dancing when she met me. You were too busy climbing the law firm ladder to help her. She could've OD'd for all you cared."

Kristen slammed her palms into Will's chest. "Out!"

Surprised, he stumbled, righted himself, and squared off with her. "You need to double up on your medication."

Beyond livid, Kristen could feel the steam building. "I said *out*, asshole."

Tina tried to insert herself again. "Don't, you two! *We're* leaving."

Appalled by Tina's announcement, Kristen gave him another shove toward the door. "You like to hit girls. Come on! You got a hundred pounds on me. Give me your best shot."

He looked at Tina as if begging for advice on how to deal with her crazy sister.

Kristen pushed again, mashing the heel of her hand under his throat. *Holy Mary, it would feel good to kick the shit out of Will.*

"Still having trouble getting it up?"

Will slapped her hand away. "Fuck you, Kristen."

It barely stung, but was all the excuse Kristen needed. She stepped back, pivoted on the ball of her left foot, and planted her shoe into Will's solar plexus. It was a sledgehammer pounding raw cookie dough.

He doubled over, gasping like an old man with emphysema, then dropped to the floor.

Before she could inflict serious punishment, Tina darted between them and wrapped her arms around Kristen's shoulders, knocking her off balance. Both women wound up in a tangle on the carpet.

Kristen shoved Tina away, leapt up, and pointed at Will. "If you *ever* hit her again, I'll find you, wherever you are, and put *you* in a hospital."

Between coughs Will nodded and raised his hands in surrender.

"Damn it, Kristen!" Tina pushed herself up. "You *are* crazy."

Kristen dashed up the stairs to the spare bedroom. She stuffed Tina's clothes into her bag and ducked into the bath, where she swept Tina's toiletries off the sink and into her kit. Kristen stormed back down. She opened the door and threw Tina's gear outside. *"Get out of here!"*

Tina stepped up to Kristen chin to chin. Her voice was oddly calm, as if she were reading a script—or finally saying what she had been rehearsing for years. "The family might've been okay, if you hadn't spilled. You never give anyone a second chance. You project all the anger you've built up over fifteen years on whoever is handy."

Kristen absorbed Tina's stare. She'd driven her sister back to Lardbucket. If Tina got hurt or even killed by the vicious bastard, she'd blame herself forever. Kristen didn't want to go crawling back to her therapist, but there was just enough truth in what Tina said to make her want to eat every pill she had.

Tina jerked a pair of jeans from her bag and pulled them on. She tugged her boyfriend up, wrapped Will's arm over her shoulder, and parted with, "Someday you're going to blow up and take out everybody around you."

CHAPTER 9

Monday, June 9

KRISTEN SAT BACK AND watched two lions, Joe Bragg and Michael Stern, rip their prey to pieces. Stern had jerked his tie loose and rolled up his sleeves, while Bragg's face shone with beads of sweat. He'd treated the hapless Dr. Gary Galway like a drug dealer. Stern hadn't been much kinder to his own client, barking at the doc when his answers were too gassy, which was most of the time. The atmosphere came close to an upper level of Dante's hell.

To add to the volatile mixture, Kristen was pissed at Stern. He had failed to ask the judge for a protective order preventing Bragg from inviting media to Galway's deposition. The presence of a videographer, a TV reporter, a sound man, and Betty Layne was obviously unnerving everyone in the room, particularly Galway. After almost every answer, Betty Layne snorted derisively, which the sound undoubtedly picked up. The best snippets of this depo— Galway's worst answers—would probably be aired on the evening news.

Bragg sneered at Galway. "And you're telling us that Mr. Layne's blood pressure was stable all night?"

"Joe, you've asked that same damn question ten times," Stern said.

"Yeah, and I want an answer."

Galway struggled. "Uh . . . That's what the nurses wrote. I've never had reason to question any of the excellent nurses at Adventist."

"I want to know what *you* think. Not the fictional story those nurses wrote."

Kristen had sat mute, seething all morning, but that did it. She erupted out of her chair. "That question is abusive! I'm calling Judge Proctor," she said, heading toward the door, cell phone in hand.

Everyone stared, shocked that the youngest lawyer had just escalated the war.

By the time Kristen dialed the courthouse number, she realized she'd made a mistake. It was Stern's client under fire and his decision whether to raise the ante. She turned and saw all eyes were on her, Stern's blazing.

Stern wiggled his finger and turned, signaling her.

She hung up before getting connected and followed Stern out of the room.

In the hall, after the door closed behind them, Stern slapped his palms against his temples. "Don't call Proctor."

"Bragg's going to get the clip about *fictional* notes on the news tonight. The first impression every potential juror gets will be that my nurses' notes are a lie."

"You'll never get a ruling today. The last thing we want is to keep this mess going, or give 'em more publicity next week."

She slammed her palms against her hips and leaned into him. "Why didn't you get a protective order?"

"How the hell could I? Betty's entitled to be here."

"TV people aren't."

"Bragg said she was a consultant. How was I supposed to know that gal worked at Channel Seven?"

"I thought the Prince knew everything."

Stern's mouth dropped open. It took him a few seconds to snap it shut. "Let's get this shit finished."

Kristen stared at him. Stern had a lot more experience, and so far, Galway's testimony was consistent with their deal. She decided to back down. She was exhausted. The nightmares had worsened since Tina left.

* * *

Two hours later, when Bragg finally gave up trying to extract a confession from Galway and they called it a day, Stern asked Kristen to meet him in his office after he escorted his client out. She offered Galway a perfunctory "nice job," tromped down the hall, and found Stern's lair.

Inside was a ridiculous stuffed bear. The ego wall was plastered with certifications framed in dark wood. Photos behind Stern's desk followed a tow-headed girl with her father's steel-blue eyes and charming smile, from toothless baby, to a toddler, to a softball and soccer player. Action shots showed the kid had talent. *Beautiful.* Kristen's irritation dissolved.

Stern returned, rubbing his temples. "Galway kept asking me when the nurse named Nancy is going to be deposed. Why's he worried about her? She didn't come on duty till right before the code."

"Both nurses in the unit will stick to their notes."

He nodded, seeming pleased. "We could use a drink."

His voice was like maple syrup on a hot waffle. He had magically regained his pizzazz and was gentleman enough not to mention their flap in the hall.

"I'm wiped out," she said.

Stern seemed indifferent. "Looks like Bragg's aiming his artillery at your people. He could concede Galway's eleven o'clock exam is accurate, claim the bleed began after Galway left, and make it a simple case of nursing error for not calling."

She decided to compromise between her exhaustion and his blabbering. *Keep your friends close and your enemies closer.*

"Meet me at the bar in The Fairmont in an hour?" Kristen asked.

The red-coated doorman opened the brass-handled door for Kristen with a flourish, like she was royalty. Stern already sat in the lobby lounge.

Once more into the breach, she told herself, as the piano player began the sorrowful "Memory."

He stood and beckoned her to his table, a four top.

She took the chair opposite, watching for any reaction that she chose not to sit close.

Stern waved at the waitress, betraying nothing.

The waitress—young, tan, and blond—hustled up. "What'll you have, hon?"

"Glenlivet and water," Kristen said. Female trial lawyers were supposed to act like one of the boys, and order accordingly.

The server gave Stern a gooey grin as she left. To his credit, Stern pretended not to see it.

"As long as they stay with their notes, we'll be okay."

"*We* again?"

"I thought *we* did pretty good today, but watch that temper."

"You got pissed too."

"Yeah. But don't pull your gun out if you ain't gonna use it," he said, making it sound slightly suggestive—just enough for her to think that, but not enough for it to sound like he meant it. "Some of my anger is manufactured for the audience. I thought you were going to slug ol' Bragg."

"Considered it." She smiled to pull her next punch. "There won't be any TV reporters at the nurses' depos."

Stern tilted his head, acknowledging her point, as the waitress returned with a glass of Scotch whiskey.

He raised his glass. "Here's to lawsuits. May our clients be rich, mad, and wrong."

Kristen laughed, sipped, and could feel the alcohol rush into her bloodstream, calming her. "Galway did a good job, testifying to the sudden arrhythmia theory."

"Yeah. We learn to smother our conscience." He leaned forward, his voice syrupy again. "You have a medical background?"

"No, but I told Pete at the interview my dad's a cardio surgeon. He didn't notice on my résumé that I switched to English lit after a rough semester in organic."

The piano player began "Yesterday." Wondering if the guy knew only sad tunes, Kristen sipped her whiskey, driving melancholy thoughts of her family away.

Puzzlement crossed Stern's face. "You don't talk like a Texan. Where are you from?"

"Philadelphia."

"How'd you get here?"

"Went to Oklahoma to play basketball. Fell in love with Austin on a road trip, so UT was my first choice for law school. Spent a year waiting tables and giving basketball lessons to kids for the in-state tuition."

"You were a jock?"

"Hardly blue-chip. Sent a highlight DVD to about fifty schools. OU invited me to walk on and arranged an academic scholarship."

"I'm impressed."

"It turned out I was too small. I quit after my junior year. But made the track team as a hurdler. Kept me in shape." She remembered all that sweat with pride, but it also kept her from dwelling on the loneliness.

He rocked back with disbelief. "Gee! Why'd a doc's daughter bother?"

She shrugged. "Stubborn Irish pride."

"Then where did that olive skin come from?"

"Mom's third-generation Italian."

"We were on similar paths," Stern said as he slugged his drink. "I finagled half a golf scholarship, joined ROTC, and delivered pizza to get through school."

"You? Give me a break."

"You're looking at the son of a barely employed trucker from a refinery town."

Kristen smiled. His large, lean hands, corded with prominent veins, could belong to a sculptor. "What's Bragg's story?"

Stern tilted his head and wiggled his glass at the waitress across the room. "Joe's a former football coach from the border, but it made him hungry. Hunger makes a lawyer."

"Then I'll be okay. In law school, I discovered frozen bread loaves at forty-nine cents. I ate one and an apple a day to stay alive."

He raised a finger. "Don't bullshit a bullshitter."

She cocked her head. "There were some dinner dates, when I got a square meal."

"When my Army money ran out, I got married."

"So your wife put you through law school?"

"Diana even got me my first big interview."

Kristen sipped her drink, feeling pensive. "You're aptly named."

"What?"

"Your name is German for *star*."

"*Kannst du Deutsch?*"

"*Ja.* Been twice and took eighteen hours in college."

"I defended the Fulda Gap from a cushy intelligence office in Mannheim before the wall came down."

"My dad presented papers in Munich and took my brother and me both times. I actually listened to the lectures. Thought I would be a surgeon." She changed the subject before the melancholy intruded. "I saw your daughter's pictures. She's pretty."

"Thanks." His pride was obvious.

Kristen felt a whiff of jealousy. Told herself it was just a passing whiff.

"What's the schedule from here?" Stern asked.

Glenlivet on an empty stomach, combined with sleepless nights, was making her lightheaded. "I put up my nurses on the twenty-fourth. Both the same day. Then we schedule Bragg's experts. One's in New York, his cardiologist. Insists on doing the depo on a Friday evening."

"I have an ol' pal there who defends docs. Gets me great show tickets and box seats for the Yankees. We could do the town Saturday."

"I'll stay with my cousin in Connecticut."

His eyes darted down. That was when he betrayed his disappointment. Kristen felt like she'd won a small battle in the ongoing war.

The waitress brought his fresh glass.

"Don't forget, Galway talked up your people," Stern said.

"But he left himself an opening big enough for your dad's truck. If Betty's notes are right, he should've been called."

"But they're nonsense."

Kristen finished her drink and looked into his eyes. "You were right. I let my temper get away." She realized she'd done what she hadn't intended. Was her admission the result of a stiff drink? Or his looks?

"No problem. I'd rather have you on my side, than against me." His eyebrows rose. "Another?"

"Got to go." She stood, telling herself she'd done well.

CHAPTER 10

LEONARD MARRS LAY SLEEPLESS, frightened. He'd been in the halfway house only a week before word leaked that he was a convicted rapist. He watched his back—he had to—but it was against the rules to lock the door in the room he slept in each night after a day of mopping floors in state buildings. At least he was alone—both his roommates got their Get Out of Jail cards that afternoon. Tomorrow he'd get two new squirrel-baits to worry about.

That meant any of the thugs in this pigsty—which had once been a ratty motel—could slip in and slit his throat without worrying about witnesses. Or jam a broken broom handle up his ass. That was common in Huntsville, but he'd dodged that particular pleasure thanks to his phony legal career. In a halfway house nobody needed a lawyer. They were on their way to freedom as long as they kept the floors shiny.

The only guys lower in the prison hierarchy than rapists were kiddie rapists. There weren't any pedophile bastards currently in residence, so Leonard was on the bottom rung. The knife that he scarfed from the kitchen lay under his pillow, a strict no-no that could get him sent back to prison faster than if he exposed himself to the tattooed lesbian who ran this place. But having a little protection was worth the risk. A guy couldn't just lie around helpless waiting to get bung-holed.

In the morning, around five, he'd be shoved onto a bus and hauled to the capitol in Austin for janitorial work. He'd have to endure the threatening sneers of fellow inmates and wonder which one was going to pork him when he got the chance.

Then there was the possibility that his big mouth had made him an enemy he didn't even know about yet. Marrs realized he shouldn't have been so cocky back in Huntsville when he'd teased stuttering Freddie Lance after getting word of the parole vote. Just because he'd had some serious allies didn't mean he could get away with his macho blabber forever.

The only thought keeping him sane was the image of Diana Stern. He could still picture her pert little nose, the wisp of hair that flowed across her forehead, and her fine tits. If he could stay alive a few more weeks and keep his nose clean, he'd be in Dallas and have a chance to meet her in the flesh.

He smiled at the expression. *In the flesh.*

His immediate concern was that he wanted to shower before dawn. Should he go now? He hated three things—body odor, bad manners, and blacks. As a kid he'd been beaten for wetting the bed. One of his mom's boyfriends had burned his arms with cigarette butts for peeing on the floor while sleeping next to their bed. His mom did nothing to stop the guy. The twenty-year-old memory still haunted him many nights, and he agonized about wetting the sheets. And the guy had been a nig-nog.

So he was conflicted. He was worried about smelling dirty tomorrow, but feared going to the showers. No telling what thug he might run into.

As if to intensify the thought process, he heard footsteps in the hallway. Not loud, but audible.

Someone stopped outside his door.

Marrs's hand slipped under the pillow and wrapped around the handle of the knife. He held his breath longer than he thought possible.

If this were an unannounced bed check, they would simply yell through the door.

After what seemed like an hour, but was only a minute, the floor creaked again. The steps faded. He started breathing again, and the hand under the rock-hard pillow relaxed.

A man could go insane here.

CHAPTER 11

TONY CASWELL STUFFED THE FILE into his briefcase, dwelling on his litany of bad breaks. He had the worst job in any law firm—the next guy struggling to make partner. All he did was churn paper, bill exaggerated hours, and go home to an empty house. So far it hadn't been enough for Jackson, Stern and Randolph. The other associate up for consideration, a woman, was a shoo-in.

Caswell didn't need the extra money. But partnership meant recognition that he was as talented as anyone else in the firm, especially Michael Stern. Tony's promotion had been tabled at the last meeting. If it didn't happen soon, somebody would be sorry—like the frat rats, whose house mysteriously burned down after Tony was blackballed.

A couple of the senior guys at the firm liked his work, but somebody important in the upper echelon blocked him, and he had a good guess who. Stern treated Tony like a mongrel begging for scraps at the back door of a greasy spoon café. Stern wasn't letting him handle anything important, and then was nitpicking every brief, every memo to clients.

Caswell wanted a lot more payback than fucking Stern's wife. And he'd promised himself Kristen would get hers too. She'd nearly fractured his windpipe and castrated him over what? A little fondling?

Talk about overreaction. Tony thought she needed a thrill, that he'd done her a favor. She should be thankful he'd decided not to file charges. It wouldn't help his image to complain about getting beat up by a girl, since begging off from the first *Layne* depo had been a big enough blow to his prestige.

He finished packing files and trudged down the silent halls, his good arm toting the briefcase. He paused as he caught his reflection in the glass of an antique print. It was bad enough he had an atrophied limb, but if his hairline receded much more, he'd have to get Rogaine.

Then there was his once-trim belly, which made him shake his head in disgust. He'd soon be fat, bald, and an alcoholic, like half the lawyers in the place. Had he gotten to work on *Layne*, he might've broken out of the seven-days-a-week paper churn and nabbed some of his own clients, maybe publicity in legal magazines.

Caswell stopped at Stern's corner office and switched on the light. The photos and certificates showed the guy's perfect life—scratch golfer, gorgeous wife, darling kid, and the best trial reputation of any lawyer in Dallas, maybe even all of Texas.

None of it was deserved. Stern came from a shithole town and wound up a king by marrying well and getting lucky in his first few cases. Tony grabbed one of the gold pens from the desk set and snapped it in two.

The moment he did, he realized his security card would indicate he'd been here late.

Shit.

His brain raced.

The cleaning crew. Sure. The cleaning crew would get the blame. He jammed the pieces in his pocket. Leave no evidence.

Tony would give one of his aching testicles to be Michael Stern. Every time he saw the Sterns' picture in the society section of the paper, Tony had a physical hurt deep inside. The desire to be popular, athletic, and successful gnawed at him, like a dog chewing a rubber bone. He was the bone.

His gaze lingered on the photos of Sarah Stern. The darling girl looked like her father, but carried her mother's class like it had been grafted upon her as a baby. She'd been at the office several times, and he'd felt proud when she addressed him as "Mr. Caswell." He thought he might like a family someday, a couple of kids, but had never found a woman worth marrying.

He rubbed his eyes, deciding nothing could be done about his misery tonight, and turned to leave when he saw an attaché case on the claw-legged writing table. Tony crossed the room, picked it up, and admired the leather and silver fittings. It was initialed *GG*, and nice enough to be toted around London's financial district.

Surprisingly, the case wasn't locked. Inside were articles from *New England Journal of Medicine*, a copy of Betty Layne's deposition, and a yellow pad filled with scribbling. Galway had forgotten his briefcase in his haste to escape.

Tony had done the preliminary workup in *Layne*, before Stern took over, and suspected something wasn't kosher. The question now was whether he could make sure his side lost and Stern got the blame, maybe even the boot out the door. But Kristen couldn't win either, or his efforts would be fruitless. The Layne case was like his school days when Caswell sat on the bench in soccer, hoping his team would lose. Except now he could influence things instead of just sitting there watching.

At the bottom of the briefcase was a nursing flow sheet form from Adventist Hospital. Feminine writing was scrawled across the page.

> *Good luck today.*
> *Everything safe. See you tonight?*
> *Been too long. Licorice.*

Caswell studied the note for a minute, then decided he should make a copy. He wondered what the note meant. And what really happened the night Layne croaked.

CHAPTER 12

"GALWAY HANDLED OUR lousy facts as well as he could, but no jury's going to love him."

Jen plopped her stocking feet on Kristen's desk. "You could see sweat above his lip on TV. Any luck baiting Stern?"

"Not sure."

"Don't give up, long legs." Jen screwed her face into a knot and imitated Tammy's high-pitched snarl. *"Even if you are short on tits."*

Kristen laughed at Jen's mimicry.

"Double-cross Stern, and you'll go down in history."

"As a snake."

"Not the worst reputation in this business. Kinda goes with the territory."

Kristen nodded. "I could tell the jury at the end of Bragg's case that after *carefully* analyzing the evidence, it's obvious poor Pain Layne's in a coma, thanks to Galway's hurry to get home."

Jen flashed a thumbs-up. "Perfect."

The receptionist, Cindy, came over the speaker. "Joe Bragg on line four."

Kristen picked up the receiver. "Kristen Kerry."

"What're your nurses going to say?"

"The truth."

"There's two kinds of truth. One sends Stern down the shitter. I bet your girls realized Layne was tanking and phoned that greasy Galway, but he blew 'em off."

Kristen frowned, but didn't reply.

"They could 'fess up and we could nail Stern and his lying doc. I could settle easy on your hospital."

"They don't say that."

"Get in their faces. You don't want to bankrupt that hospital when Stern hoses you."

"Thanks for the advice."

"Don't say I didn't warn you." Bragg hung up.

Kristen set the phone down. "Well, that was interesting." She filled Jen in.

"Maybe you should cut a deal with Bragg now."

The phone buzzed again. "Jeff Hudson, line six."

Kristen looked at Jen, puzzled. Jen smiled. "He's a criminal defense lawyer, former DA-turned-crusader. Six-five and gorgeous. Went to school with Ron."

"What does he want with me?"

Jen dropped her feet and scooted closer. "He saw you playing basketball, called me. I told him you were unattached. Forgot to tell you he'd call."

Kristen remembered the guy. He did look good, but as usual she pictured the risks.

"Want me to tell him you have herpes and bad breath?"

Kristen leaned closer to the speakerphone. "Take a number, Cindy." Kristen shrugged at Jen. "The jets on my Jacuzzi work well."

Jen chuckled. "Pete wants you to help on that drug case I'm second on. You'll get some trips to company headquarters in New Jersey on the client's dime."

Kristen felt a little nauseous. Going home was the last thing she wanted to do. Ever. Even getting within a hundred miles would tempt her to see her baby sister, but any visit would mean confronting the demons.

* * *

A week later, Nurse Nancy Wiltse slumped against Kristen's office love seat. Her forehead was creased in the center, creating a continuous line from her middle-parted gray hair to her nose. Glasses, highlighted by fake diamonds in each corner, framed her face.

"What if he asks me what Layne's blood pressure was at six?"

Kristen tried to muster her remaining patience so she wouldn't get up and shake the woman's shoulders in frustration. "Nancy, ask for the chart and tell him what you wrote."

The other cardiac nurse, Roberta Lott, touched Nancy's knee and said, "Nobody expects you to have it memorized."

Kristen kept her voice level. "Listen to my objections. There's no judge at a deposition, so you have to answer—but if I object because the question is ambiguous, or you don't know how to answer, say you don't understand the question."

"What if he asks if I have any criticisms of Dr. Galway?"

Kristen studied Nancy, trying to will the truth out of her. "Do you? I've got to know. Now."

Nancy furrowed her forehead again. "No."

Roberta smiled and touched Nancy's arm. "You'll do fine. Stick to the records."

Kristen decided to throw out a question that had been eating at her for weeks. "Has anybody leaned on you guys?"

Nancy and Roberta glanced at each other and then shook their heads in unison.

"We did everything for this patient. We knew he was on TV," Roberta said.

Nancy Wiltse's eyes went blank behind her glasses. "What if he asks whether I thought Layne was deteriorating before he coded?"

Kristen used her insinuating power voice. "Did you?"

She shrugged. "No."

"Why are you asking 'What if' questions when you already know the answers?" Kristen let some of her irritation through. "Is there something I don't know about? Did Layne's wife really unhook him from the monitor to get him to the shower? Is that why there's a gap in the monitoring?"

Roberta rolled her eyes. "People take the gear off all the time."

"But don't you get an alarm at the station?"

"There's two kinds of alarms. The loud one's for a code. The other's just a little ding. We can't run down the hall every time a machine dings," Robbie said.

Nancy nodded. "It was a routine night. I had four patients. He wasn't special."

Kristen mimicked Bragg. "Except he was dying. His heart was tamponading, compressed by bleeding. He arrested, and he's kinda brain-dead."

"What I meant was he didn't look any worse than anybody else on the unit that night."

"Did *anybody* else code?"

As both nurses shook their heads with exaggerated energy, Kristen realized Pete was right. Although she liked the nurses, and sympathized with their difficult jobs, a jury could second-guess them. They couldn't win without double-crossing Stern.

*　*　*

Stern hung up the phone as Janet stepped into his office. "Michael, the partners' meeting is waiting on you."

Stern sighed. He was in no mood for office politics. "Some people got work to do."

Janet smiled. She'd heard it a hundred times. "Remember Caswell." She glanced down the hallway. She whispered, "Speak of the devil." Janet slipped away as Caswell waltzed in toting a printout.

"I think I know what happened to Layne." Caswell spoke like he'd found the missing Mormon gold tablets.

Stern stood and came around his desk, pointing. "Are those your billables?"

Caswell nodded, then went on. "Listen. You need to hear this."

"Lemme have 'em." Stern jerked the paper from him.

Stern saw hatred reflect off Caswell's eyes, as if he wanted to rip the printout back. But Caswell must have realized that Stern was not only bigger, but was his boss.

Stern turned and left Caswell stammering. He stalked out of the office, down the hall, past the English prints, and rounded two corners before entering the main conference room. At the long cherry table sat twenty-five lawyers, all males in their white-shirted uniforms.

Senior partner John Jackson pulled an unlit cigar out of his mouth. "Now that we're all here . . ."

Stern slid into his usual spot in the middle, facing portraits of the three principal partners—Jackson, Stern, and Randolph—and scanned the agenda. "Partnership for Caswell and Faye Hill? We're scraping the bottom of the shark tank."

Jackson leaned over the table, blasting his foul breath across the room. "We promised them this year."

"The year's a long way from over."

"Michael, Tony's hours exceeded yours for the last two quarters, and we've never taken in a woman. We look like Neanderthals."

"Useless paper shuffling. He's not good enough to carry my briefcase. On *Layne*, he begs off the first depo. After I pulled him off the file, he keeps grinding bullshit hours and doing idiotic investigating."

Jackson's nicotine-stained fingers jammed the stogie between his yellow teeth. "Paper pushing pays the rent."

Stern shrugged. "I don't know about your clients, but Standard won't tolerate churning. They want results." Stern paused, knowing he was about to really piss Jackson off. "Hell, I lop some of his bills back before they go out."

Jackson's eyes bulged. "Why, for God's sake?"

"I only bill for honest work." Stern smiled, enjoying the moment. "Plus, it'll cut his year-end bonus." He slapped Caswell's time summaries on the table and began lining through entries. Stern made a *tsk tsk* sound. "Here's a good one. Three hours for a 'meeting' with hospital counsel, which was actually a date, trying to get some. Unsuccessfully, by the way."

Jackson's voice rose. "That's money you're pissing away. Not all of us have a rich wife."

Stern winked at Randolph. Everyone knew Jackson had the hots for Diana from the first time she came downtown for lunch, when Stern was a lowly associate. Jackson couldn't score even if they discovered a cure for every known STD.

"If it was up to you, we'd never take in a new partner," Jackson said.

"I don't give a rat's ass about empire building." As a couple of robots nodded agreement, Stern added, "I move to table this."

Jackson pointed at him with the mangled end of his cigar. "I told Caswell to watch you on *Layne*. He says you're taking your eye off the ball, because the hospital's lawyer is a cutie pie."

"Don't tell me how to run a lawsuit. You haven't seen a courthouse in ten years."

Jackson flushed with obvious embarrassment. "I'd hate to get a subpoena from your wife." Jackson sniffed, sounding like a quart of snot had retreated up his nose. "I'd have to tell what I know of your adventures. Her connections got you into this firm when you were green as grass. You'd be in a world of shit."

Stern couldn't decide who would be more fun to strangle, Caswell or Jackson. Maybe since one was lame and one was ancient, he could take a throat in each hand.

Jackson crammed his cigar back and mumbled through tight lips, "In this racket, you're only as good as your last win. If you let that dolly trick-fuck you and tank Galway, every lawyer in this room will say we never heard of you."

Chapter 13

Monday, June 23

STERN EYED ROBERTA LOTT, the alluring younger nurse, slipping into the witness chair for her depo, while he continued to mull his dilemma. Cut a deal with Bragg now? Settle? Or keep things rolling while he chased Kristen? Run the risk of her double-crossing him?

Most of the women he wanted quickly fell into bed with him, but Kristen's indifference intrigued him. She was under orders to entice him—he figured that out—but after two months, he'd only coaxed her into one drink. One. She had dashed off, just as he thought they were connecting. Stern guessed that once *Layne* settled, he'd never see her again. He loved to gamble, but if he continued to defend the case without making a deal with Bragg, he might wind up in a real pickle.

Kristen's first witness, Nurse Nancy, had been awful. Her stock answer, *I only know what I wrote*, stunk. Who would believe she couldn't remember anything? Did she have a TV personality in her unit every night? Who turned into a vegetable the next morning? How could she *not* remember? Kristen had remained cool, but Stern wondered if she realized Bragg was kicking the hell out of them. A joint defense in trial would sink like the *Titanic*, and there wouldn't be enough lifeboats.

After some initial softball questions, Bragg grew more intense.

"Ma'am, your notes earlier that night on your initial assessment, before Dr. Galway came in, show Mr. Layne nauseated, sweaty, and hypotensive. Did he actually improve when Dr. Galway examined him at eleven?"

The nurse's big brown eyes darted toward Kristen, seeking help her lawyer wasn't allowed to give. "The meds I gave helped. Dr. Galway was correct. He's the best—"

She stopped. Out of the corner of his eye, Stern saw Kristen tap Roberta's forearm. That was their signal.

"The best at what?"

"Everything."

Bragg smiled, and Stern wanted to laugh, thinking that next she'd say he deserved the fucking Nobel Prize.

"Ma'am, didn't you have a full unit that night?" Bragg asked.

"Yes."

"The truth is, you were busy when Dr. Galway made his eleven o'clock exam."

"Uh—"

"You don't even know whether he saw Mr. Layne."

Stern held his breath.

"I saw him go in."

Stern sighed relief, then glanced around to make sure it went unnoticed. Nurse Lott's testimony was a perfect chance for Kristen to welsh on their agreement and claim she had coached Lott as best she could. Despite Galway's fear of the nurses, their story was as good as could be expected. Kristen had either bought the deal or was sucking him in further.

An hour later Bragg concluded Robbie's depo with a snarl. "No more questions." Bragg slammed his file into his briefcase and hurried out.

Stern stood to face Roberta. "Good job, Robbie.."

"Thank you, Mr. Stern." After more assurance from Kristen,

Roberta Lott left, seeming to think she'd pleased the defense lawyers.

Kristen asked, "What'd you think?"

Stern shrugged. "Nurses always get pushed around in depos. Just like they take shit from doctors."

"I know. They sucked."

"Can't make cornbread out of turnips. Nothing substantive they said was bad. Cases come down to a battle of experts. My buddy, Ettinger, can handle Bragg." He paused. "You deserve a drink."

"Thanks, but working out will feel better. You should try it."

"Churchill said he got plenty of exercise being a pallbearer for his abstinent friends, but maybe I need inspiration. Where do you go?"

"Gold's on McKinney."

* * *

With one more agonizing crunch on the incline bench, Kristen's abs knotted tight, so tight she couldn't manage another. It had taken a gallon of sweat to rinse away the day's stress. She flopped back and stared at the NFL pennants flapping from Gold's ceiling. The air conditioning blew for all it was worth, but was still losing its battle with the heat. "Land of Confusion" by Genesis blared through the speakers, one of her old favorites.

Pulling herself up, she glanced at the free-weight area. The Fabio look-alike still fixed on her. Overt lusting was frowned on in a place so serious about exercise, but the guy must not have read the memo. She grabbed her duffel bag and headed out, but the muscleman timed his exit to meet her.

He towered over her and blocked the door. His tan skin shone, his eyes drooped like he was hung over, and he reeked of sweat and cologne. Less like Fabio and more like a desperate Saturday night bar troll.

She held her breath and slipped a hand past him to the door.

He flashed his capped teeth. "I'm Chuck, and I could drink your bathwater."

The line was far worse than she expected. Didn't anybody ever just say "Hi"? "Sorry, I shower. Excuse me." She squeezed by him.

"What's your name?"

Kristen couldn't decide how to get rid of him, but as she started toward her car, she spotted Stern getting out of a silver Mercedes next to her BMW. "That's my husband."

He-man drifted away with a scowl.

Kristen smiled, and, for the first time, was actually glad to see Stern.

As she reached her car, Stern jammed his hands into his pockets, looking sheepish. "Did I interrupt anything?"

"Not at all. I prefer men with three-digit IQs." Kristen felt his gaze creep across her. The evening breeze against her damp skin tightened her nipples against her Lycra top. She reached in her bag for a sweatshirt and pulled it on, but a second later it felt suffocating. She hated summers in Texas. By August, cars would be brick ovens.

"You look like you're burning up."

"Like Joan of Arc. How'd you find my car?"

Stern patted the hood of her BMW. "Saw the basketball on the backseat."

Kristen opened the door and tossed her bag inside.

He planted his palms on his hips. His rolled-up sleeves revealed wrists with rope-like veins. "A beer and dinner?"

"I'm wrung out and probably smell like a gym."

"Yogurt?" He pointed. "Right next door."

* * *

Stern tried to keep his ogling subtle as he handed Kristen her cone.

She was even lovelier sweaty and flushed a hint at what she'd look like under him.

Stern sat. "I try to figure out what *really* happened. My guess is the eleven o'clock exam by Galway was cursory that late. Done while Betty Layne was out smoking. The nurses had their hands full on a busy night. Betty unhooked him and his heart flutter began, leading later to the code. Your girls feel guilty 'cause of the bad result."

"Layne's crash doesn't seem to have fazed Galway."

"They teach indifference in medical school. They practice that 'Shit happens' look."

"I'm sure he aced that class."

He watched as Kristen's tongue darted into vanilla yogurt on a waffle cone.

"What if Betty's telling the truth? We send all our clients to bankruptcy."

Stern shook his head. "She's a typical plaintiff overplaying her hand." He watched her swirl the yogurt with her tongue. His imagination about what she might do with that tongue went into overdrive. It was getting harder every time he saw her not to become totally obsessed. McGee had chosen well. Much more with the cone and he wouldn't be able legally to stand.

As if she sensed his staring, she picked up the spoon. "What's your wife doing tonight?"

That was meant as a shot across his arousal, and it worked.

"This is her rare night at home with Sarah. Most of the time, she's hobnobbing or freeing felons."

"She doesn't understand you?"

Stern smiled. "Oh, we understand each other well. We get along better in different rooms."

"Aww, you should take her out." She wiggled her eyebrows. "Surprise her."

He realized Kristen was either very good at the game, or was totally uninterested. Properly chastised, he could only say, "That it would."

She changed the subject again. "Now that we know what *really* happened, what now?"

"As long as we stick to our deal, we'll be fine."

CHAPTER 14

Dallas
Tuesday, July 15

O N HIS SECOND DAY OF FREEDOM, Leonard Marrs drove his half brother Jimmy's Cherokee through beautiful Highland Park, tucked in the middle of North Dallas. Hot air from the open window blasted his face, and sweat dribbled down his sides. Thankfully trees, taller than the usual scrawny Texas variety, dangled over the street, creating shade. Streets and yards were deserted, battened down against the heat.

After weeks mopping floors in state buildings and living in a flea-infested halfway house, he wouldn't have cared if he were in Death Valley. Although it kind of felt that way.

He stopped across from Diana Stern's two-story Tudor mansion. He might have picked out her house without finding the address online, the place was so classy. Climbing ivy made it look a hundred years old. Crepe myrtle in front sported pink blossoms. On the west end of the lot, a driveway led through a stone archway to the back. A walkway parted the perfectly cut grass and led to a massive front door displaying a security decal.

From his online checking, Marrs knew hotshot lawyer Michael Stern—probably gone fat and unable to get it up—lived here with a likely frustrated wife. More investigation would be needed. He had to know who came and went and when. See if the hubby presented an obstacle.

Any plan depended on no interruptions. As he plotted, a stab of reality poked him. Diana Stern was the big time, a public official. The cops wouldn't rest until they nailed him. This would be high stakes.

As he pulled away, a wood-paneled rust-bucket wagon emerged through the stone archway and crawled down the drive. The driver was a round-faced Mexican woman. A maid? Probably full time with as much money as the Sterns had. Suddenly, a new plan coalesced in his mind.

He followed the maid at a safe distance.

* * *

Two hours later, Marrs shivered in the walk-in freezer of Jack's Truck Stop, counting cases of frozen French fries. His hands were white, and the painful cold penetrated clear to his liver.

A female voice called out from the other side. "Better hurry, honey. You'll freeze your nuts."

He stepped out, coming face to face with a woman about his age and his height, with puffed-up brown hair. Ketchup stains spattered her white well-stuffed T-shirt. Her face was streaked with sweat and laced with kitchen grime. Marrs smiled. "I think I did."

She smacked gum. "Coffee?"

"Sure."

She nodded. "Lottie Lewis. You must be Jim's brother?"

"Yeah."

"Follow me."

As she turned, Marrs noticed her pants looked like they'd been glued to her ass like wallpaper.

"We'll need ten cases of taters to get through Labor Day. Them drivers really shovel 'em in." She tucked stringy strands of hair behind her ears. "I run this place and make that asshole a mint." She smacked louder. "Let's sit down and go over the order."

The asshole must have been Jack.

She gestured Marrs toward two folding chairs by the huge steel sink. They'd been pushed close together. Despite the chill, Marrs was sweating. If he wasn't in control, women intimidated him. A guy couldn't tell what they wanted.

How he hated them.

* * *

The next day, Marrs drove downtown. He parked in a commercial zone in front of NationsBank. Inside it took a minute to figure out which elevators to take. He barely squeezed in as the doors shut, causing them to reopen and pause a couple of seconds. He could feel the glare of the other riders bore into the back of his head.

Marrs started to push the button for Jackson, Stern and Randolph's floor, but saw the number already lit. A twerp eyeballed him all the way up. Fear gripped him, as the preppy with slicked-down receding hair and a perfectly knotted striped tie continued to stare. This trip might have been a mistake. He'd just wanted a glance at the husband's digs, a feel for his competition for darling Diana, but he felt busted already. Marrs decided he'd risk a peek from outside Stern's office and then get the hell out.

After a long ascent, Marrs was alarmed that the elevator opened directly into the reception area of the firm. He'd hoped to recon the place without having to walk in, but they rented the whole fucking floor, and now he had no choice. It would look stupid—if not suspicious—to ride straight back down without getting off. Fortunately he had done some homework, so he ambled off behind the preppy VIP.

The receptionist sat in front of brass letters, which screamed the name of the place to anybody with myopia. She spoke into her headset while smiling at the fancy young lawyer.

Plank flooring and froufrou rugs told Marrs they didn't build this Taj on charity cases. Diana's hubby had to be important, and likely very busy—too busy to pay attention to his wife.

The dandy finished with the receptionist, pranced away, and used a card to open a door. The guy's left arm hung funny.

"May I help you?"

"I have a delivery for Dennis Higgins." He could see her cream-colored skin down her shirt to the top of her pink bra and figured she pissed on that lawyer wimp during lunch.

"Mr. Higgins is no longer with the firm."

Still clutching the door, the gimpy lawyer wrinkled his nose, like he smelled rotten cod. "He hasn't been here in two years. Retired because of his stroke." The attorney turned and stepped closer, giving Marrs an up-and-down eyeball search. "Who do you work for? I've not seen you up here before."

Marrs retreated. The Foodsmart shirt had been another error. Why would a law firm need a restaurant supplier? He mumbled some meaningless drivel, purposely incomprehensible.

The attorney crept nearer. "I didn't hear you."

Marrs turned and jammed the elevator button, hoping he wouldn't have to wait long. His brain searched for an answer and could only come up with, "Must have the wrong firm."

The nosy bastard snorted disbelief and kept staring. Did he moonlight as a fucking parole officer?

Marrs felt his balls retracting. After an eternity, the elevator door opened, but the creepy young lawyer's riveting eyes stayed on him until the doors closed. He'd like to go back and stab the puke with the slick new stiletto he'd bought on the street.

* * *

Later, back in his dump, Marrs studied the list of clients on Stern's website. He got up and closed the front door, shutting out the racket of kids throwing rocks at passing cars, and punched the phone number. Scouting the place hadn't been a good idea. But the guy would forget him.

"Good afternoon, Jackson, Stern and Randolph."

"Michael Stern, please," Marrs said.

"I'll connect you to his assistant."

A short pause, then, "Mr. Stern's office." This voice was older, more professional.

"This is Gene Prescott from the CNA home office. I have a new case for Mr. Stern. A major case." Marrs was pleased with how solemn he sounded.

"I can have him call you."

"Could I set a time to come down to go over the file? What's his schedule like?"

"Well, next week is tight. Let me check the week after." Marrs could hear her clicking the keyboard. "He'll be in New York that Friday. I could squeeze you in on Wednesday morning."

"Wednesday won't work. I'll be in Seattle. Any chance he could meet with me that weekend?"

"He'll probably stay in New York until Sunday. Can another partner see you?"

"I'll have to get back to you, but thanks for your help." Leering at the newspaper picture of Diana, Marrs hung up. He had a window of opportunity.

* * *

Behind his car's tinted glass, Marrs watched Diana stroll along the shops of Highland Park Village, three blocks from her house. Her yellow sundress hugged her incredible tits, but hung loose around her hips. Cute red toenails poked through sandals. A wisp of sun-streaked hair decorated her forehead. She stepped into the Escada store.

Marrs shoved open the Cherokee's door. He needed a reason for being in the area. The upscaly restaurant nearby would be a perfect cover.

Clutching the price list, he marched into Patrizio's and was greeted by the smell of tangy garlic and the din of clanging plates. He approached the skinny hostess, who was stacking menus. "I'm with Foodsmart," he said. "I'd like to see the manager."

She scowled.

Marrs added, "Please, ma'am."

She disappeared behind a door carved with a palm tree.

Marrs eyed the variety of flesh in the place. One table of women about Diana's age looked like horny, rich bitches. They laughed loud enough to crack the windows. A shapely redhead turned her legs out, her skirt riding halfway up her juicy thighs. Marrs felt moisture on his neck. His hands began to shake.

The hostess returned with no manager in tow and went back to seating customers.

He checked his Timex. After five annoying minutes Marrs wadded his list under his arm, wheeled around, and froze. Right in front of him, glowing from the heat, stood Diana Stern.

* * *

As Michael finished proofing a report to Standard on the *Layne* nurses' depos, Janet, his paralegal, shoved a stack of documents at him. "Partners' meeting at four." She pointed to the pile she'd handed him. "Caswell."

"Shit." He pinched the bridge of his nose. "Well, the girl's a lock. At least she can find the courthouse."

"You ran off the last female associate up for partner."

"She dreamed up the silly idea that I'd leave Diana and marry her."

After a long moment, Janet said, "You treated her like shit."

Stern locked his eyes on her. The woman had worked for him so long, knew so much, she seemed to think he worked for her sometimes.

Janet stared back. "You'll get us sued."

Stern decided to concede the point. "Well, Caswell's a white male. Can't get sued there." He grinned. "With my shares and Randolph's, I only need three more to shit-can him for good."

She smiled. "Want me to pick up Sarah from soccer?"

"Where's Diana?"

Janet shrugged. "Left a message, she was hung up. A church committee lunch. Asked if you could get her."

Stern considered this. Although he and Diana were observing a truce, even avoiding arguments, his marriage was doomed. Separate bedrooms. Separate lives. Diana's social life no longer interested him, and the parole thing was absurd. He wanted a son, and she couldn't have more children, so what was the point?

Fear of only seeing his angel every other weekend had held him back from taking action, even when he'd been involved with a newer model. Now that Sarah was older and so into sports, he'd have a shot at winning custody. She might even tell a judge she wanted to live with her father. But he'd need objective evidence of how good a father he was.

"Tell Randolph to vote my shares against little numb-nuts. If I don't oppose the girl, others will go along. I'm going to watch Sarah's practice. In fact, book me out every Tuesday and Thursday afternoon till Thanksgiving."

Janet nodded. "Do you know a guy named Prescott from CNA? He wants to meet you."

"Never heard of him, but schedule him in."

* * *

Pacing between the sitting room and her bedroom, Diana worked a longneck. She'd called from the restaurant and learned Michael had been at the entire practice instead of picking up Sarah when she finished. The son of a truck driver didn't know shit about soccer. When Michael was in school, nobody played it.

Knowing him, he was preparing for a custody contest. He'd find out a real fight wasn't like one of his cases. Her family would burn money, millions if needed, for the best divorce lawyers in Texas just to make sure he didn't win. When they were through, he'd be begging for every other weekend.

She finished her beer and considered her odd encounter in the Village with the attractive young man who nearly knocked her over while scrambling away. It had taken only a second to remember he was a parolee and another that his name was . . . a planet.

She stepped to her laptop, logged on to the website, and entered her password. In a minute, she had Marrs's file and photo up. Clicking over the summary of the victim's impact statement, she shivered. The young woman had been brutalized, but oddly, not penetrated, which helped Marrs get a plea deal.

He'd been so pleasant at the interview, but she wondered if he could've been what? *Flirting?* She could give the file photo to the Highland Park police. They would keep an eye on the house, if she asked. But before the printer stopped, she changed her mind. Michael had had run-ins with them, calling them the Mayberry PD, after a stupid ticket he'd fought and lost.

Diana looked up to see her husband in the doorway, staring at her. Startled, she exited out of the file, but Michael spotted the screen.

"What axe murderer were you so interested in?"

She flushed like a kid caught surfing porn. "Nobody."

"We brought home a pizza. Sarah bet me fifty bucks on some new computer game."

"You shouldn't encourage her to gamble," Diana scolded.

Stern shrugged. "I usually lose. It's better than just giving her money."

She glanced at the paper in the printer, wondering.

Marrs had run, like she'd been holding a warrant.

She wished she could still talk to Michael. Which had come first, her loss of libido or his catting around? Her own silly affair hadn't adjusted her thermometer—if three clumsy, non-orgasmic afternoons with her tennis pro counted as an affair. Being mauled by that associate, Caswell, hadn't lit her fire either. The hysterectomy was probably to blame, and Michael was a great father. So sad.

She ordered herself to forget the parolee. Mere coincidence.

* * *

Stern stared at the grotesque figures on the screen. Sarah had already killed twice as many monsters in the dungeon as he had, and was nearly out.

She flung a hand toward him. "Double or nothing?"

He'd taught her well. Too well. He dug his gold money clip out of his pocket and slapped a crisp Grant onto her palm. "You need to work on your math."

Diana sashayed into the den, carrying an empty beer bottle. "Did you clean him out?"

Sarah held the fifty up. "But he won't go double or nothing."

Diana tossed her beer bottle into the recycle bin. "Honey, I'll triple it. Let's go look at clothes."

Sarah scrambled up. "Sweet."

Stern moved to the window and watched them pile into the Volvo. He'd be smart to divorce Diana now, when he wasn't getting anything on the side. Nothing to prevent him from going for custody. No judge wanted to listen to ancient history.

Stern headed for the fridge, but stopped. Picturing Kristen's taut body, he lectured himself to get into better shape. He could watch the news while using Diana's treadmill.

Upstairs, he spotted the paper she'd printed. He grabbed it, skimmed, then blinked. Geez. This Leonard Marrs was one major scumbag. And Diana let him out? The guy ought to be dragged behind a pickup until his dick fell off.

Then another possibility.

Was she attracted to him? A crush? The guy wasn't bad looking. Was this whole parole thing a perverted fixation, like some rape fantasy? He'd heard of women writing to notorious prisoners, proposing. The idea was crazy . . . but she sure wasn't interested in sex at home.

He decided the file might prove useful, but Diana couldn't know.

* * *

Downtown twenty minutes later, Stern stopped short of his corner office, wondering why the light was on. He peered in.

Janet sat at the Victorian writing table, her chin resting on her palm, apparently staring at the framed photos of Sarah and him.

Stern spoke softly, trying not to frighten her. "Still here?"

Janet erupted from her chair, turned, then patted her chest with relief that it wasn't a murderer who startled her. At the end of the day, she looked all of her forty-five years.

"I don't pay you enough to stay this late."

She sighed. "My date canceled on me."

Her eyes glistened with that longing look he'd seen several times over their years together. Occasionally, after a drink, he'd been tempted to service her. She certainly wasn't unattractive, but it would have been out of pity, not desire. And the best way to ruin a good assistant was to screw her. She'd had the loyalty to stick with a diabetic husband through two amputations before he died. Two worthless adult kids seldom called. Sleeping with her, and dumping her afterward, would make her life worse. Better to leave her heart aching than broken.

"Copier still on?" he asked.

She rolled her eyes. His skill with the machine was a running joke. She took the file from him and returned a minute later. "What is this?"

"One of Diana's parolees she championed for release. This is the kind of sleazebucket she frees to commit more mayhem. I think she's got some weird interest in this one."

Janet handed him the file and copy. "Isn't volunteering a good example for Sarah?"

"Never thought you'd take up for my bleeding-heart wife."

"I'm not, but I hope you know what you're doing."

Stern locked the copy in his credenza. "I may come home someday and find the locks changed."

Janet sighed. "Bad news."

"Yeah?"

"Caswell got in. Jackson rounded up fifty-two shares."

Stern stared, blinking. Why couldn't they see through his phony act? Having Caswell around would be like playing Texas Hold'em with a guy you knew cheated. "One of these days, Jackson —"

"But Randolph made sure the buy-in wasn't waived."

Stern snorted. "Tony doesn't get his shares for free, like the other crybabies. That'll cut his pay for a couple of years."

"He was kicking doors. A friend at the Patton firm said he practically assaulted a girl who worked there. Documents went missing when he left."

She paused. Stern noticed her suddenly serious expression.

"He scares me. Be careful with him."

CHAPTER 15

CASEY DENMAN, NURSING director at Adventist Hospital, marched into Kristen's office. Between her severe, soldier-like short hair, the navy pantsuit that looked like a uniform, and her purse slung across her shoulder trooper-style, Kristen half expected a salute. Instead, they ran through the normal pleasantries.

Then the phone buzzed.

"Is she there?"

"Yes, come on in."

A moment later Jenny, the barefoot attorney, was in the room, hugging the ad-hoc nurse-sergeant, who towered over her.

Casey turned to Kristen. "This little pistol was my best floor nurse!"

"My charting was so creative, she talked me into law school." Jenny closed Kristen's door. "Got them?" she said to Denman.

Casey fiddled with the strap of her shoulder bag. "I've called."

Jen's eyes darted toward Kristen, then back to Casey. "I need it soon."

"You'll get it. I promise."

Kristen looked from one to the other. "What's the conspiracy, guys?"

Jen shrugged. "Casey's doing a little research."

"Research? Like what?"

"We're going to pull a few charts for an ER case Pete assigned me," Jen said.

Kristen crossed her arms, not liking the sound of this. "Sounds like charts you haven't got medical authorizations for."

Jen put on her *who me?* face. "I deposed a plaintiff's ER expert, who says he always, immediately, every fuckin' time, gives bicarb to overdose cases, even before the tox screen is back. He's plied his trade in a dozen ERs around town. We'll access the charts by physician to see if he's telling the truth."

"Have those patients given permission for you to rummage through their records? I would guess they're pretty embarrassing."

Jen winked. "We're just going to have a little look-see."

Casey slid her satchel off her shoulder, looking a bit sheepish.

"And you can get this stuff from other hospitals besides Adventist?" Kristen asked.

"We've got a mole everywhere. Folks eager to help their brothers and sisters in medicine," Jen said with sarcasm.

Kristen shook her head. "I can't believe this."

"Relax. Nobody'll ever find out . . . if the guy's not lying."

"And if he is?"

"We'll use the stuff under the table. Threaten perjury. Get him to withdraw. That greedy plaintiff will be up shit creek without an expert witness."

Kristen was appalled. If Casey weren't in the room, she'd be tempted to chew Jenny a new one. All she could do was shake her head.

"Sometimes you got to break pissant rules." Jenny left with a conspiratorial wink.

Kristen grimaced at the nursing director. "Are we going to break any 'pissant' rules to defend Layne? Do any more illegal searches?"

Casey took a seat. "No. Galway may quack like a mallard in heat and be unable to find his ass with both hands, but our girls are blameless."

Kristen stared a moment, then decided to forget Jen's subterfuge on another case and grill her witness. After two hours, satisfied that Casey was prepared for her deposition, Kristen saw her out.

On her way back, she heard caterwauling coming from Jen's office. Kristen looked around the corner. Tammy Robberson, senior adjuster for Hospital Casualty, Adventist's insurer, was snarling at Jen, who looked like a *Do Not Resuscitate* patient.

Before Kristen could escape, Tammy, overdone in jewelry, spun around and pointed at Kristen. The snarl was gone, replaced by a comical clown-face of delight. "Jen tells me you cut a joint-defense deal with Stern. Perfect!" Tammy giggled like a teenager bragging about making out with the team captain. "He'll be so shocked when we hose him."

Kristen nodded, agreeing with her client, catching Jen's sad smile. It was Jen's way of apologizing for not broadcasting a BOLO warning that Tammy was loose in the office.

Their client wagged a finger. "Remember, he'd lie to Billy Graham on his deathbed."

"I know."

"I read the Betty Layne deposition. Don't treat that whore like she's Mother Teresa. This ain't a charity. That's why you lost last time." Her lips curled in a sneer. "I'll bet Layne did his share of coke and whores."

"Stern's looking into that."

"Digging dirt is one thing he's good at."

"Thanks again for letting me handle the case."

"Just don't fuck it up."

With my shield or on it.

* * *

Stern slid Rita's enchiladas into the oven while Sarah set the table in the breakfast room. Hearing Diana's car roll past the kitchen window, he opened a Corona, telling himself not to pick a fight, even though she'd been gone two days playing busybody. He should get along with his wife. At least for now.

Sarah looked perplexed. "I heard you tell Mom she shouldn't drink so much beer."

"She's had a long trip. What do you want to drink?"

Sarah acted like she was thinking about it. "A Corona. I've had a long day."

Her straight face made him realize the temptations of booze and boys were closer than he thought. "You're so funny."

She twisted her blond braids. "If you go to New York, you'll miss my tournament."

"I'm sorry, Sugar. I'll make the next one."

The door opened. Diana walked in and kissed Sarah on the cheek.

Stern handed Diana a cold mug and tried to keep any trace of sarcasm from his voice. "Glad you're home."

Diana gave him an odd half smile and took the beer.

"Mom, can you help me with my French tonight?"

"Honey, I've got an arts meeting. When I get back, if it's not too late."

"They're up for parole?" As soon as the words escaped Stern's mouth, he cursed himself for a stupid joke in front of Sarah.

Sensing impending fireworks, Sarah slipped out.

Diana whispered, "I'm surprised I've not seen any of your family at board hearings."

He saw the glare from her blue eyes. For some bizarre reason, Stern pictured Diana at twenty-one, braless in a Theta sweatshirt, sitting across from him at Chuy's in Austin, tossing down beer after beer, her breasts bouncing as she laughed. Her pearl choker had been worth more than his family's net worth. He'd wanted her in his arms wearing nothing but the necklace.

Be careful what you wish for.

"I'll give you a chance to interview your daughter. I've got a depo late Friday in New York. Jake Rothman and I are watching the Yankees Saturday. Be back Sunday."

"Going with Kristen?"

Stern found himself tongue-tied. Diana must have a spy inside his own fucking firm. "I don't know who the puke McGee is sending."

"Pete McGee is a *gentleman*." Diana spun around and stormed up the back stairs.

Stern wanted to say that going to church twice a week only made some people hypocrites, but figured this fight should be called a draw.

He turned and saw Sarah hesitating at the door, then tiptoeing in.

Stern tried to sound reassuring. "Mom's tired."

"I guess."

"How's French going?"

"Hard. Lots of kings. Lots of people getting executed, burned, and heads lopped off."

He remembered Kristen's reference to Joan of Arc. It seemed an odd spur-of-the-moment comparison, or maybe it wasn't spontaneous. Did she identify with the martyr?

Sarah popped open Stern's briefcase. "Any juicy pictures, Dad?"

Stern peeked in the oven.

"No rotting private parts? Kids at school love nasty pictures from your cases."

Stern shook his head. "You're all sick."

Then he remembered Diana's files he'd copied, of that Marrs puke.

"Honey, while I'm gone, don't open the door unless you know who it is."

Sarah rolled her eyes. "I'm not a baby."

"Ah, but you are," he said, eyes twinkling. "You're my baby."

* * *

Thirty-five thousand feet above Missouri, Kristen took a Chardonnay from the flight attendant, then clinked her glass with Stern's. "Thanks for arranging first class."

He turned in his seat. "Standard will think I brought an associate. I booked the Ritz rooms in my name, so Tammy wouldn't bitch about the cost. I'll send your firm's half of the bill after the case is over."

"Did your New York buddy get any dirt on Bragg's expert?"

"Nothing shocking. He testifies a lot, which doesn't endear him to his colleagues."

"Which is why we're doing it on a Friday night in his apartment?"

"Yep." He smiled. "Been meaning to ask. What'd Tammy tell you about me?"

"Says you're a lying scumbag capable of murder."

"Guess I made quite an impression."

"Seems you used to represent Hospital Risk. Is she another of your heartbroken women?" Kristen watched for his reaction.

"Nah. I just got sick of her knowing more than me about cases." Stern dug into his briefcase, removed a small folder, and flipped it open. "Sarah's science paper. Microbes. I'm editing."

She took a sip of her wine. "Lawyer, golfer, carouser, dad. How do you work it all in?"

"Easy. Sarah's the most important."

Kristen smiled, wishing she had been most important seventeen years ago.

"Did you visit New York a lot growing up?"

"Yes." Kristen looked out at the puffy white clouds under the plane. The closer they got, the more spiders crawled in her brain. And the more she feared her assignment. How far to go and how should she play him?

* * *

Friday afternoon, Marrs sat on a case of tomato paste and flipped through Foodsmart's price printout. It was hard to sell food when the stench in the hot kitchen was powerful enough to be banned by the Geneva Convention.

The saggy-jowled owner of Choppin' Charlie's shook his head, reminding Marrs of an old bulldog. Behind him, a Latino kid scraped the grease trap while whistling the Mexican tune "Degüello," which the Mexicans had played at the Alamo. The kid's back pocket bulged with a switchblade.

Marrs knew how Davy Crockett felt. "I'll sell our pasta at cost, for you to try."

Steam from the boiling soup collected in beads of sweat on everybody as a roaring fan futilely pushed hot air around. Choppin' Charlie wiped his face with his filthy apron. "I don't know, son. Jimmy seemed like he never had enough time."

"Kraft has inched up the meat while you weren't looking. You're getting hosed."

Charlie smiled. "You're a real salesman, Leonard. Come back tonight late."

Marrs thought a moment. His mouth got that nasty metallic taste. Here was his alibi. *Game on.*

CHAPTER 16

"NO MORE QUESTIONS," Kristen said.

Having survived the inquisition in his Park Avenue apartment, Bragg's cardiology expert exhaled relief. The court reporter massaged her fingers, then closed her stenotype. Glaring at each other, Stern and Bragg stood and crammed files into briefcases. Kristen thought at least one hour had been wasted by Stern and Bragg bickering for no purpose.

Kristen checked the time. 10:00 p.m. She was exhausted from four hours of arguing about signs of eminent cardiac tamponade. Fortunately when the case was over, she could forget everything she'd boned up on, so she'd have room in her brain for the next case. Kristen wanted to head for the hotel and crash, but she'd agreed to have a late dinner with her "ally."

Stern seemed as fresh as a junior at the prom, since his only role had been chewing out Bragg's expert over his witness fees and jousting with Bragg himself.

Kristen loaded her laptop into her shoulder bag and followed Bragg across the marble floor.

As Bragg opened the door, Stern smirked. "Got anybody else to help you, Joe? I think we finished off this guy."

Kristen cringed. She hoped the doctor was out of earshot. He had been reasonably civil.

Bragg's face flamed. "Listen, y'all. One of you will wise up. I'll make that defendant the best deal." Bragg pointed his stubby forefingers at them, imitating pistols. "Whoever's left will get creamed."

"Won't wash, Joe. You better go back in there and resuscitate your high-dollar witness."

Still holding the door open, Bragg turned to Kristen. "Keep two hands on your purse when you're around him."

Stern looked at his reflection in the shiny elevator door and straightened his tie. "Joe, I'd love to argue, but we've got dinner reservations."

"Where?" Kristen asked.

"Greenwich Village. The Black Sheep. Very quaint."

"Did they name it for you?" Before Stern could answer her banter, Kristen tugged Bragg's elbow. "Meet us there, Joe."

Stern grimaced, but said nothing.

Kristen enjoyed the trick she played, but relished Stern's reaction more.

* * *

Inside a cab crawling south toward the Village, Stern tried to disguise his disappointment. One less chance to get something going with Kristen, but hopefully he'd have another opportunity Saturday. He also realized years of sitting at a desk and swinging a driver were taking a toll on his lower back. Tonight, his muscles screamed for Ben-Gay. Maybe he'd be better off to try again tomorrow.

Kristen crossed her arms. "Judge Proctor has sanctioned lawyers for yelling in depos."

"So? Bragg beat up our people."

"You may practice law like a pro wrestler. I don't."

She was pissed. The way she clenched her jaw and narrowed her eyes was incredibly sexy. Cleopatra probably frowned at Antony the same way. "Maybe I got carried away."

Kristen sighed, perhaps signaling an armistice. "Good guess his expert had advertised for cases."

Stern tried to stretch his back without being obvious he hurt. "There are advantages to having been around awhile."

"Yeah, I read somewhere that you did Henry VIII's prenup."

Stern smirked, encouraged. "Why'd you invite Bragg along?"

"Why not? You two can argue about who grew up more disadvantaged. I'll referee."

He paused. "I didn't want to share your company."

To his disappointment, she looked out her window, staring at the city's bustle. Maybe she didn't hear him. A grimy mist gathered on the windows. The driver flipped on the wipers, smearing the windshield.

According to Janet, Kristen wasn't seeing anyone. Nobody knew of more than a handful of dates in her six years working at Wright McGee. Apparently, she rarely saw a man twice. Janet's source had told her a McGee firm running joke about an associate returning to the office late on Christmas Eve to pick up a forgotten present, and catching Kristen grinding away. For a while everyone called her "Bob Cratchit."

They passed ice cream vendors working Central Park despite the weather. Tourists walked along sharing umbrellas. The leaves already had turned. If the weather cleared, a stroll through the park tomorrow would be delightful.

Stern studied Kristen out of the corner of his eye. Her pudgy cheekbones and slightly deviated nose added interest. He suspected a quarter would bounce off her rock-hard belly. She was also damn hard to figure out.

Stern let her odd trance continue awhile longer before interrupting. "You did a nice job today. McGee himself couldn't have done better."

Kristen turned away from the rain-smeared window. "Thanks."

Her eyes looked misty. Maybe she was simply tired, but he decided not to risk embarrassing her by asking if anything was wrong.

He frowned, took a deep breath, and closed his eyes for a moment. *Go for it, Mike. Balls out.*

"We could do a museum tomorrow. The MOMA?"

She brushed her fingers against her eyelids as if they itched. "I'll be in Stamford."

Stern hesitated, then tried to sound casual, like he would survive if she turned him down, when he knew he might not. "We could catch a show later."

"Pick out something you want to see," she said, sounding unimpressed. "Take your Manhattan pal, if you want. I'll call when I get back, but don't wait on me."

"Sure," Stern said, hoping he didn't sound as disappointed as he felt.

CHAPTER 17

Dallas
Friday, August 22

SARAH ZIPPED AND HOOKED Diana's red Valentino gown, grabbed a handful of popcorn, then plopped back onto the TV-room couch. "This shit must be important, to go by yourself."

Livid, Diana spun around and wagged a finger at her daughter. "We don't speak that way in this house."

"Sorry," Sarah mumbled.

Diana wasn't having any of it. She was tempted to haul Sarah to her feet, look into her eyes, and make her really apologize. Satisfying as that might be, she was ultimately angry at Michael for being a bad influence, for being gone, and for being so adored by Sarah.

"I'll leave as soon as the photographer finishes."

Sarah scooped more popcorn. "Is it okay if I call Chuck and see if he can come over?"

Diana's heart gunned through a few beats, but she managed to act like it didn't happen. "Certainly not."

"Just kidding. Can I spend the night with Shelly tomorrow?"

"Honey, I wanted Saturday evening with you. With Dad being gone and—"

"Blow off the party tonight, and we could do something now." Sarah crammed popcorn into her mouth and almost incomprehensibly said, "Or skip the United Way tomorrow afternoon and watch me play."

"I've made a commitment to Marge."

Sarah swallowed and shrugged. "And I've made a commitment to Shelly." The remote came up and the television volume grew louder.

Diana bit her lip. Her friends warned her that girls become monsters at thirteen. "Turn that down, please."

Sarah complied, but looked away.

Diana considered calling Marge and begging off. She did need to spend more time with Sarah before hormones completely kicked in. But it was being alone tomorrow at night that she truly dreaded, despite their security system.

For some reason, another person in the house, even Sarah, helped her sleep. Bringing Rusty upstairs didn't. His snorting and wandering kept her awake. She could drop in on her sister, but would look stupid asking to stay.

With the thought of Leonard Marrs lurking around, she actually wished Michael was home.

* * *

Saturday afternoon, Sarah's friend Becca tapped Sarah's knee as her mother's car pulled into the Sterns' driveway. "See you at Shelly's tonight."

Becca's mom turned toward the backseat. "Got a key?"

"Yes, ma'am. Thanks for the ride."

Sarah shoved open the door, slid out, and walked under the stone archway into the back yard. Rusty shook himself from under the magnolia, greeting her with a yawn. She stroked his head and walked to the back door.

Her fingers groped under the wrought iron railing leading up the steps and found the magnetic key box. She pulled it off, opened it, and unlocked the back door. The alarm didn't beep, but that wasn't uncommon during the day. Leaving Rusty outside, she stuck the box back under the handrail and entered the house.

Sarah wedged her untied cleats off and grabbed a Pepsi from the fridge. In the den, she shuffled through her CDs. Mom wouldn't be home for a while. She wouldn't have to use headphones, and could crank the music as loud as she wanted and shake the house. Before she loaded her favorites, the doorbell chimed.

* * *

The plan Marrs had for Friday tanked when the maid left early. Then, a restaurant jerk kept him waiting an hour and spent another hour putting together his order. He should have laced the shrimp with E. coli and killed everybody in the place. By the time he'd finished jacking with the seafood ticket, the Stern house sat dark and bolted down for the night.

He pressed the doorbell and shifted from one foot to another, glancing around the quiet neighborhood. This was higher risk than the original plan, but one of Jim's old Foodsmart uniforms made him look like a deliveryman. Opening a shiny silver box to displayllong-stemmed roses, he tried the storm door handle. Locked. Before he decided on his next move, the knob on the inside door turned, and the massive door cracked open.

"Flowers for Diana Stern," he said, holding out the box.

A blond girl examined him, twisting her fingers through her hair. "Leave them on the porch."

Marrs summoned up innocence. "It's too hot. They'll wilt."

The teen stared, like a fucking zombie.

His heart accelerated. The acid taste of adrenaline filled his mouth. *Come on, kid.*

After a moment she tried to unlock the glass storm door while still sizing him up, but with her attention on him, the latch didn't slide.

Now, honey.

Marrs summoned up a look of innocence. "We need to get them in water." He gently emphasized the "We."

Her fingers fiddled with the brad, but her gaze remained fixed on him.

If she pushed the latch another half inch, he'd be in. He could taste Diana's sweet flesh, feel her soft body in his hands. It would take him only a minute to get the kid out of the way. And Diana, being the good mother, would do anything to keep the girl from getting hurt. Anything.

"My mom'll be home soon. She'll get them."

The rich kid slammed the door on him like he was a Jehovah Witness.

He stood there for several moments, feeling the adrenaline drain into anger.

She would pay for her bad manners.

CHAPTER 18

New York
Saturday, August 23

WHEN KRISTEN ROSE SATURDAY morning, she'd considered checking out and spending the night with her cousin, Gina, in Stamford. Gina had been her best friend since taking her in when she was sixteen, listening to her cry, understanding her. But Gina, an assistant professor of French lit, had a new boyfriend and a faculty party that night. Kristen would have been a third wheel. She'd had enough of that Friday night, listening to Stern and Bragg argue over some old case that didn't matter. So, she just made a day trip to catch up with her old friend.

When they'd finished laughing themselves silly over the good old times (skipping the year Kristen was a refugee at Gina's), Kristen bid a fond farewell and took the train back to Midtown, since she'd missed American's last flight to Dallas. A debate worthy of Clay and Webster resumed in her mind. Room service dinner? Or Stern? The choices would only get harder.

At Penn Station, she called Stern. Perhaps there'd be no answer, and that she'd get credit for trying. She hoped he'd gone to see the Yankees or Mets with his Manhattan lawyer buddy. But Stern answered, announced he had theater tickets, and that they needed to get going in half an hour.

On the elevator up to her room, she asked herself whether this was a business outing or a date. She stepped out of her shoes as the car sped past floors. One floor before hers, it stopped. A white-haired man got on, staring at her bare feet. When the car stopped again, she raced to her room, carrying her shoes.

Inside, she pulled out the little black dress she'd tossed in for just this contingency. Next to it hung a white blouse with two rows of lace; she could wear the blouse with the slacks she'd packed. After staring into the closet a moment, she slipped into the hot number from the Neiman Marcus after-Christmas sale, faced the mirror, and did a couple of turns. She had to admit it looked pretty good. Adding her gold Byzantine earrings would catch any eye.

She swished some Scope, applied lipstick and mascara, and checked the mirror again. The old chill erupted.

You're nuts. Nobody would really want you. Or love you. At least not for long.

She tugged the dress over her head, snarling her hair in the process. The phone rang.

"Ready?" Stern's voice was melodious.

"Almost."

"I'll grab a cab."

She decided not to tell him she was half-naked with tangled hair. "Two minutes."

She squeezed back into the Needless Markup dress, dabbed Poison perfume behind each ear, brushed her hair again, and trotted to the elevator, toting her heels. *NMNS.*

* * *

In B. B. King's on Forty-Second Street, Kristen and Stern followed the maître d', Stern trailing. The saxophone player swayed to his music, which bounced off the iron grillwork around the bar. The crowd conversed and laughed. Music from *Miss Saigon* still hummed in Kristen's ears. She was glad she'd gone, and decided it was a date.

She grabbed the side of the table that would put her good ear to Stern and the bad one to the band. She felt bold, like Daisy flirting with Gatsby. "How was the museum?"

"Picked up a Monet poster for Sarah, to make a big *impression*." Stern smiled. "I thought of you when I saw this mysterious woman with dark hair in one painting." Stern inched closer. "Tell me something about yourself, something I don't know."

She could count the follicles of his beard, but didn't retreat. "My nose used to be straight. I took a knee in the face in college. You would think I'd have been smart enough not to let the trainer set it and keep playing."

"How'd you get the scars on your right knee?"

Kristen batted her lashes in mock embarrassment. "Two surgeries. High school basketball. ACL tear. Cost me a real scholarship. Later I ruptured cartilage in tae kwon do."

"Wow. Guess I'll be safe on the streets with you tonight." He smirked. "Did you have a nickname growing up?"

"*Krissy*, but in college the girls on the team called me Monk. I thought it was because I studied so much, or because I was quiet—then I found out it was short for Chipmunk, because of my chubby cheeks."

"They're precious."

She told him stories about her girls' basketball team, feeling her confidence grow with his interest, but a familiar voice reminded her, *This isn't real.* She was only following orders. It was her scamming him, and if he didn't see it, it was his problem.

Kristen smiled. "I cost us a game last spring. Got teed up when my Irish temper revolted. Worst call I'd ever seen. Wanted to strangle the guy."

"*You've* got a temper?"

She noted his sarcasm, but it had come out in jest. "If you saw me around my sister's piggy boyfriends, or blind refs in tight shorts, you'd be utterly appalled." Kristen looked away, listening to music. She could feel his gaze and remembered an old line, *Better to be looked over than overlooked.*

Breaking the spell, the waiter returned and uncorked their Cabernet.

She was starved and ordered a Porterhouse, rare. *One of the boys.*

Kristen savored the first sip, then asked, "Don't you ever feel sorry for people like Layne's family? Be honest, Michael."

Stern leaned back. "I try not to."

"Try not to feel sorry, or try not to be honest?"

"Ha ha."

She swirled the wine around in her glass. "I lost a case for Adventist last spring. Tammy wanted me to get a resident to change his story. I refused. And I had an old shoplifting conviction on the plaintiff, a lady who cleans houses and has five kids." Kristen shrugged. "Didn't use it. Couldn't."

Stern rested his chin on a palm. "I used to worry about the Laynes of the world. I defended a bad baby case for an old obstetrician once, who should've retired long before he delivered this oilman's child." He sipped, then continued, "Baby born limp as a wet rag. Couldn't swallow at three, couldn't even roll over. Dad was an okay guy, the mom an absolute saint. After three years, they still were taking turns all night sucking mucous from the kid's throat to keep him from choking. The mom quit teaching to be with that sad kid every minute."

"Did you try the case?"

"Yeah, after I busted my ass to get Standard to offer two mil, the plaintiffs rejected it. They turned it down flat." His voice trailed off. "Two was all I could get 'em to pay. Their lawyer looked like he was praying for a school bus to crash in his yard if he didn't win."

"And?"

"We convinced the jury the kid's brain damage was developmental,

122

in utero. I called a neuroradiologist. Said he saw abnormalities in the brain formed before delivery."

"Were there?"

He sighed. "I can't read an MRI. Maybe it was bullshit. Probably was. I did what I was paid to do. But when I heard that nice couple wailing in the hall after the verdict, I . . . I learned to separate myself from the people involved." Stern downed the rest of his drink. "I told myself that no amount of money would've given them the son they wanted." He stared a moment at his empty glass. "So maybe it didn't matter."

She watched him, thinking maybe there was a conscience in there, somewhere.

He shrugged. "I grew up with kids who didn't have enough money for gym shoes. Kids who *had* to eat government peanut butter at school. My clothes smelled like a refinery. Why not grab a little for me?"

Kristen listened as the band kicked into a new tune, savoring the camaraderie enveloping them. She realized the negative voice was gone. Totally gone. "Tell me about Sarah."

His expression changed immediately. "My daughter's the best kid. Good grades. Fine little athlete." Stern beamed. "Unlike some of the girls on her team, she never complains, and she'll get dirty."

He entertained her with several stories of his princess. Kristen found herself jealous. As the waiter brought salads and refilled their glasses, she debated whether to ask about Diana. *What the hell.* "And your wife?"

He didn't hesitate, like he was prepared for the question. "I'm not going to tell you she's gotten fat and doesn't understand me."

"But you've told other women that?"

Stern rocked back, looking philosophical. A new look for him. "She's had some health problems. We can't have more kids, but she's involved in more worthy causes than a stray dog's got fleas. Even though all those do-gooders annoy me, I have to say I respect her for it."

She went for broke, all in. "Then why the philandering?" Kristen fixed on Stern, determined to force an answer.

"I'm not nearly as bad as you've heard." He paused, as if giving the assertion time to stick, and ate a bite of salad.

Kristen waited, not accepting his response.

"We were both insecure when we met, but about different things. Me, socially, and her, emotionally. I was flattered the daughter of a Dallas socialite doted on a truck driver's son. I was, believe it or not, nervous as hell at the soirees she took me to. But since then, we've both grown and changed."

Kristen broke off a piece of bread. "Why not enjoy the improved versions of each other?"

"Sometimes two people drift far enough apart, they can't reach each other again. No matter how they stretch."

"That's good. It almost sounds like you were the one who did the reaching. How long did it take you to come up with that?"

He cocked his head, apparently surprised. "That's cruel."

Kristen chewed slowly, then said, "Just seeing how the witness handles the heat."

He gazed at her a second.

"I thought about you all day, what you would think of everything I saw. How much I'd enjoy sharing a day with you. A day not about *Layne*. Maybe tomorrow we could—"

Shaking her head, she stopped him. "I'm not who you think I am. Inside, I'm still the kid who fights her brother, bosses her little sisters around, and plays basketball." She tried to smile, but couldn't come up with one.

"I don't understand."

Her first thought was that she had screwed up with her mini-confession. But if she were to follow Tammy and Pete's orders to string him along, she had to keep him chasing for a few more weeks. Maybe a little mystery would help.

Stern considered her for several moments. "I know your bullshit detector is flashing. You don't trust me, but I wish you would."

The waiter reappeared and lingered, inquiring, relieving her of a need to answer. She prolonged the interruption, asking about the dressing, buying time, trying to determine how to play her role. She really liked the guy who proofed his daughter's microbes paper, but the voice returned, telling her she wasn't Daisy being courted by Gatsby. She was loony Nicole, chased by Dick Diver in "Tender Is the Night." Except Stern was more dangerous than any Fitzgerald character.

Finally, the waiter wandered off and she said, "We're lawyers, with clients whose interests are *not* identical, with a way to go before this case is over."

He seemed to accept her gentle turndown, and didn't seem terribly disappointed. He raised his glass. "United we stand."

They clinked.

As she ate her steak, Kristen considered inviting him to her room. It would get the seduction part of the assignment out of the way, and who was she saving herself for anyway? She'd even have a reason to go to confession, which she'd skipped for years. Although sleeping with Stern would be stupid, he might hold her until she quit shaking from the nightmare likely to come. This town held too many memories.

But she'd join the list of his conquests over half-hearted resistance and would feel like trailer trash the next day, screwing a married man in a fancy room he'd paid for. Worse, she'd lose leverage.

Sometime in the trial, she'd have to double-cross him, before he did the same to her. If she stupidly slept with him and more stupidly fell in love, not double-crossing him, she would be the butt of jokes for years, as the girl who got fucked twice on the same case.

CHAPTER 19

Dallas
Saturday, August 23

SITTING IN A CONVENIENCE STORE parking lot, Marrs crumpled a beer can and tossed it to the floor of the Cherokee. The heat seemed to wrap everything like a fat uncle wanting to give you a big hug. He'd risked cruising through the housekeeper's neighborhood twice last night, three times today, the last time just an hour ago. Junkers of every variety cluttered the street and lawns, but he'd spotted no wood-paneled station wagon.

He'd screwed up, not following the maid all the way to her house the first time he trailed her. But it had looked like a closed-off neighborhood, and he didn't want too much exposure. Otherwise, this weekend would have been perfect, with Michael Stern in New York. Unfortunately everything went wrong. All he could do now was sit in the parking lot, drink beer, and count smashed bugs on the windshield.

An old Camaro with a bad muffler roared in beside him. The driver killed the engine, but it sought life after death, banging and sputtering, smelling of burning oil. A brown-skinned young woman bounded out, her ass wiggling underneath running shorts. He felt eyes and saw her zit-faced boyfriend behind the wheel, glaring at him.

Marrs looked away.

A wood-paneled station wagon rolled from the maid's slum

division and stopped at the intersection. It turned left, passed him, and pulled into the side parking lot of the video store next door.

A heavy Mexican woman circled into the store.

His heart racing, Marrs bailed out of the Jeep and darted around the back of the video store, avoiding the front window. Her rust bucket sat alone.

He checked the tag.

Bingo.

The driver's side was closer to the store and the street, so he squatted at the passenger door. Salty sweat rolled into the corner of his mouth.

After what seemed long enough for her to not only rent but watch *Ben-Hur*, he heard footsteps nearing. As she got in, he yanked the passenger door open and slid inside, popping the stiletto, before she could stick the key into the ignition.

Her face contorted with shock. A scream seemed to choke in her throat.

He reached for the keys with his left hand, but she jerked them back and clawed for the door handle.

Before she could find the lever, he grabbed her right wrist and tried to shake the keys loose. "Give me the keys, or I'll slit your throat, momma."

She twisted her arm free and rotated to face him, while her left hand suddenly groped in the purse she'd set on the floorboard. She started jabbering loudly in Spanish.

He sliced through the air toward her, but she deflected the blow with her heavy forearm. He hadn't counted on her being so fucking strong.

She flattened herself against the door, still clawing through her purse, while trying to wedge her foot up to the seat and push him away.

He tightened his grip on the stiletto and shoved her leg out of his way.

Something shiny appeared in her hand. He only got a glance.

Before he could bury the knife in her, a noise erupted like a firecracker stuck in his ear. Then another.

Searing fire tore through his chest and arm. He fell from the car, landing hard on the asphalt.

His ears rang like bells had been implanted in his head.

Somehow he rolled clear before the car peeled away.

CHAPTER 20

New York
Sunday, August 24

KRISTEN DRAGGED AN ARM out from under her blanket and popped the alarm, but the infernal noise didn't stop. She realized it was her cell. She fumbled for it before she could answer.

"It's Jen."

"What time is it?" Her mouth felt like sandpaper laced with minibar scotch aftertaste. Boozing had been a futile effort to ward off nightmares.

"Nine here. You must've had a late night."

"Yes." She could imagine Jen smirking and wondering how far she'd gone in her assignment with Stern.

"We've got a big screw-up on that drug case. You know, the fucked-up kid whose mom mixed his antibiotics with asthma meds. We got noticed for depos in New Jersey, starting tomorrow. They'll last a week."

Kristen didn't understand why this was her problem. "Okay."

"Ron's secretary signed the receipt for the notice, went to lunch, got tipsy with this guy from Klein Patton, and forgot to docket it. Corporate counsel for the drug company called Pete this morning, freaking out 'cause nobody from our shop showed to preview the documents. Someone's head is going to roll."

"Ron better hop the next plane."

"Can't find him. Went camping with his son. His phone is off."

"Jeez, Jen. You're number two on this."

"No way for me to get there in time. Corporate guy will meet you at noon today."

"Today? But it's Sunday. Give me a break."

"New Brunswick. I'll e-mail you everything you need."

"We've got *Layne* stuff this week."

"We'll cover you."

Kristen winced. "I don't have enough clothes," she said, mostly to herself.

"Buy some. Call it case expense and bill the client. Get a nice room and eat well every night. They can afford it."

That wasn't the problem, nor was it necessarily that she had a boatload of *Layne* problems to take care of. Kristen had been struggling to stay sane and out of Jersey for years. Just being in New York had caused her brain to replay images of family trips best forgotten. But she had no choice. She surrendered.

"Whatever," she said, hanging up. She didn't even care if Jenny thought she was pissed. Better that than scared.

She briefly considered calling Stern. She supposed it would be rude not to, but rationalized it was too early.

* * *

Having already wasted most of Monday morning, Stern sat in his office with what his old Army colonel called the Thousand-Yard Stare. In his mind, he saw Kristen stepping gracefully out of a cab and taking his hand. Her tight black dress rode high up her showstopper legs. And she had to know they were showstoppers. *Incredible.*

Undoubtedly, McGee and Tammy had suggested she tempt him. Maybe ordered her, so he wasn't surprised she hadn't slept with him.

He figured delaying the inevitable carried its advantages for her. What bothered him was she had cut out of New York without a word, like she didn't care about her orders, or even basic civility.

Or did he miss a "tell," as poker players say? Why did such a gorgeous woman have such a nonexistent social life? No family to spend holidays with? Why no help through college? Cardio surgeons are rich. Had her family died in a crash? He had seen glimpses of melancholy in her face, both in New York and at the Fairmont when he'd joked about using her doctor dad as an expert. None of the pieces fit, but he needed to find the answer to figure out whether she was ruthless enough to shaft him before he could do the same to her.

Janet cracked his door. "Bob Russell is waiting."

Stern sighed. "Before you send him in, search for a heart surgeon named Kerry, licensed in New Jersey. Have the state board send us his file."

"First name?"

"Don't know."

Janet frowned. "Is this an expert on a case?"

"Do it today."

She blinked, possibly surprised by his tone, then slipped out.

Stern toyed with the remaining pen in his gold desk set, remembering a line from an old song his big sister used to play, about forgetting it though your heart's still burning. He knew he should forget her and represent his client.

Standard's claims manager passed through the doorway and cleared his throat. "How was New York?"

Stern stood. "We got some decent stuff out of Bragg's expert." His hand felt crunched by Russell's grip. The man had a permanent sunburn to go with his surly disposition. Maybe he was still pissed over losing at golf.

Russell dropped into a chair. "Can we win?"

Stern decided to shoot straight. "Wife was a pretty good witness.

Everybody in town thinks it's a screw-up. How could Layne lie around just fine all night, then crash with no warning whatsoever?"

"Ettinger says developing tamponades can be subtle."

"True, but since Galway didn't order an echocardiogram that night, we don't know whether it was subtle or missed."

Russell scowled. "You gettin' soft?"

The question irritated Stern, but he controlled his voice. "Just makin' sure you know the downside."

"We were going to slop this shit onto the hospital. That chickie lost her nerve in her last trial."

Stern decided to sound like George Patton "I'll dump on her right in the middle of the trial. She'll be as helpless as a heifer with a stuck calf."

Russell beamed. "That's my warhorse."

With Russell temporarily satisfied, Stern shot the breeze with him for a while, promised a round of golf the next week, and was finally able to usher the annoying client out. Stern had always thought that practicing law would be fun if not for the clients, judges, and other attorneys.

On Stern's way back to his office, Janet handed him a sheet of paper. "Only found one Kerry in New Jersey. He's just forty. Not who you're looking for, is it?"

Stern avoided her eyes, a little frightened how she read his mind. "No."

At his desk, Stern found Jake Rothman's card and called. Eventually, he got Rothman's paralegal, Donna, whom he remembered from a trip last year.

"Hi, cutie."

"Michael! Did the dirt I found on your Park Avenue whore help?"

"Priceless."

"How come I didn't hear from you while you were in town?"

"Had to hurry home for my kid's game. Do you guys do the M.D.

defense in Jersey?"

"Some. Parker and Boggs, here in New York, and a couple outfits in Philly share with us. You moving?"

"I couldn't pass the ethics exam. I'm getting an expert endorsed against me from Trenton, a heart surgeon named Kerry. Got anything on him?"

"I'll check the system." After a few seconds, Donna said, "Zilch in the expert index."

"Any chance you've represented him?"

After a minute of tapping keys, the New York paralegal said, "Nothing active. I'll check closed files."

Stern listened to more typing, feeling frustrated.

"I found a Kerry, but he was a gastro who busted a guy's colon doing a scope. Shitty mess. If it's important, I'll have a runner search files that predate this index and call other firms."

"It's vital."

Stern thanked Donna, hung up, and forced himself to get to work. As he finally got lost in a blizzard of files, the intercom buzzed.

"There's a Donna Sparling in New York calling," Janet said.

Stern grabbed the phone.

Donna spoke rapidly. "I've found two old files on a James W. Kerry from Trenton, who was a cardio surgeon. Sent a runner to storage for one. Called a Philly firm for another."

"He *was* a surgeon?" Stern asked.

"No current listing in the New Jersey Medical Directory. I called AMA in Chicago and the cardio board. Nothing. Maybe he's dead?"

Remembering that Kristen said she was the oldest kid, Stern did a rough calculation. "I doubt it."

"Well, the first is a malpractice suit against him. Pretty routine. Handled by a firm in Philadelphia. Infected sternum. Case dropped by the plaintiff."

"Doesn't sound like much of a case."

"Yeah. His CV's strong. Trained at Mass General, published on aortic grafting."

"Did he present papers in Munich?"

She paused. "Yes, it's on here."

Stern couldn't contain his excitement. "That's the guy. What's the other one?"

"A stinker. Post-op bleed. Patient died. Allegation Dr. Kerry did drugs and refused a page. The hospital was sued for credentialing him. Jake's old shop here in town got his defense."

"Ouch."

"Settled on a nondisclosure agreement."

"Can you release anything?"

"Some. The paralegal at Jake's old place said their index showed another file, a licensing board case, but she couldn't find it."

"Donna, I'm sending you a bonus. Maybe you can help her."

* * *

Stern sat in his small conference room the next day, trying to ignore Bragg's constant drumming of his chubby fingers. Puffed up and eager, Layne's lawyer seemed about to burst out of his Italian suit. The court reporter's hands rested on her machine. Everyone waited for Kristen. Soon, he'd see those green eyes again, but he had to play it cool.

The door flew open. In walked a small woman with a freckled face, her hair cropped into tiny spikes. "I'm Jenny Norton from Wright McGee."

Confusion erupted in Stern. Had McGee taken Kristen off the case? Had he already lost his chance? Would he ever see her again?

* * *

Leaving New Brunswick, Kristen slowed the rented Civic. The

plaintiff's lawyer had run out of gas early, so she had a whole day to herself. Nobody expected her in the office until Friday for Casey's depo. She was a hero. She'd pulled Jen's ass off the grill. She was also close to her baby sister, who would be thrilled to see her. It had been over a year since her brother snuck Beth out of Mom's apartment and flew her to Dallas.

One road sign read RT 1 WEST-TRENTON, the other, EAST-NEWARK. Her hands locked on the wheel. Thoughts ricocheted through her like machine gun fire off a concrete bunker. She recited from Tennyson, "Into the Valley of Death Rode the Six Hundred."

She could picture the ninety-year-old three-story house, a citadel on a lot big enough for a hunting preserve. Oaks towered over the gabled roof. The third story had been a ballroom in the Roaring Twenties. Her bedroom, in the southeast corner of the second floor, was her refuge.

She saw a patient father in Philly teaching a ten-year-old a jump shot. How loving he had been then, doting on his firstborn. A skinny girl jabbed an elbow into her younger brother's stomach and won at hoops for the last brownie, the argument more brutal than the game.

But other memories cascaded. A stinging slap across her face. Screaming behind those walls. The last time she'd been in the house was a scene that ran in Technicolor in her mind.

She dragged a duffel bag containing her important stuff. Gina sat in her car, looking scared, like she might drive off before Kristen got out the door.

Her mother wailed, "He tried to quit, but the strain is awful. You don't understand the pressure. You shouldn't have said anything to anybody. I know how you feel, but you're wrong."

Kristen shouldered past her mother and hurried to Gina's van.

"You've ruined everything."

Kristen had been the only kid with no parent to cheer her on at high school basketball games, or to have family applaud at graduation.

She'd spent her adult life deflecting questions. But she'd survived, done what she could for Tina, helped her brother get through medical school, and spent furtive hours with Beth on the phone, talking about drugs, alcohol, and boys. She repeated to herself, *NMNS. Not Mary, Not Shit.* The Kerrys were gone from Library Place, and so was she.

* * *

Stern's attention drifted as his new partner gave him a blow-by-blow of a small-fry docket she'd somehow managed to survive. He couldn't get the question out of his mind: *What happened to Kristen's father?*

Faye Hill raised her voice, as if sensing his daydreaming. He refocused on her brown eyes. She seemed satisfied he was paying attention, and continued.

Janet eased his door open. "Michael, Donna Sparling is calling from New York."

"Excuse me. I've got to take this."

Baby partner sat motionless. "I'll wait."

Stern swore under his breath. *Let them in, and they think you work for them.*

He dashed into Janet's office and picked up the phone. "Any luck?"

"Pay dirt! Big license hearing fifteen years ago."

"What happened?"

"A consent decree entered. Guy surrendered his ticket."

"Gave up?"

"It's crazy. They had a hearing after the Maguire case was settled. The unanswered pages. The order shows it lasted two days. Then the consent was entered."

Stern searched for an explanation, but came up with nothing.

"I tried to get the transcript. Jake's old firm handled it."

"And?"

"I can't. There's a confidentiality order attached to the file. The

138

transcripts are sealed."

"You're kidding!"

"No. Somebody got a separate order from juvenile court, directed at the licensing board and everybody involved. Jake said he could get disbarred if we opened it."

"Juvenile court?" Bizarre.

Stern heard pages flipping. "I've got the Petition for Revocation. He lived on Library Place in Trenton. Forty-five at the time."

"Who was his lawyer?"

"Abe Cohen. He died last year in a scuba accident."

"Donna, you did good. Got time for an ol' Texas lawyer to take you to dinner?"

"I'd make time for you."

"Hang on." Stern covered the mouthpiece and spoke to Janet. "What's my schedule?"

"Friday, Bragg's taking the depo of the hospital's nursing director," she said.

"Shit." Stern scratched his chin. "I could send Numb-nuts to sit there and keep quiet. No reason to ask anything on the record."

Janet grabbed the docket printout. "Thursday is a mediation on that cancer case."

Stern spoke into the phone, "Let's plan on Thursday. This Thursday." Stern let her excitement fulminate a minute before begging off.

He whispered to Janet, "The new 'partner' in my office can do the mediation. She'll give money away and bore 'em to death at the same time."

Janet pawed through her desk and retrieved her set of Stern's keys. "I'll tell Tony about Friday and pick up Sarah at practice."

Stern felt an anticipation similar to that of a sixteen-year-old on a date with the school cheerleader. Soon he'd have an answer to the enigma and maybe some insight into the woman.

With *Layne* critical, a trip was stupid, but the more elusive this mystery, the more somebody had tried to conceal it, the more potentially valuable the explanation.

* * *

Stern gnawed on a hot dog in a Midtown Manhattan diner. He'd forgotten mustard, but the place was jammed on a Friday, and getting up wasn't worth the effort. He called Sarah, hoping to catch her between classes. "Hi, princess."

"Daddy, you're not going to be gone another weekend, are you?"

She used *Daddy* when she was upset or wanted something she knew she couldn't have. Still, a lump gathered in his throat. "No. Let's plan our ski trip. See how the week after Christmas looks for everybody."

"Mom's mad."

"I've got the week of New Year's free."

"You guys aren't going to get a divorce, are you?"

He heard her sniff into the phone and felt like a complete heel. "No, honey. Do we want to go to Aspen?"

"Mom smashed that fancy bowl that came from Greece."

"Maybe it slipped, because it's *greasy*."

Sarah groaned. "Did you send Mom roses last Saturday?"

Stern pretended not to hear the question and talked more about skiing. *What the hell was that about?* He spotted Donna in a tan raincoat, her knobby knees protruding, dashing across the street between honking cars. Stern told Sarah good-bye as Donna walked in.

She saw him and sat at the table, which was no bigger than his briefcase.

Stern gave her a quick kiss. "Think you'll have any trouble?"

Her doe eyes blinked. "Nobody will have any reason to look for it. My friend there is reliable, but to be safe, I'll wait a few days."

Stern handed her an envelope from his room at the Ritz. "This should help weaken everyone's memory."

She peeked, but didn't count the stack of hundreds.

"Mark the package *Confidential.* Stick my FedEx number on it and use the code name."

She winked. "Thanks for last night, ol' Texas lawyer."

* * *

In her office, Kristen finished reviewing Casey's file and handed the *Layne* notes back to Adventist's nursing director. Bragg would be entitled to see everything Casey had examined to prepare for her testimony. "There's nothing in here to hide."

Casey Denman nodded. "I've been deposed by Bragg before. Lots of spray across the table."

Kristen chuckled as her phone buzzed. "Kristen, Dr. Galway's lawyer is here and wants to visit before you start," Cindy said.

Kristen hadn't seen Stern since Saturday and felt her heart race. "Send him in."

Casey slung her briefcase over her shoulder. "Meet you in the conference room."

Kristen reached into her purse and pulled out a mirror. Even if she had to resume her role, Stern was nice eye candy; his voice was easy on the ears. Hearing steps, she jammed the mirror back and looked up, only to see Tony Caswell waltz in, as welcome as a turd in her soup.

Caswell curled his nose. "I'm going to kick the shit out of your in-house expert. Your nurses were negligent as hell, ignoring Layne."

It took a moment to process this idiocy. "Did you get out of law school last week? Co-defendants don't go after each other's experts on the record. You can't jeopardize the clients over what happened between us."

He sneered.

Kristen stepped to within striking distance. "Michael and I agreed.

We're not dumping on each other."

"And Pete McGee's not here to rescue his little girl. I'd love to see the report to your client." In a falsetto voice, he added, *"I'm sorry, Tammy, but the case went to shit."*

"Tony, does Michael know—"

"Please let me keep my job, Tammy."

Kristen's anger threatened to boil over. She could feel her foot twitch. She counted to help blow off steam, focusing out the window on a jet leaving Love Field, wishing she could be Rangoon-bound.

Without looking at him, she said, "If you want to pull the plug on the agreement, go right ahead. Do whatever you think you're big enough to do, but I'll come loaded for Ted Ettinger's depo on the nonexistent echo."

"Your nurses fucked up. Stern's ignoring it because he wants in your pants. Although I can't imagine why."

Kristen could only stare.

Caswell smiled. "Payback is a bitch, *bitch*. And this is just the beginning." He turned and walked out the door.

CHAPTER 21

Dallas
Monday, August 25

IN HIS HOSPITAL BED, Marrs awoke from a morphine hit and heard his half brother's voice.

"Bullet went in on the left, shattered a rib, punctured the lung. Rib took the brunt of it or the damage would've been a lot worse. Lucky it wasn't a hollow point. Another bullet grazed his arm."

"This is potentially a parole violation."

Whose voice was that? Vaguely familiar. Zelner, his parole officer. Marrs kept his eyes shut and listened.

"Getting shot is a parole violation? Nobody reported any crime, for God's sake," Jimmy said.

"What was he doing in that part of town?" Zelner asked.

"You ought to be looking for whoever shot my brother."

"That's for the cops. My mission is easier. If he's been consorting with criminals, carrying a weapon, or anything that doesn't smell right, I'll request a parole revocation hearing."

Marrs blinked his eyes open. With every shallow breath, pain flared from the plastic drain tube sunk into his left side. "Howdy."

Zelner stepped into his line of vision. "How'd you manage to get your happy ass shot? Robbing somebody? Or trying to get a date?"

Marrs played the innocent. "Like I told the detectives, I was minding . . ." He couldn't suppress a lung-ripping cough.

"Nobody's reported anything all week. Getting shot isn't illegal. Blah-blah-blah. I want the real story."

Jimmy jumped in. "The hospital did a full tox screen. Leonard was clean, except for a little alcohol. Not enough to be legally impaired."

"Some jerk in a Camaro was having an argument with his girlfriend. Slapped her twice. I told him to cool it." Marrs coughed as lightly as possible. "Pulled a pistol and shot me. Bastard drove away."

"Nobody in the store saw a thing. Leonard's story holds up," Jimmy said.

Marrs tried to keep from blinking as the parole officer tried to stare another hole in him. "Mexican. Short hair."

Zelner glared at Jimmy. "Sorry, I'm not buying that your brother rescued some damsel in distress." He returned his attention to Leonard.

Marrs felt a stab of anxiety. Zelner was determined to send him back to prison.

"I'll be looking for the shooter. My guess is *she's* the hero." Zelner turned to leave. "I don't have time to babysit every parolee I got, but you're special."

* * *

Jim stuffed a pillow between Marrs's neck and the back of the threadbare sofa, sending a small plume of dust into the air. "Better?"

Marrs was glad to be home, even if it was the dump Jimmy had sentenced him to. Marrs eased back and exhaled through clenched teeth. He felt proud of the wounds, like the burn scars inflicted by Mom's boyfriend. "Uh-huh."

"Lottie said she visited you yesterday."

Marrs tried not to move while answering; only his eyes moved to look at Jimmy. "She a friend of yours?"

"Her joint buys a truckload every week, but I hear she's got a record." Jim blushed.

"I'll be able to take calls next week."

"Get some rest." Jimmy turned and stopped. "But I'm not going to get you a gun."

Jimmy was such a tight ass. "I gotta have it."

"I'm not sure I believe the story you told Zelner, Leonard."

Marrs shook his head and coughed, jarring the broken rib.

"What *were* you doing there?"

Marrs blinked. "Just wandering around. Nothing to do on a Saturday night."

Jimmy edged toward the front door, looking eager to leave.

"I made enemies in prison," Marrs said. "I can't just lie here defenseless in this shitty dump of yours. I need protection."

"It's against your parole rules. A gun is like a fast pass back to Huntsville, and you could be in jail, thank you very much."

"Just for here." He sucked his lips in. "Please?"

"No!" Jimmy hurried out, like Marrs had bubonic plague.

Marrs cursed, then grabbed another Oxycontin and wolfed it down. Within minutes, he was in a stupor.

* * *

The next day, between pills, Marrs remembered Freddie Lee Lance bragging about a cousin in the gun business. Marrs pushed himself up and managed to get in the Cherokee and drive. Freddie hadn't been so helpful as to provide an exact address, but the place was supposed to be two blocks east of the Cotton Bowl. After getting to the fairgrounds, he drove around, trying to guess which hovel looked like an illegal armory.

Congo music from first-class audio equipment drew his attention to a house with peeling paint and loose shingles that made Jimmy's pit seem classy. A dude who looked five months pregnant in his muscle shirt sat on a rickety porch. He sported a goatee and an open-for-business smirk. Marrs decided to give it a try.

He leaned over the wheel, trying to draw a deep breath, then managed to push the door open and get out. He shuffled up the sidewalk. Sweating after only six steps, Marrs stopped before he got too close.

"Whatcha want, man?"

The tone was menacing, but if the guy weren't selling something, he'd have run Marrs off immediately.

"I'm a friend of Freddie Lance. I was his lawyer in Huntsville. Are you his cousin?"

The dude sneered. "You don't look like no friend of Freddie's."

Marrs tried a smile. He'd found the right place, but the guy couldn't be more correct. Marrs had ragged Freddie for his stuttering stupidity. His threat on the morning of his release to look up the little sister, so he could have a taste of black meat, had probably been a mistake, but it felt so good to say it and see the look on Freddie's face.

"He said I could buy a clean piece here." A jab of pain erupted from his lung. "I wrote a brief for him. Almost finished law school before I got sent up." Marrs paused to gather his breath. "A revolver. I hate automatics." He flushed a dumb grin. "Who needs more than six shots? And a deer rifle."

The gun dealer appraised him for a full minute, then waved Marrs up.

It took him longer than he liked, but he finally made it into the shabby house. A window air conditioner battled the Texas heat, but it couldn't be heard over the rap music rattling the windows.

The dude followed Marrs in, slamming the rickety screen door, like he was annoyed at having a white customer. He pointed to a table in front of a frayed couch. The couch was stationed to watch the fanciest big-screen TV Marrs had seen outside a sports bar. Marrs shuffled to the sofa. The table had a drawer partly open, and he could see handguns inside.

Freddie's cousin strolled over.

Marrs pulled the drawer open, eyeballed the array, then selected a .32 Ruger revolver. He looked down the barrel, checking for rust. It appeared okay. "How much?"

"Two bills."

The gun was old and two hundred high, but Marrs didn't feel inclined to haggle. "Got a rifle?"

The guy snorted like it was a stupid question, escorted him to a back room, and showed Marrs quite a collection. Most were far more wicked than he needed. AKs with thirty-round clips weren't necessary. He grabbed an old bolt-action 30-30 rifle, looked it over, and made a generous offer for both weapons with some ammo thrown in.

The guy grinned, probably glad to get a sucker, grabbed a couple of ammunition boxes, and set them down near Marrs.

As Marrs pulled out his wallet, the black man's cell rang. He whipped a Blackberry from his pocket and listened for a moment before saying, "Got a friend of Freddie's here buyin' hardware." The dealer's expression went from satisfaction to puzzlement. "Honky. Small, smooth face," he said into the phone. He put the phone down and asked, "What's your name, pretty boy?"

Marrs ripped open the box of pistol ammunition and jammed two rounds into the cylinder, not taking time to load any more. The guy tossed his phone aside and reached under his belt, having to push away his paunch in the process.

Marrs got off two shots before the gun seller wrapped his fat hand around his weapon.

One slug hit his massive belly, the other penetrated below his left collarbone. Within seconds blood flowed from his mouth, and his hand quivered at his belt. He glared a second at Marrs, then fell forward, landing facedown.

Marrs helped himself to another revolver. The one he'd fired would have to be dropped in somebody's trash. He peered out the screen door, saw no one, and hightailed it as best he could to Jim's Cherokee, keeping the rifle behind his leg.

His chest hurt from the exertion, but he realized he had a bigger problem than getting rid of the Ruger. His DNA was on file, and all it would take to link him to the killing would be a drop of sweat. And whoever the arms dealer had been talking to knew there'd been shooting. Company would arrive soon. Marrs walked back to the house, trying not to rotate his neck like a periscope, but still eyeing the area. All the neighborhood welfare queens appeared to be inside beating the heat.

The house's garage teetered like a tower in Italy. He got lucky and found half a can of gasoline inside. Almost breathless, he sidled back to the house and splashed unleaded everywhere. By the time he drove away, flames were licking out the windows.

CHAPTER 22

Friday, August 29

WITH MICHAEL IN NEW YORK with his latest fling, Diana waited in Pete McGee's office, focusing on photos of his family in Vail. His pictures produced a kaleidoscope of her own memories: Michael, so handsome, striding to the green in a college golf tournament. The passion of their early marriage. The late nights worrying and then, gradually, not caring. Her peritonitis, and the end of desire.

McGee entered his office, closed the door, greeted her warmly, and sat.

"You won't tell anybody we met?" Diana asked.

"No, but remember—I'm your friend, not your lawyer."

His disclaimer was disappointing, since she'd selected Pete for one reason: he hated Michael. "I don't want anybody to know until I make up my mind."

"The guys I recommend will squeeze Michael's balls till he squeaks. And if you don't like either one, there's plenty more lawyers dying to rip into him."

"I'm not worried about money. It's Sarah. Don't mothers usually win custody fights?"

"There's no presumption anymore, unless the children are very young. Otherwise, you start even. Statistics show fathers win nearly half of contested custody cases."

Diana felt slapped. "You're kidding!"

He shrugged. "Maybe only the lousy moms get dragged to trial."

"What about his running around?"

"A factor, but not conclusive. He'd deny it anyway."

She realized she could deny her own infidelity. "A judge could take my daughter away?"

Pete hesitated, looking pensive. Diana had seen that look on lawyers many times. It meant bad news was coming next.

"With all your time commitments, Michael could argue he's the better parent."

She responded quickly. "I'm usually back by seven, and Rita's home after school."

"Rita could do the same for Michael."

Diana picked at a cuticle on her thumb. "I guess so."

"You'd probably need to give up something."

She thought aloud. "I guess I could."

Pete handed her a list of divorce lawyers he'd copied from the bar directory for her. "Talk to an expert, but make sure he prepares papers, so you can serve Michael the instant you decide."

"Why?"

"Because I know the bum. If he finds out you've been talking to lawyers, he'll file first, and get a temporary order granting him custody."

"How?"

"Sign an affidavit that you're unfit, an immediate danger to Sarah."

She flushed. "That's crazy. Could he get Sarah that way?"

"Until a show-cause hearing, and he could stall that for weeks, while he builds his custody case with public parenting."

"But I changed her diapers. Breast-fed her. I enrolled her in school."

"He could simply take her."

"Kidnap?"

"It's not illegal for a father to take a child before there's a custody order."

Diana ripped the cuticle loose. She sucked blood a second to keep from staining her pale linen skirt. "Michael *is* close to Sarah."

"Want me to call someone, so you can get in right away?"

"I'll think about it." She thanked him, then remembered the other thing. "Is Kristen with Michael in New York?"

"No, she's doing depos here today."

His answer surprised her. Maybe she was wrong. Maybe nothing was going on. Maybe she shouldn't rush into divorce. Give it another chance.

She thanked Pete and hurried out. Law offices gave her the creeps. In the hall, she sidestepped past a short, barefoot, freckled woman with strange hair, who seemed to be more than a little interested in Diana Stern.

* * *

Stern had no time to stop at the office before hurrying straight to Sarah's Friday evening game. He trotted toward the bleachers and was met by Diana's glare. A forty-dollar whore strolling into a PTA meeting would have gotten a warmer reception. He eased onto the bench next to her.

"About time you made it."

"Flight was delayed. I got here as quick as I could." The band of parents raised a cheer as Sarah's team stole the ball and pushed it up the field.

"I mean about time you made it back in town, asshole."

Stern wondered what had set Diana off. "I had to go back to New York."

Diana's pale eyebrows crunched under a wisp of hair. "Who the hell is she?"

The couple in front half-turned to take in the show.

Stern waited until they rotated back to the game. Remembering the mysterious roses Sarah mentioned, he debated his response, then decided to seek peace. "Do we have to do this here?"

Diana lowered her voice. "I can always tell. Floating, in a rush."

"I'm just getting ready for a big trial," Stern whispered.

"The 'Stern' in Jackson, Stern and Randolph will be me when I'm through with you."

Stern flinched. "Let's talk later. Please."

For once, he was innocent. In New York, Donna didn't count, since she meant nothing, and helped his investigation. Mentioning the flowers would score a point, but violate Sarah's confidence.

He kept coming back to the roses. Who would be interested in his rattlesnake wife? Though she still looked good, who could stand the stupid functions and her snotty friends? Maybe he could pay the dumb bastard to take her for keeps so he could have Sarah.

His daughter pounded the ball through the goal. Stern stood to cheer.

* * *

Before Stern could sip his Monday morning coffee, Janet came storming in.

"Christ, Michael. Ettinger's here for his deposition, pissing his pants. Our expert's getting fainthearted."

"We've got an hour. Ted will be ready."

"Something happened Friday in the nurse's depo. Kristen called demanding to know where you were."

"You didn't tell her?"

"No, but she insists on seeing you. *Now.* She's not a happy camper."

Stern stirred his coffee. He should have come into the office over the weekend or called Caswell for a report on the nursing supervisor's depo, but got wrapped up in Sarah's tournament and figuring out how to appease Diana. Fortunately, he'd more or less succeeded. Since Caswell had orders to keep quiet, he didn't see how it could have gone badly. Kristen would've made sure her witness did well. "Send her in."

Kristen stepped into Stern's office and slammed the door. "Where the hell have you been? I called you all day Friday."

Stern noticed her olive complexion had turned quite red. He smiled. "Out on another case. It's great to—"

"Don't *great* me! You've got a case more important than *Layne*? Don't you leave your people instructions, or did you tell that one-armed peckerhead to screw things up?" She paused, taking in the look on his face. "Haven't you heard what he did?"

He tried to take control. "Kristen—"

"Claiming our training programs were inadequate, our staffing ratios were too high. *On the damn record!* Bragg loved it!"

Stern felt almost as angry as Kristen looked. He took a deep breath and looked away. "That stupid shithead."

Kristen stepped closer, very close. "You had him jump my witness so you wouldn't look like the welcher. Now you can pull our deal and claim you had no choice. That the evidence is in the discovery record."

"Believe me, I've got less use for Caswell than you do. He was told to keep quiet."

"Then you need to fire his ass. Do we have a deal, or is it time to shit on each other?" She crossed her arms. "I've got some questions for your buddy Ettinger, and it won't be pretty. Bragg would love to hear about you two golfing and playing poker together. How you drafted him to serve as our expert. And I've still got time to name my own guy."

Stern blinked. "All for one and one for all."

She jabbed a finger into his chest as she bit off each word. "Don't you dare jack with me."

Stern knew he'd seen another Kristen. Maybe the real one. No melancholy uncertainty. If he hadn't known better, he would have thought she was going to slug him.

This Kristen certainly had the guts to royally shaft him.

* * *

Attorney Joe Bragg deftly positioned the pile of birthday presents around Pain Layne's wasting body so the TV camera would pick them up, along with his emaciated face and withered hands. The gifts, wrapped in Dallas Cowboys blue, would be removed after the reporter finished the stand up. The birthday cake would be eaten by the nursing home staff. Despite the valiant efforts of the aides, the place always smelled like shit.

Layne had lost sixty pounds since his code. Nourishment entered his stomach through a feeding tube. The only evidence of life was his continuing and amazing ability to breathe. When Bragg was hired a year ago, he hadn't expected his client to last long. For Bragg this was good. The longer Pain lived, the bigger the damages, since his care cost thousands a month.

Betty and her two daughters waited behind the lights for their interview. Every time Betty had been here with Bragg, she seemed more pissed than sad. Instead of tears, she set her teeth askew and scrunched her eyes when she looked at what was left of her husband. That was good, too. An angry plaintiff would hold out for more money. Bragg had been thrilled to see his client bring him the diary. It had needed only a bit of touch-up.

The daughters unfortunately had gotten the worst features of each parent. Thick and tall bodies from their dad; long noses from Mom. The girls fidgeted and looked out the window. They had quit coming months ago, as had Pain's friends, and were here today as props. Bragg prayed they wouldn't look so bored on camera.

The trial neared and Bragg hoped lots of potential jurors would see this interview and other events he had planned. Dallas County was notoriously defense-oriented in malpractice cases, but the story was so pathetic, Bragg was confident the case was his ticket to the Caribbean.

Adding to Bragg's confidence was the appearance of Kristen instead of McGee for Adventist Hospital. Not that she was incompetent—she was quite good—but a case this size surely required the senior guy. So Bragg suspected Kristen's real assignment was to hose Stern, since the pious McGee didn't have the balls to be so conniving. But Bragg guessed Kristen had no idea how ruthless Stern could be.

Bragg intended to drive a wedge between the defendants. There was no way their purported unity could hold. Eventually they would fight each other, not him. Then the jury's job would be to decide which defendant paid, not *whether* a defendant paid.

Much as Joe wanted to beat Stern, the hospital was the real target. Like what a bank robber once said, "That's where the money is." Bragg guessed Stern would be talking turkey a week into the trial. With Stern helping him, arguing the hospital had screwed up, young Kristen would get squashed like a locust under a cowboy boot. Bragg pitied Kristen. Her career in trial work would be brief.

CHAPTER 23

Dallas
Tuesday, September 16

PETE MCGEE SLAMMED A copy of Casey's deposition onto his desk. "Stern's already screwed us before we can double-cross him."

Kristen waited, hoping he'd cool down. "There's a problem between Caswell and me." She kept her voice level. "I don't think Stern had anything to do with what Caswell did. Most of Caswell's questions were totally irrelevant to this case."

Pete's eyes closed for a moment, seeming to will control. "Juries are far more likely to bust a big hospital than an individual doc. Stern's going to team up with Bragg. And Bragg's running a media campaign."

"It doesn't make sense for Stern to tip his cards." Kristen looked at her shoes, searching for a reasonable-sounding explanation. "Caswell went after Casey because of our date."

"Huh?"

She scoured her brain for a euphemism for *knocked the crap out of,* but couldn't come up with anything.

Pete appeared to decide he didn't want to know the details about the tête-à-tête he had ordered. "You listed Stern's golf buddy, Ettinger, as a joint expert?"

"Yes." She almost added *sir,* but caught herself. Those days were supposedly over.

Pete leaned his barrel chest forward. "Kristen, this is incredibly dangerous. We're the first-named defendant. We go before Stern on every witness." His voice rose with tension, "Even on closing argument. You've got to scorch Galway on your opening statement."

Kristen wanted to tell Pete to sleep with Stern himself, but instead asked, "Do you want the case back? I can second-chair you."

Pete rocked back in his seat as if he'd been offered a chance to go ten rounds with Mike Tyson. "No, but I told you how to win. Dump on Stern and that quack doc of his."

Kristen reminded herself there were other jobs. "Are you more interested in embarrassing Stern or winning?"

Pete shook his head, obviously not used to arguments from junior partners. "Kristen, you're like a daughter. I hope you're not infatuated with Stern. He'd sell his mother to al-Qaeda for a verdict."

"But if I win—"

"You can't win, unless you do what I say."

A second ago she was his daughter; now she was cannon fodder sent into battle, told *not to reason why*. Pete had no idea how many battle scars she already had. "If I don't have any discretion, you might as well send Jen and Ron."

Pete's jaw dropped. "Of course, you have room for judgment on the timing. I won't be there all the time. You'll spot the best moment."

Pete's phone buzzed. Cindy's voice came over the speaker. "Mr. McGee, Judge Proctor is on the phone. He wants to talk to Kristen."

Kristen walked around Pete's desk and picked up the receiver.

The judge wasted no time on preliminaries. "I've got Joe and Michael on the line. Mr. Bragg has filed a motion to expedite this Layne trial."

"Judge, we haven't even had the statutory time to respond and Kristen still needs to take Joe's nurse expert's deposition," Stern said.

"I had a case settle," Proctor said. "I can start you guys a week from

Monday. But I want a verdict in two weeks. And no media stunts."

"That's fine, Judge," Bragg announced.

Kristen felt panic grip her. Six days. "Your Honor—"

"My scheduling order said we'd get to this on my fall civil docket. It's fall." The judge paused, then added, "Of course, you all could settle this."

Kristen decided to play a card against Bragg. "If Joe gets reasonable, we'll talk."

In the two years Kristen had been trying cases on her own, she'd never had a case go to trial on the first day of a docket. She wondered why Stern wasn't putting up more resistance. Bragg had ambushed them and must have some pull they didn't anticipate. Or maybe Pain Layne was dying. She didn't want to be the girly-girl.

"The hospital will be ready," she said with all the confidence she could muster.

As she put the receiver down, Pete nodded. "Good decision. Stern's bluffing. Probably spent last week chasing some chick. Hang him early, and he'll be toast."

* * *

Janet handed Stern the last volume of his trial exhibit notebook. "I've numbered the old physicals. They show Layne's noncompliance with blood pressure meds and missed doctor appointments. The dirt is separate."

Stern packed the book into one of the file boxes. "I love the Cowboys' party pics with the topless dancer in his lap. And we'll nail the grieving widow with that separation order she got from ol' Pain."

"We never came up with any police calls for domestic disturbances. Maybe the neighbor who tipped off our PI was wrong."

"Try county." Stern packed his briefcase. "Get a runner to load my car and confirm with Galway that he's coming to my house

Saturday at ten."

"Kristen e-mailed. She'll be there at two." Janet stepped out.

Stern sensed the old surge of energy. Crush or no crush, the Prince could kick ass. For the next two weeks he'd sit next to Kristen, lean close and whisper, scheme with her at the end of each day, and keep an eye on those beautiful legs. Unfortunately he'd have to shaft her, even if he didn't give her the shaft. Winning trumped sex, but he still might score both if he could hold the joint defense together for a week.

He looked up as the gopher came in, followed by Tony Caswell sporting an idiotic smile.

"You saw how I cut up Kerry's nurse expert."

Stern had avoided Caswell after getting the report from Kristen on the disastrous Casey Denman deposition, knowing he might maim the nitwit. But now he had no choice. He stormed around his writing table into Caswell's face. Only the gopher's wide-eyed stare discouraged him from putting his hands around his new partner's neck.

"Listen, dickhead—you're not man enough to wear her panties. I've got her sold—we have a deal. You had your orders and did the exact opposite. When this trial's over, I'm getting you shit-canned."

Caswell clenched his fists, his face turning bright crimson. "You can't. My dad bought my shares. I'm a full partner now."

Stern laughed. "I could buy you out with what's in my wallet."

"You mean Diana could."

Stern grit his teeth. The insolence from the kid, once a champion toady, shocked him. He wanted to rip Caswell's bad arm off and beat him to death with it.

Caswell sneered, but had the sense to back toward the door. "If you're going to live on your wife's money, you ought to service her occasionally." Caswell sniffed his finger and curled his nose. "She's still fine."

In a moment of rage and clarity, it clicked. The idiot must have been the one who sent Diana flowers. Had he gotten into her pants?

Had she wanted to? His iceberg wife? With that little shit? Was Caswell the reason Diana had upped the ante, threatening divorce? It didn't make sense. He thought she had better taste than that.

Caswell slinked away. Stern stood in place, vibrating, unable to decide whether to throttle the asshole or thank him.

* * *

Kristen pushed the Sterns' doorbell. She couldn't think of a reason why this meeting wasn't at an office. If Stern was trying to intimidate her, it wouldn't work. After the Kerrys left Philly, they'd lived in a house bigger than Stern's. She reminded herself her trial record was perfect except for the case brought by the cleaning lady.

She rang again, chiming "Greensleeves." She wondered why the flamboyant Stern had such a melancholy-sounding doorbell.

A minute later, the door swung open. "Welcome to my humble abode," Stern said. He pushed open the leaded-glass outer door.

She picked up her briefcase and followed him. "Humble compared to Buckingham Palace."

Stern lowered his voice. "Galway and I are done, but he's acting like a whore in church. Help me calm him down."

He led her over a gorgeous Persian runner on the marble entry.

She imagined what the son of a truck driver must have thought the day he first saw this place. It probably didn't sink in for a few years that it was really his.

In the walnut-paneled study, Galway stood. "Have you talked to the nurses?"

"We've been over their depositions carefully."

Stern directed her to the bar, where she found a bottle of Nestea. She sat in one of the matching oxblood leather chairs near the fireplace.

"Except Roberta now remembers me offering to get a tech down for an echo. But Layne wanted to sleep and wait till morning." Galway leaned forward. "Won't she say that?"

Kristen had worried all week how to handle this new wrinkle. When Robbie called her with this new recollection, she had asked, *Are you sure?*

Kristen gave Galway an answer. "Yes, I talked to her, but she didn't say it in her depo, and you didn't document the chart." She paused, letting this sink in, hoping Galway would see the problem, and demand Stern settle. If Galway settled, she could defend the case without worrying about being double-crossed. "Bragg will call us liars."

Stern piped up before Galway could respond. "Calm down, Gary. We know what we're doing. Kristen and I have handled tougher deals than this."

She had to look away. Stern fibbing to his client was a bad sign.

Galway slid to the edge of his chair. "What would it take to settle?"

"If you want in the data bank, I can get the Standard claims board together tonight. Kristen could call her folks."

After a long minute, Galway said, "No. Let's fight."

Kristen let out the breath she'd been holding. Galway needed Stern to tell him to admit a mistake, but Stern wouldn't do it, either because he was still going after her or trying to get even with Pete McGee. She almost turned to Stern right then to say, *Quit chasing me. You're not missing anything. Let this man settle. You and Pete can compare dicks on another case.*

Galway's cell rang. He answered, listened a moment, then clicked off. "Got a post with changes. Have coverage, but I'd better go see him."

"Sure, Gary. You're ready, even if Bragg calls you first thing in his case." Stern rose and escorted Galway out.

Alone, Kristen explored the room, scanning the rows of books, mostly histories. An old sea battle print of sailing ships blasting away at each other hung over the fireplace. Dramatic lettering showed it was done in London, 1811, and was dedicated to Horatio Nelson. The ornate mantle looked like an antique imported from a European hunting lodge. Not unlike his office. All very Stern.

"Are you going to try a case with my dad?"

Kristen turned and saw the girl in Stern's office photos, toting a duffel bag. She sported the strong Stern nose, blue eyes, and confident expression. She had to be pushing five-seven, even at thirteen. Her shorts revealed long tanned legs and powerful quads a fitness trainer would love. The sun-drenched ponytail was darling.

"You must be Sarah."

"Yeah."

"I'm Kristen." She walked across the room and offered her hand, which the girl gripped firmly. "Your home is beautiful. Have you lived here long?"

"Since I was in first grade."

"I hear you're a fabulous ballplayer."

"Dad exaggerates."

The line was spoken so straight-faced, Kristen laughed, instantly liking the girl. A stand-up comedian couldn't have done better.

Stern reentered. "I see you two have met."

"Becca says I can come over now." Sarah hoisted her bag over her shoulder, paused by Stern, and pecked his cheek.

"Have fun, princess. Mom'll pick you up in the morning."

"Love you."

Stern's voice mellowed. "You too."

Sarah smiled at Kristen. "Nice to meet you. Good luck next week."

"Thanks." Kristen tracked Stern's gaze following Sarah out. A collie watching his lamb. Stern knew boys would soon be intruding, diverting her attention from her doting father. After that, college. Behind all the bluster lay sadness. The door chime now made sense.

"She's delightful," Kristen said, adding with a smile, "Obviously she got her looks from her mom."

Stern chuckled. "For sure."

"How come you didn't fight Bragg for more time?" she asked.

"Because Bragg must've called in whatever chits he had with the judge to get this trial on so quick. I doubt Proctor will give him any more breaks; I also doubt he'll let him put on a show. Contrary to the crap they teach in law school, trial judges control the little things. The little things add up to victory or defeat. All the shit in the casebooks you have to read means nothing."

Kristen wondered if he had a deal already cooked up with Bragg.

"Great job with Bragg on the conference call the other day," he added. "Let Proctor think Bragg's greed is forcing a trial. Let's work on voir dire so we can coordinate our questions. One set for the dummies and another for the bright jurors."

His tone surprised her—the same as he'd used with Sarah, like she had a microbes paper. Serenity enveloped her, making her glad she'd come. Despite the ambience, she spoke the obvious. "I think Galway wants to settle."

"Layne's contracted a nasty infection. The nursing home moved him yesterday. He may not last long. Bragg'll come off his fifteen-mil demand before the week's out. We're better off starting trial and talking settlement after Layne cashes in."

Kristen peered into his eyes, searching. "With our deal on?"

"Of course."

* * *

Leonard Marrs fidgeted in the parole office waiting area, folding the receipt for his monthly supervision fee. Three seats away, a black dude with gold earrings bobbed his head to the rhythm from his headset. Marrs thought they were only a generation away from bones in their noses and missionaries in their stew.

Next, there was a wrung-out woman. She let loose a desperate smile, which he didn't return. To her right, a slob in a dirty T-shirt coughed, hacked, and blew his nose. His mushy arm was decorated with a tattoo of a topless woman. Undoubtedly, it was the only woman he'd ever had touch his skin.

Finally, Zelner, in his usual black suit, pushed open a heavy glass door, zeroed in on Marrs, and barked, "You!"

Marrs pushed himself up and followed his parole officer through a maze of cubicles until they reached Zelner's.

The parole officer pointed to a chair. "Gotten shot lately?"

Marrs sat. "No, sir."

"Besides protecting women, just what do you do all the live-long day?"

"I call on Jimmy's customers and make deliveries."

Zelner pushed his glasses up. "It occurs to me that to find out what you're really doing, I should be checking with these restaurant folks instead of your half brother."

Zelner looked like he'd discovered Colonel Mustard with the candlestick in the conservatory.

"I'm doing good." Marrs spotted a photo behind the parole officer of him next to a pretty little thing, both in running shorts with numbers pinned to their tank tops. She looked luscious. He'd love to tug those shorts down to her knees. "I stay real busy."

"That's what worries me. Bring me a log of your time for this next week. Signed by the people you see. In fact, let's do it *every* week."

Tired of playing supplicant, Marrs white-knuckled the metal arms of the chair. "Why don't you cut me any slack? Jimmy's sales—"

Zelner pounded his desk, rattling the photos. "Because I'm not buying your act."

Marrs imagined splashing gasoline around Zelner's house at 3:00 a.m., tossing a match, seeing the flash of combustion, and watching Zelner crawl out with flames leaping off his ass.

"I'll be checking when you least expect it."

As Marrs turned to leave, he stared with disbelief into the next cubicle.

Freddy Lee Lance sat facing a female parole officer. His arms were still as thick as Marrs's thighs, his legs as big as tree trunks. The Grim Reaper decorated a bicep.

Freddie seemed to sense the stare and swiveled around. His big dark eyes narrowed. As he slowly rose out of his chair, the parole officer—not much smaller than Freddie—pushed him down, but had trouble convincing him to stay put.

"Friend of yours, Marrs?" Zelner asked.

"Uh . . . no, sir. I'll see you next week, sir." Marrs hurried out, taking the stairs instead of waiting on the elevator.

What's the world coming to when a cop-shooting nigger gets paroled?

* * *

Tuesday, September 26

Kristen knew that Monday's voir dire went lousy. One prospective juror had blurted that nurses and doctors cover for each other, and all of them lie in records. Several other possible panel members agreed. Bragg had grinned like a fat kid with a tray of warm cookies.

Kristen had gotten the loudmouth excused without using a valuable preemptory challenge, but she had invited the problem by asking one question too many. Like a rookie. She'd beaten on herself half the night for the silly mistake. The final panel was one Bragg had to be happy with. Several of the men watched local sports and liked Brook Layne.

Decision time.

Pete and Tammy sat on the first gallery row, hyped up like blackjack players sitting on a nineteen. This was Kristen's first opportunity to hose Stern, the one chance she'd have to get licks in before he could do the same to her.

Kristen walked to the lectern with two versions of her opening statement outlined.

Ladies and Gentlemen, when Brook Layne arrived in our hospital ER at five in the afternoon, his lab work was abnormal; he was nauseated and light-headed. These are troubling signs for a man with a new heart valve. Dr. Galway was called from the emergency room and told about the signs and symptoms. He admitted the patient, issuing routine telephone orders, but didn't come in to see Mr. Layne until eleven that night, six long hours after Mr. Layne arrived. Although Mr. Layne's blood pressure had stabilized, he still felt, in his words, "terrible."

Every cardiologist and heart surgeon knows the first weeks after valve surgery are the most dangerous until the warfarin levels are stabilized. Warfarin is a blood thinner, necessary for the artificial valve to work correctly. Dr. Galway knew the only way to fully evaluate a patient like Mr. Layne is to do an ultrasound of the heart, like pregnant moms receive to see their babies. This test is called an echocardiogram.

With a doctor's order, our hospital can perform that study any time. Dr. Galway elected to leave the hospital, go home, and sleep, without ordering this critical test. He left Adventist's nurses instructions to take vital signs every hour and call if Mr. Layne's condition worsened. The nurses did that, but they can't order tests. Tests would show that blood needed to be drained off Mr. Layne's heart sac and save his life. At eleven that night, there was still time to prevent the tragedy. But this wasn't done. Ultimately, Dr. Galway is responsible, not Adventist Hospital.

She took a deep breath and glanced to her right, where her fearless leaders huddled safely behind the bar. She looked left at Stern. He was relaxed, with his elbows on the table, fingers interlocked. Her heart thundered. She sensed everyone's puzzlement at the delay.

If she pounded Stern now, he'd never be able to double-cross her, and would maybe never recover from the blow she inflicted.

But the image of him in his study saying good-bye to his daughter, then helping out with the voir dire questions, flickered into her mind. She told herself she'd have a clue, a warning, before Stern bailed on their deal. She could hammer him with more impact after some evidence was in.

She spoke softly, "Ladies and Gentlemen, on behalf of the entire staff at Adventist, we extend our sympathy and prayers to the Layne family." Her voice gained strength. "But you'll be told at the end of this trial that you can't base your decision on sympathy. Instead, you must find in favor of both Dr. Galway and Adventist Hospital, because Mr. Layne's injury sadly could not have been prevented, despite the best of care he received from his doctor and his nurses."

* * *

In her office after finishing the day, Kristen lay on her love seat, shoes off, and crunched a Snickers. Tonight she had to review both versions of notes for the cross-exam of Galway tomorrow, assuming Bragg put Stern's client on in his case-in-chief. As they'd left the courthouse, Stern had assured her that everything would go as planned. But she would be ready if the dam burst.

As she swallowed the last sumptuous bite, Pete and Tammy marched into her office and closed the door. Kristen wished she'd taken her work straight home from the courthouse.

Getting up, she motioned them to sit. Tammy remained standing.

Pete sat on her desk. "Kristen, that was a nice open, but you missed the best chance."

Tammy waited a moment before erupting. "Goddamn it! Now we'll have to sweat every witness who might hose us!"

Pete flinched, but didn't contradict the client.

Kristen bought time by slipping on her pumps. "I thought it would look staged without any evidence in. If I fought Stern and Bragg for two solid weeks, the verdict could be astronomical. I can ease into it when my nurses testify."

Pete stroked his chin. "You could be correct. It might look spontaneous. Galway's probably going to be called in Bragg's case. Do you have a read of Stern?"

Kristen knew what he meant. *Is Stern so eager to fuck you that he'll hold off a week?"*

"I think things are under control," she said.

Pete nodded. "I'm sure you have lots to do tonight." He left without looking back, closing the door behind him.

Tammy walked closer and pointed a long red fingernail. "You better not botch this, or you'll never get another job in this town."

* * *

Late on the third day of the trial, Kristen's neurons fired at maximum. Her heart raced, and she thought she herself might need a cardiologist soon. She hoped there was a good one around.

On the witness stand, Dr. Galway's hands rolled and unrolled a stack of papers marked "Exhibit 1," the records from Layne's first night in the hospital.

Bragg leaned over the lectern. "Doctor, can we agree that the nurses' notes that night and the descriptions that Mrs. Layne wrote look like they're for two totally different patients?"

Galway clenched his hands around the paper even tighter. "I guess."

"And if my client's diary is correct, you should've been called that night?"

Galway squinted. "If—*if*—they're correct."

"And *if . . .*" Bragg let the word linger, mimicking Galway, "the nurses had any concerns, you'd want them to call you."

"Yes."

"Because you're a dedicated, caring physician, and you'd want

169

to know."

"Certainly."

"No matter what time it was."

"That's part of being a doctor."

"And nobody, not one nurse, not one living soul from Adventist, this giant hospital, called you the entire night, while Mr. Layne, a hero to a million sports fans, was bleeding and dying, desperate for a doctor, did they?" Bragg raised his forefinger and pointed at Kristen.

Before Kristen could object to the absurdly argumentative question, Galway blurted, "No, sir."

Kristen tried to look unfazed while thinking, *You bastard!*

CHAPTER 24

Tuesday Night

STERN FINISHED HIS PHONE conversation with Bragg and hung up. He pulled a Corona from his office mini-fridge and handed it to Galway. After being held late by Judge Proctor to finish Galway's testimony, Stern's back hurt too much to sit. He probably had a bulging disc. His butt was numb, and after three days he wondered if this trial was really worth the trouble.

"Gary, you didn't follow the script. You were supposed to add, 'There was no need to call me.'"

"Sorry." Galway unbuttoned his tight collar and changed the subject. "What'd Bragg want?"

Though still annoyed, Stern shrugged. "We got a firm offer of four mil if you testify the nurses should've called you around one, and that you could've saved Layne, had you been phoned. That means Bragg would probably take between two and three."

Galway slugged down a good third of the can. "I knew that's where he was headed. The way he was complimenting me—"

"Was a setup. He wants the jury to shoot the moon against the big hospital."

"I thought that was the plan."

Stern opened a bottle for himself. He figured now was the time for a little CYA. "It is, but we'd be better off waiting till next week.

They'll return fire, and they've got plenty of bullets." Stern gulped beer. "Nurses can't order an echocardiogram or stick a needle in his chest to draw off fluid. That was your job."

"But nobody told me he was crashing."

Stern wiped his lips with his shirtsleeve. "If the defendants start pissing on each other from the get-go and then ratchet up every day for weeks, the verdict can blow up on everybody."

"Are you protecting their dreamboat lawyer?"

Stern pictured Kristen. Sitting close to her for the last three days, brushing against her, inhaling her breath, the trial was almost as intimate as sex. For his client's benefit, he banged his can down. "I don't give a rat's ass about her. But, contrary to popular belief, cases don't turn on who's the best bullshitter—but who's got the best evidence."

Galway slammed his fist on the table. "Goddamn it, Stern, you talked me into this fucking trial."

Stern clenched his teeth. "You want to go into the data bank with a three-mil hit? This early in your career? If you do, I'll call Bragg back. *Right now!*"

Galway, sucking his lips like a little kid, looked away. "Not unless that hospital pays twice what I pay. I want everybody to know they were the ones who blew it."

"And they're saying they won't pay as much as you." Stern let the dilemma soak in a second. "I won't cross-examine you tomorrow. I'll put you on again next week. Let's hear the rest of Bragg's evidence. Then we've got the weekend to cut a deal."

* * *

Kristen glanced at the jury, who seemed riveted. A few leaned forward on their swivel seats, watching Betty Layne testify. Dressed in a tailored turquoise suit with white buttons, she sniffed and rubbed her long, thin nose. She'd grown bangs since her deposition; they covered the birthmark near her hairline.

Bragg's voice had grown raspy after five days, but he was full of intensity, biting off each word. "Are you absolutely certain of these findings you recorded the night your husband was admitted?"

"Yes. As a mom, I've taken temperatures and pulses."

Bragg flourished his reading glasses through the air, something he did whenever he wanted to emphasize a point. "And the blood pressures you've written?"

"I watched the monitor when the nurses were out of the room." She glared at Kristen. "Which was all the time."

Bragg's eyes followed his client's.

Kristen held her gaze steady on the witness.

"Did you ask the nurses to call the doctor?" he asked.

"I begged them."

"Did they ever call him?"

"I don't know what they were doing. They weren't in our room."

"The hospital's lawyer, Ms. Kerry, told us in her opening statement they were monitoring him with telemetry."

Betty Layne dabbed an eye. "Electronics can't tell how sick a man is."

"She also said that you must have unhooked the monitor so your husband could shower. And that's why there's a gap in the monitoring."

"Why would I undo the monitor if I thought he was in trouble?"

Bragg paused, obviously letting the answer settle in. "At any time that night and morning, before breakfast, did you see Dr. Galway?"

Betty rotated to laser Galway. "Absolutely not."

An hour later, after hearing sobbing stories of the Layne kids' depression, Judge Proctor ordered a recess for Betty to regain her composure.

Stern pulled Kristen into an alcove down the hall. He tapped her elbow. "This'll take a deft touch, but it's all yours. A woman taking her on will look better."

"Don't you want to cross her about not seeing Galway?"

"If I get into it again, it'll just give her a chance to make another speech about how indifferent we were."

"What about the separation order?" Kristen asked.

"Hammer her. She's made her marriage sound like Bogart and Bacall."

"The jury likes her. It could backfire."

Stern chortled. "That birthmark is probably a permanent bruise the tight end left on her."

"Show her the pictures of the victory party?"

Stern edged closer. "Shove them down her throat. You've got the flair to pull it off. You know, act shocked, absolutely shocked, that ol' Pain Layne, a Baptist deacon, would have his hands on another woman. Especially one with forty-D's."

A shiver zipped through her. Was he setting her up to be the heavy, picking on the poor widow? Pissing off the jury, so his backstab would go down easier?

Shorty, the bailiff, rounded the corner on his rickety legs. "Time."

In the courtroom, Betty Layne fixed on Kristen as she approached the lectern. Kristen wondered if the woman ever blinked. By the time Judge Proctor barked at her to proceed, she still hadn't made up her mind how to handle the plaintiff. It was unlikely she could shake the story Betty told, but it would look terrible to concede. Maybe Stern had dropped this role on her because there was no good way.

Kristen spent half an hour crossing on the events of the night before Brook Layne cashed in. The woman had a fabulous memory for detail. Kristen felt like she was jacking up threes from thirty feet in front of a hostile crowd. Every shot an air ball.

"Nurse Nancy Wiltse documented that at six she came into the room and your husband was returning from the bathroom without his portable monitor. Are you saying the nurse is lying?"

Betty smiled slightly. "She must have my husband confused with another patient."

Kristen wanted to curse. Betty hadn't fallen into the trap of looking unreasonable. The question had bounced right back at Kristen. Keep going and risk looking even worse? She snuck a glance at Stern and got no reaction.

"You're not telling us that Nancy and Roberta didn't care about your husband, are you?"

"Not at all. I think the hospital had too many patients on the floor and was understaffed."

This was getting worse. Kristen had to surrender, but decided to try to inflict some damage in retreat.

After a short pause Kristen smiled. "I want to talk to you about your marriage. Would you say you and your husband were close?"

Betty drew back in the witness chair, as if she suspected a trap. "We were each other's best friend."

Kristen felt the jury's glare. They liked the woman, or at least were giving her the benefit of any doubt. *Drive the paint, girl.* "Brook played football for the Cowboys. They had some pretty wild parties, didn't they?"

Betty's eyes gaped open.

With the bawdy photos in hand, Kristen stepped closer to the witness.

Bragg flew out of his chair. "Judge, I don't know what she's got, but all exhibits were supposed to be exchanged a month ago. I haven't seen anything about football parties."

Judge Proctor wrinkled his capillary-lined nose. "Counsel?"

Kristen glanced at Stern. He made no move to help, but she was ready. "Your Honor, I don't intend to offer these pictures of Mr. Layne, shall we say, having a good time without his wife, but I'm entitled to show them to the witness to refresh her memory of Brook's propensity to have a *very* good time."

Bragg shook his jowls. "She's testifyin'. I strongly object."

Kristen glanced at the jury. Their attention couldn't have been more aroused if a stripper had arrived to do a table dance. She caught Stern's wink of approval.

Kristen decided to prolong the moment to get her money's worth. "Before we get to parties, you do agree there were times in your marriage when you claimed Brook was abusive?"

Betty fidgeted in the chair, her eyes searching the ceiling.

Kristen folded her arms and raised her voice. "Can you answer, ma'am?"

Betty struggled a minute before blurting, "No marriage is perfect."

"Including yours?"

* * *

Janet handed Stern a beer from the mini-fridge.

Stern popped the can, downed some of it, and felt some of his stress dissolve. But he was worried he'd need to see a spine surgeon soon. "I'm afraid Bragg kicked the shit out of us."

"You creamed his cardiology expert."

Stern forced a smile. "You always say that."

"Kristen hammered Betty. I loved the shock on her face. I saw a juror roll his eyes when she said all that happened before Brook found Jesus."

Stern's brain was a torrent. He'd kept himself clean by not crossing Betty Layne. If the jury thought it was unfair to mar Pain Layne's reputation, the blowback would hit Kristen. "Yeah. Thought Bragg was going to shit. Got to hand it to Kristen. She's going to be the best someday. A real dynamo."

"I don't think the jury liked Galway."

Stern collapsed into his chair and rubbed his eyelids. "Can't imagine why they wouldn't adore the hairball."

"Michael, why not settle? Dumping on the hospital would mean total war with Wright McGee and Hospital Risk."

Stern stared at the ceiling a second. "We're in a helluva bind. Between us and the hospital, Bragg wants the moon. I've oversold Trapper John on the allure of a backstab, and Kristen says Tammy won't pay nearly as much as Galway's policy limit." Stern sipped his drink. "Anything going on here?"

"The usual crabbing and an odd message from a woman who didn't leave a name. Said, 'Remember the morphine case.'"

Stern's whole body weakened. He tried to hide the tremor in his hands. Tammy was threatening him over a case eight years ago, when he'd defended a hospital her company insured. A patient arrested after a morphine injection, likely an overdose. Tammy's hospital had supposedly lost records the DEA made it keep on every milligram of narcotics.

Suddenly, the records magically reappeared before trial. The plaintiff's lawyer had threatened Stern with sanctions, but he was able to show he wasn't behind the mysterious discovery. He'd suspected the records were phony, but offered them as exhibits anyway.

Janet stared at him, quizzical.

He composed himself. He'd be damned if that bleached whore was going to rattle him. Her threat made him more determined to screw Adventist, McGee, and Tammy.

"That guy from CNA called," Janet said. "He is *begging* to meet you, dangling some big case. I told him you'd be in trial all next week. He offered to meet you on a weekend."

"I may need all the clients I can get after next week."

"He didn't leave a number, but I retrieved it from caller ID." Janet pushed the message slip toward him. "You'll pull through. Never spit the bit." Her eyes searched his face. "Also, there was a bizarre message from a Betty Davis in New York."

Stern sat upright. "Yeah?"

Janet stuck her glasses on, then read from a message slip. "*Found the transcript. Really nasty.*" She put the note down. "What's this about?"

Stern tried to look blasé. "You got me."

"A FedEx package came today. Stamped *Confidential*, so I didn't open it."

"I'll look at it later." Stern, managing to look unconcerned, took the number for the CNA adjuster and tossed it onto the growing pile of crap on his desk. "Gotta go. Sarah's team is gonna kick ass on the Garland kids." He paused. "Just win, baby, just win."

* * *

Parked in the commercial zone, Leonard Marrs spotted Stern's Mercedes tearing out of the garage underneath NationsBank. Judge Proctor's clerk had been helpful over the phone to a "member of the media," telling him the judge would keep the jury even later than usual on Friday to finish the plaintiff's case. Stern probably had to hump his secretary and throw back a couple of drinks before heading home to face the family.

Unfortunately, Diana would be at an arts function, according to the society pages. He knew their kid would beat them all home unless she had a game. He'd found her schedule on the league website, so he had an idea of where she'd be. He contemplated becoming a youth sports fan and laughed to himself.

As he looked up, a green Porsche sped out of the garage. The slick-haired driver stared as he roared by, like he was imprinting Marrs in his mind. It took another second for Marrs to realize it was the same smug asshole who'd given him grief when he'd played deliveryman. The one with the wilted arm.

* * *

The sound of slamming car doors jerked Marrs's attention away from his instant coffee to the filmy front window of his brother's rental house. Zelner and a huge uniformed cop marched across the crabgrass toward the front door.

Marrs's belly jumped into his throat.

They pounded on the door.

He waited a minute before opening the door with a forced yawn. "You guys are up bright and early."

Zelner pushed past him and stormed in. The cop followed, his trigger finger scratching a mole on his temple. Marrs caught the name on the cop's badge: McKinnon. He was big enough to play for the Cowboys.

"Been out buying guns?" Zelner asked. "So you can return fire next time?"

Marrs set his mug on the rickety lamp table. "No, 'course not."

"A gun dealer in the hood got shot last month. Cops found a witness who saw a white man and a Jeep Cherokee parked in front of the dude's house. Ten minutes later the place was on fire." Zelner jerked his thumb toward the door. "That's a Cherokee. And you're a white guy."

Marrs's stomach knotted, but he met Zelner's stare. "I think they only sell Jeeps to white guys. How many Jeeps are there in this town?"

Zelner looked ready to get the rubber hose, but McKinnon's stone face cracked into a nasty grin. "I'm sure you don't mind if we look around?"

"My friend, Sergeant McKinnon, is off duty," Zelner said. "We're asking for your cooperation, unofficially."

McKinnon could beat consent out of a Navy SEAL. Marrs had buried his armory under overgrown cedar bushes in his neighbor's yard, next to the beat-up cyclone fence. He'd carefully replaced the sod, disguising the upturned ground. Since he was a parolee, these Dudley

Do-Rights could conduct a "reasonable" search without a warrant.

Marrs had to gamble. He spread his arms as if he had nothing to hide. "Help yourself."

CHAPTER 25

KRISTEN BLINKED AT HER digital alarm clock, not believing what she was seeing. Did she really sleep late without a single Ambien or Lortab? She curled her pillow under her shoulder, grabbing another minute of bliss . . . until she remembered Stern wanted to see her before he left for a softball game.

She rolled out of bed, pulled on jeans, stretched and groaned, then headed downstairs, her bad knee popping. She was starved, subsisting for the past week on coffee, the occasional Snickers, and a glass of wine at night, laced with a sleeping pill.

Today was the best she'd felt about herself since her team won mid-high regional, maybe since her dad took her to hospital rounds, the day she decided to be a surgeon. Before everything crashed. She'd survived the first week of the biggest malpractice case ever. Her deal with Stern held. Bragg had rested his case. The reporter from the paper had confided he gave them a chance to walk. There was still time to double-cross Stern, if she had to.

The doorbell rang, breaking her trance. Thinking Stern must have decided to go early and stop by, she padded to the door and opened it without looking to see who it was.

On the welcome mat, Tina stared at her flip-flops, then looked up, displaying a stitched lip to go with a purple eye.

"Yo, Krissy."

"Yo, yourself, Philly girl."

"I feel so stupid. I'm sorry for what I said. You were right about Will . . . and our family."

Kristen drew Tina into a tight embrace. "You were right, too. I'm a little uptight."

Tina mumbled into Kristen's shoulder, "Will you take back a rehab slut?"

Kristen shushed her. "Is the Pope Catholic?"

Tina stepped back, sheepish. "I scarfed money from Will."

"Why?"

"How'd you like to sit on the corner every day for two years, trying to sell his shitty paintings? If I'd worn a bra, I wouldn't have unloaded a single one."

Kristen smiled. "Always wondered how you two ate."

"Said he'd kill me if I ever took anything."

"Great. One more thing to worry about."

* * *

Kristen parked in front of the walkway snaking to Stern's house and got out. Planning on running later, she wore shorts with revealing side-slits. For only the second time, Stern would see her hair untied—her best catch-an-eye look. She looked forward to seeing him. Whether she stabbed him in the back later or not, it was nice to be desired. For once, Tammy had been correct.

Feeling déjà vu, Kristen leaned against her BMW and absorbed the scene. Stern and Sarah playing catch in front of a host of red impatiens sent her mind retreating twenty years before her family moved to Jersey. *Go straight to the hoop. That's it, sugar. Use your left hand.*

Michael snagged a throw in the webbing of his glove, breaking her trance.

"Nice arm," Kristen half-shouted.

"Not bad." Michael lofted a towering fly.

Sprinting toward Stern, Sarah made a slick basket catch and flipped the ball back to her dad.

Stern pointed toward the front door. "The articles are up there."

Feeling some disappointment that he hadn't really looked at her, Kristen walked to the porch and picked up a folder tied with a rubber band.

He strolled closer. They locked gazes, but only after he finally considered her in her entirety. "Ettinger wants to use these. Tamponade is hard to spot and all that. Most post-op bleeding stops without intervention."

"Our deal still on?"

"What do I have to do to get you to believe me?" He smiled. "See you Sunday."

Walking back to her car, Kristen called out to Sarah, "Hit it hard!"

The girl grinned, showing braces, and gave a thumbs-up. "Will do. You give 'em hell."

Kristen matched her thumbs-up. She hoped she had a daughter someday. That one would do.

* * *

With the office empty on Sunday morning, Stern finally had the privacy to delve into the contraband from New York. Associates trying to impress him might drift in later, but he'd be on to *Layne* by then, with the Kristen Kerry family secrets locked away. He sipped coffee, propped his feet up, and tore open the FedEx package. He spotted young Dr. Kerry's photo on his original license application. He was good looking, with Kristen's big eyes.

Too excited to read verbatim, he skimmed. It seemed Dr. Kerry had started heavy boozing after leaving a teaching position in Philly and entering private practice in New Jersey. He stayed on the sauce, despite detox at a substance abuse facility for doctors in Atlanta. Later he'd alternated Valium and speed to get him through his busy days. A dead patient had been the result.

He went on to the second volume, feeling like he was peering through the keyhole of his big sister's bedroom door. He told himself he should run the whole thing through a shredder, screw the hospital, and be a hero. Get laid another time. Another girl. Nobody would ever know he'd taken this secret peek into someone else's life.

But temptation prevailed, curiosity blending with voyeurism. Why would the bastard surrender his license *after* fighting through a snot-slinging hearing? Why not plea bargain before trial? Ninety-nine percent of troubled doctors do. Take probation and dry out again. They always give a doc three or four chances.

And Donna's cryptic message. What was *real nasty*? Everything he'd read was bad, but not unheard of, especially for an impaired physician. He'd had several guys like Kerry for clients and had gotten them sent off to clean up. So had Donna's boss, Jake. Donna knew the drill.

He flipped from the back. His hands went rigid when he saw the name of the last witness called by the prosecutor.

Why her, for God's sake? She was a kid then, a teenager. He read a few pages. So, that's how they proved he hadn't answered his page. His own daughter's testimony would settle it.

As he read more, his pace slowed and his throat tightened. Kristen's testimony was so vivid, he could only read snippets at a time, disgusted.

> *I can barely hear out of my left ear. That was from when he hit me on a family trip to New York . . . No, the first time was when I found pills like I'd seen kids sell. He accused me of stealing his medicine. He slapped my face . . .*

Like a spectator to a gory car crash, he couldn't pull himself away.

There were many times he was on call and drunk. He had so much to drink the night we lost the State Championship, I had to drive him home. I was fourteen. I scratched his car on a light pole.

Stern had to put it down a minute and gather himself, before continuing.

He hit me so hard in the stomach that I threw up. His pager rang the whole time. He got so mad, he threw it against the wall and broke it.

"Do you need a recess, young lady?"

"No . . ."

My mother saw my bruise. She knew Dad was drinking. She was on some of the same drugs. I know she took Valium.

He realized science was wrong. The center of emotion *is* the heart, not the brain, for his whole chest cavity felt scorched. Her own mother had been ignoring the abuse, sacrificing her firstborn on the altar of social status. *Joan of Arc. Perfect.*

He thought *he'd* had a tough childhood. They never had enough. Shabby clothes. Dad never worked any day he could fish. Stern had gotten *whuppins*, but none left permanent scars.

Now, when he pictured Kristen, he didn't see a sexy doll, but a terrified kid. He wanted to time travel, steal her away, and make sure no one ever hurt her again.

* * *

Sunday night, after a long day in Stern's conference room, Kristen stared at the ridiculously dramatic portraits of the Jackson, Stern and Randolph partners looming over the table. She realized she'd tuned out Ettinger's discussion and had to shake herself alert. Beer with the pizza

Stern ordered had been a bad idea.

Stern rolled his conference room chair back and stood. "Okay, Ted, we're ready. You go on first tomorrow."

Ettinger, the gangly cardiologist and their joint expert witness, rose and gathered his file.

"Explain and teach," Stern counseled, "but make the jury think being a doctor is damn hard. If they think medical decisions are easy, they can second-guess."

"I can honestly say this is a judgment call, if the man's signs were properly recorded by the nurses. I would've ordered an echo, but with carriers screaming about costs, I can see why a guy might wait for more symptoms."

Stern handed the doctor his coat. "If Bragg wants to call Galway and Kristen's nurses liars, let him. All he's got is a diary written by a greedy widow."

The cardiologist turned to Kristen. "And you'll start me on the nurses?"

"Yes, Doctor. We go first, then Michael."

"You two look wrung out," Ettinger said.

Stern nodded. "It's been a long ol' day. If he asks if you know me socially, tell him every doctor needs to know Mr. Stern these days, with all the frivolous lawsuits being filed."

"Got it. Nothing about golf." The doctor said good night and shuffled out.

"Good job tonight, kiddo," Stern said.

Kristen remained slumped in the conference room chair. "I'm totally wasted," she said. "Can I spend the night here? Then I could make sure you don't meet with *our* expert in the morning." She smiled and stretched her feet under the table, searching for her shoes.

"If you're like me, once you hit the sack, you'll be trying the case in your head all night."

"I've got pills."

He dropped into the chair next to her and reached for her ankle. She started to jerk back, but her reflexes were slow.

He pulled her foot up to his lap. "This is better than a pill."

She found herself perplexed, unsure why she wasn't rejecting him, and curious where this was leading. She was too intrigued—and tired—to retreat.

Stern stroked the ball of her foot with his thumbs, then kneaded the soft underside, and rounded off at the heel. He pulled her short crew sock off. "Good-looking foot. High arch, straight toes. Too wide for an aristocrat though. But I guess Joan was a country girl."

She was glad she had treated herself to a pedicure before the trial.

He worked up each toe, caressing, squeezing, then gently pulling. Finishing at the notch of the Achilles tendon, he made circles with both hands around her ankle. Taking the other foot, he began anew.

Her eyelids grew heavy. Sensations of pleasure migrated up to her brain, circled there, and delightfully lingered. He gave her foot a final squeeze and eased it to the floor.

Stern rose, but she felt nailed to the conference chair. He stepped behind her, squeezed her shoulders, and began working her tight trapezius muscles with his thumbs.

Helpless under his hands, her chin collapsed to her chest.

Stern's fingers crawled into her hair and massaged her scalp, deadening her senses to the world. There was no trial, no worry over who was going to screw whom.

Just as she would have succumbed to anything, Stern stepped around, took her hand, and pulled her to her feet. "Big day tomorrow."

He'd spoken just above a whisper. His fingers lingered, tangled with hers.

Her heartbeat quickened. Was he moving closer? His lips looked delicious.

Kiss me. What are you waiting for?

Her breath halted.

He moved no nearer.

She told herself to forget it.

Get real. He's married. And you're crazy.

She grabbed her sneakers and socks from the floor, putting them on while sneaking a glance to see if he was disappointed.

Stern, seeming unperturbed by the close call, picked up her briefcase. "I'll walk you down."

When they reached her car, parked near his Benz, she fumbled her keys onto the concrete.

Stern retrieved them, tapped the lock button, and opened the door. "We'll get 'em tomorrow."

Perhaps it was the beer, the camaraderie, the rub, or just the years of deprivation, but suddenly she felt insanely assertive. She touched his shoulder, leaned forward, and stood tiptoe. Feeling petite, she brushed her lips across his. To her astonishment, he backed up, smiled, and said good-bye.

Kristen got in, started her BMW, put it in gear, and looked back one last time. His expression puzzled her. No studly grin. Rather, he appeared thoughtful. She hadn't kissed that many men, but all had responded positively.

Probably plotting when to turn on me.

CHAPTER 26

NEITHER KRISTEN NOR Stern saw Caswell. Parked on the far side of NationsBank's underground garage, waiting for them to come down, Tony was nothing if not patient.

His guilt-ridden father, who'd spent Tony's childhood trying out mistresses in exotic lands, had bought stock in Jackson, Stern and Randolph for his son. Tony Caswell was the equal of everyone in the firm, except Jackson and Stern, who hated each other. If Tony could find the right dirt, he might soon watch Stern clean out his desk.

Seeing Stern and Kristen get off the elevator, he scrunched lower in his seat. She walked to her car like she was dazed, like Stern had fucked her silly. Tony wondered how they could possibly justify screwing around the night before their case-in-chief began.

If they lost *Layne*, and if Tony ratted out the lovebirds, then Hospital Risk, Adventist, and Standard would be looking for new lawyers. What an opportunity. He would remind them that he'd warned everybody that Stern was more interested in dipping his stick than doing his duty for his client. Their little kiss was totally disgusting.

Tony waited until both left, then got out of his car and used his security access card to ride the elevator up to the dark seventy-third floor. A pizza box and beer bottles cluttered the main conference room table. Caswell looked around, checked the trash, and found nothing interesting.

In Stern's office, little seemed amiss. He rifled through Stern's desk, trying to preserve the same semblance of order. Tony rotated the massive leather chair and tugged on the credenza doors, finding them locked. Strange to secure this and not bother with the desk. He examined the lock, figuring he might pick it with a paper clip. But if it broke, he was dead meat. The access card would identify him and the time he entered.

Searching around the computer terminal revealed no spare key. He couldn't imagine what the so-called Prince was hiding. He pawed through every desk drawer, his fingers clawing to the corners for a key. Walking across the hall, he flipped on the light in Janet's office.

He remembered she picked up Stern's kid, his cleaning, and guessed she threw in a weekly blow job. Caswell smirked. Now that he was a partner, he'd get a better-looking, younger version.

After combing through her bottom drawer, he found a ring holding three keys—one to a house, a Mercedes key, and a small brass jobbie. There was tape on the house key with numbers written on it, maybe an alarm code. He went back to Stern's office and tried the credenza. *Bingo*. Philip Marlowe couldn't have done better.

He found brokerage and bank statements in Stern's name only. An envelope crammed full of hundred-dollar bills. It looked like Stern was preparing for a divorce, keeping separate accounts and a lot of cash. Caswell spotted transcripts from a New Jersey case. He flipped a volume open, read a little, and realized why the bitch was crazy. Tammy and Pete might want to know more background on their hotshot partner, who apparently had no loyalty to doctors or family.

Caswell tossed the Kerry stuff aside and pulled out a manila folder. It contained what looked like a parole file on a scumbag named Leonard Marrs. Caswell gnawed a knuckle, staring at the file photo, wondering where he'd seen this dog-eyed dork. He scoured his brain.

It took a minute to remember the phony deliveryman, the same spook casing the garage.

Tony perused Marrs's file. Convicted of sexual assault and kidnapping, he was on closely supervised parole. Why was Marrs hanging around? What was he planning? No good, that's for sure. Sniffing around Diana? With her family money, she made a great target, but obviously this guy didn't have the brains to arrange a kidnapping, much less a payoff, without getting caught.

Caswell copied Marrs's folder before returning it to the credenza. He decided to get duplicates made of the keys and slip them back in Janet's desk early in the morning. As he locked the credenza, he wondered if there might be another angle. What if Stern didn't want a divorce, but was looking for his own payout? Maybe find somebody to kill his wife so he could grab her millions? Then run off with Kristen? At first, Caswell found the idea incredible, especially trading Diana for Kristen.

But after more thought, Tony decided Marrs would be a blue-chip recruit and Stern could clean up nicely. Kristen might be involved, too. Or she could know about the plot and be guilty of abetting.

If true—and it was a big *if*—his best revenge would be to make sure they got caught.

* * *

Marrs sat inside Jimmy's Cherokee on the Cabell Elementary School parking lot in Farmers Branch. He was pissed at himself for going to Lottie's for some home cookin' and been lucky to escape the truck stop gal's attempts at romance. Worse than her paws were the incessant questions. He'd finally confessed he was an ex-con, although that didn't faze her. He found her disgusting, but she fit into his plan as a backstop. And he'd gotten a decent meal out of it.

He spotted the jogger, silhouetted against the glimmer of dawn, crossing the baseball field a hundred yards away. Marrs rested his rifle on the open passenger window, the barrel an inch out of the Jeep. His pulse racing, he exhaled and squeezed the trigger, but only heard the tap of the hammer.

Marrs couldn't figure out what was wrong. He had tested the stolen piece by firing into phone books on the floor.

He jerked the bolt back, ejected the unspent bullet, chambered another round, then zeroed in again and pulled the trigger.

Click.

Nothing.

He frowned. He'd been pointing down when it fired correctly. Perhaps the pin wasn't making center contact while held at ninety degrees. He pounded the butt against the floorboard, then jerked the rifle back to the window.

Zelner had already dashed behind the building.

"Fuck!" Marrs threw the gun into the backseat and started the engine.

He was back in Jimmy's rental dump in thirty minutes. He ran to the house, paying no attention to the sports car across the street, and grabbed his shovel. The sun was up by the time he walked through the back door with the weapon wrapped and reburied. He was spent. Breakfast sounded good.

"Don't move. Don't even turn around."

Marrs stopped. The voice came from his left, from the room he used for an office. Without turning his neck he attempted a peripheral look, but couldn't see the intruder. He tried not to sound frightened. "What do you want?"

"You got a thing for Diana Stern?"

Marrs didn't answer, but he felt piss dribble into his shorts. His stiletto was in his back pocket. He could get to the intruder in two seconds, but that might be too late if the guy had a gun. Could it be a cop? A Zelner plant? He thought of McKinnon, the cop the size of a garage.

"Who are you?" Marrs asked.

"Maybe you've been hired to kill an inconvenient wife."

"Maybe you should get the fuck out of here."

"I'm here to help, but if you turn around, you're dead."

Marrs heard the unmistakable click of a pistol hammer being retracted. His butthole tightened.

"Now listen. I've got a plan that will make us rich, and you can still have some fun with darling Diana."

Despite his fear Marrs resolved to sound tough. "What's it to you, asshole?"

"Shut up. I'm the best friend you have. I'll keep you out of prison."

Marrs leaned forward against the rusty kitchen sink. He wiped sweat from his lip, and decided to hear the dude out. Not like he had a choice.

CHAPTER 27

Monday, October 6

SECOND WEEK, AND SO FAR Kristen's gamble had paid off. Dr. Ettinger, their joint expert, had charmed everyone on direct and was handling Bragg's cross with aplomb. But she wouldn't take a full breath until it ended.

Bragg draped his rotund body over the lectern and paused. Seeing it was 5:30, Kristen worried Bragg had to have something good left to justify keeping everyone late.

Judge Proctor cleared his throat. "Anything else, Mr. Bragg?"

"A bit more, Judge." Bragg smiled. "Dr. Ettinger, did you say that somebody had to have, in your words, 'screwed the pooch, for Layne to have croaked'?"

Ettinger hesitated, and sipped on his cup of water.

Kristen peeked at Stern, who looked unflappable. She didn't feel so calm.

Somebody must've ratted to Bragg, and now it was Ettinger's chance to dump on the hospital.

"You're under oath and subject to the law of perjury," Bragg boomed.

The cardiologist finally spoke, showing little distress. "Mr. Bragg, I think everyone initially guessed something had gone wrong. If I said that, I shouldn't have. One can't express an opinion that's worth anything without careful examination of the record. I've since done just that."

Bragg sputtered, trying to cut Ettinger off, but the witness continued.

"Mr. Layne's compression of the heart that occurred when blood built up in the space between his heart muscle and the sac covering the heart was slow and subtle. Combined with the interruption in his monitoring and a sudden arrhythmia, this was a disaster that good caregivers couldn't prevent, even if they were standing right there. It's impossible to achieve perfection in any medical setting."

Kristen made sure the breath she'd held came out quietly. She stole a glance at the jury. Maybe a couple had bought the explanation, but some scowled disbelief.

"What you really mean," Bragg said slowly, "is that you've got one opinion when shooting the breeze with your doctor friends or playing golf with Mr. Stern, and another when you're paid to come to court."

Kristen saw deflation in Ettinger's confidence. She prepared to object, but Stern continued to take notes. Perhaps better to ride out the storm.

Ettinger took too long to say, "No, sir."

Bragg turned to the jury and smirked. "No more questions."

Kristen noticed several jurors had crossed their arms. A bad omen.

Judge Proctor announced the end of the day, dismissed the jury, and hurried out, his clerk, reporter, and bailiff right behind.

Tired, but relieved it hadn't gone worse, Kristen stood at the defendants' table and stretched.

After the last juror left, Tammy Robberson, Adventist claims super, shoved open the low swinging door separating the spectators from the bar, and stamped up to the defendants' table.

Stern winked at Kristen, grabbed his briefcase, took Galway's elbow, and led his client out.

Tammy waited until Bragg and Betty Layne left before saying,

"Well, Ettinger didn't fuck us. So my plan's on track."

Kristen loaded her briefcase and spoke without looking at her client, "I'm not sure how well it went. Did you watch the jury?"

Tammy grabbed Kristen's arm. "Show some balls, girlie."

Kristen didn't know what to say. She'd always given honest, reasoned advice. But now? "Tammy—"

"I talked to our girls today. They're ready to go."

"That's my job."

"You tellin' me how to run a case? Layne's in multiple organ failure and won't last long. No future medical expense. Just a dead guy with a widow cute enough to find another old football player."

"Tammy, if Layne dies tonight, let's talk settlement with Bragg."

Tammy stepped closer, her nose just under Kristen's chin. "Bullshit! You be ready to cut Stern's balls off when I give you the signal. Casey's testimony is perfect. I can't wait to see Stern's face when he watches his nuts bounce off the floor."

Kristen bought herself some time with, "Whatever you say."

"Every lawyer in town will salute you, girlie-pie."

Kristen couldn't delay the decision much longer. Soon she would either have to welsh on her deal with Stern or refuse the direct orders of a client and her boss. She attempted reason.

"Tammy, what makes you think we can skate this if we blame Galway? Stern will hammer us right back."

Tammy pushed Kristen's shoulder. "Get out there and charm the TV shits. You're good at that. Jurors will watch the news tonight, even though they've been told not to."

"Right." Kristen noticed Casey, her courtroom representative for the hospital and star witness, had heard every word.

Casey nodded at Tammy, walked to the back of the courtroom, and lingered.

Tammy snarled more encouragement, then left with Casey.

Kristen lugged her gear to the gallery gate where Tina waited.

Tina shook her head. "This reminds me of table dancing in front of drunk soldiers." She had nailed it. Kristen was naked in front of jerk-offs demanding more and more.

It took her another moment to realize Casey had no reason to meet with Tammy tonight. Her nursing director was supposed to be preparing for her testimony on Wednesday. So why leave together? Like spies arranging a drop.

Kristen dug into her purse and handed Tina her keys. "Get my car and follow the bitch with the baubles and the tall nurse. See if they stay together. I'll bum a ride later from Jen and see you at the house. Don't let them spot you."

"Okay, boss."

Tina's voice sparkled. Maybe, thought Kristen, there was hope. The eye had progressed to light purple. Swelling in her upper lip had improved. "Put the shades back on. You look like shit."

"How much do I get to bill?"

"I'll take it off your rent."

* * *

At eleven that night, Kristen thanked Jen for the ride and hurried through pouring rain into her townhouse. A tropical storm had wandered up from the Gulf, drenching Texas, filling in cracks in the earth and bringing life back to brown trees. By the time she got inside, Kristen's worsted wool skirt smelled like a wet dog. Her white blouse pasted her skin, making her look like a coed on South Beach for spring break.

Tina lounged on the couch, nursing an Amstel, watching *Sleepless in Seattle* for the hundredth time. Her bare feet rested on the Chippendale table. Her toenails were painted a color not found in any big box of crayons.

Kristen shivered. Goosebumps rose. Tina obviously didn't worry about the electric bill. Kristen quickly peeled out of her wet clothes down to underwear.

"You missed yourself on the late news."

Kristen grabbed a throw blanket off the couch and wrapped herself. "How'd I look?"

"Almost had me believing your hospital isn't guilty."

Kristen sat next to Tina. "Almost?"

"No luck spying, by the way. I didn't see them."

Kristen considered this. "Probably my paranoia." Kristen lay down. "Pop my back."

"Wasn't it eerie when Bragg asked where the doctor was while the patient—"

"Don't even go there, Tina."

"Sorry." Tina sounded thoughtful for a change. "Funny, but watching Stern all day, I could swear he likes you. You know, *really* likes you."

"You think?"

"I'm pretty sure. I've seen that kind of pining look a few times. Still going to shaft him?"

Kristen tried to process Tina's opinion and couldn't decide whether to accept it at face value. Tina knew more about men than she did.

"Either that or you'll have to give me pole-dancing lessons."

* * *

Caswell sat in the gallery waiting for the fireworks to begin. Mug shots of former judges going back a century stared at him. The old guys with handlebar mustaches looked like they could have been defendants, instead of jurists.

Dallas County had the ugliest courtrooms in Texas, monuments to the tasteless sixties. The low acoustic tile ceiling and scuffed linoleum made them look like an old 7-Eleven, one needing to be refurbished.

Caswell studied the lawyers. He hoped that since Stern had already nailed Kristen, he'd do it again by double-crossing Kristen, perhaps as soon as that morning. Tony wanted to watch Kristen's career collapse when her lover dumped all the shit on her. He wondered if she'd lose it completely. Cry or take out Stern with some karate-chop crap?

At the plaintiffs' table, Bragg looked confident, his doughy body hanging over his chair. He looked like a walrus. One question lingered in Tony's mind: How crooked was Bragg and how appreciative would he be of help? Enough for Tony to flee this shithole?

The next witness, Nurse Roberta "Robbie" Lott, roosted on the first row, just down from Caswell. To complement her lovely milk-chocolate skin, her pale blue blouse and soft linen jacket had likely been selected by Kristen.

Robbie fidgeted, crossing nice legs, and dug into her jacket pocket, rattling cellophane. She slipped a handful of black jelly beans into her mouth. He smelled licorice.

* * *

"How was Mr. Layne when you left?" Kristen asked, glancing right, signaling Nurse Lott to turn to the jury.

"He was sick. But he was stable. I assumed he would go home the next day after his medicine was adjusted. Most patients in our unit go home after one day."

Kristen felt like she'd stolen a pass and made an uncontested layup. For all her nastiness, Tammy could evaluate a witness. Robbie was a star. Two male jurors leaned forward with interest. They might actually have a chance.

Time to decide whether to ask about what she suspected was a lie. A total lie. She glanced at Stern, saw his gorgeous hands resting on the defendants' table. *We band of brothers.* "One more thing, Nurse Lott. You didn't see Dr. Galway examine the patient?"

"No. I saw him go into Mr. Layne's room, before I went to the nurse's station to catch up on my charting right before eleven."

"Did you overhear any conversations between Dr. Galway and Mr. Layne?"

Bragg launched himself out of his chair, jabbing his chubby forefinger. "Objection! Hearsay."

Proctor snarled, "Sustained."

Bragg plopped down and folded his arms over his chest, looking satisfied that he'd squelched this problem.

Kristen was ready with an exception in the evidence rules. "Did Dr. Galway offer an echocardiogram, and did Mr. Layne decline the test until morning?"

Bragg jumped up. "Judge, she's disobeyin' your ruling!"

Kristen spoke evenly, "Your Honor, this is an action, not a statement."

Proctor nodded in admiration of Kristen's trick. "Overruled."

Robbie Lott's hand touched her full lips. "Yes. Yes, he did."

* * *

Stern fought the impulse to shake his head. Had Kristen actually bought the absurd story of the undocumented, offered-but-declined STAT echo? After twenty years, he knew horseshit blindfolded and asleep, but if Galway wanted to spread manure, who could blame his lawyer for supplying the rake?

He wondered if she asked the question to show her adherence to the cause, to set him up for a backstab, or if she actually believed that nonsense?

Kristen gathered her notes and strode to the table. She eased into the chair and let out a shallow breath. Perhaps seeking assurance, she glanced in his direction.

Stern scribbled *Sehr gut* on his pad and pushed it toward her.

Remembering the Jersey transcript, he felt a surge of nausea. He could still recite some of the sickening testimony. The more he tried to forget it, the more it stuck in his brain, like a bubblegum rock tune.

He wished he'd never lusted for her, wished he could do something, anything, to undo all that pain. How could she have fled home, finished high school, gotten a scholarship, and made it through law school all on her own? *One tough cookie.* He ordered himself to quit thinking about the transcripts or he'd turn into a sobbing fool.

As Bragg lumbered up to cross Robbie, Stern recognized himself as the drunk at a poker game, way down on the night and playing another bad hand. He'd seen that kind of dumbass at the table many times, shoveling chips in, raising the stakes, hoping the river—the last card—would bail him out.

The longer he played, the more likely he'd have to hurt Kristen. But instead, he stayed in the game, didn't make Galway settle because he couldn't leave the action, couldn't peel himself away from her.

His choices were to keep his clients—and his image—or chase the vaporous aura of a woman who'd given no indication she was the least bit interested in him beyond doing her job and following her orders.

Why was he making this harder than it had to be?

* * *

That evening Stern slung his suit jacket on his couch and grabbed a beer from the mini-fridge. He pictured the sly smile Kristen gave him as they left the courtroom. A setup, role-playing, or did she like him? *Christ, you're acting like a high school kid. Snap out of it. She is Pete McGee's torpedo aimed straight at you. You could lose your whole practice, dip shit.*

Janet came in, interrupting his thoughts.

"Big news. My source at Parkland called. Layne died an hour ago."

"About fucking time."

"They finally got a culture report from the throat swab. C-diff. In his blood, too."

Stern frowned.

"That's odd, isn't it?" Janet asked.

"Yep. Real odd."

"What now?"

Stern grabbed another beer and handed it to Janet, his brain in turmoil. He knew Bragg would have to announce to the judge tomorrow that *Layne* was now a death case. The stakes had actually dropped, but since it would take less to settle, Galway might insist that the whole mess go away, so he could go back to making money.

"Want me to call Kristen? Galway?"

"No, I'll handle it," Stern said.

Stern thought a minute. Tammy wouldn't be a problem. She and McGee were after his hide and wouldn't want to quit. But he had to get to Galway quick and make sure his client continued the play. The curtain couldn't close now or he might never look into those green eyes again.

CHAPTER 28

IT TOOK A MINUTE TO GATHER his nerve, but Leonard Marrs put the Cherokee in park and moseyed up to an old Buick Electra. The wire wheel spokes gleamed. He saw his reflection. In his pocket, he supposedly carried the Sterns' house key, assuming his new friend had kept his word. Jimmy was going to Hawaii, leaving Marrs the extra car and the accounts to service. Time to shit or get off the pot.

Jungle-bunny music blasted through the car's open windows. The black kids had parked several spaces away from the other cars in the Wendy's parking lot, probably to protect the relic from door dings. The driver looked at him and said something he couldn't understand. The others laughed.

Marrs cleared his throat. "Hey, guys, want to make some easy money?"

"Say what, man?"

"I got twenty bucks." He waved the bill.

The kid next to the driver snorted. "For what, man? We ain't got no blow."

He forced a smile. "A few hairs from you."

"Huh?"

Marrs pulled the baggie from his pocket. "It's for a science class.

Got to have black hair to test, have to be pulled out, not cut. Put 'em in the bag."

The driver shook his head. "You on something strong, man."

* * *

Parole Officer Lyndon Zelner hopped into McKinnon's car and grabbed a powdered donut from the sack on the console. "I know Marrs is up to something."

McKinnon rolled his massive shoulders. "Prob'ly." He ripped open a sweetener and emptied the packet into his coffee. "Homicide has a make on the gun dealer killing. A competitor. They got prints off part of the back porch that wasn't damaged, gunpowder residue on a shirt, and DNA. Perp drives an SUV. Not a Cherokee like Marrs, but the same color."

Zelner stared for a second at the moonlight reflected over White Rock Lake. "Just because this guy was there sometime doesn't mean Marrs wasn't."

"Homicide's happy. They want that gangbanger off the street. They don't wanna hear about your baby-faced pervert."

Zelner fiddled with the string on his running pants. "Okay. We drew a blank. I'd still like to take that little dump apart board by board."

A smile flickered for a second on Sergeant McKinnon's face. "We gave it a pretty good look. He may have a stash somewhere else."

Zelner popped the door handle. "I could sic that Lance kid on him."

McKinnon grabbed Zelner's arm. "That would be dangerous. To you."

"Marrs is loose because they've put liberal women on the board."

"If it went bad, you might go to jail."

"How could it go bad? Freddie could rip Marrs apart in two seconds. I could even arrange an alibi for Freddie."

McKinnon shook his head, showing his displeasure at the idea. "I'll ask the dispatchers to be on the lookout for Marrs and tip the detectives in sex crimes. If I hear anything that sounds like him, I'll be there in a flash. And make sure he gets nailed."

"Marrs is worse than that pimp we sent back, after those pussies sprang him. Bet you a steak that stockbroker wasn't his first."

"And I'll bet you a six-pack the next one won't live to tell about it."

CHAPTER 29

A FTER THE TRIAL adjournment for the day, Tony Caswell sat in the Adventist Hospital risk management department. Disappointed that Stern hadn't pulled the trigger, he'd decided to see if he could figure out the *Licorice* note.

> *Good luck today.*
> *Everything safe. See you tonight?*
> *Been too long. Licorice.*

He studied the original chart he had access to thanks to the joint defense agreement. Bragg's associate had taken a documents depo months ago for the plaintiff, but had only counted the pages and made sure they had a complete copy. He doubted anyone had looked at it since, at least not like Tony would.

After pondering the likely scenarios, Caswell—in a moment of deduction worthy of Mike Hammer had concluded something had happened to derail the system. Galway could've ordered an echo and gotten the results by phone, even if he had been in a hurry to get home. So far, no really credible explanation for why a non-invasive test hadn't been done, had surfaced from any of the parties in the case. Bragg claimed Galway didn't care. Maybe he didn't, but it wasn't likely he wanted to be sued either. So Stern and Kristen had to contend that an echo wasn't necessary—a weak story in Tony's mind.

When Caswell had done the preliminary work—before Stern jerked the case away from him—an aide had confirmed to Tony she'd seen Galway on the floor at eleven. She didn't have a dog in the hunt and had no reason to lie. But he'd seen Betty Layne testify. The widow was too credible to have made it all up.

Layne's admission was before Adventist switched entirely to electronic charting. Caswell found Galway's progress note, summarizing the 11:00 p.m. exam. It was right above the entry the next morning, describing Layne's crash on the customary form scribbled on by the docs. Galway had written his third progress report after surgery two hours later, in black instead of blue.

Caswell flipped to the nurses' notes. Robbie's writing flowed in a swirling style, identical to the *Licorice* note. He squinted through his magnifying glass. The width of the pen's stroke looked the same for entries until 10:30 p.m. Then a different pen, one that leaked just a little, was used until the end of Robbie's twelve-hour shift at 6:00 a.m. It was still her handwriting, but the same pen used by Nancy to write her note that began at 6:00 p.m., before the code. Why would two nurses have the same pen?

Tony found no evidence of indentation on Robbie's page. If Nancy's sheet had been on top of the clipboard, pressure from her pen would show on the underlying page. Her wordy summary ended on the last line, like she had been determined to take up the whole page.

He thumbed to the flow sheet that summarized vital signs. Although the dots and lines on the temp and blood pressure chart weren't signed, Robbie must have made the entries until 11:00 p.m., since the same pen appeared to have been used. But around the time the pen on Robbie's notes changed to match Nancy's later entries, the check marks on the flow sheet became slightly smudged.

Caswell returned the chart and hurried to the elevators. Upstairs on the heart floor, Caswell found Robbie at the nurse's station in the cardiac step-down unit.

Robbie spoke into the phone, "Send another up." She hung up and muttered to herself, "By all means. I've got plenty of help."

"You look overwhelmed."

"You got it."

He introduced himself and pushed his card toward her, assuring her that he worked for Stern.

Roberta Lott cocked her head for a second. "Yes, I saw you."

"You were a great witness."

She smiled with obvious pride. "Thanks."

"Can't believe they made you work tonight."

An old man in a stained robe and worn slippers, his IV preceding him on wheels, doddered toward them. His family circled him, as if afraid he'd cut them out of the will before he died.

Caswell waited until the herd passed, then said, "We need your nurse's license for an exhibit tomorrow."

Robbie stepped around the station. "I'll get my purse."

Caswell followed her through a door marked *STAFF*. Robbie hurried past a table cluttered with *People* magazines and empty coffee cups to four rows of green metal lockers.

Robbie rotated the combination lock right half a turn while Caswell peered over her shoulder. She opened the locker, pulled out a purse, and flipped through her wallet. She removed a laminated card and handed it to Caswell.

He stashed the license into the inside pocket of his sport coat. "Thanks. I'll get it back to you tomorrow after court."

She shoved her purse back, and gave the lock a half turn to the left.

"Got a new patient coming," she said, standing.

"I've got a long night ahead, too." He pointed at the coffeemaker by the door. "May I?"

"Sure. It'll keep you up a week," Robbie said as she left.

Caswell strolled to the pot, poured himself a cup, and emptied a packet of sugar into it. After listening a moment, he stepped back to the lockers, squatted at Robbie's, retraced the half right turn, and popped the lock.

* * *

He spent ten minutes rifling through the obvious places in Robbie's apartment. Then he grabbed a chair and stood on it to probe the top shelf of the bedroom closet. He jumped off the chair and raised the mattress on each side. Tony tucked the sheets back, then looked inside every shoebox, finding only size eights.

Surely she kept the first version for insurance against being dumped by a rich doc going back to his wife, or him finding a new darling on the side, but was it here?

Sweating in Robbie's hot apartment, he located the electrical switch box in the kitchen and tugged it open. Empty. He checked under every table in the apartment, but nothing was taped underneath. All the carpet was tacked down. He realized it could be stowed with a friend, and he'd wasted his time. He asked himself what Harry Bosch would do.

The refrigerator pulled him like a magnet. He horsed it out a few inches and stuck his good hand into a tangle of cobwebs. Caswell locked onto an envelope, liberated it, and undid the tin clasp, finding two pristine pages of original nurses' notes on an Adventist form.

Jackpot.

CHAPTER 30

KRISTEN'S BREAKFAST PREP session with her nursing expert, Casey Denman, had been like preparing Marie Antoinette for the guillotine. Again, Kristen had two outlines for Casey's testimony, but Casey didn't seem any more enthusiastic for the "shaft Stern" version than the joint defense "sudden arrhythmia/nobody could've done anything" story.

Kristen left her witness in the courthouse snack bar and hurried upstairs to corner Stern before court commenced. If she could somehow talk everybody into settling, she wouldn't have to pick someone to screw. Galway was the weak link in the chain holding this insanity together. Unfortunately she couldn't talk to the nervous cardiologist without going through Stern.

She found Stern at the defense table in Proctor's court and signaled him outside. They walked down the crowded corridor, past other courtrooms and a hundred anxious people hoping for justice or praying it be denied, until they reached an empty alcove.

Kristen whispered, "When I told my star witness Layne died yesterday, she started dancing on hot coals. Suddenly, it's 'Maybe the doctor should have been called' and, 'This lab result is troubling.'"

"Kick her ass! With Layne dead, we're okay."

"This gambling is crazy. I bet Bragg now will take something under six. That's less than three each."

One of the jurors, a guy in jeans and a Western-style shirt, snaked through the horde and walked past them toward the courtroom without making eye contact. Kristen knew that was a bad omen.

After the man was out of earshot, Stern said, "We're not doin' that bad. Ol' Ted was great. We hammered their New York cardiologist last week. And nobody liked Joe's old-bag nurse expert."

"If Casey bombs, I'm in trouble, and you've still got to put Galway back on. He's got as much charm as a muddy hog in his pen."

"You're sounding like a Texan." Stern winked at her, which she found annoying. "Look, we've stuck together great. Bragg thought he could pry us apart."

"Oh, give me a break! Your client wants to tank me and the hospital to save his bacon. He's the last witness, and you can't control what he blurts out."

"If we win this together, we'll be the biggest heroes—"

"Let's offer four. Split it fifty-fifty. I'll go to Pete, override Tammy. Betty may jump on it or come back with a counter of seven."

"I talked to my guy last night. Galway will never consent to settle, if Tammy won't double what he pays. His policy with Standard requires his okay to pay a dime."

"This ego shit is stupid." Kristen clenched a fist. "*Make* him settle, damn it. Something's rotten."

Stern shrugged. "It doesn't matter. I know Tammy. She will never authorize paying as much as my guy does. That would feel like a loss to her."

Kristen felt steam building in her. "I'll worry about my asshole. You cover yours. Get his permission!"

Before Stern could respond, Shorty, the bailiff, crept up to them. "Judge is ready."

* * *

Janet watched Stern from the gallery. Nobody knew him better than his paralegal. In trial, he continually eyed the jury for reactions to the witnesses and lawyers. He was an actor, hungry for applause, peering through the stage lights for reassurance. She'd seen him change his entire tone because of one juror's body language. But this case, especially this second week, was different. He seemed oblivious to the panel, his attention never straying long from Kristen.

He tensed his shoulders every time Kristen rose to speak, relaxed when she finished, and smiled when she did well, like when Sarah fielded a hot grounder. Janet had seen him panting for a woman before and realized this wasn't lust, but something quite different. Janet wondered whether the odd package from New York had something to do with Kristen.

Behind all the bluster was a damn good man, if he could rid himself of hoity-toity Diana. Michael needed a woman who knew how to hunt, fish, and bop him upside the head when he got out of line. From what she had learned about Kristen, Janet doubted she knew how to bait a hook.

But Kristen had savvy. The pretty black nurse had charmed everyone. The other RN with the fake diamonds in her glasses had crept to the stand like a rattlesnake was waiting for her, but Kristen had gotten her through it. Bragg had tried to make her look indifferent to Layne, but she seemed more forgetful than uncaring.

This morning, the Adventist nursing director, Casey, had testified on direct. More than once, she'd looked like she had more to say than what Kristen asked. Janet had noticed Casey making eye contact with Michael's former client, Tammy, in the gallery. Once, Casey blurted that Galway could easily have gotten an echo done at 11:00 p.m. At that point, Janet thought the deal between the defendants was going to blow up, but Kristen hadn't pursued the suggestion. Janet saw Michael relax with relief, and she also saw Tammy's scowl, like she was plotting an assassination.

Bragg continued to hammer Casey on cross. Everything she said had been perfect, as if scripted, but Janet thought something was funky about her demeanor.

"So you're telling us that nurses don't respond to every monitor alarm?" Bragg asked.

"The screen at the station would've shown the disconnect if Mrs. Layne had taken the monitor off. That wouldn't be the same as his heart stopping or going into arrhythmia. Patients disconnect themselves often. Sometimes accidentally. We try to get to them promptly."

"Convenient that this *disconnect* happened shortly before the code, isn't it?"

Kristen hopped up. "Objection!"

"Sustained," Judge Proctor bellowed.

Bragg seemed to take a minute to lick his wounds. "Have you ever diagnosed a cardiac tamponade, Nurse Denman?"

Casey shifted her weight. "Yes."

"Nurses can and do find tamponade?"

"Well, I've suspected it, when a patient showed signs."

"Such as nausea, a history of—"

Kristen stood, stopping Casey's response. "Objection. Your Honor, we've been over all this for hours."

Before Proctor could rule, Bragg's jowls shook as he said, "Withdrawn. Ms. Kerry is correct. We *all* know by now what the symptoms are of a heart being squeezed by bleeding. And it's up to the nurses to call these signs to the attention of the physician, so he can diagnose and treat the patient, right?"

"Yes, sir."

"And y'all never alerted anybody about Mr. Layne?"

Casey's eyes stayed fixed on the far wall.

Bragg smirked. "Nothing else, judge."

* * *

That evening, Kristen ate a ham sandwich in her office, her first real meal all week. She held it over her desk, careful not to drip mustard. She craved the calories, but her guts were like revolutionaries in a basement, plotting an uprising.

Tammy Robberson marched in, her hair a new shade of bleach. "We're runnin' out of time to hose Stern. I had Casey ready to cut loose against Galway on your direct, and you just went merrily on. Are you even listening to your own witness, sweet pea? 'Dr. Galway could have easily gotten an echo done at eleven.' Stern was sitting on a platter."

Kristen put her sandwich down. "Tammy, Casey acts scared to death. Everybody sensed it. I have to redirect her in the morning, and Bragg gets another crack at re-cross. I recommend we settle. I'm putting it in writing and sending a copy to Adventist."

Tammy stomped to the edge of Kristen's desk and pointed, jangling a silver bracelet. "You horny little bitch! Doin' Stern, while you should be preparing your witnesses. You want out, so you can play hide-the-hot-dog with a clear conscience. You don't want to follow orders because you've fallen in *love*."

Blood surged to Kristen's head. The enormity—the absurdity—of this sucked her breath away.

"You're insane."

"I got a tip from a pretty good source." Tammy curled her pug nose. "We ain't settling. We ain't going to offer fifty fuckin' cents. I won't have us wimping out, while Stern bangs my drug addict lawyer, then brags about it all over town."

"What?"

"I wonder what Pete would think of all the shit you take. You could open your own drugstore."

Kristen stood up from behind her desk. "First of all, we haven't touched each other. Second, my records are *private*!"

"Nothing 'bout my lawyers is private, princess. Either fry Galway tomorrow on Casey's redirect or clean out your desk and get a job airin' up basketballs." Tammy spun on her high heels, stalked out, and slammed the door shut behind her.

Before Kristen could breathe again, Cindy, the receptionist, buzzed her. "Nancy Wiltse called you. Asked if you needed her nursing license."

Still shaking, Kristen stared at her intercom. "Huh?"

"An attorney was at the hospital last night asking Roberta Lott for hers. She doesn't remember his name. Said he was kind of nice-looking."

Kristen struggled to make sense of what Cindy was saying. Nobody claimed her nurses weren't properly licensed. Did Bragg have a PI out? No lawyer, in any of the three firms involved, had any reason to want the nurses' license cards. Tammy prowling through her life, a ridiculous accusation, one more chance to follow orders, and now a snoop on the loose. She'd love to beat the crap out of somebody. Tammy, Pete, Caswell, even Stern. Anyone would do.

* * *

After another day of watching the trial in Bragg's office, Caswell felt like Sam Spade in *The Maltese Falcon*, with Bragg playing Sydney Greenstreet. It wasn't much of a stretch.

Behind his mammoth desk, Bragg sipped decaffeinated tea. "This better be good. I've got to prepare for Galway's testimony tomorrow and my throat's sore."

"What would it be worth to guarantee a win?"

"I *am* winning."

"I mean blow the roof off the courthouse. Get Stern and Kristen disbarred."

Bragg's chubby fingers swirled the tea bag in his cup. He poured in another half spoonful of honey, and finally looked up. "I haven't got anything personal against them. Stern's a bastard, but so am I. As for Kristen, she seems like a pretty good girl."

Caswell's voice rose. "I can prove they lied."

Bragg chuckled, shaking both his chins. "Lawyers are paid to lie."

"The whole defense is a fabrication."

Bragg's eyes narrowed. "What exactly do you want?"

Caswell wasn't sure what to ask for. He didn't want to sell himself short, but didn't want to run Bragg off, either. "A fourth of your fee," Caswell mumbled.

Bragg shook his head.

"You can hit them for millions," Tony added.

Bragg stared at him, then enunciated clearly, "If you have evidence of perjury, you should tell Judge Proctor."

"You think I'm taping you?" Caswell tapped his briefcase on his lap. "I've got the smoking gun right here. I'll take a check, postdated after you win."

Bragg smirked but didn't reply.

"I'm out to get Stern and Kristen. The money's not important. You can pay me later. Whatever's fair."

"Huh?"

Angry and frustrated, Caswell couldn't understand why this fat toad didn't get that he was offering two vacation homes, gift wrapped.

"Want me to strip? Show you I'm not wired?"

"I got work to do." Bragg flipped his hand at Caswell, as if removing lint from his suit.

Caswell got up, thinking what a dumbshit Bragg was. He remembered some Chinese military philosopher had said to strike your enemy at his most vulnerable point. The *Layne* angle wasn't panning out. But he had a more lethal weapon in the arsenal.

* * *

Kristen was exhausted. She had wasted two hours pacing and cursing. Every time she rehearsed the questions that would blow up the joint defense, she pictured Michael's *Sehr gut* note and the way he'd looked at her. Could Tina be right? If so, how could she possibly do this?

But maybe he still planned on beating her to the draw. His charm was probably just an act. Like Pete said, he'd sell his mother to terrorists.

She decided to drive past Bragg's office on her way home. If Stern's silver Mercedes sat outside, her decision would be easy. Casey would torch Galway.

A two-story white colonial on Maple, a mile north of downtown, had been converted into Bragg's office. It was typical of expensive Dallas houses built in the twenties, when Highland Park was prairie. The place next door had been moved, and the lot had been paved for parking. No Mercedes in the lot, only an Escalade she'd seen Bragg drive to a depo, and a Porsche like Tony's. A figure drifted out of the building. One she recognized.

Caswell? Shit!

She slammed her brakes and leapt out.

Caswell spun around, bug-eyed, and ran toward his car, as if fleeing a posse.

She sprinted as fast as she could in pumps, but Caswell reached his car before she could catch him.

"I know the truth," Tony shouted as he jumped in and slammed the door.

Suddenly, she got it. The stink wasn't from the rat she expected.

"*You* wanted Robbie's license? Why?"

Caswell started his Porsche, rolled his window down, and yelled, "*You and Stern are toast!*"

CHAPTER 31

KRISTEN DROVE HOME, her brain fogged over like a nineteenth-century London night. Had Caswell been working with Stern and inadvertently leaked the plan to hose her and the hospital? Or was Caswell freelancing? Did she have an edge on Stern that she could hammer him over the head with? Or should she be loyal and tell him what she saw?

A worse problem penetrated the confusion. Had they both suborned perjury by putting liars on the stand? Would they get disbarred?

Kristen found her sister nursing a beer and watching *Shakespeare in Love*. She hit the stop button and bounced the story off Tina, whose great advice was to sleep on it.

Even with an Ambien and Xanax cocktail, Kristen flopped around for six hours before giving up and dressing at 5:30, well before fall daylight. She had two cups of coffee, then drove to Casey's house, feeling like she was plunging into a dark abyss.

Half an hour later Kristen stood on her porch. She pressed Casey's doorbell, waited a minute, and hit it again.

Wrapped in a bathrobe, Adventist's nursing director answered her front door. "Kristen? What's wrong?"

Kristen strolled in. "Funny thing happened last night. I caught Tony Caswell sneaking out of Bragg's office, claiming he told Bragg 'the truth.'"

Kristen watched Casey's expression morph from uncertainty into a grimace of realization. Half a minute of painful silence passed before Casey turned away, unable to look her lawyer in the eye.

Kristen poked the air with her finger. "I want it all. If I have to find 'the truth' myself, I'll see to it everybody involved is prosecuted. *Including you!*"

Casey's mum response confirmed Kristen's suspicion. She wanted to jerk Casey around, but instead tried reason. "Look, if you tell me what's going on, we might be able to limit the damage. But if Caswell keeps blabbing, it'll be too late."

Casey collapsed onto her couch, rubbing her forehead. "Promise to keep me clean."

Kristen sat next to her. "You know I can't guarantee anything."

"Then why should I—"

"Because you'll fucking go to jail!"

Casey's broad shoulders slumped. "I'm sorry, Kristen. I wish I could. By the time I knew, Tammy had the story locked in."

Kristen got up. "Okay, I gave you a chance. You go down with all the rest."

"I didn't invent the fable."

Kristen pivoted toward the door. "Doesn't matter. You perjured yourself. You lied."

Casey jumped up to follow. "But I had to go along."

"If we tell the truth now, we can both save our licenses."

Casey drew a deep breath, looked away, and spoke to the wall. "Galway's been sleeping with Roberta. On the night Layne was admitted, they went to a hotel across the street." Casey shook her head. "During her shift."

"Christ, why didn't they just grab an empty room?"

"They used to, but Robbie's in love. Wanted to have 'The Talk.' Believed Galway might leave his wife for her. That night was the first time she ever left."

Kristen closed her eyes. "Before Galway's exam?"

"Yes. Robbie told me she needed to leave. I thought it would be all right for an hour or so. She said every patient looked okay. She's a competent nurse. It was my night of the month to work a shift, so I thought we could cover for her. I felt bad for Robbie. She was in too deep."

"But?"

"But 'The Talk' didn't go well. He told Robbie he wouldn't get a divorce. Hurt the kids and all. Then about midnight, his wife starts looking for him. Their daughter missed curfew or something. She was in a panic. Comes to the hospital. I had to tell her he'd just left, so he can't return and see Layne. He hightails it to beat the wife home."

"So he never went back?"

"And neither does Robbie. She was a basket case."

"Criminy."

"I checked the monitor myself a couple times, asked an aide to look in on Layne, but I got swamped with director crap to catch up on. So I called Nancy to come in early. Layne didn't look bad from my station, but I never assessed him." Casey drew a hard breath. "I told Robbie I want her out of my hospital when this trial is over." She rolled her eyes. "I even heard they're seeing each other again."

"And Betty Layne's diary?"

"It may be accurate. Nancy and Robbie rewrote Robbie's notes to make everything look fairly normal. I don't know where the original record is."

"Why's Nancy involved? She didn't have to lie."

"Galway promised her director of nursing at the heart center he's invested in. It'll be a big promotion."

"And Tammy's known all along?"

223

"Yes, and administration didn't exactly discourage the cover-up. Galway is number two in cardiac admissions, so he generates bucks and they don't want him to leave." She shook her head. "Believe me, I didn't know Layne was that sick. I suspect Nancy didn't pay a lot of attention after getting dragged out of bed early and facing a twelve-hour shift on top of finishing Robbie's."

"Does Stern know?"

"I don't know. Tammy doesn't trust him. Supposedly when Stern represented Hospital Risk years ago, they had a falling out. Galway may think he can sweat this out without telling his lawyer, but from what I've heard of Stern, anything's possible." Tears gathered in her eyes. "Kristen, you have to protect me."

"You're going to Canterbury with this Nurse's Tale."

Casey shook her head. "I'll deny everything."

Kristen pulled her pocket recorder from her jacket, and held it up to Casey's nose.

"Get dressed. You're coming with me, so you won't get lost."

Kristen grabbed her cell from her purse and left Tammy Robberson a message to meet her at the office ASAP.

Casey dressed and rode with Kristen downtown, arriving at Wright McGee before eight. Kristen parked the nursing director in the waiting area with orders not to move, delivered like a pissed-off marine drill sergeant.

Kristen assumed Tammy got her message and had reluctantly obeyed. As Kristen walked toward her office, she debated how to throw water on the Wicked Witch of the West.

The instant Kristen opened her door, Tammy bellowed, "Whatdya mean, *telling* me to meet you here early?"

"We *are* going to settle this case."

The adjuster wrinkled her nose. "Stern's client won't—"

"I don't care what he won't do. We're going to meet Bragg's latest demand. The whole eight mil and pray he'll still take it." Kristen thrust out her hand. "Give me a check."

"You're fucking crazy."

Kristen couldn't resist a smile. "Maybe, but I also know the story. The *whole* story."

"Whatever you heard was bullshit." Tammy's lips curled. "Just because Casey is Jen's buddy doesn't make her an angel. She invented the whole scam. You think Adventist wants to be known for killing an All Pro?"

"And I suppose you wanted to come clean?"

"Well we're better off going balls out now. The case is almost ready for the jury, and you still got time to hose Stern."

Kristen flipped open her briefcase and retrieved an extra subpoena she'd gotten in case of an emergency. She scribbled *Tammy Robberson* on it and thrust it at her.

Tammy stepped back. "You can't call me. I'm not listed as a witness."

"I just endorsed you." Kristen flipped open Tammy's cashmere jacket and crammed the subpoena into the inside pocket. "Be there in an hour."

"Go fuck yourself!" Tammy whipped the subpoena back out and tore it into shreds, sending paper floating to the gray carpet.

For an instant Kristen fantasized about ripping out Tammy's bleached hair and stuffing it in her mouth, but decided she had better head for the courthouse instead. "If I had time, I'd make you eat every single scrap off the floor."

Tammy ran out like a bull at Pamplona was chasing her.

Kristen grabbed her briefcase as her pal Jen ran in and slammed the door. "Have you lost it?"

Kristen elbowed Jen aside. "Out of the way."

Jen sidestepped to block her. "Casey will lose everything. *You'll* lose everything."

"Jen, I recall an oath—"

"Honey, every goddamn hospital is gettin' its tits squeezed by insurance and the feds. They can't afford an RN leaning over every patient or calling a cardiologist every time a patient barfs. I spent twelve years in the trenches. It's a thankless, shitty job, where people do the best they can."

"They lied."

"All bastards lie. If Betty Layne gets rich, every cocksucker will think the courthouse is a casino." She clamped Kristen's wrist. "Her little diary exaggerated his condition, probably at Bragg's suggestion. It perfectly describes a developing tamponade. Real life's not so perfect, so get your pretty ass over there and fry Galway."

Kristen locked her hands on her hips. "This isn't a *pissant* rule. It's a *felony*."

"I'm telling Pete."

The room spun as Kristen grabbed a yellow pad from her desk and scribbled. "Then take my resignation with you. You and Pete finish the trial."

Jen froze, before blurting, "I'm telling Casey to leave."

Kristen grabbed Jen's wrist and squeezed hard. Very hard. "You do and I'll get your license too, and you can go back to giving enemas at your *shitty* job."

* * *

Two steps after Kristen and Casey cleared courthouse security, the nurse planted herself on the scuffed floor. "I'm not going up there."

Kristen clutched Casey's shoulder purse strap and jerked her toward the elevators.

The bigger woman pulled back, dragging Kristen with her. "I'll be fired."

"There's a nursing shortage."

The leather strap stretched as far as it would go. "You're supposed to be our lawyer."

"My first duty is to justice."

"That's Girl Scout crap. Go up there and nail Stern."

Keeping one hand locked on the strap, Kristen clamped Casey's arm. "Tammy told me you're the one changing records."

Casey paused. "That lying whore. She wanted you on the case, 'cause you're good-looking enough to hook Stern, and rookie enough to follow orders."

Kristen dug her nails into Casey's wrist, making sure it hurt. "You guys picked the wrong girl."

Casey's face reddened as she tried to twist away. "Let go!"

Litigants, lawyers, and jurors gathered to watch the spectacle. Most stared open mouthed. One man whistled. Another hollered for more.

Casey slammed a hand into Kristen's shoulder, rocking her back, but Kristen tightened her grip on the nurse's wrist, spun her, clamped her throat, and wedged Casey's arm up her back until she shrieked, utterly helpless.

"If I have to drag you up there with a broken arm, I will."

Gasping, Casey bent backward, trying to relieve the pain.

The wide-eyed crowd was transfixed, but no one made an effort to intervene.

Kristen levered Casey's arm harder. A little more and her shoulder would dislocate. "Do *not* jack with me."

Casey managed to choke out, "Okay."

Kristen let go of the nurse's neck and eased her arm down, sending a message that Casey's immediate health remained in Kristen's hands. Kristen steered her to an elevator.

Upstairs, Kristen planted her witness at the defendants' table. Satisfying herself that Casey was too scared to flee, Kristen marched toward the judge's chambers, where the lawyers were to meet for the jury instruction conference.

She considered pulling Stern into the hall and telling him

everything. Maybe she owed that to her fellow musketeer, but she told herself he was like all of them. A liar. This was Jersey all over again.

As she stepped in, Proctor glared at Kristen. "It's about time."

"I'm sorry, Judge, but we can close a day early. The truth doesn't take as long." She turned to Stern. "I'm sure you don't want *your* liar to testify again."

She watched carefully for his reaction. Had all the unity talk been bullshit? Had she learned another lesson in trust? As in, *never trust anyone*?

Stern's forehead wrinkled. "Huh?"

* * *

Kristen walked into the courtroom and spotted Pete, on the front gallery row, frantically beckoning her over. She detoured, leaned over the rail, and whispered to him, "Next time, sleep with Stern yourself."

She left him speechless and stepped to the lectern, feeling like she was on an airplane in a death spiral. No choice now but to ride the disaster all the way down.

"Nurse Denman, tell the jury what happened the night Mr. Layne was admitted. I mean, what *really* happened." Kristen picked up Defendant's Exhibit 1, the medical records, and slammed the pile of paper back down, startling everyone in the courtroom. "Not this fairy tale."

The jurors leaned forward.

Bragg sat perfectly still, arms resting on the plaintiffs' counsel table, his chubby fingers interlocked.

Stern and Galway slumped, looking like they hoped Scotty would beam them up.

Sucking her lips, Casey's gaze met Betty Layne's. "First, Mrs. Layne's notes may be accurate."

Betty's eyes swelled with tears. Bragg handed her his maroon pocket square.

"Our records that night were falsified. Dr. Galway was at the hospital, but never saw Mr. Layne."

There was a collective gasp. The big juror in the redneck shirt and jeans clenched his fists against the knees of his Levi's. The young Latina's face knotted in anger.

"Did Nurse Roberta Lott watch Mr. Layne closely? Did she tell us the truth when she testified?"

"No. She left the hospital with Dr. Galway around eleven. They went to a hotel across the street."

"She lied in this courtroom?"

Casey's vision seemed focused on the far wall of the courtroom. "Yes."

The gasp, sounding like a collective *Oh my God*, was loud. Louder than if Galway had dropped his pants and mooned everyone.

"Did Roberta Lott and Nancy Wiltse switch the records?"

"Yes. They wrote an entire new page of notes to cover themselves."

Kristen gritted her teeth, turned, and glared at her bosses in the gallery. "Your Honor, Adventist rests," she said, slowly enunciating each syllable.

Judge Proctor glared with fury at Stern. "Anything *else*, Mr. Stern?"

Stern mumbled, "No, your honor."

An hour later, Bragg leaned over the lectern, winding down his long closing. "Ladies and Gentlemen, we've spent two weeks hearing lies. While Brook Layne was in desperate need of a doctor—a cardiologist—Dr. Galway and his nurse were in a hotel trying out the mattress."

Bragg pointed toward the defendants' table. "They lied to cheat the Layne family. The proper punishment for such behavior is for y'all to bring back your verdict in the amount of fifty million dollars." Bragg strutted back to the plaintiffs' table like John Wayne returning to the saloon after a gunfight.

Kristen sat frozen, clueless how to close the case for the hospital. Apologize? Beg? Surrender? How do you sweep up, after the whole parade stops to shit in the street? She had scribbled a few of Bragg's phrases on her legal pad, but organizing any thoughts seemed hopeless. Maybe Stern hadn't known, but he was as good an actor as John Wilkes Booth.

Sitting in the packed, silent gallery, Jen and Pete looked like *they* were developing cardiac tamponades. She wanted to kick the shit out of the two shysters who got her in this mess, but panic redirected her attention to the fear of having to stand and say something coherent. All she could think of was suggesting the jury give a little less than what Bragg wanted—not a good pitch under the circumstances.

Two reporters next to Pete took notes. A platoon of ex–football players occupied two rows, shoulder to shoulder, glowering. Kristen spotted Tina, wearing sunglasses, smiling encouragement. Reckless Tina. Had she been on the *Lusitania* after the torpedo hit, she would have grabbed a beer before heading for the lifeboats.

As Bragg plopped down, Stern slid a note toward her. *Waive your close. I'll eat this.*

Kristen pushed against the table to stand, but Stern whispered, "*Please*, Kristen."

She remembered the warnings about Stern. Now was the time to salvage the wreckage by creaming Galway. If she waived and Stern torched the hospital, the hospital could go bankrupt. She would be the joke of the Dallas bar for years, might never find another job. But one didn't have to live in a slick townhouse. Life would go on, even if she waited tables. Someday, maybe she'd find a man who liked to read Dickens and play basketball.

Judge Proctor cleared his throat.

She glanced at Stern. How would he handle closing this disaster? Instead of a suggestion, he looked at her with a strange expression, almost like how he looked at his daughter.

He whispered, "Waive, please."

Somehow Kristen managed to stand. "Adventist waives close."

Proctor asked her to repeat what she'd said.

Bile filled her guts. She prayed she could get through the next half hour without soiling herself or throwing up. "We waive."

"Mr. Stern?" Proctor asked, glaring like he preferred not hearing a peep from Stern.

Stern rose and began walking, his posture that of an officer reviewing troops as he walked along the jury rail to the lectern.

The jury, as one, had their arms folded. Their anger at listening to lies for nearly two weeks was riveted on him.

A minute of wretched silence passed before Stern spoke. "That was an excellent argument by my longtime adversary. But, folks, Mr. Bragg is only partly right. Let's make sure we punish only the guilty."

Stern paused.

Kristen feared she was going to toss her breakfast on the defendants' table. She glanced back at Pete and Tammy. It looked like they were plotting her murder. Maybe they were. Hopefully the security screeners had spotted their weapons and she would have time to run when the trial finally ended. She could e-mail her resignation.

Stern continued, "Dr. Galway's conduct was despicable. The yarn he told to cover it up was worse. He even lied to his insurance company, paying me to defend him.

"He controlled the two nurses. If these women had blown the whistle, they might have gotten fired. My guess is Nurse Wiltse got pressured or bribed into this mess. Nurse Lott probably began the affair because of Galway's manipulation. *'My wife doesn't understand me.'* I've seen it happen. So have you. When powerful men exert their will over others, whose fault is it?"

Stern paused and looked at Casey.

"Nurses have the toughest job at a hospital and don't get to join country clubs, buy second homes, or take vacations in Rome. Dr.

Galway knew his patient needed to be seen. He could have called for the lab results, ordered more tests, but instead took Roberta Lott away from her duties."

Stern sighed.

"I'm to blame, too, for not asking enough questions, for not finding the truth."

Another long, painful pause. Kristen didn't believe this was really happening. Surely she'd wake up soon.

"But please, exonerate the nurses and their hospital. Their courageous lawyer told you the truth, as soon as she discovered it. She embodies the finest principles of the bar and our judicial system." He offered a thin smile.

"Principles are too often the subject of cynical abuse. If we had more lawyers like her, there'd be less need for folks like you to take time from your jobs and families for jury service."

What the hell? Kristen thought she'd stumbled into a Kafka story.

Slowly, Stern let his gaze meet each juror's eyes. "Please find for Adventist Hospital."

CHAPTER 32

AS THE JURY FILED OUT, Kristen turned to Stern and garbled a weak, "Thanks." Then she got up and spent the next hour in a restroom worshipping the porcelain goddess.

Tina rubbed her back. "It'll be okay, baby. We can go back to Philly."

Kristen's cell phone rang, and she pushed herself away from the toilet, glanced at the screen, and answered.

It was Shorty. *"We have a verdict."*

Since her career could be measured in minutes at this point, she wondered if she should tell Tina to find a realtor who sold townhouses.

Kristen checked herself in the mirror, decided looking like a med school cadaver didn't matter, and hurried to the courtroom. Stern arrived a minute later, with Galway in tow. She stole a glance, but Stern seemed focused into deep space. Galway looked ready to implode into his own callow skin.

Shorty led the jury into the courtroom, his arthritic legs slowing the procession to a creep. Kristen's foreboding increased with every rickety step.

Judge Proctor riveted his eyes on the only juror wearing a tie, who held the verdict form in his hand. "Mr. Sneed, are you the foreman?"

"Yes, sir."

"Have you reached a verdict?"

"Yes, sir."

"Please hand it to the clerk."

The clerk, who for two weeks had been annoyed at all the inconveniences of the trial, whisked the verdict from the foreman. Her hands shook as she read. "We, the jury, empanelled on our oath, on question one find in favor of the plaintiff and against the defendant, Gary Galway, MD."

A murmur rushed through the nearly full courtroom, followed by silence. Bragg leaned toward Betty Layne and whispered, then squeezed her shoulder.

Kristen held her breath.

The clerk continued, "Question number two. We find in favor of the defendant, Adventist Hospital."

The courtroom echoed with noise as if all had blurted, *Holy shit.*

Kristen barely heard the next part.

"Question three. We fix damages at eighty million dollars."

* * *

Stern had never seen Bob Russell's size-eighteen neck so inflamed, even when Stern sank a thirty-footer to beat the claims manager.

Russell pounded Stern's desk. "You cost us millions and probably got this doc charged with perjury."

Stern squeezed the arms of his chair with his little remaining energy. "Bob, Proctor will cut the verdict down by—"

The claims manager beat the leather inlay again, cutting Stern off. "Did you fall in love?"

"I'll say it again. There's nothing between us." Stern fought for control. "Standard's not likely to get stuck for much more than the policy limit. We believed the insured." Stern looked at Galway, slumped in a chair, holding his head in his hands. "Even when the insured lied to his carrier and his lawyer."

"Stern, this is a fucking *disaster*."

"Dr. Galway never told me he'd fabricated an exam."

"But Galway says you talked him out of settling!"

Stern bit off each word. "It would've helped if we'd known why he wanted to settle."

"Everyone thinks you've gotta be humping the hospital's darlin' lawyer. Why else would you save their bacon? We could've gotten help paying this, and wouldn't look like the town saps, if they had gone down, too." Russell flung his beefy hands toward the ceiling. "You had to play Sir Fucking Galahad."

"You think *I* enjoy losing?"

"You'll be disbarred for suborning perjury."

Stern massaged his temples. "I didn't know he was lying. I assume you didn't either."

A flash of panic crossed Russell's face. "Of course not."

Stern smirked in disbelief.

As if to confirm his guilt, Russell wheeled around and kicked the stuffed bear, then walked to the window and stared toward the once-trendy hundred-year-old brick warehouses in the West End. "I'm asking the board to terminate your representation of Standard. You'll make a great divorce lawyer. Work out your fees on the couch." He stomped out, heaving the door shut, rattling Stern's certificates.

"That's some gratitude for all those years buyin' him whiskey."

Galway finally dropped his hands from his ashen face. He seemed to struggle for a response.

Stern spared him. "I can't handle your perjury charge. It would be a conflict." He shrugged. "Besides, I may be indicted with you."

Galway dropped his head to his knees. A gurgling sound rose from his throat, as if he were choking on a furball. "You were supposed to protect me."

"And I asked you more than once if the records were accurate."

"I wanted out."

"Damn it, Gary, you should've told me the truth."

"What now?"

"You'll need a new lawyer to handle a bad-faith claim against Standard and negotiate over your personal assets." Stern flashed a smile. "You can sue me for legal malpractice."

Galway took the hint, stood, and shuffled out.

Relieved to see the lying bastard leave, Stern castigated himself. He had to admit this whole debacle started from chasing a babe who didn't want him. A smart one, beautiful, but totally messed up in the head. Then he'd screwed up by caring. And the weird part was, he *really* cared.

He trudged to his mini-fridge, grabbed a beer, popped open the can, and gulped. The cold brew didn't wash the sour taste of fear from his mouth. If Diana left him, and his clients bailed, he'd be playing golf on municipal courses. Now he knew why some guys blew their brains out. Maybe he ought to give Janet his gun.

A soft knock echoed from the door.

Before he could respond, Janet entered and eased the door shut. She sucked her lower lip in and stepped toward him.

Stern pointed toward the fridge. Instead she slipped behind him and began massaging his shoulders.

* * *

Kristen lay sprawled on the love seat in her office, wiped out, unsure whether to celebrate or cry.

Pete paced in front of her, his speech droning on and on. "Despite the fabulous outcome, indictments of the nurses will be bad for the firm's image."

Kristen wanted to say, *No shit, Sherlock. I told everybody something stunk. Including you.*

Instead, she continued to listen.

"Of course, I'm proud of you. You did the right thing. Such shocking lies."

Kristen hadn't heard such utter bullshit since the last time she went to happy hour alone and put up with fifty lame pick-up lines. But she was too douched to call him on it.

Jen asked, "Think Stern got scared of a perjury conspiracy charge? Decided to cut his losses?"

Pete ignored Jen's question. "I've got an idea. Go to the mountains. The slopes aren't open, but my place in Vail is lovely in the fall. Gets you away from the media, the DA, and the bar association. You can't answer their questions if you're not here."

"Thanks, but—"

"I'll get the keys and a map." Pete stepped out.

Jen followed.

A minute later, Jen tiptoed back in, carrying Pete's keys. "Congratulations."

Kristen rolled her head toward her ex-friend, allowing her expression to carry the disdain she felt.

Jen's lips moved as if she were considering several opening lines before trying out, "I'm so sorry about what I said."

Kristen just wished Jen would get the hell out. She couldn't bring herself to respond.

After a minute of painful silence, Jen said, "I forgot to tell you who consulted the old man about a divorce."

Kristen closed her eyes, in no mood for gossip.

Jen clucked her tongue. "Stern's wife. I thought it was her. Checked Pete's calendar. *Diana Stern.*"

"Divorce? How do you know?"

"Tear-streaked makeup. Pete's bar directory was opened to the section on divorce lawyers. Wasn't here to discuss SMU alumni."

Jen lingered a moment, smiled self-consciously, then departed.

Kristen got up and trudged around the corner, where Tina waited in Kristen's paralegal's office. "Sorry to be so long. Everybody had to help on the post mortem."

Tina stood and hugged her older sister. "And?"

Kristen drew warmth from Tina's arms. "They can't decide whether I'm Benedict Arnold or Nathan Hale, so they've sent me into exile."

Grinning, Tina stepped back. "I love being on the lam."

They walked down the main hallway, and Kristen pushed open the double doors of Wright McGee. "Let's get dinner and book a morning flight."

Tina tapped the elevator button. "Kristen, you shouldn't take *me*."

"Huh?"

"There's a dreamy-looking man who's nuts about you."

"He's married." She said *married* like she would say *leprosy*.

"Barely. I overheard."

"He's still married."

"Till the wheels of justice grind. Why not take him and have a good time? Just once."

The elevator arrived. Kristen followed Tina in. "Because I wouldn't have a good time."

"How do you know?"

"I don't want to feel responsible for busting up his home and hurting his kid."

"Sounds like the *piñata* already burst." Tina looked into Kristen's eyes. "You don't have to get mixed up in his life. Besides, it's time you quit feeling so damn *responsible*."

Kristen's gaze dropped to her feet. Tina sounded like her shrink.

They walked to the garage in silence, until Kristen asked, "What sounds good?"

"Didn't you see the way he looked at you before his closing? Like that English officer in *Last of the Mohicans*, right before the Indians torched him."

Kristen unlocked the car. "You watch too many old movies."

"Really, Krissy, you don't have to get *involved*. Just a weekend." Tina's eyebrows rose suggestively. "An older guy will know what he's doing."

Kristen rolled her eyes as she got in the car. "You're oversexed."

"If a guy had done that for me, I'd feel—"

Kristen slammed her door. "I don't want to be obligated to any man."

* * *

Stern found Sarah in the game room, her tan arms bare in her sleeveless uniform shirt. He tugged the sun-bleached hair sticking through her ball visor and kissed her cheek before she twisted free.

"Are you okay, Dad?"

Her glow seemed to contain captured sunshine. Sadness swept over him. He imagined her graduating, leaving home, getting married, and felt terribly lonely. Soon she'd be gone, have her own family, and he'd be praying for a call.

Stern wiped his eye. "Had a bad day. How was school?"

"Boring. I got to change. Mom's taking me to get invitations for my Halloween party."

He started to ask for details, but she left.

Diana traipsed in. "You're home early. Did they close the bars for an election I missed?"

"Have you let all the hoods out?" Stern almost regretted his catty remark as he noticed her slacks hung off her hips. Was she dieting for Caswell? In that moment, Stern decided to beat the little shithead to death with his bare hands.

"You may be interested to know, we're going to start teleconferencing interviews. I'll only be in Austin one day a week."

"Fabulous." Stern slung his suit jacket over his shoulder and headed upstairs.

Diana followed him. "Seeing some bimbo in New York this weekend?"

Stern slowed, prepared to launch into her about Caswell, but stopped himself. Knowledge was power. No use spilling what he knew now.

Diana plowed on, "You might as well. Sarah and I will be busy. She's having a slumber party Friday, and I canceled on Junior League Saturday, so we could see *Phantom*."

Stern stopped. "Getting ready for the custody fight?"

Diana smirked. "No, praying for lightning on the golf course."

"That's a bit vicious, even for you."

Her voice simmered with pent-up anger. "The truth is, I quit worrying whether you'd make it home years ago."

Stern closed his eyes. There had been times he might have eaten his steering wheel or been shot by a jealous husband. He shuddered. He had lived too recklessly. Time to grow up. Imagining Caswell's claw hand on Diana suddenly made him want her. Show her what a real man could do. For her age, she certainly looked good.

"Honey, let's get counseling. For Sarah's sake. Or we could go to Paris. Leave Sarah with her cousins."

She glared. "Your offer is too late. Years too late."

Somewhat disappointed, but feeling less guilty for having tried, Stern asked, "Aren't you curious how the trial turned out?"

"Saw the news." Diana grinned. "Nice work, Prince."

Stern's face flamed. He realized why she was so hostile. She was getting her ducks in a row for a divorce and was soothing her conscience. It's easier to dump a spouse and cause a kid pain if you're convinced the guy's scum.

He actually didn't blame her.

* * *

At La Calle Doce, the beer was cold and the seafood enchiladas were hot. Tina finally quit playing matchmaker during dinner, and they avoided talking about the trial. Kristen found herself enjoying Tina's raunchy dancing stories.

Not as experienced with alcohol as her little sister, Kristen let Tina drive home, but sobered up enough to buy plane tickets online. Upstairs in her bathroom, she peeled off her sticky trial clothes and filled the tub. Her body felt like she'd played every minute of a triple overtime game. A hot bath sounded heavenly.

She switched on the jets and inched in, propping her heels on the maroon tile at the end of her tub. Time floated by as rosemary-scented bubbles quivered against her breath, and water pounded her neck. Gripping the faucet lever with her toes, she shoved it up and left, cascading more hot water into the tub.

Against her closed lids, she could see Stern asking her to waive closing.

Was she imagining it, or was there a glint of moisture in his eyes? She remembered the odd expression on his face Sunday night after she kissed him. Maybe she'd totally misjudged him. Did he really care about her? Or was he simply covering himself against a criminal charge?

Her fingers ventured down her slick, soapy body, stopped at her knee, and started back up again. She pictured his big hands, with the beautiful veins, and imagined them on her.

Tina was right. It had been too long.

Just as her fantasy got rolling—or maybe she had dozed off—a tap on the bathroom door jarred her back to reality. "Krissy, are you okay?"

"Yes. I'm getting out." Kristen stepped out of the tub, toweled dry, and wrapped herself in a robe.

"Sorry, but you'd been in there an hour." Tina looked at her with obvious suspicion.

Embarrassed, Kristen said, "It's a beautiful night. Want to sit out on the balcony?"

Kristen padded through the bedroom, pulled out the bracing rod, and slid open the glass door. Stepping out, they sat looking at the narrow greenbelt and creek behind Kristen's townhouse.

"Why don't you call Michael in the morning?"

Kristen picked at her robe. "NMNS. Not Mary, Not Shit." She looked up at her sister. "I don't know."

"Come on! Do I need to kick *your* ass?"

* * *

Friday, September 29

Kristen counted the giant red tubes in the Lieberman art pile outside Stern's building. Anything to buy time. Remembering her trips with her father, she realized why in Europe, they build statues of heroes and poets, but they don't in Dallas. Here, *heroes* don't write symphonies or win wars; they play football or drill oil wells. And hope to avoid indictment.

Tina nudged her out of her trance. "Game time."

"I don't know about this."

"Want me to take it up?"

"No."

Tina shoved Kristen's shoulder. "Go, girl."

Kristen hoped a lunch replacement sat at reception and she wouldn't be recognized, but popped on her Oakleys anyway. Wearing jeans, she hoped to pass for some firm's gopher.

"I'll be humiliated."

Tina smiled. "Then we dance together. The Kool Kerry Sisters."

Kristen rolled her eyes, got out of her car, stepped into the early fall warmth, and walked to the marble lobby of NationsBank. Icy sweat trickled down from her pits. She caught a crowded elevator resounding with Muzak.

Snaking an arm through the other passengers, she hit the button for seventy-three. She pulled the sheet of pink stationery from her envelope and reread her note, written to avoid calling and getting rejected personally.

> *Michael, I'm sorry. I know you're having a hard time. Can I make it up to you with a weekend in the mountains? I've got tickets to Denver on American at 4 p.m.*

The elevator stopped and a man carrying take-out Chinese got off. She mulled over the situation. The tone was too damn servile. No need to play the supplicant or apologize. After all, she'd warned Stern and tried her best to get him to settle. Tina was right—quit feeling responsible for everything.

The elevator halted again. No telling how many eyeballs her message would pass under before it reached Stern, assuming he got it in time. She wadded the pretty paper, jammed it into her pocket, and contemplated chickening out. She could picture him laughing, telling his partners she'd finally succumbed. He'd do her a favor and service the lonely girl, then report all the details later.

The elevator stopped at seventy-three. She started to push the button for the ground floor, but knew Tina would discern her relief and put her to shame. And she'd berate herself the rest of her life for cowardice.

She stepped off and walked toward a young woman in the reception cubicle; fortunately, Kristen hadn't seen her before. The receptionist lifted her head an inch, hardly acknowledging Kristen, while speaking into her headset.

"I need some paper, please," Kristen said.

The receptionist transferred a call, clawed through a drawer, tore off a sheet from a yellow pad, and thrust it at Kristen.

She wrote as quickly as she could think in German. Even Janet wouldn't know what she'd said.

*Michael, kommst du mit mir mile hoch Stadt. Ich habe ein gemut-
lich Haus fur uns in der Berg. Nur uns. Gehst du der Flughafen.
Zeit ab vier. Luft Amerika. Joan d' Arc.*

"Please take this to Mr. Stern now."

"He's in a conference."

Kristen flipped up her sunglasses, locked her hands on her hips, and slapped the girl with her power stare, usually reserved for whoring expert witnesses. "Then hold it between your knees until he gets out."

The young woman flinched. "I will make sure he sees it."

Out of the corner of her vision, Kristen saw Tony Caswell strolling down the main hall, wearing a lavender shirt.

Popping the shades back, she hurried to the elevator.

CHAPTER 33

EVERYBODY STERN PASSED in the Jackson, Stern and Randolph corridors had some pressing reason not to look up and speak. *Bastards.*

Wearing yesterday's wrinkled white dress shirt with khakis, he strolled into his office and slung his sport coat on the sofa. He considered calling Kristen, but decided against it. He'd made her career. The sooner he forgot her, the better. He needed to concentrate on the coming custody fight, not a silly crush.

Janet walked in, carrying a stack of new pleadings and letters. "How you doing?"

"Couldn't sleep, so I teed off at dawn. We still in business?"

She eased the pile of papers on his writing table, careful not to let any slide off. "So far."

"Thanks for keeping the wolves at bay."

"There's also a note I can't read, with a flight itinerary."

"Probably Bragg's idea of a joke."

"An assistant DA wants to see you and, he says, 'your lawyer.'"

Stern squinted and pushed the skin on his forehead. "Right, I'll jump on that."

Janet smiled. "Jackson called a partners' meeting for next Thursday."

"Any more good news?"

"Galway's new lawyer wants to see you before you talk to the DA." Janet rearranged layers of paper. "Here's that bizarre note."

Stern took the envelope and tossed it on his desk. Janet left as he dropped into his chair. He touched the privacy button on his phone to block incoming calls and began shifting through the blizzard. After an hour, he lost interest. It would all wait. He'd made an appearance. Nobody could call him a pussy for hiding at home.

Before he could leave, his door flew open without a knock, revealing Caswell, smirking. "Was that skinny wench worth losing your clients?"

It took Stern a second to realize this was his chance to knock the kid's teeth out. He rose and hustled toward Caswell. "Come on in and close the door, *pard*, so we can talk."

Caswell's eyes bugged before he scurried out into the hall.

Stern followed the little snot, but Janet darted out of her office and blocked his way. "It's not worth it, Michael."

He started to go around her, but she planted her hands on his chest. "That guy from CNA is on the phone again. Said it's urgent he see you."

Stern decided maiming Caswell wouldn't look good in family court during the custody fight. "Guess he hasn't heard. Schedule him for next week. I'm outta here."

Janet squeezed his hand. "Call me if you need anything this weekend."

"Will do." As Janet returned to her station, he went back to his office and pulled on his jacket. The pretty handwriting on the mystery envelope drew his attention. He picked it up and peeked in, thinking it odd to use legal pad paper with the envelope. As he read it, mentally translating, he was flabbergasted. He stared at it, imagining the emotion she'd wrestled with, the courage it took for her to initiate this.

Janet returned. "Michael, now this CNA guy wants to know if you could meet him this weekend. He's a royal pain in the ass." She frowned. "Are you okay?"

He cleared his throat. "This weekend?"

"That's what he said."

He checked his watch and calculated the time. He might make it.

But should he? Was he biting off trouble he didn't need? Would he be handing Diana free ammo?

He decided he'd start for the airport and make up his mind on the way.

"Tell him I'll be out of town."

* * *

Kristen and Tina waited for a cab to the garage where Pete stored his Explorer. The weather in Denver was brisk, but not cold, a wonderful change from Dallas.

Kristen's cell phone rang. She dropped her gear, pawed through her purse, and answered the call. "Yes?"

"Sorry I missed your flight," Stern said. "I found another. I can be there in two hours."

Kristen's heart fluttered. Just when she'd gotten comfortable with rejection, with sitting on the bench, the coach had sent her in with the game tied.

Tina's eyeballs glowed. "Michael?" she whispered.

Kristen nodded. "That's great. Where should I meet you?"

"I'll call when I land. Wait there."

Kristen managed a meek, "Okay. See you then."

Tina pumped her fist. "Loan me a credit card. I'm off to Aspen to find a ski bum. And have a *very* good time."

Kristen sucked a long breath. Too late to chicken out now.

* * *

Marrs slowed the Cherokee as he neared the dump the munificent Jimmy rented to him. He spotted a long pimpmobile down the street from his house. A black guy stared out the windshield for a minute before driving off.

Marrs released his death grip on the wheel. For an instant, he'd imagined it was Freddie, but Zelner couldn't tell Freddie where he lived. It was against the rules. And the black man didn't look big enough to be Freddie Lee Lance . . . did he?

Leonard decided the smart move was to abandon this pigsty and relocate his base of operations to Jimmy's place. He pulled up, dashed inside, grabbed the few things he needed, and headed north.

Thirty minutes later, he surveyed Jim's ticket to respectability with disgust. Fake logs huddled in the fireplace. The beige carpet melted into the off-white walls, decorated with boring landscapes in tacky glittering frames. The furniture was brown vinyl, and the kitchen reeked of Comet. Nobody could guess their mother was a whore.

Diana's hubby was supposedly out of town. Jim gone for the week.

He held the key to Stern's house and the alarm code, delivered by mail. His "partner" seemed to have held up his end of the deal. So far.

But who was this new pal? How did the wise-ass know he wanted Diana? And was the guy's plan for collecting their dough by wire to some foreign bank going to work? Why should he trust someone he'd never seen?

Maybe Zelner and a platoon of cops would pounce the instant he strolled into the Sterns' house.

Marrs remembered the prison law books. Entrapment. Pure and simple. But if the monster at the rental house really was Freddie, Zelner had probably also given him Jim's address.

Marrs decided to take truck stop gal, Lottie, up on her offer.

* * *

Marrs pulled the musty sheet up to his chin, cursing himself over letting the nasty harlot crawl all over him. Whenever he failed in bed, he wanted to use a knife on his wrist and watch his miserable life flow away.

Lottie sat up, the sheet falling, exposing massive, drooping tits. She stroked his hair. "It's okay, babe."

He turned his head, but she continued to pet him like a dog.

She scooted off the wet spot where he'd shot his wad. "Hey, it's only Friday night."

He guessed his wasn't the only stain on the sheet. "I got plans Saturday."

Lottie fumbled under the sheet and began stroking his thigh. "You're so cute."

He fought back his revulsion. Amazing he had even gotten hard. He hated women, their teasing and lying. How they pretend not to want sex, then demand a guy satisfy them.

She crossed her arms against nips the size of saucers and squinted. "Been meanin' to ask, how come you're wantin' me to sign your log book for tomorrow? You never come in on the weekend."

"Just want to keep my parole officer happy."

She crammed gum into her mouth. "Ain't been no goody-goody myself. Juvenile detention for shopliftin'. Got in a little trouble when I was twenty. Grand larceny pleaded down. I still get mighty tempted, seein' all that loot Jack rakes in. Bastard cheats on his taxes and pays me squat."

Marrs nodded.

She spoke between smacks of Bubble Yum. "Bet Jimmy was a sweet little boy who said 'scuse me when he farted."

He felt despair. "Mom's next bastard beat the snot out of me every other day," he said. "Jimmy was long gone, to a nice house and a new stepmother."

"What were you in for?"

"Trying to get rich."

"Didn't hurt nobody, didja?"

He met her examining eyes. "No."

Continuing to work her jaw, she tucked one side of stringy hair behind her ear. "I'd like to grab enough to quit slingin' hash browns. One little caper, where nobody gets hurt, and whoever loses money won't miss it."

* * *

In Minturn Country Club outside Vail, a glass of Chateau Margaux drained some of Kristen's tension from riding two hours with a man who didn't exactly seem excited to be with her. She wondered whether this had been a huge mistake. He'd been so quiet, distracted. Where was the confident, ballsy hustler? Why hadn't he kissed her like lovers in the movies do when she picked him up?

"Tired?" she asked.

"Sorry, didn't sleep last night."

"Trouble with Standard?"

"Yep, and the firm."

"I should've called you before I went to Proctor." She berated herself a second after she spoke. Guilt would be an adversary all weekend, and it didn't need any help from her.

He smiled. It was impossible to tell whether he agreed with her, or thought it didn't really matter. She reminded herself to quit worrying.

"There's other bloodsuckers."

"Caswell figured it out first," she said. "He was at Bragg's the night before we closed."

His face turned red. "He's probably sleeping with that pig Tammy tonight, hustling business."

Kristen shook her head. "She's not going to have any cases to pass out when I get through with her."

"I don't know. Some people love to hire crooks."

She stared at her wine glass, swirling the red magic around. After a minute of awkward silence, she gulped the rest. Another glass with the half Xanax she'd taken and she'd be lit, which might be a good plan.

* * *

Kristen retrieved Pete's key, unlocked the door, and flipped on a light. Woven rugs decorated lovely polished wood floors. Family portraits lined knotty pine walls. The high ceiling was anchored by bare wooden beams. A wide stairway circled up to a balcony in front of the bedrooms. "Nice."

Stern carried their things in and locked the door behind them. "Always knew McGee overbilled. How 'bout a fire?"

"And a nightcap."

Michael began building a fire from wood stacked by the fireplace. Among several bottles in the antique icebox, Kristen found brandy. She poured some in snifters, then sipped liquid fire, hoping it would relax her. After all, this should be fun and it had been a long time.

Kristen toted the glasses to the fireplace. Flames cracked to life. "You're a pretty good Boy Scout."

"Nah. They kicked me out for organizing a poker game on a campout."

Kristen handed Stern his glass. He sipped with an oddly somber expression on his face. She worried that he looked like he was mentally heading for court. No evidence of lust.

Rip my clothes off. Please.

Since he wasn't attacking her, she rummaged through a Wal-Mart sack and withdrew a bottle of Vaseline Intensive Care. "I owe you. Take off your shirt."

He smiled, but it seemed empty. "If you insist." He unbuttoned, revealing firm pecs, and stretched out on the rug, facedown.

Kristen pulled off her boots and dropped next to him. She kneaded his neck, admiring his razored hairline. His back was gorgeous, muscular, and hairless. She bent to work his shoulders, then decided it would be easier to sit on his butt, and hopped aboard. She slid her hands up and down his spine, admiring his broad shoulders, then massaged the hard tissue on each side of his spinal column.

Burning pine sap popped and hissed in the fireplace.

Her hands forced low moans of pleasure from him. After awhile her arms grew tired. She danced her fingertips over his bare back, slipped off him, and nestled closer to the fire.

He sat up. Blue eyes locked onto hers. His lips approached, making a butterfly landing before taking off. Her lips followed and they met again, locking together.

She felt tingling warmth surrounding her as he wrapped his arms around her body.

His hand cupped a breast. Her breath caught. His fingers traced the edges of her nipple. It stiffened, sending a current pulsing through her.

Her shirt fell away. His mouth roamed her chest. *Oh my God. Wonderful.* She grabbed his belt, but tugged the wrong way. The snap seemed welded shut. She wanted to be assaulted, wanted to feel his unbridled passion.

* * *

Stern's tongue roamed Kristen's skin, tasting the faint musky smell usually so sensuous . . . but not tonight. He told himself to just do it.

How many times? How many women? He'd lost count before he married Diana.

But she's different. No, she's special.

Don't think about the problems Sarah's going to have. Yeah, don't think, idiot.

Anxiety barricaded the valves he needed to get things working.

Though he used all the usual tricks, he couldn't get it to do what he wanted. It only wiggled.

Come on!

She raised her bottom from the floor, helping him pull her jeans off. Her face flushed, her breath was rapid, but no sound came from her. Only the steady crackle of the ebbing fire sliced through the silence. How he wanted her to moan, tell him she really wanted him.

She reached for him, she caressed his penis. A month ago he would've committed murder for that touch, but now nothing happened. Nothing.

He settled onto her, praying nature would take over. He had rarely failed to satisfy a woman, but a voice kept screaming she wasn't *any* woman. Her hands clasped around his ass, but still nothing stirred.

This was turning into Dunkirk, instead of D-Day.

"What's wrong?" she whispered in his ear.

He lifted his head, couldn't think of what to say.

"Is it me?"

"No."

He'd blown it. He should have never opened the envelope. Her history had become his nightmare.

"I'm sorry. Guess I'm just beat."

"You don't need to apologize."

He pushed himself up, then touched her fingertips. "I wanted it to be perfect for you."

"I'm not seventeen, Michael."

"You are so beautiful, *Joan d'Arc.*" He walked his fingers between her breasts and pecked her lips.

"I want you to know, I didn't ask you to come because I won. I didn't deserve to win." She covered herself with her shirt, seeming to choose her words carefully. "But what you whispered to me, was a *beau geste.*"

He tried to sound casual. "Maybe this *beau geste* legionnaire needs a good night's sleep."

"Just tell me you want me. Tell me it wasn't manipulation. A conquest that didn't meet expectations."

You stupid fuck! She craved reassurance, and he knew exactly why. Leaving her naked by the fire, their affair unconsummated, was the worst thing he could have done.

He struggled for an answer that wouldn't sound like he felt sorry for her and wished he'd missed the flight. "More than I can say. This is new for me."

"Please."

"No, really . . . I haven't slept . . . *been* with someone I care about in a long time. A *very* long time."

She made a face of exaggerated perplexity. "I thought you said you slept by *yourself* every night at home."

In spite of his embarrassment, he found himself laughing.

* * *

Moonlight illuminated the Victorian iron footboard. How many couplings had it witnessed? Thousands? But not tonight. Kristen had hoped things would reignite when they got in bed, but Michael had fallen asleep inside a minute.

She could feel his pulse in the hand resting under her breast. Two hours ago, she'd been shivering with apprehension. Now she felt disappointment. Deep disappointment. Who'd have thought Michael Stern would wilt? Maybe he felt guilty. Perhaps they were both too wiped out to make the sparks fly. After months of sexual tension, maybe the reality couldn't measure up. And they were stuck with each other for days.

The little negative murmur whispered that it was her fault, that she wasn't exciting enough, that she was too inexperienced. Her breasts weren't big enough. Her touch wasn't sexy enough. A good lover would've known what to do.

But the therapy-trained voice argued she'd done okay. NMNS. Asking him to come here was the biggest chance she'd ever taken with a man.

But she dreaded tomorrow. What would they do all day? Stare at each other and wonder whether he was overrated as a stud or she was doomed to spend the rest of her life with batteries?

She got up, found an Ambien in her bag, and washed it down with brandy. Several swallows. Before getting back in bed, she stopped and stared through the parted shutters. Trees towered over the cabin. The night wind rustled the bare Aspen branches, dropping clumps of snow. Billions of stars illuminated the clear sky. So beautiful. *You wanted too much. Trumpets and wild passion. Silly dreamer, nothing ever measures up to fantasy. Should've met him at the Fairmont and then gone home.*

CHAPTER 34

THE AROMA OF PERKING coffee and the sound of sizzling bacon infiltrated Kristen's dull senses. She opened her eyes, hearing Stern in the kitchen on the phone.

"Honey, I'm sorry I'll miss the game . . . You and Mom will have fun at the show . . . That's fine, if it's okay with Mom . . . Good luck today, and don't forget to pick up your room for Rita to clean . . . Love you."

Kristen sat up, lecturing herself. What a major mistake, taking him from his daughter. First, the sex fiasco. Now, she was playing homewrecker. Michael's wife would think she'd been doing her husband for weeks and would subpoena her, if Diana didn't shoot her first.

Stern walked in carrying a mug. "You're alive? I wasn't sure you'd come around."

She stretched. "Too much to drink. Didn't hear you leave." She didn't add that she'd slept late because of the full Ambien she took out of frustration. Probably wouldn't help his ego.

He set the steaming coffee on the nightstand.

"Thanks."

"I'm starved. Drove to the little store on the highway and picked up bacon and eggs. Got this swell sweatshirt."

She squinted. It had some kind of seal with the word "VAIL" and

"Elevation 8150."

She took the mug and allowed the aroma to wake her senses.

"We'll need a good breakfast where we're going," she said.

"Strolling around Vail?"

"No, Lake Whitney."

He blinked. "Where?"

"I read about it while I was waiting at the airport. It's supposed to be stunning. Two thousand feet up from the trailhead."

He frowned. "Sounds more like torture."

Kristen hopped out of bed and kissed his cheek. "Just think how good the hot tub will feel when we get back." She figured they couldn't dwell on their unrequited affair while busting their rears up the mountain.

* * *

Stern had been working his abs and hitting the treadmill the last few weeks to help his back and had lost a couple of pounds in the stress of the trial. Until last night he'd thought he could pass for thirty-five, but now feared Kristen thought he was more like seventy-five. Maybe he could find a doc in town to prescribe Viagra.

He stared at his new hiking boots shuffling over the slushy Aspen leaves. The wind whistled through the trees, not muting his labored breath. He sucked in all the thin air his lungs could hold, but still couldn't grab enough, like air didn't reach the bottom. His legs wobbled with each step. He didn't want to trip again. At least his chin had stopped bleeding.

Ahead of him Kristen's tight butt barely wiggled with each sure step down the trail. Her hair was banded and topped with a Yankees cap, her jacket was tied around her waist, and she wore no gloves. He couldn't imagine why she wasn't cold. It had to be near freezing. Was she trying to completely wear his ass down?

Kristen turned her head and slowed, giving him what he hoped was an encouraging—not derisive—smile as puffs of condensed breath rose around her flushed cheeks. He squared his shoulders and tried to disguise his agony.

Half an hour later, when they finally reached the SUV, he collapsed on the passenger seat, his legs too unsteady to drive. Kristen flipped the heater to high and slid the Ford into gear. Too drained to fight the rough road, his body bounced against the door. They finally reached the pavement, so he could rest his cheek against the cold window, too tired for conversation. After fifteen minutes, she pulled into the same small grocery where he'd bought breakfast.

"Coffee and a snack?"

"I can't move."

"No problem."

She sprang from the Explorer and returned with steaming Styrofoam cups and a package of Oreos.

Soon, the caffeine and sugar revived him enough to think he might survive the Vail Death March.

At the cabin Kristen unlocked the door and held it for him, as he staggered past her. "Maybe we went too far."

"No, I'm fine.

"I'll check the hot tub."

Stern decided alcohol might ease the agony. He shuffled to the kitchen and grabbed two brews from the refrigerator. Opening them, he called after her, "Beer?"

Hearing no response, he limped upstairs to the bedroom door she'd left ajar. Without thinking, he elbowed it open. He caught Kristen pulling her sweatshirt over her head, shedding her t-shirt. She tossed the clothing aside and faced him, clad only in jeans. Her brown nipples pointed at him, olive skin shining with sweat. Her jeans flared out, showing off hard abs. More beautiful than if she'd been wearing a Versace gown.

He expected her to turn away, but she stood still, watching him drink her in. Her casualness in not having bothered with a bra, and the way her full lips rose into a sly smile, heightened the eroticism. In that instant, she again became the woman he'd once desperately wanted.

And he returned to being the man he thought he was.

* * *

The hot tub water and cold air fostered delightful contentment in the afterglow of having a man she really liked. In the excitement, she'd even forgotten NMNS.

Michael, standing next to the cedar ledge, punched numbers on his cell phone.

"Odd for Sarah not to call back after a game." He waited a minute, and spoke into the phone. "Hi, honey. Hope you won. Call me." He clicked off, set the phone on a redwood stool, doffed the robe they'd found in the closet, and eased in, one leg at a time.

Kristen admired the view. *Nice.*

After lowering himself into the hot gurgling water, Stern pulled Kristen's foot up to his mouth and planted a kiss in the middle of the soft underside. He swirled his tongue, making her giggle, and sucked each toe, sending pulsing current up her leg.

He dropped her foot and scooted close, between her legs, his expression serious. "Kristen—"

Sensing more information coming than she could yet handle, she put a finger to his lips. "Michael, I've been fed a lot of shit by men trying to get me in the sack, and I've struggled to get close to anybody. You don't need to say anything." She smiled. "I'm already here."

He slipped his arms behind her and kissed her. As she felt his renewed arousal, her heart sped.

Certainly no Virgin Mary, but sure as hell not shit.

CHAPTER 35

Dallas
Saturday, October 11

LEONARD MARRS JOGGED toward the Sterns' Tudor mini-mansion. Parking too close risked a nosy neighbor remembering his car, but runners along the tree-lined street weren't suspicious. His shirt hung out, hiding his pistol, knife, tape, and twine. He glanced around one more time and saw nobody. Rich pukes were probably watching football, yardmen done for the weekend.

He strolled up the walkway to the front door. When he reached the porch he slipped on gloves. Not hesitating, he inserted the key and turned. It opened, just like the dude said. Marrs slipped inside, closed the door, and tapped in the alarm code that came with the key.

His "partner" had no idea how much fun Marrs had planned. *Two* kidnappings would really pay. With luck he could even screw the guy out of his half.

He exhaled a long breath and listened. If this was an ambush at least he was armed. Though he'd gotten a burr cut just for the occasion, he tugged on a hairnet to be safe. A baseball bag sat near the door. He snatched an aluminum bat out of it and hurried over the Oriental runner through a living room big enough for a basketball court.

Casing the downstairs led him to a study lined with books and pictures of old ships. Hoping to nab some spare cash, he searched inside the desk and found only stationery printed *Jackson, Stern and Randolph*. Thinking it might come in handy, he folded several sheets of the paper, slipped them into his shirt pocket, and ducked into the kitchen.

Marrs snagged a beer from the fridge, twisted off the cap, and gulped. The brew didn't slow his pounding heart or wash away the nasty metallic taste in his mouth. A Dallas Zoo calendar hung above the phone. In Saturday's box somebody had scribbled over *Junior League* and written *theater with Sarah*. He remembered the danger of saliva and poured the rest of the beer down the sink. He ran water over the bottle to eliminate any DNA.

A car door slammed in front. He darted into the living room, edged to the picture window, and saw the Stern girl in a ball uniform getting out of a black BMW.

She strolled under the arch and into the backyard.

As the car drove away, he grabbed the bat and stationed himself next to the back door.

He watched through a window as she trotted up the back steps, then fished under the iron handrail, pulled out a box, unlocked the door, and replaced the key. The kid nuzzled the dog back outside and stepped in.

At the instant she closed the door, Marrs swung the bat into her leg. She screamed and went down. The fun would start soon.

* * *

Sated with trout, good sex, and Chardonnay, Kristen slept dreamlessly. No pill necessary. She woke Sunday to the wind slapping flecks of icy rain against the window. Michael's hand cupped her breast. He got up and pulled on her arm, so Kristen climbed out of bed and followed him into the kitchen.

He tapped the kitchen counter by the sink, and she gave him a quizzical grin. He slipped his hands under her arms and lifted her up, then lay her gently over, positioning her head on the edge of the sink. She wasn't sure what he was doing, but she knew two things—sleeping with this man would be habit-forming, and the tongue was mightier than the sword.

Michael tucked a rolled towel under her neck and turned the tap. Warm water soaked her hair, while cold air seeped through the window above the sink and ice peppered the glass.

"Maybe we'll get snowed in," he said.

"Fine with me. They told me to take some time off while they figure out how to deal with a 'hero.'"

"A unique problem for a law firm."

His hands molded mounds of shampoo lather and stroked her scalp. He ran more hot water and added shampoo. She sank into a stupor of complete pleasure. He ever so slowly rinsed and conditioned her hair, finishing with a vigorous toweling before pulling her up.

She locked her hands around his back and pressed her cheek against his chest.

"I never trusted before. Really trusted. I took a gamble." She fought the urge to cry. "I'm afraid . . ." Her voice cracked slightly. "I'm afraid you'll patch things up when we get home and go back to business as usual."

He smiled, the Sarah smile. "Don't be silly."

She listened for a minute to the sleet bouncing off the windows. "You're the one with a home and a kid."

"Diana's made up her mind and so have I. I won't get less than joint custody out of any judge."

"Won't I be in the way?"

"You two sports fanatics will hit it off great."

"Can't you still salvage your marriage?"

He didn't answer immediately. Instead he peered out the window. Seconds crawled like hours. She dreaded what he might say.

Finally, he answered, "I've thought a lot. Diana was my security, a ticket to the big time I didn't think I could get on my own. Maybe I couldn't. But I've spent the last twenty years trying to prove I could have been something without her. Now I just want you. You and Sarah."

"How do I know there won't be another young lawyer someday, working a case with you, traveling together?"

His face flushed. "You've changed me. Please believe me."

She examined him, wanting to believe, but not sure. She lost focus and spoke into his sweatshirt, "I should tell you, before we get too carried away, I've had some problems."

She hesitated, wondering whether divulging too much would run him off. "My parents are nuts. My dad kept my mom medicated and locked up like Mrs. Rochester. I left home before I finished high school. I've had to take in one immature sister and support a messed-up brother in med school. My baby sister's in the custody of my insane mother, but supervised by the state. I've tried to sneak her to Texas. I may have to go to Jersey for a hearing and ask for custody."

She watched for a reaction, saw none, and wondered why she was telling him this, all of this, all at once. It took months for her therapist to coax it out of her. But his arms squeezed her gently as if it was okay. She closed her eyes and continued.

"I have terrible nightmares. Horrible monsters ripping my clothes. Drowning in front of people. Sometimes I wake up screaming."

His hand lifted her chin and he kissed her, stopping her confession. "In mine, they discover I didn't pass the bar. Send me back to Beaumont to shag golf bags for rich duffers."

"Michael, I'm serious. You need to know what you're getting into. My family's—"

"It doesn't matter. But, if we ever get in another mess, let's keep our stories straight."

* * *

Monday, October 2

Rita dropped her Safeway sack on top of the rubber *Happy Home* mat on the Sterns' back porch. She thought it *raro* that the concrete was wet. It hadn't rained in days. She inserted her key, turned it, and pushed on the door. As she cracked it open, water rushed over her sandals and down the steps. Hot air and a rotten smell—like raw hamburger left in the sun—flowed out with thousands of gallons of water.

"Mrs. Stern?" Rita yelled.

Silence, except for the flood pouring through the house.

She sloshed into the kitchen, but halted when she saw Rusty, on his side, his fur matted. Rita cupped her nose, gagging on the stench. She stepped around the dead dog, splashing through the mess. Her finger mashed the panic button on the alarm panel.

* * *

Stern punched his home number again, calculating that Sarah should be out of school and home. Maybe she lost her cell. Not unusual. He tried the landline. Listening to the ring, he stared at Vail Mountain, coated with snow well down the timberline.

"Yeah?" It was a raspy male voice.

Stern started to click off, but then asked, "Is this the Stern residence?"

"Who's this?"

"Michael Stern. I own the goddamn place. Who the hell are you?"

"Detective Burrows. Highland Park Police. Where are you, Mr. Stern?"

"Vail. What the hell's going on?"

"You need to come home. Now. We have an emergency situation."

The cop's voice fadey, like he was hanging up.

"What emergency?"

"There's been a crime."

Panic rose in Michael's chest. Hoping for the best, he asked, "A burglary?"

"I'm sorry, but your wife's been murdered. And your daughter's missing."

CHAPTER 36

KRISTEN FEARED MICHAEL was having a heart attack. She stayed close to him, until some color finally returned. She threw their gear together while Michael sat by the fireplace, palms covering his face. Then they hurried to the SUV. After telling him everything would be okay, and sounding stupid for it, she kept quiet for the next hour.

The only sound was the wipers shoving sleet into the corners of the windshield. Her heavy foot and four-wheel drive sped them east along I-70, passing every other vehicle.

Finally, Michael jarred the morbid silence. "You should wait for another flight."

Kristen's first thought was that he was dumping her. No need for a casual girlfriend during the crisis of his life. "But—"

He put up a hand. "You need to stay out of this."

"Michael, I want to do anything I can to help."

"I know, baby." He paused, then turned his head to her. "The husband's always a suspect when there've been marital problems. They've probably already talked to Diana's family. They'll be all too eager to say I'm an asshole. So will her friends. The police will be at the airport to make sure I don't take the next flight to Cancún."

She absorbed this. She understood, but how to tell him she needed to be needed? "I can testify we've been here all—"

"No. I can handle the Highland Park knuckleheads. I'm just praying Sarah's at a sleepover."

"Me too." She doubted kids did sleepovers on Sunday nights, but Michael needed to maintain enough hope to get home.

In the Denver suburbs, traffic slowed. Kristen darted in and out of lanes, drawing one-finger salutes. "Want me to call a lawyer to meet you?"

He leaned his cheek away from the cold glass. "I'd look guilty. Better to be completely cooperative." He stretched his arm and brushed her hair. "Stay low. I'll call you."

* * *

Kristen stood in a gaggle of onlookers across the street from Michael's house. All the way to Dallas, she'd clung to a reed of hope that the whole thing was some awful stunt played on Michael by some lawyer he'd beaten, or was Galway's attempt at revenge. It couldn't, of course, be that simple.

Michael's front door opened. She shielded her eyes from the red pulsating lights of the police cars.

A phalanx of cops spilled out of the house, led by a heavy man in a green sport coat. In the middle, Stern plodded along, his vision cast at his shoes. The formation parted as it reached an unmarked cop car. The fat guy opened the door. One of the uniforms clamped a hand on Michael's elbow and helped him in.

She asked herself if it was her fault. Would Diana be alive if she hadn't taken Michael to Vail? Would Sarah be safe up in her bed? The trust problem erupted. Did the cops really think he was involved? Did they know something about him that she didn't? Had she inadvertently provided him an alibi?

She staggered to an oak near the sidewalk and planted her palms against it. After a few staccato breaths, she threw up on the grass between her hiking boots.

* * *

In an office cluttered with bowling trophies inside the Highland Park police station, Stern watched Detective Rick Burrows suck on his cigarette once more before starting the video interview. Burrows offered a phlegmy thanks for Stern's cooperation. A green sport coat stretched over the cop's beer belly. His thin hair had been combed strategically to cover as much of his dome as possible.

Stern worked at staying focused. He'd tossed down several drinks on the flight home, before being intercepted by the cops at the airport. They'd hauled him home to examine the scene, to see if he could provide any observations, then driven him here. He gathered his remaining strength and spoke evenly, "Let's get going so you can find my daughter."

"When did you last speak with Diana?"

"Thursday night, after work. I left the house Friday, before she got up."

"And Sarah?"

"Saturday morning. I called to tell her good luck in her game. I tried several more times later and on Sunday, but got no answer on her cell phone."

"Okay, Mr. Stern, where were you from Friday night until nine tonight?"

"I already told you, I flew to Denver Friday for the weekend and stayed in a cabin near Vail with a friend."

"Girlfriend?"

Stern drew a breath and nodded. For some reason it occurred to him how unfortunate it was for this cop that he couldn't transplant some hair from his eyebrows to his scalp.

Burrows's partner added, "You were having an affair at the time your wife was murdered?"

Stern matched the detective's stare with his own. "That's correct."

Burrows's volume strengthened. "Who with?"

"What difference does it make? I can prove I was in Colorado all weekend." He imagined Kristen's photo on the front page and the headline "Girlfriend Establishes Husband's Alibi"—or worse, TV news reports showing her dragged in for questioning.

"How long have you been having an affair?"

"I've had lots of affairs. I'm the cad of the century, but I didn't kill Diana! She was the mother of my only daughter."

He paused, hoping common sense would have some impact on these mental midgets. He saw no reaction, and decided to get aggressive.

"Have you got people looking for Sarah? Or are you just planning on beating a confession out of me?"

"You traveled by yourself. We've checked the flight." The detective blew out a smoke ring. "Did you meet the woman there?"

Stern thumbed his temples, wondering when this torture would end. He'd give all Diana's money, as well as his own, to see Sarah in front of one of her dumb video games.

"I have to have complete candor, Mr. Stern."

"I don't want her name leaked to the media." Stern slammed his back against the frame of the steel chair. He knew they'd find out anyway, but wanted them to focus on Sarah. "Why won't you tell me exactly what happened to Diana? I have a right to know."

For a minute, Burrows sat mute and drummed his nicotine-stained fingers on the metal table, then almost whispered, "Who owns the cabin?"

"Look, a young woman with frizzy blond hair at Rob Roy's outside Beaver Creek will remember me. I was in twice Saturday. Groceries will be on my credit card. Also at a Wal-Mart west of Denver."

"Can anybody else verify you were in Colorado?"

"I ate at Minturn's in Vail Friday. Another credit card receipt."

"I have to have the whole truth. This is a murder investigation, not one of your bullshit lawsuits." Burrows puffed a cloud of smoke. "How'd you get that scrape on your chin?"

"I tripped on the trail." Stern noticed his hands shook, like he had Parkinson's. He clasped them so the cops wouldn't notice. Much more of this and he'd either punch the cop or start bawling. "Somebody must've known where the key was on the back handrail. That's how they got in."

"The killer used it and put it back?"

"Burrows, I—"

"I'll find your broad eventually." Burrows's flabby jowls rose. "A tomcat always leaves clues. This game you're playing is making me mighty suspicious."

Stern prayed for control. "I'll do anything you want."

"We'd like for the post office to hold your mail."

"Sure, but what happened to Diana?"

"And tap your phone."

"Be my guest."

"Will you put up a reward? Say ten thousand dollars?"

"Ten lousy grand for *my* daughter? I'll make it a cool million. Cash."

It took Burrows a minute to gather another sneer. "One more time. Who were you with?"

"Find Sarah, and I'll tell you."

Burrows wagged a finger. "If you're going to withhold pertinent information, I'll have to consider you a suspect."

"Fine. Dandy. I'm a suspect. Frame me for anything, but you know the whole time I've been here, I haven't seen my kid. And you haven't been looking for her while you've been jacking with me. So if something happens to her, it's on your fucking head!"

CHAPTER 37

Tuesday, October 14

STERN SPENT A SLEEPLESS night at the Hyatt, with calls from shocked friends and family keeping him busy. Burrows called around eleven, telling him he could return home.

The steam-cleaning people's equipment whirred in the family room. In the kitchen Rita cleaned. Stern thought what a fine lady she was, working nonstop without complaint on the killer's mess. The lowlife had dragged a garden hose inside, sprayed everywhere, stopped up the sinks, turned on every faucet, and flooded the house.

Outside, the storm front that had escorted Michael and Kristen out of the mountains maintained a steady drizzle against the leaded-glass window. His mind conjured the image of Sarah lying in the rain without a coat.

His cell rang. He answered with hope and dread.

Burrows skipped the pleasantries. "We've put together photos of sex perps and relatives of cons Diana denied parole. Can you come and take a look? It'll take all day."

* * *

Kristen ducked through the rain and stepped over a rubber hose twisting its way from a Steamatic truck parked on Stern's driveway.

Returning Michael's medical articles would be her excuse, if anyone asked. In the twenty-four hours since leaving Vail, she'd eaten little and hadn't slept.

She was going insane. She did her best to follow Michael's orders and lay low, but she couldn't be more scared for Sarah than if the girl were her own. Surely Michael couldn't have had anything to do with Diana's death, but the little voice of mistrust gnawed at her.

Kristen had called Jen and asked her to pump her pal, Hudson, whom she'd tried to set Kristen up with, for information, what the police were thinking. Jen was more than eager, since she liked gossip, but she also wanted to get back into Kristen's good graces. The criminal bar was a tight-knit group, always sharing scuttlebutt.

Jen called back three hours later. She had learned that the police were concentrating on the relatives of men who had been denied parole, but still hadn't ruled out Michael as a suspect. At least one detective thought Diana's money, their public arguments, her seeing divorce lawyers, and Michael's refusal to name his girlfriend, added up to a hired kill. The place had been drenched in water and bleach, which indicated that whoever did it knew something about forensics.

All this sounded exciting to Jen, who thought Stern must be guilty.

Kristen closed her eyes. A movie ran in her mind. She saw the staring neighbors, the cops, the tape, and could taste vomit wanting to rise up. She tugged her hair, trying to shake her head clear. Finally she pushed the doorbell. It chimed "Greensleeves," as she'd heard three long weeks ago.

The door cracked open. A Latina—fortyish, stocky, with distrust plastered on her pretty skin—peered through the slight opening.

Kristen thought the housekeeper's name was Rita from overhearing Michael talk to Sarah. She took a flyer.

"Rita, I'm Kristen Kerry, a friend of Michael's. Is he in?"

The woman kept a tight hand on the edge of the door. "Gone to police station."

Kristen drew a deep breath. "Can we talk? I'm so worried."

"You with newspaper?"

In her most plaintive tone, Kristen said, "No, I work with Michael. I'm a lawyer."

After looking her over again, Rita opened the door.

Kristen pulled off her wet jacket and trailed the housekeeper over the buckled hardwood floor. The beautiful entry runner was gone. Disinfectant didn't completely mask a lingering odor of death and mildew. Kristen followed Rita into the kitchen.

Rita pointed. "Drinks in refrigerator." She turned away and began wiping a countertop, cleaning off fingerprint powder.

"Got an extra rag?" Kristen hoped she wouldn't have to clean up blood, but wanted to feel useful.

Rita handed Kristen a sponge. "Big mess."

"Is there any news?"

Kristen dabbed soapy water from the sink.

"No news. Very bad man took Sarah." Rita crossed herself. "I pray for her."

Rita had more faith than Kristen could muster, but she made the sign of the cross, too. Jen had reported that the cops, because of the brutality of Diana's murder, doubted Sarah was alive. So far they hadn't called the FBI kidnapping team.

Kristen debated what to say, then blurted, "What was Diana like?"

Rita studied Kristen again, but after a second smiled. "Great lady. I work for her four years. She give me big bonus every Christmas. Help my Raphael find work."

At a loss for words, Kristen picked up a decorative bowl, then asked, "Did you see anybody suspicious around the house?"

"I tell police I know nothing. Nobody strange around."

Kristen hoped to stall until Michael walked in. The Steamatic people were collecting their gear.

Rita said she had to pick up her kids. She gathered groceries from the refrigerator. "Mr. Stern tell me to take what I can use at home. Stuff will spoil here."

Kristen wondered if that meant Michael had given up hope. She tossed the wet sponge away and helped Rita bag three sacks of food. Kristen grabbed one and, stepping gingerly on the damp tile floor, followed Rita through the back door.

Trying to carry two sacks, Rita struggled to retrieve her key from her purse. The purse fell to the concrete, scattering its contents on the back steps. A small nickel-plated pistol landed in the pile of brushes, makeup, and junk.

A sheepish look consumed Rita's face, like she was hiding more than the weapon. She looked away, set the groceries down, and refilled her handbag.

"Hope you've never had to use that," Kristen said.

Rita found her key chain in the clutter and locked the deadbolt.

Rita noticed the silver cross hanging from Kristen's neck, which Kristen had worn since coming home. Rita started to speak, halted, then said, "I need priest. Go to confession."

Kristen thought Rita was going to cry. She took Rita's hand. "Did something happen?" Kristen nodded encouragement. "I'm a lawyer. I can't tell anyone."

Rita closed her eyes, and her body shook. When she spoke, it seemed to be more to the Holy Spirit than to Kristen.

"I shoot man weeks ago. He try to steal my car."

Kristen gasped. "You must've been so scared."

Rita squeezed Kristen's hand, perhaps a thankful gesture, then walked to her station wagon with the bags, Kristen following.

"Did you tell the police?"

"No." Rita opened the door. "Don't happen here. Near my house."

"You never reported it?"

Rita tossed her purse in the car. "Don't want trouble over my gun."

"They wouldn't have charged you."

"Well, I don't want trouble. My friend, who stays with me, not legal. He good, just not legal. Police make trouble. Man got what he deserve."

"Did you kill him?"

"Don't know. Never think I could use gun. Raphael give it to me."

"What did he look like?"

"Small. Angry. But why he want my car?"

"Rita, when did this happen?"

"Was Saturday night. Kids at gym dance." She flushed. "Raphael send me to get some tapes for us."

"Could it have been the weekend Michael went to New York?"

"Yes. I don't cook . . . Man had long knife."

Jen had told Kristen the blade used to kill Diana wasn't domestic, more like a gangland stiletto. She eyed Rita's car. The muffler was tied on with baling wire; the windshield was cracked and the outside half of the car was rusted. Rita was right. Why would anybody steal it, especially at the risk of getting shot?

"Could I see the knife?"

"I throw away. Very sharp. Thin and long, like bad men carry."

"Do you keep the Sterns' house key on the chain with your car key?"

"Si."

* * *

That night, at the Galleria shopping center, Kristen watched the ice-skaters trade near misses. Every kid Kristen grew up with was better than any of them, but like most Texans, they probably thought themselves fabulous.

Standing next to her was Tammy Robberson, the once-fearsome, now contrite, former client. Kristen gave her a totally fake smile.

"Why'd you want to see me?" Tammy asked.

The tables were turned. The former claims terror had nobody to castrate and no tits to cut off. "Are you going to jail?"

Tammy shook her head. "They've agreed to defer, if nobody rats me out at the *Layne* hearing. Might even get on with State Farm after probation."

"You could cheat everybody on their storm claims. Wouldn't that be fun?" Kristen was enjoying this. "I might be willing to help you, but I need a favor."

"What?"

"I need some ER records of gunshot patients."

Tammy stuffed her hands into her jean pockets. "That's pretty ballsy for Ms. Righteous. You know it's illegal."

Kristen squinted. "I doubt you should be lecturing me on what's illegal. So don't get snotty. The DA and the judge would like to know what you told those nurses to say."

"You can't. Lawyer/client privilege."

"You've watched too many bad lawyer movies. Perjury isn't protected communication."

After letting Tammy sweat a minute, Kristen pressed her notes, containing the possible dates and hospitals, into Tammy's sticky palm. She'd decided to include the two Saturdays before and after the New York trip to be safe. "Hurry. It's kind of important."

Tammy squeezed Kristen's arm. "Cover me in the hearing."

"Please?"

"Please."

* * *

Wednesday

Stern led Diana's family to the front pews in Highland Park Presbyterian Church, as the pipe organ jarred the shoulder-to-shoulder crowd to their feet. Stern felt every set of eyeballs trained like laser-guided missiles on him.

Did they believe he killed her? What did they think he'd done with Sarah? Sent her to camp? Was she going to hop off the church bus Saturday, toting her beadwork?

Diana's younger sister sat next to him, but left a foot between them, like he had a communicable disease. Little did she know, if he hadn't intervened, Diana would still be in the morgue, waiting for the autopsy to be finished. The overdone box they were staring at would have been empty.

He remembered their honeymoon in Maui. She had looked luscious, blond, and tan. Other men stared, making him feel on top of the world. They laughed then, teased each other. Taking Sarah home from the hospital had been joyous. Diana had helped him get his big interview at the law firm that became his own. How proud he'd been to have her on his arm at those first office Christmas parties.

The poor boy had married up. Way up.

As the minister droned on about God's will, Stern tuned out what he considered nonsense and counted to himself. He knew that in abduction cases where there'd been a murder, the chances of finding Sarah diminished every hour. And it had already been five days.

* * *

Detective Burrows clicked his phone off. "We got a positive ID from the girl at that convenience store outside Vail for Saturday."

Assistant DA John Livermore held the yellow pad against his nose, sniffing ink and dye. His skin had a jaundiced hue, close to matching the paper. He sat slump shouldered, as if the weight of his job overwhelmed him.

"Let's summarize what we got. Stern didn't do it. Even with the heat cranked up and the flood, Saturday noon is the earliest time of death."

"Cashier says the second time she saw Stern, he was with a looker, tall, brunette."

"Diana Stern was stabbed and nude, but there's no evidence of sexual assault. Lab guys think the perp might have forced her to scrub before he stabbed her."

Burrows shook a Marlboro out of his crumpled pack and lit up. "If he's so damn clean, why is Stern covering for his babe?"

Livermore shrugged. "She's married? Doesn't want a jealous husband to find out?"

"Nobody who knows him thinks he's noble, not even his partners." He puffed out smoke. "For every bloodthirsty pervert, there's ten greedy, horny husbands. Diana was rich, and he's got a girlfriend." He stuck the cigarette back between his lips and muttered, "I can't stand the guy. Acts like the King of Siam. He gave my officers grief a year ago over a traffic ticket he could pay with pocket change."

"But his kid's missing."

Burrows scoffed. "Supposedly. There's been no ransom demand. For all we know, she'll turn up, a little scuffed up, dropped off by somebody she never saw or can't remember. A *kidnapping* gives Stern the greatest alibi ever."

"Maybe you shouldn't work in Highland Park, since you hate rich snobs so much."

Burrows harrumphed.

"There may be more cheating husbands than murdering sex fiends, but Diana Stern put herself in front of more than her share of scum."

"Why would somebody she *paroled* want to kill her?" Burrows took another long drag. "I could see some psycho developing a crush, but we never got any stalking reports. She had a state contact number to report any harassment."

"You think Stern's clever enough to buy the job, make it look like a pervert, and hide his daughter? Make her *think* she's been kidnapped?"

Burrows grinned. "Sure do."

"His girlfriend may have the kid or know where she is. It's wild, really wild, but until we find the kid, we can't rule it out."

Burrows pushed off the chair arms and shuffled to the door. "DPD will regret letting me go when I bust this open."

"Just between us," Livermore said, leaning across his desk, "I applied at Stern's firm six years ago. Didn't even get a form letter from those assholes. But don't tell." The ADA reached into his bottom desk drawer and pulled out a flask. "Somebody might claim I'm conflicted. And I want this puppy."

CHAPTER 38

Thursday, October 16

A FTER ESCAPING DIANA'S family and spending another
evening at the police station looking at photos of convicts and
their brothers, Stern got up early, unable to sleep. He caught his awful
image in the bathroom mirror—eyes sunk into their sockets, hair
plastered on his skull, cheeks collapsing from hunger. The shower he'd
had before the funeral had been his first since leaving Vail, and he
didn't care if he had another one.

Stern retrieved the morning paper. He flipped through it, looking
for news on the investigation, since the cops weren't telling him squat.
The story had retreated from the front page to the local section. *Police
Pursuing Leads in Stern Murder.* He snorted skepticism.

He poured coffee and wandered into his library. Coffee and booze
had been his only sustenance since getting back to Dallas. For the
hundredth time, he flipped through the scrapbook he'd compiled since
Sarah played Tball. He stared at the sequential shots of her perfect
swing. *She would play on ESPN. If they found her.*

The book started his eyes watering again, but he didn't bother to
pray anymore. God obviously didn't have time, while running the
universe, to give a shit about him. All his sins squared didn't merit this.
Despite trying not to, he wondered what the murderer was doing to
her. He imagined a knife and blood. An erection. Sarah helpless. Tears

ran down his cheeks. He poured Irish whiskey into his java, hoping to close the cinema in his brain.

The doorbell chimed.

He blew his nose and shuffled into the entry. For a fraction of a second, the remote, impossible possibility that Sarah stood at the door leapt to his imagination. He hurried, only to find the police. Stern motioned them into his study. The same dork who operated the camera in his first interrogation trailed mutely behind Burrows.

The detective plopped himself down under Stern's favorite Trafalgar print. He placed his recorder on the ottoman and switched it on.

"We have more questions."

Stern exhaled, counting *questions* as relatively good news. "Any leads?"

"We're getting hundreds of tips."

"Then why are you here and not chasing those tips?"

Burrows ignored Stern's question, as usual. "You tried a case and had a bad outcome last week."

"Bad outcome? I got the holy crap kicked out of me."

"Wouldn't that hurt you financially? We heard your best client is terminating you."

"I've got all the money I need. And I'm tired of Standard and arrogant doctors."

"What happens to Diana's money?"

Stern glared at Burrows as the man searched his jacket pockets for cigarettes. "No smoking." As a concession Stern added, "Please."

The cop hesitated before making the cigarettes disappear again.

"Does the money go to Sarah or you?"

"I've been pulling down nearly a million, year in and year out, for twelve years. I bought Apple stock at twenty. I shorted the dot-coms."

Burrows glowered impatience.

Stern counted on his fingers, making sure he didn't forget anything. "Twenty million goes into a trust for Sarah. As best as I can remember, the church gets five, SMU eight for some endowed chair. Hockaday and breast cancer about the same. I get the rest and the house. Forty or fifty after taxes. Maybe sixty, I haven't bothered to add it up."

Burrows loosed a whistle of amazement. "Assuming she wasn't trying to change her will before she died."

Stern shrugged. "Maybe she did. I wouldn't know about that."

Burrows smirked. "I've got witnesses claiming you and your wife were going at it pretty good at one of Sarah's soccer games a month ago. A friend of Diana's says your wife was deciding which lawyer to hire to kick your ass."

Stern kept his voice level. "Do you honestly think I wanted the mother of my thirteen-year-old daughter dead? That I could ever look into Sarah's face again after that?"

A blank look crossed Burrows's face, like Stern had asked him for the square root of nineteen, but he plowed ahead. "Another pal of Diana's, Marge, says—"

"I'm a bum? That's not news."

"We hear you had an affair last year with an associate at your firm."

"Yeah. She got pissy, threatened to sue, and left when we didn't make her partner."

Burrows's running buddy, who until now hadn't said a word, piped up. "Did she go to Vail?"

"Haven't seen her since she quit."

"You have a new partner who's attractive. Are you covering for her?" Burrows asked.

"She drives me nuts."

Burrows drew a long breath. Stern guessed the real question had to be coming.

"How does Kristen Kerry figure in your plans now?"

Stern kept his eyes steady. The dumbasses had done some homework. "I don't know."

"One of your partners says you two have been doing a lot more

285

together than trying a case."

Stern locked his teeth for a second before answering. "Tell Caswell he's full of shit, but he already knows that. Frankly, if I was going to murder anybody, it would be him."

Burrows's saddlebag eyes blinked surprise. It took him a minute to restart the inquisition. "He says you two worked together late several nights."

"Correct."

"And he saw you two getting it on."

"He's lying."

"Your partner, Jackson, says—"

"Jackson wants me out; now he sees his chance. Burrows, you've found all my enemies. Why don't you find my daughter?"

"Did Kristen go to Vail with you?"

Stern felt a chill run up his spine, but focused on the cop. "I think I'll call my congressman and ask him to get the FBI on this, since you can't handle hundreds of leads."

Burrows continued, oblivious to Stern's taunt. "I couldn't find Kristen today. She hasn't been at work and wasn't home. One of your neighbors says a woman matching her description was across the street, barfing her guts out on their lawn Monday night." He slid to the edge of the leather chair. "You did all you could to help her client win the trial. She just happened to buy a plane ticket in your name, although you didn't use it."

Stern heaved a sigh. "Be easy on her. She's a good girl."

Burrows beamed as if he'd just won the lottery. After a long moment of triumph, Burrows reached into his faded green coat. He retrieved a photograph encased in a plastic sleeve and plopped it on Sarah's scrapbook cover.

Stern, guessing it was another worthless hood, ignored it and glared at the cop.

Burrows snickered knowingly, like he held the secret of what happened to the Templars.

Sick of cops and mug shots, Stern glowered back, determined not to play the cop's little game.

After a long minute Burrows said, "You might want to take a peek."

Stern rolled his eyes and picked up whatever was so damn valuable.

It took him a second to figure out that the petrified kid with matted hair in the photo was Sarah, holding yesterday's paper in front of her. "Oh Lord."

He covered his face to keep some dignity, but couldn't staunch the tears. He bawled and choked on his phlegm, holding the picture to his chest as if it were Sarah herself.

Burrows waited awhile, before speaking with all the emotion of a CPA reviewing a 1040. "We intercepted this in your mail. With a note, telling you to wire four million dollars to a bank in Costa Rica by noon Friday."

Stern rose, sniffed, and wiped his face, his joy turning to anger. "You asshole! You must've had this last night. Do you have any fucking idea what I've been through? How hard it is to sleep? To keep from slitting my throat? You hung onto this until I'd given you Kristen, you bloated prick."

Stern shoved Burrows, hoping the cop would slug him, so he could strangle his fat neck. Burrows pushed back. Stern could tell the fat boy had little muscle strength.

Burrows's running buddy stepped between them, planting a palm on Stern's chest. "Hold it!"

Stern readied himself to whip them both, consequences be damned.

Burrows backed away and turned toward the door. "I'm eager to hear what your 'good girl' has to say."

Stern wiped his nose with his sleeve. "When this is over, I'll see to it you're writing parking tickets in Gainesville."

"Yeah, we'll see who's where."

* * *

In his half brother's house, Marrs jammed his hand under the waistband of Sarah Stern's softball pants, grazed it across her thin patch of pubes, and poked a little. Girls didn't do much for him, but maybe he ought to initiate her into the ways of the world.

She tried to twist away from his probing fingers. "Please don't! It hurts."

Her screeching annoyed him, so he pulled away. Wasn't much fun anyway. He had considered wearing a ski mask around the kid, so she couldn't ID him later, but they itched and he'd already decided she wasn't going home, at least not alive.

She scrunched up, groaning. "I need to pee."

"Again?" He didn't want a mess, so he untied the cord around the girl's ankles and pulled her up from the floor.

She crumpled back to the carpet. "My leg hurts bad."

"You'll live."

He dragged her to the hallway bathroom, backed her into the toilet, and pulled off her ball pants and panties.

She sat, shivering. "Can you untie my arms? They hurt too much to go."

Marrs wished he hadn't killed Diana. She would've been much more fun to keep around than the brat. Sometimes the best plans are lost in all the excitement. His mystery partner would be pissed. He'd begged Marrs not to hurt Diana, but they'd be rich soon and everybody dies sometime. The guy was obviously a pussy.

"Please, sir."

He freed her arms.

"Don't look."

Turning his back, he kept an eye on her in the mirror. After an interminable wait, piss came. He scarfed the kid's drawers and tossed them in the cabinet under the sink. They might come in handy if he needed further proof for Stern that he had the girl. Or he could just cut off a finger.

But as he slammed the cabinet shut, she rocketed up and scooted along, half naked, on a leg and a half, through the den toward the front door. For a second he stared at her little bottom, amazed at her quickness.

Marrs hurried after her. She had already reached the front door. "Stop!"

The kid couldn't halt her momentum, and slammed her palms into the front door. She stepped back and pulled, but the latch chain stretched tight and held. She fiddled with the chain, while looking back in terror.

He caught her by the neck and flung her to the carpet as hard as he could. To his surprise, she wasn't hurt and crawled away. Even on hands and knees she moved fast. He hollered for her to stop, but she kept plowing along, nowhere really to go.

She shouted, *"Help! Help!"*

How fucking annoying could she get? It took him five quick steps to catch her. In his rage, he reached for the closest object, a baked-clay flower vase, and slammed it against her head.

She collapsed without a sound.

* * *

Kristen shook herself alert. She had fallen asleep in her gym clothes on top of the bedspread, only intending to rest her eyes for a minute. She stumbled into the bathroom, turned on the faucet, and splashed cold water on her face.

Tina came in, beaming for the first time since returning from Colorado. "Michael called! He got a photo of Sarah in the mail, holding yesterday's paper. He's supposed to pay a ransom by tomorrow."

"Christ, Tina, why didn't you wake me?"

"I told him you haven't slept for days. That all you've done is run, shoot baskets, and pace all night. He said to let you nap."

She wanted to do anything she could to help. But there had been nothing to do.

"He also said to tell you that when this is all over, he wants to go to Lake Whitney again with the Maid of Orleans. What does that mean?"

Kristen smiled. "Code, I think, for getting together."

"He sounded pretty wrung out. Said he told the cops you two were involved, so you'll get questioned. Also, he didn't think they knew squat. Overwhelmed with too many phone-in tips."

Tina waved an envelope.

"And the pug-nosed bitch with the wrist baubles brought this by. Said, 'Do the rest of the fucking research yourself.'"

Kristen grabbed the envelope from Tina, tore it open, and pulled out a printed list of hundreds of names. Tammy must not have narrowed the billing codes beyond trauma. "I've got to go to Austin. I might figure out who's got Sarah."

"How?"

"The housekeeper shot a guy trying to steal her car, but never reported it. He might've been after a key to the house."

"Somebody tries to carjack the housekeeper so he can kill Michael's wife?"

Kristen ignored Tina's frown. "I think it happened the weekend we went to New York for a deposition. It wouldn't be hard to get a lawyer's schedule. Wright McGee prints dozens of copies every day that end up in the trash."

"Why not tell the cops what you think?"

"I promised Rita I wouldn't. Plus, having these names is a little bit illegal." Kristen stared at herself in the mirror. Her red puffy eyes and pale skin would scare Dracula. She looked like the kid who, once upon a time, got the shit kicked out of her after catching dear ol' Dad snorting coke. Whatever she had to do, she'd do it for both Sarah and that frightened girl from New Jersey.

"Why Austin?"

"Because Diana Stern met a lot of weirdos. I can imagine one falling in love."

* * *

Three hours of hard driving later, Kristen and Tina watched the parole board public information clerk stare as the printer sputtered to life. Over the next minute, it spat reams of paper. Kristen had managed to charm the clerk into producing the information without a formal open records request, which would have taken weeks.

The clerk checked her watch for the umpteenth time, folded the list, and handed the stack to Kristen. "This is every prisoner whose parole was voted on in the last two years. On the right is the date of release." She stood, shooing them out. "If there's no date, it's pending or denied."

Kristen rose. "Thanks."

"Good luck on your law review article."

Kristen nodded, happy that the cover story had been bought.

Tina followed Kristen out. "There are thousands of names. It'll take days."

"We'll scan both lists into the database program in my office."

* * *

Kristen tapped her keyboard and looked at the screen with anticipation. Bingo.

"We've got a match! Leonard Marrs. Aggravated assault, kidnapping, and rape by instrument. Released in July."

Kristen pulled up the hospital site and used her firm password and the patient ID number from Tammy's list to hack into Marrs's patient chart.

291

Tina leaned over Kristen's shoulder and read aloud:

"Patient is a thirty-year-old white male. Presents with gunshot wound, lateral torso and arm. Is alert and oriented, but in some distress. Denies use of street drugs. Admits consuming two beers. Denies street drugs. Lives alone. Recent parolee. Does not know his assailant. Surgery team called. Police notified."

Kristen picked up the phone and punched the number of the police hotline. Before it rang, she hung up, realizing they could identify the caller.

"Let's find a pay phone, since we just committed a federal crime that could get us ten years."

"*You* committed a federal crime. I was an innocent bystander."

Kristen deleted the lists from her computer, logged off, and hopped up. "Come on."

She led her sister to the back door of the Wright McGee offices and locked it once they were on the other side.

Tina pushed the elevator button. The car arrived immediately, and they reached the ground floor, avoiding security by taking a side door.

Kristen pointed up the deserted street. "There's a phone at the Hertz station."

They hurried along the empty downtown sidewalk and found an unbroken phone.

Kristen fished for change in her purse, and slid the coins into the slot. An irritable-sounding man answered. She pictured a cop munching on a Bavarian cream doughnut. "I've found a suspect on the Stern case. Leonard Marrs. He's a rapist paroled by Mrs. Stern."

"Hang on a second. We're taking notes on another call."

Other calls at ten o'clock? They were overwhelmed. By the time the police sorted through another tip, Sarah could be dead. If Michael paid the ransom tomorrow, the kidnapper had no incentive to keep Sarah alive. She hung up. "Let's go."

"Where?"

"We're going home to get my pistol. We're going to find her."

"You've got a gun?"

"Welcome to Texas."

"Kristen, you've lost your fucking mind."

"Yes, but in its current condition, it can't go far." Before Tina could argue further, Kristen added, "After killing Diana, he's not going to let Sarah live another minute longer than he has to. He's already staring at the death penalty for killing a public official."

"I don't want any part of this."

Kristen gripped her sister's arm, digging her nails into Tina's wrist, like she'd done for more than twenty years. "Come on, Tina. I need help."

* * *

Freddie Lee Lance shoved open the door of his Bonneville. He studied the first address on the slip of yellow paper the parole officer had given him. Spotting a faded number on the house next door, he slowly did the arithmetic and satisfied himself that he had the right place. Marrs's house sat dark, the blinds open, but he grabbed his gun from under the seat anyway.

Lance levered himself out and tromped his size 13E's across the empty, cracked driveway.

Two houses away, scrawny Latino kids leaned against a dirty pickup, smoking and laughing. As their eyes met his, he glared, and they shut up.

He took another look around before reaching the crumbling front steps.

Freddie looked through a tiny window in the door and saw nothing but greasy film on the glass. Whipping out a piece of brass the size of a swizzle stick, the professional burglar jimmied open the rusty lock so fast, it looked like he'd used a key.

CHAPTER 39

FROM HER CAR, KRISTEN surveyed the block. Tiny frame houses were nestled together, yards jammed with old cars and littered with trash. Marrs's castle hunkered down in total darkness. Two houses down, a stereo blared "Bohemian Rhapsody." Next door, kids who should've been in bed sat under a street light jabbering.

Tina slunk lower in the passenger seat as a train whistle ricocheted down the narrow street. "Okay, *Poirot*, we found it. Now, do the little gray cells say, 'Call the cops?'"

Kristen stared at the dump for several minutes before deciding.

"The driveway's empty, there's no garage, and it's dark inside, so he must be gone. I'm going to take a look."

"Maybe he rides the bus. Maybe he's asleep with a gun under his pillow."

"His employment is sales. He'd need a car to sell anything. The records say he lives alone."

"And we all know records *never* lie."

Kristen couldn't argue the point, so she let it pass.

Tina grabbed Kristen's arm. "These cracker boxes are three feet apart. The neighbors will hear you, if they don't spot you."

Two phone numbers for Marrs appeared on the hospital chart. The prefix on one looked like a mobile. Hopefully the other was a landline into this house. Kristen punched the second number.

"People around here don't call the cops," Kristen said. "Besides, I can handle most men."

"You haven't competed in years. According to you, the only guy you 'handled' lately was a one-armed wimp. This guy kills."

Kristen let the phone ring until she got the machine, then clicked off. "If you see anybody coming, ring me. I'll spring the instant I hear it and be out before he gets on the porch."

She retrieved the flashlight, the Browning, and her Yankees cap from the console, then walked to the trunk and pulled a screwdriver from the tool kit. She was churning out so much adrenaline, her hands shook.

She handed the pistol, butt-first, through the window to Tina. "Careful. It's chambered. Double-action. You don't need to touch the hammer, but flip the safety before wasting anybody. Move over and be ready to peel out."

Tina shoved the gun back. "I'm not having a thing to do with this."

Kristen wanted to smack Tina. Under the adrenaline rush, she could only count to three.

"Tina, I've got to have a lookout." She wanted to add, *You fucking owe me*, but instead let her expression say, *Help, or I'll break your thumbs.*

Tina rolled her eyes and took the pistol. "You must be off your Xanax."

"Give me a break."

Kristen tucked her hair under her ball cap and turned away from the car. It took all the bravado she could muster to stride up Marrs's cracked driveway, but she had the element of surprise. No way would he expect her.

At the side of the house, she was greeted by the stench of dog shit a second before the neighbor's big, snarling mutt darted from behind a wheelless pickup and leaped at her. Only the short chain link fence kept her from being mauled. Her heart bounced off the inside of her sternum. She flattened herself against the side of Marrs's house, squeezing her Kegels to keep from pissing her pants. So much for the element of surprise.

She kept still, hoping the dog couldn't or wouldn't scale the fence.

After an interminable minute, it dropped its paws from the fence, but kept barking.

Breathing again, Kristen crept to the back of Marrs's house. She turned the corner and peered into the first dark window. Seeing nothing, she jammed the screwdriver through a gap from the casement, turned the latch, and pushed. Nails in the sides of the frame stopped the window. She walked to another and got the same result. But the tumbler on the back door looked as decrepit as the house.

Lights came on next door. Kristen ducked behind an overgrown bush. A strip of cloth parted, revealing a pair of searching eyes. After an anxious minute, the place went dark again.

When the blast of war blows, imitate the tiger.

Kristen hurried up the steps to the back door. She aimed at the lock above the knob, rocked back on her left heel, kicked, and blasted the door open. The stereo down the street kept blaring Freddie Mercury's "We Are The Champions." The dog barked, but inside nothing stirred.

Brandishing the screwdriver, she switched her flashlight on and tiptoed in. On her third stride, a loose board under the buckling kitchen floor creaked. Her heart revved. She froze, but heard nothing else. Another plank groaned as she continued.

The place smelled like wet cardboard. A sweep of the beam around the main room revealed cases of pasta and a computer monitor on a rickety table. Porn magazines lay over the keyboard. A roach scurried from the light, then disappeared under the baseboard. On the table, a thick laser-printed pile of paper listed the prices of everything from apples to zucchini. Brochures and business cards identified the company as Foodsmart and the salesmen as Jimmy Johnson and Leonard Marrs.

She crept into a hallway and opened a closet. A rust-stained hot water tank sat silent. She wiped off her prints with her jacket sleeve. In the tiny bathroom she knelt and examined the dirty gold vinyl floor with the narrow beam, finding short brown hairs that made her cringe. The toilet seat revealed a few more strays, none blond.

The bedroom closet sported a few wrinkled shirts, draped over hangers. Bending down to look under the lumpy bed, she sneezed. As she opened her eyes and sniffed, the flashlight illuminated a newspaper clipping among the dust bunnies. She grabbed it and studied the faces in the *Morning News*, swallowing hard when she read the names in the caption.

She slipped the clipping into her windbreaker and forced herself to take one more look around. Walking through his house was like wading barefoot through a sewage plant, fishing in shit for used condoms.

Kristen spotted a hatch in the hallway ceiling, and pushed a flimsy chair from the kitchen toward it with her foot. Standing on it, she checked her watch. Already three minutes. She used her elbow to pop the cover. She poked her head through and flicked her light toward the dark attic. Nothing but used tires and boxes, none large enough for a five-foot-something girl.

A car sped down the street. Somebody shouted. She dropped the lid back. Hurrying out the shattered door, she ran back to the car so fast that the dog didn't have a chance to maul her.

Tina pulled the stick into drive as Kristen piled in. "Didn't think you were going to get past the Hound of the Baskervilles."

"We got the right guy, but no sign of Sarah." Kristen grabbed Tammy's list and held it to her flashlight as Tina peeled out. "Marrs works with or for somebody named Jim Johnson."

"The NASCAR dude?"

"Not that classy." Kristen scanned Marrs's admit sheet from the hospital. She clenched a fist in the air. "Jim Johnson's address is here. He's Marrs's guarantor! From the zip, this place is out north. Let's pay a visit." Kristen dialed the number in her cell. "I'll see if anybody's home."

"Kristen, this is crazy."

"It runs in the family."

After four rings, a machine answered and she clicked off.

"We've got a chance to grab her. Now. Not when the cops decide to do something."

"What if Sarah's buried behind the dirtbag's house?"

"Drive!"

* * *

Wearing latex gloves they'd bought at a late-night drugstore and clutching the Browning automatic behind her back, Kristen tapped Johnson's doorbell. The lackluster 1970s one-story brick rancher seemed an unlikely venue for a kidnapping. Again the place was dark, not even a porch light on.

Tina pressed herself against the buff brick next to the storm door. "How do you know he'll answer?"

Kristen hit the button again. "If he's innocent, he will."

"What if he's clean?"

"He can tell us."

Tina snorted in exasperation. "Even if Johnson knows something, how are we going to get him to talk? Expect me to seduce him?"

Kristen rolled her eyes and mashed the bell again. "Our advantage over the police—*Miranda* doesn't apply to us."

"What if he answers the door with a shotgun?"

"We're sorry. We got the wrong house."

Although Tina drove her nuts, Kristen knew she was right—absolutely right. She had no real plan, and the thought of dying, of

299

never seeing Michael again, made her legs heavy, almost paralyzed. But without Sarah, she and Michael had no future.

Kristen knew people in this neighborhood did call the cops. She had an idea.

Thirty minutes later, she smiled at the chubby locksmith as he wedged himself out of his miniature Toyota pickup.

"Thanks for coming. I feel pretty stupid, locking myself out."

He gave the sisters an up-and-down and beamed. "Happens ever' night." He reached into the pocket of his camouflage hunting vest, pulled out a tin of Skoal, stuck a pinch in his mouth, then waddled up to the front door of Johnson's house. His metal tool kit clanked on the concrete porch. Kristen flinched, but no lights came on.

"This ya'll's house?"

"Yes. I'm Kristen. Kristen Johnson."

"I'm Tee-na."

Tina did an admirable job of sounding like she'd been raised in Texarkana instead of Philly.

The locksmith eyed the cursive letters *JJ* engraved on the brass door knocker on the front door and sucked his cheek in, getting an extra buzz from his snuff. "You know, in a nice neighborhood like this, I ought to ask for an ID."

Kristen dug through her purse. "I haven't changed my name on my license since Jim and I got married."

He jiggled a wire in the lock. "My third wife took a year to change hers."

Kristen nodded at Tina. "Hotshot here was married four years and never changed hers."

Tina drawled, "Reckoned it wouldn't last a month."

"Let's see." Kristen pawed through her purse. "Did I leave it here? The keys might be with my wallet. You know how us girls are."

The guy looked up from his work. "I better take down your tag number."

Kristen nudged Tina.

"The car's all I got from the bastard, except for a black eye and the clap," Tina blurted.

The locksmith threw his head back with a belly laugh and pushed the door open. Kristen joined in the merriment. It was a damn good line. Perhaps the guy would forget about tags and IDs. Kristen paid him, glad she had gotten extra cash for Vail.

Still chuckling, he piled into his truck without another glance at the BMW, and drove away.

Kristen tugged on gloves, pulled the Browning 9 mm from her purse, and pushed it toward Tina. "Park by that house across the street with the *For Sale* sign. It looks empty."

"You keep it. I'll be all right. This neighborhood's okay."

Kristen patted the cell phone in her jacket. "I'll search. If I don't find her, we'll wait for Johnson. Call me if you see anybody coming."

"How do you know nobody's in there?" Tina asked.

"Well, nobody honest could be, after all this commotion."

"And we're not after anybody honest. You want to fucking die?"

"If I don't come out, get Beth away from Mom as soon as she turns eighteen." Even Tina was more responsible than their mother.

Tina stuck her forefinger at Kristen's nose. "You'd *better* come out."

Kristen motioned for Tina to go.

Tina gave her older sister a last pleading look, then left for the car.

For all her bravery—for Tina's benefit—Kristen was plenty scared. Hesitating in the doorway, she realized she could go to the police with the newspaper clipping. Maybe that would be enough to get them moving. She would live, regardless of what happened to Sarah. She'd already done a lot for her lover. More than anybody could expect.

But Sarah could die tonight, before the cops listened. Sarah might be only feet away.

The question was simple. Like Hamlet's. Live or die? Take action or suffer the consequences?

An image flashed through her mind—Sarah's funeral. Michael sobbing. Her teammates and friends hysterical.

The awful picture stiffened her limbs and stilled her guts. She couldn't live with wimping out.

Once more into the breach. Close up the wall with our dead.

CHAPTER 40

HER RIGHT HAND GRIPPING her automatic pistol, Kristen shined her flashlight with her left and tiptoed through the house. She could turn on the lights, but kept the place dark, so anyone returning wouldn't be alerted. Slivers of streetlight penetrated the half-open blinds and helped a bit.

In the family room, a Naugahyde sectional had been pushed apart. Newspapers lay scattered. The dining area had no place to hide anything. A quick look in the kitchen revealed a pot on the range caked with dried beans, and bowls piled up in the sink. Somebody had missed the trash with two crumpled beer cans. A den off the kitchen loomed empty.

In the first bedroom, her beam caught a kid's bed shaped like a sailboat, with teddy bears on the spread. The closet was cluttered with Legos and more stuffed animals. The room beside it had been converted to an office. Nothing there. Next, a smaller bedroom, all tidy, appeared ready for a guest. Zilch.

Reaching the master bedroom, she saw linens had been flung back onto the carpet. An oil landscape of prairie cows hung over the bed. Family photos cluttered the dresser. She started for the bathroom, but decided to check the walk-in first. Bright women's dresses, which looked to be at least size sixteens, draped over hangers on one side;

men's duds hung on the other. She dropped the beam of her light to the floor.

Rope and a roll of duct tape lay tangled in a pile.

She picked up a tangled chunk of used tape and held it to the beam. A long blond hair adhered to it. She smelled urine.

Her flashlight caught a big round object against the wall, partly covered by hanging clothes. She retreated to the closet door, closed it, and flipped the switch. An Oriental runner was rolled up, tied with string, and bulging with something inside.

Hail Mary.

Sticking the pistol and the flashlight in her windbreaker, her heart thundering, she hurried to the rug, knelt, and looked down the end.

My God!

Before she could unroll the carpet, the closet door flew open. She turned to see a huge black guy, then an enormous sneaker flying at her.

She twisted away, but the foot caught her in the ribs, knocking her against the rug.

She groped in her jacket for her pistol. Before she could grip the handle, another shoe pounded her chest, blasting the air from her lungs.

The giant leaned over and grabbed her wrists.

Gasping, her body slow to answer her commands, she tried to buck her hips and wedge her knee up to kick him off, but he wouldn't budge.

He grinned at her helplessness.

The monster slapped one cheek, spinning her face. He leered and backhanded the other. Her face felt on fire, but his blows freed one arm. Just as she reached the pistol, he pounded her temple. The closet light flickered.

The intruder jammed a cold steel barrel under her chin.

It took a second for her rattled brain to analyze her predicament. No options.

She let herself go limp and whispered, "Okay."

Accepting her surrender, he lowered his handgun and shoved her flat on the floor. He sat on her belly, and pinned her arms with his legs. The goon fished in her pocket and pulled out the Browning. Holding it at eye level, he beamed, short a front tooth. "N-nice."

His breath, smelling of bacon grease and rotting teeth, made her gag.

He patted her other pocket and lifted the phone. Standing, pointing his gun, he motioned her to roll over.

She managed to flop onto her belly, praying to the Blessed Mother Tina had heard or seen something.

* * *

Marrs checked the block before getting out of Jimmy's car. Rap drifted from the shooting gallery up the street. Fag music competed next door. Lights from the dump next to it suggested the household's elderly citizens were awake and petrified behind their barred windows. No sign of Freddie or a pimpmobile. The other guy he'd seen was probably a loan shark collector.

The manager at the Cactus Grill said he could only meet him at midnight. Really? Midnight? So then when he got there, the asshole had to see the *entire* price sheet . . . which Leonard left in the rental dump. But it was important to keep everything looking normal for another day. Soon he'd be in Costa Rica shopping for villas.

Marrs climbed the crooked concrete steps to his house, inserted the key, and pushed the door open. He switched on the overhead fixture, casting a pale light through cobwebs and dead bugs inside the globe. As he scooped up the printout from the table, a breeze swept in from the kitchen.

He saw fresh wood splintered out where the doorjamb once met the dead bolt. He intended to inspect the damage, but realized the cop-blaster probably had Jimmy's address.

* * *

Marrs drove up the block and spotted an ancient car, complete with fins, parked six houses down. Unless bootleggers were back in vogue, it didn't belong in this neighborhood. Marrs drove around and parked the Cherokee on the street north and parallel to Jimmy's. He got out and grabbed the electronic garage door opener.

The house behind Jimmy's was dark. Hoping the dog slept inside the house, he slunk up the driveway to the backyard stockade fence. He eased the gate open, listened for a moment, then snuck into the neighbor's backyard. Hearing nothing, he dashed across the yard, dodged a swing set, and assaulted the back fence. In a second, he was scraping his hands on rough wood, but on top and over. He ran to Jimmy's back door, which opened into the den.

* * *

Inside the closet, the black man planted his knees on Kristen's spine, and tied her hands behind her back with cord and tape from the floor. He rolled her over.

"Who y-you, b-babe?"

Kristen suspected the thug wasn't Johnson, but still had no idea who he was. Was he with or against Marrs? Did he have any idea Sarah was there? She decided *against and no.*

"I'm after Marrs."

He wormed a hand under her shirt and squeezed a breast. "That g-give us somethin' in common."

Kristen couldn't shake his hand off. "He hurt a friend of mine."

"That so? He fuckin' killed m-my cousin."

He stroked her butt with one hand, squeezed a cheek with the other, then dug a finger into the crease of her jeans.

"N-nice ass."

She jerked and tried to kick him, more from reflex than thought. He tapped her jaw with the butt of his gun.

"My guess be, b-baby-face out looking for a d-date. Bet he be back here soon." One mammoth hand lifted her by her waistband, the other fumbled with the snap on her jeans. "Relax, babe. You g-gonna love black snake."

She bit her lip, fighting a scream. Her heart threatened to blow out her chest cavity, which hopefully would turn him off. She pressed her pelvis back to the carpet, but his grip easily held her up. The snap popped. Her zipper clicked down fast, a ripping noise.

She pleaded, "The cops are coming. He's wanted for murder."

Without bothering to untie them, he pried her sneakers off. His greedy fingers clutched the elastic band of her underwear, the scraggly fingernails scratching her. "Now I be d-doubtin' you called the po-lice before l-lyin' your way in. I heard ever'thing with that lockman." He yanked her jeans and panties to her knees.

She smelled his sweat, sensed his excitement. She'd known pain from basketball injuries, blows she hadn't blocked in martial arts, but knew nothing would compare.

Hail Mary, full of Grace.

"Quit wigglin'!" He tugged her jeans and drawers off, one leg at a time. His massive hand wandered over her crotch. The sensation of his touch sent her into a choking gag reflex. She wanted to fight, risk death to keep him from her, but told herself resistance would only make pain worse.

"Ever take it in the b-back door?"

She tried deep breaths to keep from shrieking. If Sarah joined in her screaming, made any noise, she'd be another victim.

A zipper sound.

Hail Mary, Full of grace.

She tried to send her mind elsewhere, to think of anything but this, but couldn't. Terror stayed right with her, gripping her like she was in a vise, making every breath difficult.

A rattling noise on the other side of the house penetrated the closet.

"Fuck! There he b-be." He shoved himself off her, pulled her by her hair, and slapped a piece of duct tape over her mouth. Hurrying to tape her ankles together, leaving her half-naked, he said, "You be r-real quiet. I'll take care of that p-pervert and b-be back."

* * *

Peering inside, Marrs spotted the hulk creeping through the family room taking a position for an ambush in the kitchen. Freddie would think Marrs was entering from the garage. He hit the remote again. With the rattle of the closing garage door providing sound cover, he slipped his key in the den back door and unlocked it. His timing perfect, he eased the door open the instant the overhead banged down on the concrete floor.

Crouching, his sweaty hand choking his revolver, Marrs dashed inside.

Near the kitchen door into the garage, light from the window over the sink silhouetted the ex-con. Marrs dropped onto his belly and fired.

Return fire erupted from the kitchen. He felt air swish above him.

Marrs emptied his last rounds.

Silence.

Dead silence.

Marrs lay still, watching the kitchen for a minute before getting up and switching on the light. Freddie's massive carcass lay slumped against Jimmy's refrigerator, his hand near a nickel-plated automatic pistol. A faint sucking noise came from the big man's chest. His mouth gurgled pink foam. His last heartbeats spread crimson blood over his white shirt.

Marrs's instinct told him to run. But he thought for a second. He'd shot a prowler. No crime here, just a dead cop-shooter in violation of his parole. They might even give him a bounty. He could claim the gun was his brother's, perfectly legal inside a law-abiding citizen's home.

They had nothing to tie him to the Stern case, nothing for it to even cross their minds. Zelner couldn't make trouble, since he'd obviously given Freddie the address. Parole boy had no idea Marrs had serious cash stuffed in the closet.

But to be safe, he decided to hide the kid in the attic before calling the cops. He guessed they'd half-ass glance around, but wouldn't bother to look there.

* * *

Hearing gunfire, Kristen redoubled her efforts to get free. She worked her wrists raw, back and forth. Using all her strength, she still couldn't stretch the cord and tape enough to free her hands. She tried to pull her knees up, lever her wrists under her feet, and get her hands in front, where she could use them.

Shit. She wasn't limber enough and was too tall.

Whichever desperado survived the shootout, she was going to get raped and slit from ear to ear. She hoped Tina sitting in her car across the street could hear gunfire from inside a closed house, but she doubted it.

Think.

Kristen saw a large nail driven into the wall, about five feet above the floor, serving as a belt rack. If it was in a stud, and not Sheetrock, she might be in luck. She backed and bounced, stretching her hands high, but missed the nail. Not even close.

She spotted a wicker clothes hamper, struggled toward it, dropped back to the floor, and kicked it over. By pushing off the wall, she was able to scoot the bin across the carpet under the nail. She staggered up and bunny-hopped on top of the bin.

There were enough dirty skivvies inside that the sides held. From a squat, she leaped, stretching her arms, straining her shoulders. On the second try the cord hooked around the nailhead. It bent, but held on the way down, tugging the cotton rope enough to loosen a hand.

Kristen shook off the rope, ripped the tape from her ankles and mouth, and pulled on her panties and jeans.

She tore the string on the rug apart. Two spins of the carpet revealed Sarah, tied and gagged.

She felt Sarah's neck. A pulse. *Thank God.*

She made sure her nostrils were clear, and decided to leave her out of the way of the coming fireworks.

Catch your breath and think.

If the black guy won the shootout, her only chance would be to get out before he returned for his entertainment. He was armed and far too big to fight. But if he lost, she'd have surprise on her side against Marrs. From what Rita described, she could take him. She switched off the light, cracked the door, and listened.

"Stupid fucking nigger."

No stutter. Marrs.

If she fled now, the guy would know he was busted and kill Sarah. Slip out and try to find the big dude's body . . . and hopefully her pistol? Even if the black man fired it, instead of his, her Browning held thirteen rounds and she hadn't heard that many shots.

The words grew louder, the voice closer. "I'll fucking kill Zelner."

She stepped back and assumed a combat stance. Despite her exhaustion, a last dose of adrenaline surged through her, sending energy back to her sloggy legs. Her heart went to ramming speed. The next few seconds would determine whether she and Sarah lived or died.

The bedroom light came on. *Holy Mary, give me strength.*

The closet door opened, revealing a short, wiry man. He blinked with astonishment at this unknown woman with a battered face. Kristen planted her bare left foot on the soft carpet. She thundered her right sole into his knee at the instant he started turning away.

Damn it! She'd missed a square blow that would have shredded every ligament.

Howling, Marrs collapsed.

Maybe she hadn't done all that bad.

She gathered her balance and kicked at his nose, but he spun away. She only grazed cheekbone.

Tina was right. She spent too much time in the office. The guy should already be toast. Or maybe fear had sucked her strength away.

Frustrated, breathless, she reminded herself this was the human debris who'd kidnapped Sarah and killed Diana.

Take him apart! No excuses.

The guy had experience. He kept his pelvis rotated slightly, making his crotch a harder target. Going for the knockout, she drove her foot again at his head, missing as he backed into the bedroom.

She followed. This time she aimed for his sternum, a bigger target, hoping to knock the wind out, paralyze him. But he had fast hands. His wrist slapped her ankle aside.

His parry gave him time to stagger up, using the wall for balance, listing to his good leg. He dug into a back pocket and came out with a knife. She reset herself, shielded her torso with her left arm, and punched at his nose with the heel of her right palm. A shattered nasal septum ended most fights.

But he ducked, thrusting up with his knife, causing her to hit his forehead. The blade caught her sleeve, nicking her arm. She felt a sting and a trickle of warm blood.

You're fighting like a green belt rookie!

Before she could strike again, he retreated farther into the bedroom, making half-thrusts with what looked like a switchblade, obviously hoping to sucker her into a mistake. The guy had fought before.

Any blow she delivered now risked her getting stabbed. She could try to kick the weapon out of his hand. Heroes did it in the movies.

However, Marrs was no stuntman hired to make it look easy. Still, a cut foot was better than a stuck belly. She faked to her right, rotated left, focused on the knife, and kicked.

He dodged and slashed, ripping her jeans, nicking her ankle. The blade was incredibly sharp and so was the pain.

Marrs circled the knife, creating a more difficult target. "Come and get it, sweetheart, whoever the hell you are."

This battle was stupid. *Find your pistol, dummy.*

Her cell rang. It had to be on the black guy. She backed toward the noise, kicked to cover her retreat, gained a couple of feet, then turned and sprinted. Fast, as fast as she'd ever run.

Marrs couldn't keep up with her on one good leg.

She followed the noise into the kitchen and spotted Bigfoot, reeking of shit, leaning against the refrigerator in a pool of blood, his eyes open. She started to grab the pistol next to his mammoth hand, but the slide had locked open, empty.

The sound of coughing neared.

Careful not to step in the puddle, she rummaged in the black man's jacket and found the ringing phone, but not her pistol.

Marrs shuffled, dragging a leg, mummy-like, into the kitchen, his face a portrait of pissed-off pain.

She was cornered against the wall, blocked by the fridge and the body. If he got in close, he'd have the advantage. She wouldn't have room to maneuver or kick.

Marrs limped closer, cautiously, slicing air with the knife, but showing respect for her ability. "Got you now, cutie."

Her gun had to be in the goon's other pocket against the linoleum. Fright surged as she struggled to lift the dead man's shoulders. He had to weigh three hundred pounds.

She looked around and saw a set of kitchen knives in a wooden holder between her and the killer. She might beat him to them. *Might.* He was slow, but closer to the blades and probably a lot better in a knife fight.

Marrs giggled and edged closer, seeming to gain confidence or sense her fear. "That your pal there? With the empty gun? Ready to join him in hell?"

She used her knee to wedge Bigfoot's torso up, and found her Browning pistol stuck in his pants. The big pistol caught on the pocket. She couldn't jerk it free. *Shit!*

Marrs stopped, now looking uncertain.

With one last effort, Kristen ripped her double-action automatic out, tearing the pocket. She had to step back to keep from falling. Her bare foot landed in the thug's warm, sticky blood and slipped. Kristen caught herself awkwardly against the fridge.

While she struggled to stand, Marrs hobbled out of the kitchen.

She braced herself against the cabinets, but her wet sole slid again, taking her to her knees.

Shit!

Her fingers struggled to flip the safety. She grabbed a cup towel from the fridge door handle and wiped her sole with it. Her weapon ready, she tore after him. She was Joan storming the medieval walls of Paris.

Before she got through the den, she heard a ripping crash, almost as loud as a shot.

"Kristen?"

She ran toward the racket, reached the front entryway, and saw Tina, flushed and waving a tire tool. The front door leaned in on its hinges. "Tina, get behind me! He's in here."

Keeping her pistol poised, Kristen headed for the walk-in, Tina trailing.

"I saw lights. Then you didn't answer."

"You did well. Stay close," Kristen whispered.

Kristen guessed Marrs must have used all his ammo; otherwise she would have faced a gun instead of a knife. Was he looking for bullets?

Or had he fled through the open den door?

She whipped around the corner in the hallway, pistol in front.

Clear.

She ran to the master, hesitated at the door, then exploded into the room, ready to fire.

Nothing.

She opened the closet. No Marrs.

"Give me a hand."

Maintaining her grip on the pistol, Kristen unrolled the rug.

"Holy Mary and Joseph."

"Carry her. I'll lead us out."

* * *

His knee aflame, Marrs limped out of the den to the side of Jimmy's house. He staggered behind the neighbor's minivan and listened through his labored breath. Hearing nothing for several seconds, he risked a glance.

Two chicks fled Jimmy's house, the kid draped over one's shoulder. The vigilante trained her weapon around like Sarah Conner in a *Terminator* movie. They settled the kid into the back of a car across the street and pulled out fast.

Marrs's brain went into overdrive. *Who are those cunts?* Were they with Freddie? Zelner? How'd they get in? Not legally, he decided. Maybe they wouldn't be eager to report their exploits.

He remembered the name the second one hollered. *Kristen.* How he'd like to slice her into bass bait.

He started toward Jimmy's Jeep, getting the idea he could still float the prowler story. Maybe Stern had already wired the money. Marrs wouldn't hear from his "partner" until morning, and if he fled tonight, he would be on the run broke. If the money was already in Costa Rica, he could get paid tomorrow, assuming he could bullshit his way out of the Freddie problem. If he didn't report the shooting, he'd give Zelner the excuse to stop him at the border.

Limping back to the house, he recalled everything he'd learned in Huntsville. Once inside he ran the vacuum carefully everywhere, washed the toilet with bleach, then found a thirty-gallon plastic garbage bag. He stuffed the duct tape, rope, and ski mask in with old newspapers for bulk. In the kitchen, he spotted a bloody towel the chick used and tossed it in. Marrs even remembered the vase he'd bonked the girl with and added it to the bag. He hobbled down the street to a neighbor's dark house and added his bag to a pile of lawn bags next to the curb.

His knee shredded, he could barely climb the back fence to retrieve the Cherokee on the next street. It would be suspicious not to have a car here when the cops arrived. After retrieving the Jeep, he loaded the Oriental rug and the Hoover. With each step he thought his kneecap would fall off. A strip mall four blocks away had a dumpster behind it. Some bum would later use the rug as a blanket and have no clue what it was worth.

Back at Jimmy's, he took the spoon and bowl the kid had used and jammed them in the dishwasher. He wiped the woman's footprints up with bleach. He doubted he could walk much more on his injured leg, but took one last look around, satisfied he'd fooled any dumb cop. His knee injury and swollen eye from Wonder Woman constituted evidence of his struggle with the burglar; the smashed front door was proof of a break-in.

As long as the kickboxer didn't flap her mouth, he'd be okay. People don't readily admit to breaking and entering with cop-shooters. If she was a Zelner plant sent to help Freddie—a likely possibility—she'd have to keep quiet. A gamble, but he could sell sand to Arabs.

Marrs dialed 911.

* * *

315

Tina screeched the car to a stop at the ER entrance to Methodist Hospital.

In the backseat, Kristen kept her arm draped over Sarah's shoulder and repeated, "You'll be okay. We'll call your dad."

Kristen let go of Sarah, pulled on her Yankees cap, tucked her hair underneath, and stuck on sunglasses. Tina ran around the car and helped lift the girl out.

"Stay here, Tina," Kristen said.

Kristen hoisted Sarah onto her shoulder and carried her through the automatic doors. In the waiting area, she passed a miserable-looking guy holding a compress to his head, a mom rocking a bawling baby, and a dozen others. Kristen hollered at the annoyed-looking intake clerk in a cubicle that *this was a real emergency.*

After a minute of bickering from the woman, Kristen found the disguised release button next to the admitting door. She pressed it and headed for the examining rooms, blowing past the triage nurse, who stuttered a protest as Kristen hurried by.

Kristen found an empty room. Supporting the kid's head, she eased Sarah onto the exam table. The round-faced triage nurse and the intake clerk followed her into the room, both barking about breach of protocol.

"She's Sarah Stern. Call her father, Michael Stern, in Highland Park, then call the police."

Mouths open, the women stood silent.

"Now! Please!"

After another moment of staring, the nurse finally grabbed the phone. Kristen noticed Sarah's pupils reacted to the bright light, narrowing to pinpoints. *Thank God.*

Another functionary stormed into the room. "You'll have to register this patient. Please step back to the front."

"I've given you her name. She may have a skull fracture." Running fingers over Sarah's head, she found the lump with blood-caked hair and raised her voice over the nurse's telephone discussion. "She's been in and out of consciousness. I found her this way. She's not my kid! I can't sign your forms."

The triage nurse hurriedly finished some instructions into the phone and grabbed a blood pressure cuff. She shooed the info takers out, saying it could wait.

Together they pulled off Sarah's shirt. Kristen noticed a spot of blood on her own sleeve and hoped nobody asked about it.

Kristen helped the triage nurse wrap the cuff around Sarah's arm.

A craggy, heavy woman in scrubs hurried in. "Do we need security?"

Trying to keep a hand over her face and sound harmless, Kristen said, "We'll need somebody trained on the rape kit."

They seemed to size Kristen up and decide she wasn't a threat.

"We're okay. Go get Judy. Tell her to hustle. We can't cath her until she's done. Go to my station. I'll take over here." She asked Kristen, "Who are you?"

Kristen pretended not to hear and continued to describe Sarah's condition.

Before the question could be repeated, a striking woman about Kristen's age with copper-colored hair stepped in. Kristen was relieved as she spotted the "M.D." after the name *Howell* on her hospital ID badge.

"What's going on?"

Kristen reported without looking at the doctor, "Not fully oriented, maybe a skull fracture. Glasgow probably no better than nine. Possible internal bleeding, probable rape. I'm sure she's dehydrated and may need mannitol. She's had the head injury for a while, possibly days. Knee feels very swollen."

The young physician found the crusty gash on Sarah's head, then issued orders in a staccato voice. "CBC, Chem 20, UA, tox screen now, then get her to radiology stat. Plain skull, CT head and abdomen. Type and cross match. This is the Highland Park kid the police have been looking for?"

The nurse nodded at Kristen. "That's what she says."

The doctor glanced at Kristen, then pulled a penlight from her pocket and shined it in Sarah's eyes. "Tell Judy to hurry." The doctor bent closer to Sarah. "What's your name? Sweetie, tell us your name."

The nurse said, "BP's ninety. Pulse 120."

Kristen knew those numbers were abnormal, but thanked the Blessed Mother when Sarah mumbled and tracked the doctor's hand. The doctor urged Sarah to talk while she pushed on the girl's abdomen, then listened to her heart and bowel sounds with her stethoscope. The nurse swabbed an arm. Starting the IV didn't appear to cause Sarah to react to pain. Not a great sign.

But to Kristen's profound relief, she heard, "Sarah Stern." The sound was just above a whisper, with considerable delay from when the question had been asked. But it was heartening nevertheless.

Dr. Howell smiled. "That-a-girl."

The saline began. Color slowly returned to Sarah's face. Kristen decided the situation was under control and slipped toward the door.

The nurse pulled off Sarah's baseball pants, tugging past a nasty purple knee. Sarah wore no panties.

Another nurse, thin and middle-aged, arrived toting a white plastic container the size of a shoebox. Kristen shuddered, knowing what would happen next.

"Find the on-call pediatric neurosurgeon. Did anyone call the cops? Tell anesthesia we may need to go right away. I want her head and belly scanned before we mess with the kit," Dr. Howell ordered. Her voice softened when she turned back to Sarah. "Tell us where it hurts, Sarah. You're going to be okay, but we need you to stay with us."

Kristen slipped out through the commotion, hearing, "Where's the woman in sunglasses?"

She reached the exit without being stopped. Every carb in her blood had been spent; walking out felt like finishing a marathon.

Outside the first automatic door, Tina was jabbering into a phone on a desk. The desk was empty, given the time of night. "Just send a car. The case is wrapped up on a platter. You've got his name and address. Barney Fife could handle it."

Tina slammed the phone down. "Didn't want you getting any dumb ideas, like going back after that asshole."

Kristen tugged Tina outside, heading for the car.

"Aren't we going to wait for the police?"

"No."

Tina trotted to catch up. "We've got to make sure this Marrs gets convicted. You can't be afraid we'll get busted for breaking into that place or messing with hospital records."

Kristen got into the BMW. "We might. Better to shag."

Tina hesitated on the other side. "What about the other guy?"

Kristen dabbed her swollen lips and checked her ankle. Her sock was stained, but the bleeding had stopped—same with her sleeve. "He got what he deserved. Bet they fought over their ransom." She motioned. "Get in."

Tina shook her head. "The paper and TV will be here. We'll be famous."

"Don't be stupid."

Tina eased into her seat and closed the door. "Stern will be so grateful."

The dam burst. All the emotion Kristen had contained that night—emotion over the search, the near rape, the fight—spilled into tears streaking down her cheeks. Her whole body shook.

"It's so . . . so hard for me." She sobbed, tried to inhale between each word. "If . . . Michael wants me . . . loves me . . . me . . . not for—"

Tina slipped an arm around Kristen's shoulder, squeezed, and finished Kristen's speech. "For saving his kid."

Kristen managed to nod, her crying intensifying. She struggled with the ignition, her hand too palsied to insert the key. Her head collapsed against the wheel. The tough girl—too small for the paint, but who rebounded with the bigs, and who once trained to fight competitively—was done.

"I'll drive."

Kristen cried through hands plastered on her face.

"But I'm afraid we're going to get in trouble."

CHAPTER 41

MARRS KEPT HIS INJURED leg iced and elevated on Jim's lounger while the police huddled, whispering to each other, in the kitchen. So far, they'd been considerate and sympathetic, apparently buying the shot prowler story. Perhaps they were glad he'd saved taxpayers serious money.

The Dallas PD homicide detective finished inspecting the bullet holes behind Freddie, then said something to the uniformed guys who'd answered the 911 call. They bobbed agreement. The photographer shot pictures of Freddie from every conceivable angle, like a Pulitzer awaited him.

The Hispanic detective walked back to the den and spoke to Marrs, "I'm sure the DA will call this self-defense. Want to come in and give a statement while they get the body out?"

Marrs wiped an eye. "Feel so terrible. Killing a man."

He watched for a reaction to his melodrama, saw none, and debated whether to divulge knowing the stiff on Jim's kitchen floor. Zelner had undoubtedly told Freddie where to find him and wouldn't admit to setting up this rendezvous. But Marrs knew that if the cops suspected more than an honest homeowner plugging an anonymous intruder, they would have probable cause to search both his houses.

Before Marrs could decide, the busted front door flew open. Without any invitation, a tall, broad-shouldered, uniformed Dallas cop marched in. He had a boot-camp haircut and a mole on his temple, which looked like it was leaking brake fluid. "Need help?"

Marrs had seen this guy before.

The detective seemed to recognize the big cop and stepped back, appearing almost intimidated. He shook his head. "We're good."

"Sure?"

The detective hesitated. "Yep."

The newcomer asked, "Mind if I use your pisser?"

"No problem." Marrs pointed at the small bathroom off the den.

The detective held up a palm. "Not here. Part of the scene."

The big cop thumbed like a hitchhiker. "Back there, okay?"

Marrs hesitated. "Uh-huh."

The storm trooper disappeared down the hall.

Marrs's mind raced until he remembered.

Zelner's buddy.

The plotters now knew Freddie failed.

Sweat trickled down his butt crack.

He wasn't safe around either his parole officer or his enforcer.

* * *

Friday, October 13

Stern looked up from his sleepless stupor to see Burrows enter the surgical waiting room at Methodist Hospital and rumble toward him. He carried a paper cup of coffee, also sporting droopy bags, as if he, too, had been up all night.

Stern stood on wobbly legs, his reserve tank of energy empty.

Burrows offered no formalities, as if no time had elapsed since their last little get-together. "How's your daughter?"

"In recovery. They drained a hematoma under her skull."

Burrows stroked his mustache. "Never heard of a kidnap victim deposited at a hospital. How'd she get here?"

Burrows's cigarette stench annoyed Stern almost as much as his phony concern. "No thanks to the police."

"How much ransom did you pay?"

Stern rubbed his dry eyes. Since the question hadn't the dignity for an immediate response, he waited another moment before replying. "You got half the force following me. You'd know if I hit an ATM for fifty bucks."

"I stopped at your girlfriend's house late last night. Nobody home. Where's she been?"

Stern had decided to wait until a civilized hour to call Kristen with the wonderful news. He answered honestly, "I don't know."

* * *

Banging on the door jarred Kristen awake. She removed the ice pack from her throbbing face and pushed her limp body from her couch, where she'd dozed off to the early morning news. She had lived the last week on shallow naps—lingering nausea prevented real sleep. It was just as well. Nightmares of the big goon tugging off her pants were likely, if and when she slept again.

She opened the door to find a fat man with an out-of-control mustache, and eyebrows that looked to be mating. He was badly in need of a shave. He dug into a sport coat the color of pond scum, and his ragged, dirty fingernails produced a badge.

"Ms. Kerry, my name's Burrows. Highland Park. You've been hard for me to find."

She remembered seeing him at Michael's house Monday night, then realized he had spotted her eye and swollen lip. Too late now. She flipped the latch and pushed the door open. "Coffee? I just got up."

Burrows nodded, stomped in, then stalked her into the kitchen.

While she filled her Krups coffeemaker, he stood silent, but uncomfortably close. His wrinkled gray slacks were too short to hide his lime-green socks. Kristen guessed he hadn't made the top ten best-dressed cop list.

The coffeemaker sputtered into action, spitting out a full cup. She motioned the detective to sit.

He settled in with a groan. She forced herself to look calm, and pushed the mug across the table.

Burrows pulled out a pocket recorder and flipped it on. After a short preamble establishing permission to record, he asked, "What happened to your face?"

"Pickup basketball gets rough." The lie flew out. She instantly regretted it.

He looked skeptical, so she added, "Some big girl I'd never played with before didn't like my rebounding and took a poke at me."

The bushes on his forehead rose. "Where were you yesterday? And last night?"

Kristen doctored her coffee, trying to get a grip. Would confessing lead to opening up her whole life? They might not believe the truth. They'd figure only a lunatic would have done what she did, and they'd be half-right.

"At the Y, playing ball, out to eat with my sister. My firm wants me to stay away."

The cop frowned. After a moment he asked, "Are you and Stern having an affair?"

She felt like a boxer pinned against the ropes, unable to get away. "I guess. We spent last weekend together."

"Were you with him in Colorado?"

She cradled the warm mug and sat across from the detective, reminding herself of the advice she gave her own witnesses. *Just answer the question that's asked.*

"Yes."

"The whole weekend?"

"Every minute."

"When exactly?"

"Friday night until Monday afternoon when we got back to the Denver airport."

"How'd he get the cut on his chin?"

"He fell. He's a better golfer than hiker."

"Did he call home?"

Kristen sipped her coffee. "Several times."

"Who'd he talk to?"

"I believe he talked to Sarah Saturday morning."

"Did he ever talk to his wife?"

"I don't know."

Burrows stared, making her wish she could run for the border, then said, "Someone, possibly an accomplice, brought Stern's kid to the hospital last night, then disappeared. Any idea who?"

Accomplice?

She stalled, sipping coffee. He had to be joking.

"And you think this person was in on the murder?"

"Who else would know where the kid was?"

She realized the guy was determined to look for conspiracies under every rock he stumbled over. He had probably solved Jimmy Hoffa's murder in his spare time.

She argued with herself to tell him, then decided it would look worse now. She'd already lied, committing another crime. He had a script and was reading straight from it. She didn't have a copy.

Could somebody ID her? Emergency rooms are busy. She tried to guess what physical evidence they would have to link her to Johnson's house. Had Sarah left prints or DNA in her car? Did they record the tip calls?

Answers didn't come. Her brain had short-circuited from exhaustion.

Burrows sipped coffee, then announced, "There's no forcible entry, and the alarm didn't sound, so I can't rule out a murder-for-hire."

"After Sarah was kidnapped?"

Kristen had nearly added, *you dumbshit*, but stopped herself in time.

"What an alibi! My daughter was taken, so I couldn't have done it."

Kristen's mouth dropped open. She wondered why this bozo was sharing his theories with her. Did he think she was going to give him Michael, if he argued enough? Or was he trying to talk himself into this idiocy?

Her stare locked onto Burrows. For a moment, neither blinked. It was a contest Kristen was determined to win.

"What else?"

Burrows forfeited. "Tell me about your affair."

At first, she thought he wanted to know if Michael was good in the sack. She had to repress a grin. "I asked him on Friday afternoon. He missed my plane, took another flight. He had absolutely no idea before last Friday that I was going to invite him." The smile came despite her effort. "He didn't think I was even interested."

"Did you two discuss how he could get his inconvenient wife out of the picture?"

Kristen ground her teeth, trying to keep her temper under control. "Look, Detective, we had one weekend. One weekend. Michael and I haven't talked since Vail."

"Why not?"

"He's been busy."

Burrows kept staring, like he was dreaming up new plots.

"Are you a Yankees fan?"

Somebody remembered her cap. *Crap.* "No. Phillies." The hat would be burned the instant he left.

"Can I get your photo for my file?" He used his cell to shoot her. "You have no idea who brought the girl in?"

She weighed the alternatives. Would she get disbarred for burglary? For violating federal privacy laws? Would this crackpot think Michael *had* hired Marrs if she came clean? If Tammy denied helping her, and Rita denied shooting Marrs, how could she prove Michael hadn't told her where to find Sarah? In Texas she'd have to prove her innocence, Constitution be damned.

"No clue."

* * *

After leaving Kristen Kerry's slick townhome, Burrows returned to the Highland Park station, where he sipped his sixth cup of coffee since he'd gotten the middle-of-the-night call from Methodist Hospital. As he'd done every morning after Diana Stern was found murdered, he sorted through notes taken by the night guy manning the tip line.

It looked like the usual garbage they'd gotten since Stern announced his million-dollar reward—crank calls telling them to look for Al Capone or Bonnie and Clyde. And lots of names of ex-cons.

As he got up for a refill, he spotted two different messages on Leonard Marrs. The intake described the second caller as highly agitated. She'd even given a vague location where Marrs lived and where his brother's place was. Burrows went to the printout, showing the caller's phone number.

The first came from a pay phone downtown. The second . . .

A sip of coffee went down the wrong pipe. He coughed.

Methodist Medical Center. *Shit and shinola.*

The time listed was five minutes before he received word the Stern kid had been brought in by an unknown woman, described as tall, early thirties.

Burrows played the original recording.

He shook his fist. The voice on both calls sounded like Kristen Kerry. He'd flipped the sodden house upside-down before Stern came back from Colorado, but turned up only a dead woman in a bathtub and a lot of crap collected by rich people.

A lawyer might not keep secrets at home, but his office could be a different story.

Assuming it was Kristen on the tip line, what was the connection with this Leonard Marrs character, who the caller had helpfully added was a convicted rapist?

Burrows called his assistant and told him to get a warrant, then find what he could on Leonard Marrs. Burrows drove downtown.

Two hours later, after he and one of the uniforms had pawed through Stern's desk, Burrows tugged on Stern's credenza. Locked. Burrows's hopes rose, since the papers in the desk could have been sent to recycle, for all they were worth.

They had negotiated with a nasty-looking partner, some old fart named Jackson, and reached an agreement without having to call the judge. They could search all common areas, Stern's office, and his paralegal's office. The other lawyers' cubbies and client files were off limits as privileged.

Burrows was surprised that Jackson, though concerned about client secrecy, seemed eager to help, like he was thrilled Stern might go to prison.

He remembered what Stern said in their last conversation. *Jackson wants me out; now he sees his chance . . . you've found all my enemies.*

Lawyers were even more cutthroat than he thought. "Who's got the key?"

Tony Caswell, the young partner who'd been feeding them background information, piped up. "There's one in Janet's desk."

The pup attorney played eager beaver, darting out and returning quickly. He tossed a brass key to Burrows. Another one of Stern's enemies? Apparently he had more of those than friends.

Burrows popped the doors open. For a couple of minutes, he rummaged through an unassuming pile of account statements, tossing them all on the floor.

At the bottom was a folder. Inside was a copy of one parolee's file. *Leonard Marrs.*

* * *

That night, sitting in an unmarked car, parole officer Lyndon Zelner helped himself to one of Sergeant McKinnon's doughnuts, hoping the sugar would relieve his building fear. If word leaked he'd given Freddie not only the okay, but the locations, to go after Marrs, he'd lose his job and maybe go to jail. His good deed—trying to save who knows how many women from Marrs—wouldn't go unpunished.

"I can't believe it. Of all the rotten luck! Marrs killing Freddie."

McKinnon scratched the mole on his temple. "Glad he's dead. Goddamn cop-shooter."

"Yeah, but Marrs has my balls in my pocket. He knows I gave Freddie his address."

McKinnon snagged the last powdered sugar donut, crammed the whole thing in his mouth, and mumbled, "We may have somethin'."

He reached into the glove box of his cruiser, retrieved a cellophane bag containing a wad of soft material, and tossed it to Marrs's parole officer.

Zelner caught the baggie. Inside was a pair of panties labeled, Victoria Secret Pink on them. With two daughters of his own, he guessed the owner was about thirteen.

"Found them under the sink in a bathroom at his brother's house. Brother's wife must weigh two hundred, from the size of her getups in the closet. They do have a girl, but there's blood on 'em. From the pictures I saw in the house I don't think their kid has hit puberty. 'Course they could belong to a friend."

"Think he's gotten into girls?"

"Somethin' else odd. When I got there, Marrs was icing his knee like somebody had kicked the shit out of him. Freddie wouldn't have bothered with his leg. He would've just blown the little perv away."

"Okay. We've got evidence. We only need a crime."

"Why not stick 'em in his place, then stumble over 'em at your next drop-in? Looks like a parole violation to me, even if you don't have a vic. Bring another officer, so you got a witness. Won't even have to identify 'em to send him back to Huntsville."

"Let's go."

Thirty minutes later, after Zelner hopped back in the car, McKinnon pulled away from the slummy house that Marrs's brother rented to him.

"Any trouble?"

Zelner's hands were still shaking from his close encounter with the snarling dog next to the house. "Didn't need your pick. Back door was busted open."

McKinnon frowned. "That could be a problem."

"Doesn't matter. My next pop-in visit will turn up a pair of girl's undies in the home of a sex offender."

McKinnon gunned the car faster.

Zelner breathed relief they'd pulled off the stunt.

McKinnon's cell rang. He answered with a growl. Zelner watched his expression change from annoyance to a shit-eating grin.

"What is it?"

McKinnon clicked off. "You're not gonna believe it."

"What?"

"You're not gonna fuckin' believe it."

"Goddamn it, McKinnon, what?"

"Your pervert client is a person of interest in a murder-kidnap."

"What murder?"

"You know, I told pals in other units to be on the lookout for him?"

Zelner was ready to scream. "What murder?"

McKinnon drew a long breath, prolonging Zelner's agony. "Seems

Highland Park got a couple of tips about your boy."

"Highland Park?" It took Zelner a second to connect the dots. "Diana Stern! Holy shit."

"And her thirteen-year-old daughter was kidnapped and probably raped."

"Think we should leave the panties there?"

"Absolutely. We just provided the Stern case foolproof evidence. Marrs will be executed."

CHAPTER 42

Friday, October 17

MARRS HAD HALFHEARTEDLY taken a few food orders while waiting on word from his "partner." Mysteriously, the cell number the guy had given him had gone dead.

The sound of banging on Jim's front door interrupted his anxiety.

Marrs dashed to the entry and spotted a whole squad of cops.

"Mr. Marrs, police. We have some questions."

Marrs opened the door, playing the role of cooperative citizen who'd defended his castle against the scum of the earth. "Sure."

The cops elbowed their way in. The lead guy wore a green coat buttoned around a balloon belly and looked like he hadn't slept in a week. Two uniformed Dallas patrolmen flanked him. The same plainclothes detective who'd popped in after Marrs plugged Freddie trailed the pack. The uniforms rested their hands on their batons, like they were expecting orders to beat the shit out of him.

The Hispanic guy, who had been at Jim's, read the *Miranda* rights.

Marrs decided to take the offensive. "Texas says I got a right to defend my home. Penal Code section 9.32."

The lard-ass frowned, looking surprised by Marrs's brilliance.

Marrs guessed DPD would summarize everything for the DA for a final decision, and that they'd already run his own record.

"Purely a coincidence, but I think I saw that ape in prison. Heard he shot a Dallas cop investigating a burglary, put him in a wheelchair."

Beer-belly asked him why he'd been in the slammer. Marrs answered truthfully, penance plastered on his mug.

"I'm Burrows, from Highland Park."

Marrs squeezed his sphincter tight. He'd assumed these guys were investigating Freddie's death. They had no more reason to tie him to the Stern case than to the Ripper murders, unless Wonder Woman had blabbed. But the news said she disappeared the night she brought the kid to the hospital. And, of course, the news always reported the truth.

"Where you working?"

"For my brother, selling food."

The cop tongued an unlit cigarette. "Keep you busy?"

"Barely time to take a dump."

"Keep records?"

He reached into his back pocket and pulled out his log.

The cop snatched it.

"I work every day."

The cop looked unconvinced. "Even weekends?"

"Sometimes. Last Saturday, I had a big order to take out to a truck stop. Then I went for a late dinner with a friend who works there." Marrs realized he'd volunteered too much.

Burrows flipped through the book. "Lots of calls in my little town."

Marrs shrugged. "That's where the money is."

"Who recommended your parole?"

He met the fat cop's puffy eyes. "I don't understand why you're talking to me."

"Who recommended your parole?" he repeated. "Was it Diana Stern?"

"I was real sorry to hear she died."

"Mind if I borrow this diary?" Burrows asked.

"It ain't copyrighted."

The younger DPD detective stepped forward. "I checked with

334

Freddie's parole officer. Says you and Freddie didn't care for each other. Kind of coincidental a prowler picks the house of a guy he knows and goes in armed. And we reached your brother in Hawaii. Says he doesn't own a revolver."

"Zelner was trying to get me killed. He and that big cop have been framin' me for every crime in this town."

"What were you and Freddie up to?"

"I want a lawyer."

"Did you and Freddie fight over the ransom?"

"I said I want a fucking lawyer. *Comprende?*"

The uniforms jerked Marrs around, face against the wall, and cuffed him. Marrs felt his pecker retract into his pelvis. He could get the big lethal needle.

* * *

Kristen, toting a four-foot-tall stuffed panda, spotted Michael leaving Sarah's hospital room. No point staying apart now, and she craved his touch. She'd slept a little last night, and had smeared moisturizer and concealer on. She hoped she looked somewhat presentable.

She had no idea how he'd greet her in his greatest crisis and feared it might be easy for him to forget her under the circumstances. *Maybe he's already forgotten me or is hitting on a nurse.*

But he beamed, motioning her closer, though he looked ready to crash on the nearest floor.

Despite her determination not to become emotional, tears blurred her vision as she rushed to him. She put the panda down and embraced him, never wanting to let go. In the next second, she felt guilty. His daughter should be his concern, not her.

"How's Sarah?"

"Better."

He kept her in his arms so long, she began to think she could stay forever. With one more squeeze, he stepped back and looked at her.

"Baby, what happened to your face?"

"Basketball. Took a couple elbows, playing with sloppy men."

He squinted, examining her wounds. Kristen prayed he would buy, at least for now, her weak explanation.

She changed the subject back again. "Tell me about Sarah."

"Her vision is normal. There's no more bleeding in her head; the patellar fracture isn't displaced. What did they call it? Only a hairline at the plateau. With a cast, the joint's going to be okay." Stern sniffed. "The worst was telling her about her mother. She's getting Ativan. Thank God, she fell asleep again."

"I'm so sorry." Kristen took his hands in hers. "I was worried about brain damage when the TV said head injury."

He grimaced. "Her recent memory is completely gone, but that's a blessing. It couldn't be good."

She struggled with the question on her mind for days, hoping and praying for a *no*. "Did he?"

"They don't think . . . he . . . just some bruising."

She thought he was going to cry, and realized they had no future. Sarah, even after she healed physically, would be his only concern—should be his only concern. How could she invade their lives, lever herself into a home with a girl who'd been assaulted and her mother murdered? Her dreams of Michael were just that—dreams. It had only been a weekend.

Sarah wasn't stupid. She'd suspect something had been going on between this new chick and her father before Diana died. There'd be talk at school. The stories would get juicier by the day. What could Kristen do in such a horrible situation? Redecorate?

Under her breath, she cursed the bastard who had stolen Vail from them.

"Michael, if I hadn't taken you, this wouldn't have happened."

"I think he was stalking. He'd have struck sometime."

336

"You shouldn't have tried to keep me out of it."

"I love you. I wanted to protect you."

Her brain stopped.

Had she heard him right? *He loved her?* After everything he'd been through?

Her hearing wasn't that bad. Much as she longed to repeat his words, her inner voice screamed "retreat." What if she went all in and it didn't work? Michael would dump her and she'd be shattered.

"Sarah needs you, Michael. All your energy."

"I don't want to lose you. I'll make it work."

Kristen debated whether to tell him about her interview with the fat cop. His idea had to be lunacy, but mistrust lingered, as always. "Burrows came to my house yesterday. He has some crazy conspiracy theory."

His face flushed, his fists clenched. "Idiot cops."

Kristen nodded, feeling reassured by his anger.

Stern seemed to search her face. "Nobody knows who brought Sarah to the hospital. In all the excitement, they let her walk out. Christ, I want to thank her."

She was tempted to tell him, to bathe in his gratitude. He would be hers as long as she wanted him, if she confessed. But would that love be real? Could she commit to him and love in return? And just as importantly, could she trust him?

She decided to keep quiet. She declined his offer to go to the cafeteria for lunch, chatted awhile, and left before Sarah woke up.

* * *

Burrows tossed a cigarette butt into the weeds around Marrs's grimy little house. The county lab people wouldn't let him inside and were treating him like a security guard from the jewelry store. But soon every lawman in Texas would know Rick Burrows.

Before going inside, the county criminalist finished outfitting himself like a spaceman and said, "With the door busted open, anybody could've waltzed in here. A defense lawyer will claim whatever we find was planted."

Burrows sighed, exasperated. "We're checking with the neighbors."

"Bet people here won't be too chatty with the cops."

Before Burrows could continue the argument, the lab guys traipsed inside.

He had time to smoke another before the skinny nerd from county, who hadn't argued with him, yelled, "Got something!"

Burrows took one step into the dump, seeing the crime scene guy holding a pair of tongs, which locked on a dripping cellophane baggy full of cash.

"Found it in the toilet tank. The money looks dry enough to fingerprint."

"There's a pair of girl's panties in the bedroom closet," another lab tech called out.

Burrows grinned. For the rest of his life, he'd never have to buy his own beer, if there was a cop in the bar wanting to hear how he nailed a rich, sleazy lawyer.

* * *

Wednesday

Marrs sat cuffed to the chair in the jail conference room. The place was bare except for a bolted-down table, two chairs, and an empty paper coffee cup full of cigarette butts. A fly had come to its end in the corner. He'd already talked to his appointed attorney that morning. So who was the new lawyer?

A guard opened the steel door and a big guy strutted in. Though at least six-five, his suit fit perfectly, like it came from a special store for tall assholes. His tie was powder yellow, and he sported a cocky smile that suggested he was used to winning babes, as well as cases. His long fingers grasped a single legal pad.

Marrs strained to recall where he'd seen this stud.

"Remember me? Jeff Hudson. I'm a criminal defense lawyer now."

It hit Marrs like a baseball bat to the nose. "You sent me to prison!"

He smiled. "And now I'm here to defend you."

"I got a public defender."

Hudson laughed. "Rookies and do-gooders. I'm for real. I get two hundred grand for a murder defense, but pay me whatever you can."

Marrs squinted. "Is this a setup?"

"You're in big trouble, my friend."

"Thanks for the news flash. Why do you want my case?"

"I want to get a rogue cop." He flashed the winning smile again. "Plus, this case will be big news." He leaned his body over the table. "When I heard that McKinnon showed up after you shot that burglar, I suspected something fishy."

"He wandered all over the house without permission. Practically got out the rubber hose and rammed it up my ass."

The fancy lawyer nodded. "I don't doubt it."

Cursing himself for forgetting the panties, Marrs had concluded McKinnon had grabbed Sarah's britches from the bathroom while pretending to piss. Setting him up for a kiddie rape charge was likely Zelner's backup plan.

The attorney continued, "Every ADA knows McKinnon's dirty, but they all want convictions, so they find a way to live with themselves. I want to shut him down."

"My other lawyer told me they found that girl's panties at my house. I never saw them in my life. McKinnon musta gotten 'em and planted them."

Marrs wished he could tell him he'd never had the kid at his own dump, but figured the lawyer would work harder if he thought Marrs really was innocent.

"DNA proves they were Sarah Stern's."

"I'll tell you who killed that nice lady. Freddie Lance. Wasn't there kinky black hair found in the Stern house?"

"That's what I heard."

"Zelner and McKinnon put that gorille on me. Or Stern did, to cover paying that monster to kill his wife."

"They found money in your house with Stern's fingerprints on it."

"But not my prints! They stashed that, too. How could I get it to my place without touching it?"

Hudson wrote on his pad and stroked his chin.

"I have an alibi witness, too," Marrs added. "Name is Lottie Lewis. I was at her apartment the night the Stern lady died."

Hudson made another note. "Are you and this Lottie involved?"

"Just friends."

"That's not a good alibi."

"They're trying to find an easy mark. Why don't they settle on Freddie?"

"They think you and Freddie Lance were partners."

"What? He was after *me*. Got my address from my favorite parole officer. Zelner and that dirty cop are Laurel and Hardy. I was just a fall guy. Stern probably spotted me in his wife's files and guessed I'd be an easy mark after he'd hired Freddie. Freddie came to kill me. With me dead, the whole case would be put to bed."

Marrs noticed Hudson's hands quiver. He'd sold the guy.

For the first time since he'd been thrown in the slammer, Marrs began to hope he might see daylight again.

* * *

Detective Rick Burrows blew a ring of smoke. It dissolved around the jaundiced face of John Livermore, the assistant DA, who was assigned to big murder cases.

"Told you I'd get that snob."

To emphasize the point, Burrows slid the evidence file across the table. The warrant for Stern's office, which everybody thought was silly, had produced Marrs's parole file. The search of Marrs's house had found forty hundred-dollar bills—six with Stern's prints—and Sarah's panties.

Livermore sniffed his yellow pad. "Marrs could have stolen the money from Stern's house."

"But—"

"Four grand's not much to get a rich wife killed. Even for someone like Marrs."

Burrows couldn't believe the ADA didn't congratulate him. He started to argue about how the four grand was a down payment or that more could be hidden elsewhere, but Livermore waved him off.

"The bigger problem is, outside of the panties, we don't have much on Marrs. That cash hasn't got his prints. His house was wide open when you got there. Thanks to the flood at the Sterns' mansion, we got no fluids, no fibers, no hair. Anything Marrs left washed down the street when the maid opened the door."

"Zelner says Marrs is slick enough to plant the black hair we found on the back stairs above the waterline."

Livermore plowed ahead without responding. "And the worst news is, Stern's kid can't identify Marrs. Fibers on her clothes are from an expensive Oriental rug and there ain't one in Marrs's brother's house, let alone his. The dark hair on her shirt doesn't match Marrs or Freddie."

Burrows coughed and took a drag from his Marlboro.

"I'm not going to discuss this case with you, after they cut out your throat."

Burrows sucked a last puff. "Listen to the call-in tip again. It's Stern's girlfriend. She had to be in on the deal from the get-go." Burrows slapped the cassette into his tape player. "Stern probably prearranged to bring the kid in after the hit."

Livermore contorted his lips in doubt. "But the girl was so roughed up. Had to have head surgery."

"Maybe Stern's original plan didn't include taking the kid, but she was there and saw Marrs. If the gal who brought the kid in was a hero, not in on the deal, then why not collect a million?"

"Are you after Stern because you can't stand the residents of Highland Park, who pay you, or you don't like him in particular?"

Burrows mashed the half-smoked cigarette on Livermore's steel desk and tossed the butt in the trash. He tapped the play button.

"Barney Fife could handle it."

He clicked off. "Sounds like Stern's girlfriend to me."

Livermore hesitated. "Marrs and Lance duke it out, call time, then get out their rods and start blasting each other? Absurd." Livermore focused on Burrows again. "Marrs got clocked by somebody else that night. And isn't it funny? Stern's girlfriend looks like she's been in a bar fight the day after all this comes down."

"Maybe Stern realized the kid was in more danger than he'd planned. Marrs was demanding more money and threatening to kill her. Stern sent his girlfriend to get the kid, since he was under surveillance. Marrs didn't want to turn loose of his insurance policy."

Livermore pressed his yellow pad against his lips. "But where does Freddie fit in? Whose side is he on?"

"Freddie was a *freelance* Marrs hired? Perhaps Marrs screwed Stern by taking the kid. Stern thought his daughter would be gone. Marrs figured he could get a lot more money for the kid than he got for the murder."

"And Kristen Kerry arrives to rescue her *after* Freddie and Marrs shoot it out?"

Livermore tapped his pad against his forehead. "If Marrs starts sweating, he'll finger Stern. Contact surrounding states and the feds for similar unsolved rapes and murders. Marrs is our guy. We got to prove it so we can turn up the heat on Stern."

Burrows nodded. "I'll keep working on the lovely, but bruised, Ms. Kerry and ask the FBI for a voice comparison with the tip line call."

Livermore nodded. "I wish McKinnon hadn't butted in. For once we didn't need him."

* * *

Burrows parted the swinging tin doors into the truck stop's hot kitchen. A vat of grease popped and sizzled as a kid dropped a rack of french fries into the slimy pool. So much smoke and grease filled the air, he didn't need a cigarette. A woman in a ketchup-stained white T-shirt and tight jeans turned away from a stove lined with a battalion of grilling hamburger patties.

"Lottie Lewis?" Burrows asked.

She mopped her forehead with her splattered apron. "You a food salesman?"

Burrows whipped out his badge. "No, Highland Park PD."

She blinked. "You're on the wrong side of town."

She motioned him to follow and led him into a tiny office cluttered with industrial-sized boxes of pancake mix. They sat on steel folding chairs. Burrows flipped on his recorder, blathered the preliminaries, and asked if she knew Leonard Marrs.

She unwrapped a stick of Doublemint. "He's our food dude."

"He claims he was here Saturday afternoon, and you two went out that night."

She crammed the gum between her teeth. "That's right."

Burrows watched her gaze drop. "Did he sleep at your house?"

Showing no embarrassment, she smacked her gum. "Yeah."

"You know he's a suspect in the Stern murder?"

Her face gathered into a look of innocence. "That's what I done read in the paper. But I know Leonard could never do something like that."

Burrows stared. Based on the descriptions from the ER, she couldn't be the rescuer. "Do you have any idea who brought Stern's daughter into the hospital?"

She seemed startled. "No. Ya think I'm psychic?"

Burrows examined her and decided he believed her. Nobody could act that well.

"If you ask me, you oughta be lookin' at the husband. He probably had his wife insured for millions and had a hot new girlfriend."

Burrows nodded.

* * *

Tired of sitting at home worrying, Kristen went downtown to work. She found the stack on her desk shorter than expected.

"Welcome back. Ready to hit it again?"

She looked up, seeing Jen hesitating at the door. Kristen tapped her finger on the paper in her in-box. "Pretty thin gruel. What have you guys been doing with my share?"

"Didn't want you overwhelmed." Jen shuffled closer, as if hindered by a ball and chain. Or afraid she'd get slapped. "I owed you at least that." Jen clasped her hands together. "Krissy, I am so sorry. I don't know how to tell you."

"I'm giving my notice today."

"I was afraid you were going to say that." Jen covered her face. "Kristen, give Pete another chance. All of us. You know I really care about doing right. The good we do outweighs—"

To avoid an argument Kristen held up her hand to stop her, and said with little conviction, "I'll sleep on it."

Jen pushed her fingers through her cropped hair. "The police have been here."

"About Tammy's charges?"

"No, the Stern murder."

Kristen feared she failed to look unconcerned and felt examining eyes. "What'd they ask?"

"If you and Stern were involved. Why I thought Stern threw the trial."

Kristen managed to stifle panic and ask, "What'd you tell them?"

Jen smiled. "I said you'd never let a parking ticket go overdue."

Kristen smiled. "Thanks."

"And that you'd never get involved with a sleaze like Stern."

"Anything else?"

Jen shrugged. "Lots of background stuff. I told him I'd only known you four years. Said you worked hard, liked playing ball, read a lot." She thought a moment. "Oh yeah, I told him you have a black belt."

CHAPTER 43

IN THE METHODIST HOSPITAL boardroom, Burrows handed six photos to the triage ER nurse—one was Kristen Kerry's bar directory picture; another was Stern's paralegal, Janet; and the remaining four featured attractive female cops.

Her plump, pleasant face scrunched with concentration. Sliding the pictures back, she shook her head. "Do you have any idea how many people we get in here every night?"

Burrows passed the photos to the admitting clerk. The needle-nosed woman shrugged, pointing at Kristen. "Maybe. Like I told your partner that night, she had on sunglasses and a Yankees hat. Hard to know exactly what she looked like."

Burrows exhaled his disappointment.

The automatic door swished open. An attractive, late-thirtyish, fair-skinned and freckled woman entered, her name tag identifying her as *Amy Howell, M.D.*

Burrows introduced himself and handed the pictures to her.

She sat and studied the photos while tapping a copper-haired temple. After a full minute she pointed at Kristen's. "Perhaps her, but it was hectic. She'd be the closest."

Dr. Howell pulled another brunette from the stack, a policewoman, but not Janet. "Could be this one. We had this kid who'd been on TV and in the paper. We needed a rape exam. The girl was near shock. I had to get consults and a CT. We could have lost her." She shrugged. "No time to do a third degree on the person bringing her in."

Burrows sucked his lips in disappointment. "Yeah."

"It didn't occur to me she wouldn't stay around."

Wrinkling the skin of her forehead, the admitting nurse added, "I do remember, she was very sweet with the girl. Like the kid was special to her. Not like a kidnapper."

Dr. Howell added, "Whoever it was knew some medicine. Maybe she's a nurse or is married to a doc?"

"What?" Burrows asked.

"She gave me a near-perfect report, knew we'd need mannitol for brain swelling as well as the kit. Calculated the Glasgow scale. She'd worked in hospitals before. I'd bet on it."

* * *

Sitting on her bed, Kristen stroked the concave tip of the top hollow-point 9 mm bullet in the clip, imagining the pain the bastard would have felt as a slug ripped into him and came out flat, the size of a quarter.

Tina stepped in, a newspaper under her arm. She saw the pistol magazine. "You're wishing you'd wasted that scumbag."

"Yes."

Tina flung the paper's local section at her sister. "Look at this! *Police Still Searching for Mystery Woman.* You think the cops are going to drop it? Let you say, *Oh, sorry about that*?"

Kristen stared into space. "It's my fault. I'm crazy. I can't trust anybody. That morning the detective came, it was easier to lie."

"You're not crazy. Dad started jonesing and Mom only wanted to hang onto the credit cards."

Kristen rubbed her eyes, trying to expunge the vision. "Remember the day after we got back from that last trip to New York, before all hell broke loose? I jammed my finger during basketball practice, came home early, and caught him fucking Evonne."

"The woman who cleaned the house?"

Kristen's voice came from a tunnel. "Yes."

"No wonder the place was never clean."

Kristen's gaze clouded. "I saw his erection. He screamed at me, but I couldn't move. I was so shocked. Then he jumped up and hit me. Hard. I ran to my closet. The same with Sarah in that walk-in. Waiting. Petrified."

"And you did the right thing, when you told those cover-up jockeys on the licensing board what he'd been doing that night they paged his ass. They didn't have any choice but to shit-can him."

Kristen tossed the clip aside. "Whenever I felt good about myself, Dad kicked me down. Michael was the first man I ever connected with."

"Kristen, you and Michael had an *affair*. Affairs don't last. I know. There's lots of okay guys around, and you won't have to rescue their kids. I wanted you to go to Vail and have fun, loosen up, not get mixed up in a murder. If you want to fly to whatever shithole Dad's in, sign me up, but call that cop."

"We've got a problem. He's trying to set up Michael and even me. Like we conspired to kill Diana."

Tina's hands flew through the air. "I told you to stay at the hospital!"

Kristen grabbed Tina's arm. "Nobody paid attention to me. We're better off sweating it out now."

"You sound like that bleached bitch you used to work for."

"And I know who's feeding bullshit to the cops."

"Who?"

"The little bastard I beat up months ago."

Tina covered her face and mumbled, "Next you'll want to shoot him."

* * *

Saturday, November 4

The early November wind whipped leaves through the air as Kristen walked toward the bleachers where a knot of parents huddled together, cheering on their daughters. She slowed her steps, tempted to turn back before being noticed. She could chicken out, say she'd gotten tied up.

What a sick joke.

She jammed her hands into the pockets of her windbreaker and slouched, making herself a bit smaller, but continued on. Michael had insisted they start acting like an item, everything out in the open, cops and gossip be damned.

This would be her first public appearance with him. Was a month since Diana was killed enough time for a shred of respectability? Knowing the legal community's penchant for gossip, folks likely thought they'd been carrying on for years and that Kristen had slit Diana's throat herself.

After her head surgery, they had scoped Sarah's knee. They'd kept her for a week, probably because of who her father was, as opposed to keeping her due to her condition. Then she was transferred to a rehab facility. It had been a way to get more casual mental evaluations without sending her to a psych hospital.

Although she hadn't told Michael she loved him, she knew she did. She wanted more time with him, wanted to feel normal, share a home. Maybe on a romantic night they would talk about kids. She was sick of being a furtive fugitive. So, despite her doubt they had a future, she had agreed to come to Sarah's first game since leaving the hospital.

Stern turned in his seat, spotted her, and waved. Too late now. She spurred her steps and settled next to him on the end of the third row. The other parents looked her over, some with clear disdain. Michael didn't introduce her to anyone. Annoyed, she wondered if he didn't know how to describe her. Girlfriend? Accomplice?

"How we doing?" she asked.

"Down one—zip."

"And our star?"

"Better than I'd hoped." Stern shook his head, belying his words. "She can run a little. She's got atrophy in the leg, but is holding up."

"Does she have permission to play?"

Stern pursed his lips. "Sorta. I talked the doc into it. Thought it might help." He pointed to the field and beamed with pride at the short-cropped girls. "Her team got haircuts to match hers and insisted Coach start her."

"That's so sweet."

Kristen spotted Sarah wearing a padded knee brace. Her feet danced in anticipation. She stopped a pass and faked; then, limping slightly, she dribbled past the opponent guarding her, but lost the ball. In a second the competitors were charging to the other end.

Sarah's face contorted in agony over such an easy steal.

On the next ball out of bounds, the coach pulled her out.

Kristen felt the other adults' sense of helpless embarrassment, watching Sarah's emotional overreaction. Except Kristen knew how it felt, like the night she couldn't stop crying over a jammed finger.

* * *

Parked across the street from the field, Detective Rick Burrows tapped the end of his Marlboro against the wheel of his unmarked car, stuck it into his mouth, and lit up. After a drag, he hacked crap from his lungs and swallowed. He wiped slime from the windshield with his coat sleeve and watched the Stern kid hobble out of the game. Burrows thought Stern overplayed the role of concerned father.

Burrows wondered why Kristen Kerry, who seemed bright, had the bad judgment to be involved with such a sleaze. Marrs's parole file, the prints on the cash, and the panties were almost enough to give Stern an appointment with a needle. The morning after Sarah's rescue, Kristen looked like she'd gone ten rounds with the welterweight champ. The basketball story was a lie. She hadn't used her pass that night at the YMCA. The locksmith had called after seeing the paper. He nailed the ID.

They had her phone records. Kristen had foolishly called the lock man, Marrs, and Johnson with her cell.

An obvious scam—philandering bastard hates his rich wife, leaves town with his lovely babe days after his wife sees a divorce lawyer. Happily for hubby, before a petition is filed, wife gets sliced. Although the kid's abduction got a little out of hand, it ended when a mysterious rescuer brought the kid in, but couldn't stick around to collect a million bucks.

He had been second-guessing his decision not to bring Kristen in for a station grill and hit her with a search warrant. But from what he'd learned, she was too tough to be intimidated and wouldn't have been dumb enough to haul the kid in her own car or bring Sarah to her house.

Burrows guessed the big-time lawyer's eyes would eventually wander. They had before. He'd get caught and their Tinkertoy romance would collapse. Confronted with Burrows's evidence, Kristen would hand him Stern on a silver tray, to avoid her own life sentence.

* * *

As he made the turn off Oxford, Stern spotted a Ryder truck blocking his driveway. Janet stood next to it. Stopping at the curb, he shoved the door open and bounded out. "What's going on?"

He recognized the mangy errand boy from his office getting out of the rental truck.

Janet tugged on his sleeve. "Michael, we need to talk."

"Mr. Stern, where do you want me to unload all this stuff?" the kid asked.

Stern pulled his arm free. "What *stuff?*"

"Your personal things." The kid jerked his thumb toward the rear of the truck. "I got it all in here."

Janet planted her thin body between them and pushed on Stern's chest. "Jackson had them pack everything last night. They quit arguing over how to break the partnership and just bought you out. I've got the paperwork and a check."

The kid flung open the back door. Another oaf appeared and jerked a dolly out.

"They emptied your office. Even all your closed files in storage."

"Just like that?"

"Jackson thought they could keep the clients if they threw you out. Randolph resisted, but the youngsters went along."

"I'm sure they're happier than pigs in shit. And you?"

"I got a month's pay."

Dumbasses! They canned the best paralegal in the place.

He pulled her to his chest and wrapped his arms around her. "You've always got a place with me."

Janet broke the moment by fishing in her briefcase and pulling out an envelope. "Here."

Stern tore it open.

"Those bastards! They're valuing the firm at half of what it's worth."

"Michael, forget it. You don't need the money."

He ripped the check into shreds, letting the pieces float to the ground. "Maybe not, but there's no reason I should bend over for a screwing. This looks like a Jackson and Caswell stunt. They're going to be damn sorry."

CHAPTER 44

KRISTEN, MORE NERVOUS than when standing before a jury, held Michael's back door open for Rita. Kristen had urged him to play golf for the first time since Vail and had volunteered to stay with Sarah. He needed an outing. But she dreaded the questions—*When did you and my dad start going out? Do you love him?* Christmas was looming. It wouldn't get easier.

She feared silence just as much. To Sarah, she must be *old*. How do you talk to a girl who had been through living hell? Was this a babysitting gig? Or a visit with a friend? Or a nursing assignment? She should decide, since she volunteered for it.

The maid called out, "Bye, Sarah. I see you Tuesday."

Out of sight, Sarah yelled, "See you, Ri."

Rita paused on the back steps. "Mr. Stern seem happy this morning, and Sarah some better, too. She eat my pancakes today. But still too thin. I pray every night."

"Me too."

"She's in her *padre's* room. I have hot cider on stove."

Kristen thanked Rita, watched her off, went to the kitchen, and poured herself a steaming cup, tempted to spike it. Michael's house held the warm memory of Thanksgiving. Sarah had spent the day and Thursday night with cousins, Diana's sister's kids. Kristen's brother had flown in. Her siblings hit it off with Michael. Alcohol, old stories, and jokes flowed freely. Sleeping with Michael that night had been heavenly.

For some reason, the cops had retreated. Kristen hoped they were scouring for evidence against Marrs, but she was probably wrong. Taking the newspaper photo of Diana from Marrs's house had been stupid, probably not the only dumb thing she'd done that night.

Jeff Hudson, his new lawyer, had filed motions to exclude evidence that Kristen hoped were go-through-the-motions stuff. To keep busy while they waited for whatever shoe was about to drop, Kristen stayed at McGee, but didn't get much work. Maybe they didn't trust her. She should probably give notice soon and start looking for a job.

Sarah sat next to the fireplace, pulling files out of boxes. The clutter practically covered the massive new Chinese rug. Her hair had grown long enough to lie neatly on her scalp. There was the wonderful smell of Christmas—the tree, cinnamon candles, the cider Rita had made. Instrumental Christmas music was playing—Mannheim Steamroller.

"Hi, Sarah."

"Hi." Her voice seemed detached. "Mom loved this CD."

Kristen had no idea what to say. Michael had said she'd been turning down invitations from friends, sitting around morose. He hoped Kristen might perk her up.

"We could go shopping later."

"I don't know. Not feeling like it."

"We don't have to go anywhere. I brought a book I can read."

Sarah smiled. "I told Dad it would be okay for you to come over."

That made Kristen feel good, so she smiled. "What are you doing with all this mess?"

"Helping Dad sort through his office stuff."

"Want some help?"

"Sure. If files have a blue tab, they're closed. Yellow tabs are open, but I haven't found many of those. Dad says they're stealing his cases."

"Look at all those old depositions." There had to be a thousand.

"Experts. I'm organizing them. Lawyers from all over ask him for copies. He should just keep discs, but he's too old-fashioned. Janet explained it to me when I was at the office last summer. I was going to be a runner when I got to be sixteen."

"I'm sure he'll have another firm."

"Maybe you two could start one."

"As long as we call it *Kerry and Stern*."

Sarah grinned. "Let's tell Dad we insist. Girls rule."

"Someday *Stern, Kerry and Stern*. You be the first *Stern*."

Sarah laughed. Relief flooded through Kristen. Maybe, just maybe, things might work out.

Sarah picked up another stack of transcripts. "I didn't know these could be *secret*."

Kristen cocked her head. "What?"

"These two." Sarah studied the cover. "It says, *Sealed by Order of the Court*."

* * *

Working on Saturday, as usual, Jeff Hudson studied the Marrs investigation file the DA had finally coughed up. Finding the section on Lance's death, he reviewed the autopsy.

Four gunshot wounds. Tox screen clean. Nothing tied Lance to Stern, except Marrs's theory and maybe a few negroid hairs in Stern's house. Tests on those were pending. Caucasoid hair found upstairs only matched the Stern family. So far there was no evidence Marrs had been in the Sterns' little shack.

From what he'd seen of his client, *multicultural* wasn't a word that came to mind. He and Freddie were as likely to be partners as Rush Limbaugh and Bill Clinton. So, Marrs's claim that his parole officer set him up to be killed by Lance, while bizarre, might be true, although

Hudson knew not to believe much of what his clients said.

Sarah Stern's panties were the key. DNA from urine and blood confirmed they were hers. If Marrs was guilty, he wondered why nothing but the panties and cash had turned up. The place hadn't been cleaned in months, but still no other physical evidence of the girl was found in Marrs's pigsty. No hair, not even a flake of skin. The only reasonable conclusion was the kid had never been there. And although more tests were pending, nothing from Johnson's house had been linked to Sarah.

Hudson wondered if McKinnon had planted them. Was he that crooked? Hudson checked the inventory of stuff taken from Stern's house by Highland Park PD. Dirty clothes for scent and DNA. Including . . . panties! But were they the same pair? There was no return inventory, at least not yet. If he could keep them out of evidence, he could walk Marrs right out of the courthouse.

Hudson read on. Rug fiber on Sarah's shirt matched a common carpet found at Johnson's, but other fibers, from an expensive rug, matched nothing. There were thousands of carpets in town identical to Johnson's, so that didn't mean a thing. The Oriental entry runner from Stern's house, which the kid was probably bundled in, hadn't been found.

A long brunette mystery hair had been lifted off Freddie. Identical hairs were removed from Sarah's clothes. The rescuer? Hudson wondered why they hadn't attempted to get DNA off them. Sometimes hair didn't make a good sample, but it looked almost like the cops were holding back a broader investigation, as if waiting on something else to surface. Or they had a theory they weren't ready to disclose.

Interviews of Diana's friends described Stern as a philandering jerk seen arguing with his sweet bride in public, but a devoted father. It seemed he was a successful malpractice attorney and quite a Casanova.

Hudson went rigid when he read the name of the current girlfriend. The bitch who never returned his call.

Jenny at Wright McGee had fished him for inside info, supposedly for her partner. He thought she meant McGee. Instead, it was for Stern's mistress.

He had a duty to tell the DA about Jenny's calls.

* * *

Whistling "Free Man in Paris," Stern strolled in his back door. For the first time in weeks he felt hopeful. His ambivalent agony over Diana had faded. The few times he'd held Kristen were almost as good as Vail. Thanksgiving with her crew had been the drunken hoot he needed. He genuinely liked wacky Tina. His round of golf relaxed him—no annoying, ungrateful clients.

The cops had left him alone for a while. Sarah seemed happy for Kristen to stay with her. The overnight with cousins had gone fairly well. Perhaps Sarah would want to spend some of Christmas break at her aunt's, and he could take Kristen to Cancún. Getting out of Dallas and onto a beach sounded marvelous. He'd savor other men's jealous stares at the bikini-clad Kristen and feel young again himself.

Sarah stood at the kitchen counter, spreading peanut butter on Ritz crackers. "Hi, Dad."

"How late did you sleep?"

"Till ten. What'd you shoot?"

"A lousy eighty."

She smirked at him. "Want me to dump the sand out of your shoes?"

He squeezed her shoulder. Teasing was a good sign. It looked as if she was starting to regain weight.

"Where's Kristen?"

"In your room."

Sarah's mood left him upbeat. They could order pizza later. Shoot hoops. What an evening they would have.

He found Kristen in his study by the fireplace, staring at nothing with a face of granite. Utterly perplexed, he stepped closer and spotted the two volumes in her lap, the ones Jake's paralegal had scarfed from Jersey.

He hadn't been back to the office since Diana died, and had forgotten about them. He tried to think of an explanation, some reasonable story, but his brain was a black hole. His heart rate accelerated. Optimism evaporated like wet footprints around the pool in July. He knew this was bad. Very bad. Terror gripped him.

Her eyes finally focused, turned up at his face, and pierced him. "You son of a bitch."

The words were said quietly—probably for Sarah's benefit—but distinct enough.

He stepped closer, whispering, "Honey, I'm so sorry."

"You mean, you're sorry you got caught." She rose and pulled on her windbreaker, still keeping her voice low. "How were you going to use this garbage? Blackmail me? Take this shit to McGee if I didn't sleep with you? You're just another liar, like Pete and the docs on the Jersey Medical Board."

Stern held up his palms. "Kristen, please. Things have changed. I've changed. I love you."

"You really outdid yourself. It must have taken a lot of sneaking around to get your grimy mitts on these."

He tried to take her hands, but she jerked away. "Kristen, I'm so, so sorry."

"I'm curious." She stopped a second, her voice dripping with sarcasm. "Who'd you have to bribe or fuck?"

"Baby—"

"Didn't you stop to think there was a damn good reason to seal them? To protect a kid, a kid not much older than your daughter?"

"Kristen—"

"Did you share these with the guys at your office? Everyone have a good laugh?"

She was a cobra, hissing at him. For all his skill at talking clients out of trouble, he couldn't conjure a defense. He sputtered apologies that sounded pathetically lame.

"Please, please, don't go."

"We are *finished.*"

She bolted, carrying the transcripts with her.

CHAPTER 45

Monday, December 15

AFTER GIVING KRISTEN a couple of days to come to a simmer, Stern rang her doorbell. She hadn't returned his calls, but her BMW was in the driveway. He still hadn't come up with a reasonable explanation for his snooping. The truth was he'd been obsessed with her mystery, her evasiveness, about how she could be so tough one minute and melancholy the next.

Getting anything useful for *Layne* had been unlikely, and he suspected it at the time. Inadvertently, what he'd learned had eventually led him to love her, but he had no idea how he was going to explain any of this.

He pushed the button again, hoping that if she opened the door, he could absorb enough anger that the volcano would burn itself out.

She jerked the door open. "Get out!"

"Baby, I know you feel betrayed."

"Don't call me *baby*."

He clasped his hands together. "I got it before the trial. Before Vail."

She spat the words, "Give me a fucking break."

"Kristen, I love you."

Kristen shoved his chest. "Out!"

Stern gripped her arms, but her wrists flew up inside his and slapped his hands away.

"Don't touch me."

He saw the fury of a wounded leopard. The way she positioned her hands, balanced herself, made him think she was going to hit him. He made no effort to protect himself, deserving whatever she wanted to dish out. If taking a beating was the price for forgiveness, he'd happily pay.

Stern waited until she finally lowered her hands. "Can we talk inside? Please?"

She thrust her nose an inch from his chin. "Did it ever occur to you that a judge decided nobody needed to know I was beaten by my own fucking father? That my mom did coke? Did you see that I had to drive him home when I was only fourteen? That I wrecked his precious car and he let a man die while he slapped me around?"

She stopped for breath. "Did you not think that I never wanted anybody, and I mean any-fucking-body, to know I got my dad's medical license revoked?"

Plenty of lava remained. Stern felt like the scumbag of the century.

She erupted again. "The first thing I heard about you was that you cheat. But I had no idea how low and dirty you played."

She slammed the door in his face.

* * *

In Livermore's ADA office, Burrows thumbed the stop button, turning the television screen to snow. He popped out the surveillance tape, taken from a camera hidden across the courtyard from Kristen's place, and beamed at Livermore. "Told you. Give 'em some line, they'll run themselves over the dam."

Livermore tapped his yellow pad before responding. "Just because she's pissed at him doesn't mean she'll cooperate. She has to say Stern told her where to get the girl."

"Give me a little more time, and she'll be fryin' Stern in an iron skillet. Probably caught him trolling."

Livermore nodded.

"See that slick move she gave Stern? That stance? Bet you a buck, she fought Marrs before grabbing the hostage."

Livermore tossed his pad on the desk. "How much heat can we put on her?"

"Threaten her with obstruction of justice. She lied to me."

"Marrs double-crossed Stern, so Stern sends his jock girlfriend to get the kid?"

"Yep. She gets there after Freddie and Marrs have already shot it out over how to split their cash."

Livermore reached for his flask. "We'll have blowback if we give Marrs a deal to get Stern. Even life without parole." He paused. "But— and it's a big *but*—if we announce Freddie killed Diana, that the Negroid hair in the house is his—"

"We could cancel the DNA. It's only mitochondrial anyway. Not a hundred percent. Who cares about a dead cop-shooter?"

"The stories still have to make sense." Livermore stared into space a minute. "I'm worried about the suppress motion. Hudson acts like he's got something up his sleeve."

"Huh?" Burrows thought those motions were routine.

The ADA stood and peered out the window of the Frank Crowley Courts Building to the stately Victorian-style Old Red courthouse built in the nineteenth century. "While you're downtown, run over to Jackson Randolph." Livermore carefully enunciated the firm's new name. "Press Caswell again. He's our link to Kristen before the murder."

"Roger that."

Livermore turned back to Burrows. "I got problems with your theory. A big problem. I got daughters myself. But we have leverage with Kristen, if she wants to keep her license. You bag her and get the right story, and I'll get you an ironclad indictment of that arrogant bastard."

* * *

Thirty minutes later, Burrows watched Tony Caswell rocking on his squeaky executive chair. Caswell wore a green and yellow regimental tie, slung loose around his collar. His skin had a pasty hue. Dark lines circled his eyes. His shirt collar looked two sizes too big. Burrows thought the guy had aged ten years since he first met him.

"Are you certain they were involved before Diana Stern was killed?"

"Like I told you, I saw them during the Layne trial, before the verdict, ripping each other's clothes off. Overheard them talking about how wonderful it would be if Stern wasn't married. Disgusting."

Burrows nodded encouragement, but found Caswell's accent irritating. He suspected juries would, too.

Caswell sneered and added, "Kristen asked Stern if he had a prenup with Diana. Said she wanted to quit practicing and live in Europe. Check the security system. Late Sunday night during the trial. It'll show I was here the same time they were."

Burrows absorbed this new detail. It troubled him that Caswell's memory got better each time he talked.

"The lawyers who work with her disagree. They say she never dated anybody seriously in the six years she's been there."

"Well, *duh*. She was seeing a married man."

Burrows saw why Stern couldn't stand the guy. "You don't like her, do you?"

Caswell shrugged. "She's a total bitch."

She turned him down, he thought.

Burrows decided to sidestep that for the moment.

"Is she going to get you in trouble with Judge Proctor?"

"Nothing I can't handle."

"And Stern blackballing you for partnership pissed you off, didn't it?"

"I would've made it anyway. I protect clients. I tried to warn him she's flaky, but he was too much *in love*. Dumbass must've felt sorry for her."

"Huh?"

Caswell leaned closer. "She testified against her own father in a medical license hearing when she was a teenager. Claimed he beat her and was a drunk."

It took Burrows a minute to process this and concentrate again. "Her father?"

"I saw the transcript. Board was after him for patient abandonment. She claimed he was abusing her when the hospital was calling him. Poor bastard resigned his license. Stern had it in his office, even though it'd been sealed by a New Jersey court."

"Where'd he get it?"

"Probably stole it, knowing him."

They hadn't paid much attention to depositions, once they found Marrs's file. Burrows pretended to go over his notes. Something smelled, but the kid was helping nail a scumbag, and he'd take it. "What were you doing looking in his office?"

He hesitated. "Getting a file. Do it every day."

Burrows noted the delay and didn't like it. "Kristen's quite attractive. Anything between you two I need to know about?"

"Uh . . . one date. Never called her again."

"Do you know if she's into some kind of karate stuff?"

Caswell's hand flew to his throat. "Yeah. I heard that."

Burrows thought the reaction strange. "Did Stern ever express a desire to end his marriage?"

"He catted around like a frat boy."

Burrows was trying to determine how many axes Caswell had to grind, and it sounded like he had a garage full of them. He decided to float the obvious question, the one they had to be ready for down the line. "If he got away with it, why would he kill his wife?"

Caswell leaned back, squeaking his chair. "Easy. Kristen wouldn't settle for being a concubine and wanted Diana's money. Probably close to a hundred million."

Burrows checked his notes and spotted another question he needed to ask. "Does Kristen know her stuff on hospital cases?"

Caswell shrugged. "Yeah, I'll give her that."

Burrows guessed that, somewhere along the way, Kristen or Stern had rubbed Caswell's nose in his own shit. Bad as he wanted to believe him, he wondered how credible their star witness was.

Burrows decided not to share his doubt with Livermore.

* * *

As the doorknob of Janet Wharton's duplex turned, Burrows stamped out his Marlboro and kicked the stub into the purple ajuga next to the porch. He'd met Stern's Girl Friday the day Diana's body was found, but his questions then had been about anybody she'd seen around the house or office. Today's agenda was different.

Janet opened the door, eyes slit with wariness.

He flashed his badge and reintroduced himself.

She invited him in with bare civility.

Burrows plopped onto a tufted wingback chair that looked like it had been recently recovered. The place was impeccably neat, perfect for a person who managed details for her boss. Even the throw pillows lined the couch smartly.

"A few more questions, ma'am." He tried a smile of reassurance, but she didn't respond. He knew he was in enemy territory. Burrows guessed she was in her midforties. She was attractive, if not pretty, and he wondered if she'd ever had an affair with Stern.

"How can you be positive they weren't involved before Diana died?"

She sat on the chair's twin and crossed her thin legs. "Why would he be checking Kristen out, if he'd already slept with her? Michael

368

asked me to get information on her. I called a friend who worked at her firm."

"When?"

She stumbled. "I don't remember for certain."

Burrows watched her eyes. She held his gaze like she believed what she said, or at least wanted to. "Do you know how he found a transcript on Kristen's father?"

This time she blinked. "I have no idea."

"How would you describe the Sterns' marriage?"

She rubbed her palms on her jeans. "They had what I'd call . . . a truce. They didn't hate each other."

"Did you know she'd talked to lawyers about divorce before she was killed?"

She blinked again. "No."

"Stern says you had a key to his house."

"Uh-huh. Kept it in my desk."

"Did you lock your desk every night?"

She raised her chin, seeming to realize something. "No. No need, really. External security is excellent."

"How many times did Marrs call the firm?"

"I didn't know he did."

He knew she was dancing with the truth and decided to show a card. "The caller ID log shows twice. Guess they keep that to make sure no chance is missed to bill clients."

"Maybe Marrs was the guy checking Michael's schedule, supposedly from an insurance company. I wondered if he was legit."

"Did he leave a number?"

She touched her lips again. "I don't remember."

Burrows scooted to the edge of his chair. "Did you ever give Stern the number?"

"I don't remember."

Burrows puffed up. They'd found a carbon on her old-fashioned message pad. "Did you know Marrs's parole file was in Stern's credenza? Did you copy it?"

Her head tilted and her eyes drifted up, as if manufacturing a lie. "I don't know."

"Did you bring Sarah to the hospital?"

"No, but whoever did was a hero."

Her denial was so resolute, Burrows floated, "Any idea who did?" She hesitated a second. "No."

* * *

Janet paced through her house, as if that would help her think. She tried to summarize what she had heard and what she suspected.

There'd been no forcible entry.

Scuttlebutt had it: cash had been found in Marrs's house with Michael's prints.

The parole file with Marrs's contact information was in Michael's credenza. She tried to remember details of the file she'd copied that night. It had to be the same one.

Were there reasonable explanations that would absolve Michael? She had locked his football winnings in his credenza many times, and had often taken money out to pay the bookie. Anyone in the firm could have stolen the money, grabbed the file, and nabbed her key to his house with the alarm code taped to it.

Questions rattled around her brain. Who would want Diana murdered and Sarah kidnapped, then try to frame Michael? How had this Marrs character gotten involved? Did somebody hire him?

She went to the kitchen and poured another glass of iced tea. Michael Stern had been her life for years, filling not just her days, but her dreams, subbing in her imagination for whoever might temporarily share her bed after her second husband died of diabetes.

The cop seemed determined to get Michael and tie in Kristen. But who'd hire a thug to kill his wife on the possibility a woman he'd never slept with would fall for him? Especially when the rich wife let him get away with skirt chasing, and he had plenty of money of his own?

A hot romance, going on long enough to consider the murder of a rich, inconvenient wife, bolstered the police theory. She doubted anything had been going on before the verdict. Michael was busy running Sarah around, building his custody case.

A passerby could have found Sarah, after she'd escaped, and didn't know about the reward. Although Kristen fit the cops' conspiracy, Janet didn't think Kristen had the moxie to pull off a rescue from a killer in the dead of the night. Unless Michael knew where Sarah was. That thought made her cringe.

Janet pondered her most important question—was Kristen in love with Michael? Was he in love with her?

Obviously, Kristen brought the mystery plane ticket to the office, so maybe they were getting it on in secret. Would they last? A fourteen-year age difference. Once the hot coals of lust burned out, Sarah's demands would annoy Kristen. Surely Michael didn't want diapers and sleepless nights again. The odds were against it.

Still a chance.

CHAPTER 46

Thursday, December 18

THREE DAYS AFTER THEIR stormy front porch scene,
Kristen sat next to Stern in the same courtroom table they'd
occupied for two weeks. Now *Layne* seemed to predate the
Reformation. She kept her arms folded against her chest and ignored
him. At least fifty lawyers from a dozen different firms packed the
gallery, eager to witness the bloodletting. They could have sold tickets.

At the other table, Bragg fiddled with his silk tie and drummed
his fat fingers. Kristen guessed Bragg had known enough that night,
after talking to Caswell, to trigger his duty to disclose any known
perjury. She suspected he had held back, knowing that if he lost
the case, he could rush in with allegations of lying and get a new
trial. Bragg's yacht was in jeopardy in this hearing, as well as Stern's
license and a bunch of people's freedom. Even Shorty looked edgy,
fidgeting in the bailiff's chair.

Judge Proctor entered, rocketing everyone to their feet.

Proctor cleared his throat as the gallery sat.

"Let the record reflect counsel for all parties are present. I know the
DA has an inquiry under way. I've waited for his conclusions, but have
decided to look into this whole business myself. I still have jurisdiction."
The judge paused before adding, "Ms. Kerry, come up please."

Kristen rolled her chair back, stood, and approached the bench.

Her legs wobbled. She hoped nobody noticed.

"Ms. Kerry, I don't usually ask lawyers to take the oath, but . . ."

"I understand, Your Honor." Kristen raised her hand and was sworn in by the clerk. She then sat in the witness stand and adjusted the microphone.

"The court notes your integrity."

"Thank you." Kristen's voice came out reedy. This was tougher than she'd anticipated.

"First, do you have any evidence that Mr. Stern had prior knowledge of the conspiracy to deceive this court?"

Kristen's eyes met Michael's, but he looked away. Was it shame she saw on his face? His shirt collar didn't seem quite as starched; his tan appeared faded.

The bastard would crawl on his belly and lick the bottom of her shoe to keep his license or be forgiven. The first man she'd slept with in years had turned out to be a sneak. This was her chance to get even.

Anger roared in her gut, but unfortunately she had nothing to offer the judge.

"No, Your Honor."

"What do you know about Ms. Robberson's involvement?"

"I don't have any proof she instructed the nurses to lie. They all told me the same version." This was technically true, but certainly not likely.

"Do you have any information indicating she knew *any* witnesses were lying?"

Kristen made sure her voice didn't quaver, though she hated what she was doing.

"No, sir."

Lying was like free throws. You get better with practice.

Kristen spotted the pug-nosed former adjuster in the back of the courtroom slump forward, obviously relieved Kristen had held up her end of the bargain.

Proctor peered down, his brow crunched in skepticism. "Do you know of any lawyers who knew about this perjury and supported it or failed to notify the court?"

For an instant, she considered ratting out Jenny or Pete, but there had been good times— beers after work, celebrating wins over expensive dinners. Besides, a well-aimed rifle shot was better than a shotgun blast.

"Yes, Your Honor. Tony Caswell, at what's now Jackson Randolph." She remembered his threat about *paybacks*. "It was when I retraced his steps that I learned the truth."

Caswell, from the third row, mouthed, *You're dead, bitch.*

* * *

In the same courthouse, Marrs's Motion to Suppress evidentiary hearing was underway in Judge Wallace's court.

Jeff Hudson leaned over the lectern and pointed at Sergeant McKinnon. "Your shift's over, but you drive to Mr. Marrs's brother's house after he shot an intruder. That's odd. Isn't it?"

The Dallas PD sergeant shifted his powerful frame from one hip to another. "I was close. Heard the radio. Thought they might need help. I had no idea your client killed Diana Stern."

Hudson nearly flew out of his Gucci loafers. "Your Honor!"

Judge Wallace scowled. "Officer, just answer the questions."

Hudson had to take a moment to calm down. "Had you ever met my client before?"

McKinnon stroked the eight o'clock shadow on his Neanderthal jaw before replying. "Don't think so."

"You just happened to be in the area and decided to back up?"

"Yes, and I just happened to need to urinate."

"Your Honor, move to strike as nonresponsive."

Judge Wallace closed his eyes and ran his palms across his bald dome. "Move on, Counselor. I know what to ignore. Officer, this is an evidentiary hearing. Stick to the facts concerning the admissibility of the evidence."

Hudson's voice carried sarcasm. "Did you find any evidence that Mr. Marrs had killed anybody besides a convicted burglar?"

The cop shrugged. "Wasn't lookin' for any."

"Never met my client before?"

McKinnon scratched an odd misshaped mole on his temple. Hudson wondered if he had skin cancer.

"Don't think so."

"Never been in his house?"

Looking annoyed at the whole business, McKinnon hiked a shoulder. "Don't think so."

"Have you ever spoken to Mr. Zelner about Mr. Marrs?"

This time the sergeant hesitated, searching the ceiling for an answer, and Hudson knew he'd hit home.

"Sergeant?"

"We talk about his clients some." McKinnon seemed to realize he'd screwed up and added defiantly, "I didn't go to your client's house. Never been close to there. And I don't know anything about any kid's undies."

Hudson stepped closer to Judge Wallace. "Your Honor, no more from this witness. I call Lyndon Zelner."

McKinnon was excused, and hurried from the courtroom like his ass was on fire.

Jeff Hudson couldn't contain his excitement as the bailiff retrieved Zelner from the holding area, where he'd not been able to hear McKinnon's testimony.

Entering the courtroom, Zelner trudged to the hot seat in front of the Lone Star flag. The parole officer's hand shook as Judge Wallace administered the oath.

Hudson boomed, "You're Mr. Marrs's parole officer, Mr. Zelner?"

"Yes."

"You're an officer of the law?"

Zelner shifted his butt from one cheek to the other in the witness chair. "Yes."

"You've been to both his house and his brother's?"

"It's my job to see my clients and their homes. Sometimes when they don't expect me."

"Sure. Did you ever drop in to question him about a murder of a gun dealer?"

Zelner looked around, as if hoping for help. "Yes."

Hudson stepped around the lectern. "And you found no evidence that he'd shot anybody?"

Zelner glanced at Assistant DA John Livermore. "I guess not. But we didn't have any scene equipment."

"We? Was there a policeman with you that morning?"

Zelner's chest rose up and down quickly. Blood drained from his face. He had misspoken and knew it. Hudson thought the guy might faint. It was likely McKinnon and Zelner had rehearsed their testimony, contrary to court rules, but Zelner probably had a conscience.

Hudson jumped into the pause. "I'll advise you, Mr. Zelner, that a neighbor saw you and a tall DPD officer on a Saturday morning. A neighbor with a big dog." Hudson smiled. "And, of course, you're under oath."

"Yes. Sergeant McKinnon. He's a friend of mine."

"The same officer who denied ever going to Marrs's house." Hudson let that statement settle.

The judge ripped off his bifocals and glared, a silent warning.

Hudson was up to two touchdowns and still had the ball.

"And did you know a parolee named Freddie Lee Lance?"

"He wasn't assigned to me."

"That's not what I asked you, Mr. Zelner."

Zelner took off his glasses and cleaned them on his shirt.

"Mr. Zelner?"

"I may have seen him in the office."

Hudson moved closer, daring the witness to lie. "You got Mr. Lance's phone number from *his* parole officer and gave him Mr. Marrs's address, so Lance could kill him, didn't you?"

Zelner looked like a mouse caught between a cat's paws. "I did talk to Lance's officer. We wondered why they didn't like each other. But I didn't give Lance any—"

"Do I need to call Mr. Lance's officer, who loaned you Mr. Lance's file?"

"Uh . . . no, I just wanted to contact Lance, find out what he knew about Marrs. Maybe help us learn who shot him."

Hudson glanced at the judge. Wallace was clearly appalled. Hudson had found gold. He decided to gamble.

"And this same neighbor will testify that late the same night Freddie Lance got shot . . ." Guessing, having a fifty-fifty chance of getting it right, Hudson decided Zelner did it. He had an excuse to be at Marrs's dump, and McKinnon was obviously a coward when his butt was on the line. ". . . A thin man in warm-ups, wearing glasses, came to Marrs's house."

"I may have made a surprise visit that night," Zelner blubbered. He looked like a heretic facing the rack.

"What were you carrying when you went to the busted back door, causing the dog to raise a ruckus?"

"Uh . . . just a file."

Hudson had them. He was going to walk Leonard Marrs.

* * *

Tony Caswell's Beretta rested on his lap. He slouched low in his Porsche and peered through the darkness at the Silver Spur Saloon. Orange neon light bathed the beer brewers' logos festooning the bar's windows. A din of redneck noise, passing for music, could be heard a block away.

The parking lot was full of pickups, but he saw no one. All the yahoos were inside, slurping cheap suds.

The cryptic text said, *I KNOW. Meet at 11 Silver Spur.*

When he called back, the number was dead, likely from a throwaway cell. After considerable debate over whether it was Marrs's girlfriend, or Kristen, or even Stern, he had decided to come, but well armed.

He glanced at his Rolex—ten after and nobody had approached him. He sure as hell wasn't going inside the dive.

He wiped his palms on his slacks, then tapped his keys back and forth. Though he'd parked a good distance from the entrance to be safe, he wondered if that had been wise. His car stuck out like Angelina Jolie at a Camp Fire meeting. Caswell realized he hadn't thought things through clearly. He should've backed into the parking space, in case he needed a fast getaway. But that was only his most recent mistake.

He needed alcohol, and lots of it, lately. Caswell reminded himself that all he'd done was push things along faster. It wasn't his job to play Wyatt Earp at the Stern house. Whatever Marrs had been up to before Caswell intervened would've happened anyway. His goal had been to hurt Stern in the worst way, by kidnapping the kid. Once they'd gotten paid, he'd assumed Marrs would let the girl go without much fuss. Despite the rationalizations, he kept having visions of Sarah being assaulted.

Caswell had no idea Marrs was going to kill Diana, since the crime Marrs had been sent up for hadn't been murder. Tony had read the file and knew Diana would likely get poked and fondled, but Marrs hadn't been able to keep it up long enough to rape his first victim. Caswell thought Diana could use some excitement. Had he known *Layne* would end Stern's career, Tony would never have messed with the scumbag.

The idea of taking the daughter had been his, but Tony hadn't wanted the kid to get hurt. Scared maybe, but not hurt. And they hadn't gotten the fucking ransom. Still, he had hosed Stern but good.

Even if they didn't charge Stern, suspicion would haunt him forever. Nobody would ever partner with him. The country club would probably find an excuse to drop him. The swiped bills from Stern's credenza had paid dividends far beyond their value. Even better, the stink had spread to Kristen, thanks to her eagerness to get at Stern's baloney.

Piled on top of Tony's guilt came panic. Kristen was jeopardizing his license to practice and possibly his freedom. He'd taken the Fifth when Proctor called him to the stand. But "the nickel" was practically a confession. Every eye in the courtroom had been trained on him.

He had to destroy Kristen's credibility to keep his ticket. If the cops wrapped Kristen into Stern's murder-for-hire charge, the Bar wouldn't buy the story of a lawyer indicted for conspiracy to murder.

The police hadn't said—or maybe they hadn't figured out—who had brought Sarah to the hospital, but Tony figured Kristen had been the heroine. Caswell had spent hours since the hearing trying to think of anything else he could tell Burrows that would help him rope Kristen in, but was out of plausible tales and couldn't risk his credibility any further.

He stopped ruminating and decided it was dangerous to stay in this hellhole. Caswell drained his Frappuccino and ejected the clip from his pistol. If he got pulled over on the way home, an unloaded gun in the car wouldn't be a problem.

As he twisted the key, a shadow bundled in a long coat appeared at his window. Its face was obscured with a kerchief over the mouth and a Stetson pulled low to the eyes. He couldn't guess the height or size of this made-up stagecoach robber. But Tony's throat clenched shut as the apparition produced a six-shooter in its gloved hand.

Caswell's belly lurched. His arms palsied. He couldn't decide what to do—shift to reverse and back away, or reload his Beretta? If he'd had two good hands, he might've done both. He chose the stick, but the ghost's gun went off two feet from his ear, deafening him before he could shift gears.

His shoulder jerked from the punch of the bullet, costing him his grip on the knob. Blood misted over the passenger seat. Piss streamed between his legs. He tried to grip the pistol, but the strong arm hung uselessly, worse than his other.

Less than a second later, before he could beg for his life, another shot erupted. Shards of tooth enamel, saliva, and blood sprayed the dashboard.

His hand flew up to the gaping hole in his face.

Another bang.

The orange lights went black.

CHAPTER 47

PAIN RACKED BURROWS'S chest as he listened. His shaking finger clicked off his cell phone. He fumbled for a cigarette, dropped it, and picked it up off the floor. Burrows finally lit it, then sucked in a nicotine calm. He'd count himself lucky if he survived the next hour.

"What the hell is it?" Livermore snapped as he walked in.

The Park Detective's voice shook. "Mesquite PD found Stern's former partner, Caswell. Shot three times. Only witness, a drunk redneck from Waco. Puking outside at the time. Thinks he saw a cowboy. Caswell's wallet was still in his pocket. No prints. No nothing."

Livermore's eyes ballooned. "Where was Stern?"

"Home. I've had him watched. Unless he floated out through his chimney."

"Yeah, but I bet your spies can be fooled." Livermore unscrewed the cap on his flask. "Could be a robbery gone sour."

Burrows took another drag on his Marlboro. "Sounds like a cover-up kill. My only witness to their horizontal mambo before Diana got slashed, their talk about prenups and Europe, gets shot outside some cowboy saloon."

"I want county lab people all over that scene."

"Mesquite said they didn't find diddly. No shell casings, no footprints on a concrete lot. No hair. Shots fired from two or three feet. Nothing in the car."

Livermore shook his head. "Another reason for my plan."

Burrows surveyed the ADA's office. Steel desk and file cabinets, thin nylon carpet, vinyl chairs, and plastic plants. Not a natural substance in the place. No wonder Livermore wanted out. "As long as you're willing to take the fall, if it goes bad."

"I'm vested. If it works, I could be in Congress." He picked up his phone and snapped, "Send Zelner in."

Burrows peered out the grimy little window toward the infamous Dealey Plaza, where Kennedy got shot, as Livermore slurped a mouthful, hid his sauce in his desk, then sprayed something smelling like peppermint in his mouth.

Shuffling in, Zelner seemed to have shell shock.

Livermore wasted not a second. "Judge Wallace is going to rule today on Hudson's motion. It's obvious you and McKinnon have been lying. Did you knuckleheads plant those panties? The cash? I know you nimrods went off half-cocked on that gun dealer."

Zelner shook his head. "I can't believe ballistics couldn't match the dealer's killing with the gun he shot Lance with."

Burrows rolled his eyes. "Marrs got a new piece. They're as easy to find as grape bubblegum."

Livermore got in Zelner's face. "I'm not going to suborn perjury and get disbarred. If we lose the motion today, we'll look like fools as well as crooks. It'll hurt every prosecution for years. This county has already had enough bad publicity on the DNA exoneration cases to last a century. For the last time, did you?"

Zelner stalled a minute before he spoke to the floor, "Only the panties. Not the cash. I wanted him off the street."

Livermore threw his yellow pad across his office. "Idiots! If McKinnon had just left them at the brother's house, we'd have Marrs by the balls. Now I'm supposed to advise the court that you lied."

"McKinnon thought . . . wasn't thinking about the Stern case. I . . . we assumed Marrs had found an underage girl . . . statutory rape." Zelner seemed to realize he was only digging himself deeper and shut up.

A minute of silent agony crawled by before Livermore said, "The issue now is, how do we turn this to our advantage? How can we nail Stern, his sweetheart accomplice, and Leonard Shithead Marrs in the bargain?" Livermore tapped his pigeon-colored temple for a second, as if calculating the speed of light. "If we dismiss the charges, can we keep him under surveillance for a couple of days?"

Zelner's jaw dropped. "Let Marrs go?"

Burrows pretended the idea was a surprise. "Wow! It'll have to be a Highland Park job, since he wasn't charged with anything by Dallas PD. We'd need volunteers, outside our jurisdiction."

Livermore nodded. "It's a gamble, but if we release him and schedule a parole revocation hearing for early next week, we might bait him into action."

Zelner waved his hands. "That long? He'll flee."

"Or lead us to the co-conspirators. As of today, we've got another murder likely tied to this caper. Marrs didn't do it, unless he escaped and broke back into jail."

Zelner shook his head. "He'll kill somebody else."

"I want all of them, not just your pervert parolee. We can refile charges on Marrs, hopefully with enough evidence to overcome your asinine shenanigans. Maybe Stern's kid will regain her memory."

Burrows slapped the table. "Let's gamble. Marrs might hook up with Stern, demand his dough."

Zelner regained some color. "God, I hope your supervisors know what you guys are doing."

Burrows scrunched his face into what he hoped was a thoughtful expression. "Marrs's half brother is willing to help. We'll put a GPS tracer on his car and tail Marrs the instant he leaves jail."

"Why not put an ankle bracelet on him?" Zelner asked.

Livermore rolled his eyes. "He's not out on *bail*. In an hour, there won't even be a charge against him." Livermore snorted. "Thanks to you and your pal, Frankenstein."

Burrows added, "It's not that risky. We've searched his little dump and know he doesn't have a weapon. We only have to keep track of him for three or four days."

"Something else." Livermore stroked his chin. "I'll call in an IOU with the court clerk. We'll file the dismissal late Friday. Keep it out of the paper till Sunday."

Zelner shook his head. "I don't think you understand this guy."

* * *

Marrs's knee ached with each step as he trailed Jimmy to his car. He knew his release was a setup, that the cops were keeping close. Sure enough, a goober with aviator shades sat at the curb across from county lockup in a white four-door, eyeballing them.

Marrs guessed Jimmy's new helpfulness meant the bald bastard had volunteered to play junior auxiliary policeman. Did they give Brother Jim a plastic badge and toy gun?

He didn't have much time until the parole hearing to get the jump on Wonder Woman and teach her some manners.

After reading the paper, it had taken Marrs only a minute to connect some dots and figure out that the dead lawyer in Mesquite, who had worked with Stern, was the man who came into his home with a gun and made him a deal he couldn't refuse. His *partner*. It only made sense that Stern or his girlfriend had taken out the poof-sounding Caswell.

There was still a lush island in Marrs's future, if Stern cared enough about his concubine to pay. But now Marrs wouldn't have to split the dough.

As they reached the parking garage, Marrs said, "I got shit to do downtown. I'll grab a bus home."

Jimmy looked around like he needed instructions from the shadows. "I'll run you where you need to go."

"I don't want to put you out."

Jim shook his head. "I'm not in a hurry."

Marrs smiled. Yeah, right. His half brother even crapped in a hurry. "Great."

They strolled to County Administration and the assessor's office inside. Twenty minutes later, Marrs scanned the screen. Kristen Kerry did okay. Nice condo. The court clerk's office turned up no divorce or lawsuits.

He decided to walk over to Municipal Court, though that seemed as likely to hit pay dirt as searching the post office *Wanted* posters. On the way, a stiff in a plaid sport coat followed about fifty yards behind. The guy might as well wear a sandwich board that said *cop*.

Soon a young woman with a funky hairdo, tattoos, and nose rings tapped her keyboard in the city court clerk's office, while Jim sighed and paced. She hit the icon, stepped to the printer, then pushed a sheet over the counter and hurried back to her desk.

Marrs picked it up. "Assault and Battery?"

She ignored him.

He called out, "Dismissed?"

"Whatever the computer says."

He parted with a sarcastic smile. In the hallway, he looked at the printout and wondered who the hell Will Fett, the complaining witness, was.

Marrs told Jim he needed to piss and ducked into the restroom. He pulled out his cell phone, which the jailers had helpfully returned fully charged, and punched the phone number on the court form.

After two rings, a gravelly voice answered.

Marrs tried to sound professional. "Are you the Will Fett who filed an assault complaint against Kristen Kerry?" Getting no response, Marrs added, "I'm investigating some trouble she's in, in Dallas. I see you live in Santa Fe."

After another pause, the man on the other end said, "She's nuts. Attacked me. I was just taking her sister home."

"Why'd they drop the charges?"

"I didn't have time to stick around for the hearing."

"The sister's in trouble, too."

"The whole family's crazy. Tina cleaned out my bank account when she ran back to Texas." Fett's volume rose. "Owes me five grand, not counting what I spent on her. I could tell you enough about that family to make you gag."

Marrs realized this guy might be useful. "I can help you get your money back."

"Who are you again?"

"An investigator hired by the dead gal's life insurance company."

"Dead gal?"

"Kristen and her boyfriend killed the guy's wife. Now they want to collect on her policy."

"You're shittin' me!"

"I'd like you to come back to Dallas and help. There's a big reward."

"What do you need me for?"

"I need somebody I can wire who can talk to those chicks and get me evidence."

"How much is the reward?"

Marrs wondered what number would appeal to greed without making the dude too suspicious.

"Fifty grand."

Half a minute of silence passed. Marrs cursed under his breath.

Finally, Fett said, "I was actually leaving Amarillo when you called, so I could hit up a few galleries out there.

* * *

Kristen knew the jig was up when she opened her door. Reluctantly she invited Burrows, his partner, and the guy he introduced as an assistant DA inside. She'd seen Livermore on TV and knew he was assigned the Marrs case. Television hid the dandruff sprinkled over his black suit jacket as well as the capillaries on his nose.

She felt resigned, and real stupid.

They trailed her to the kitchen table, where Burrows draped his bulk over one of her ice cream store chairs. He looked so wrung out, his mustache might crawl off his face in search of fresher meat.

Burrows's younger partner wore a sharp tweed sport coat and skinny tie. Too well dressed for his job.

Livermore tossed his yellow legal pad on the table and dropped onto a chair with an expression of disdain. His skin looked like he was drinking himself into the Johnnie Walker Hall of Shame.

Kristen bought herself a minute by offering coffee.

Livermore waved her off, but the detectives accepted.

She poured three mugs, then pushed two toward the cops.

Burrows pulled his pocket recorder out and flipped it on. After *Miranda* preliminaries, he asked, "Ms. Kerry, are you going to admit you brought Sarah Stern to the hospital?"

Surprised at how calm she felt, like facing a firing squad with a last cigarette, she raised her mug and sipped.

Livermore pointed. "You're looking at a felony for obstructing an investigation."

"I can demand hair and compare it to the strands we found on Sarah's clothes." Burrows's voice gained ferocity. "I got voice comparisons from the tip line and your cell phone records, showing calls to Marrs's house and to a locksmith."

She was doomed, felled by her own flaws. Like a Greek tragedy. Her license was gone either way, but maybe if she spilled the beans, they'd stop focusing on Michael and put Marrs on death row. Not that she cared about Stern, but it would be a shame for Sarah to become an orphan.

Her attention drifted for a second. She whispered, *"Out of danger, we plucked this flower."*

"Huh?" Burrows looked like she had just spoken Japanese.

"Sorry. One of the Henry plays." Her voice strengthened. "Yes, I brought her in."

Livermore's face puffed into smug satisfaction. "After Stern told you where she was?"

"No. He didn't know." His smarmy know-it-all attitude made her want to bash the ADA's bulbous nose in, but she reined in her anger. She spent the next five minutes describing the mission, from Rita through Tammy and the night in hell, leaving out nothing.

Burrows and his young partner listened without interrupting while Livermore scratched notes on his yellow pad.

"Stern didn't help you?"

"He had no idea. He still doesn't."

Livermore sniffed in obvious disbelief. "Why didn't you call the police?"

"I did. You were *busy*."

"You took a hell of a risk. Faced two killers. Why?"

She sipped, staring at her sunshine-yellow walls. "I honestly felt I had a better chance of getting Sarah back alive, at that moment, than a SWAT team would days later. If he had hidden her, maybe I could make him tell me where she was. Not likely he would've told *you*."

"You asked your friend, Jenny Norton, to get information about the investigation from Jeff Hudson."

"I just wanted to know if the man I hooked up with had his wife murdered."

"Do you have any evidence on Leonard Marrs? Anything that you've withheld?"

Kristen got up and walked into the living room. Inside the entry closet, under a stack of unfinished *New Yorkers*, she retrieved the clipping of Diana she'd found under Marrs's bed. Holding it by a corner, she returned and handed it to Burrows. "I'm sure you'll find Marrs's prints on this. It was under his bed."

Burrows opened his briefcase and pulled out a plastic baggie. With the blunt tip of his pen, he slid it into the bag.

"Why the hell didn't you leave it there?"

"Give me a receipt for the clipping," Kristen shot back.

Burrows slowly scribbled on a small pad, as if trying to calm the atmosphere, then tore a sheet off and handed it to Kristen. "Where were you Saturday night?"

"Here with my sister."

"All night?"

"Yes."

"Do you own a gun?"

"Yes. A Browning nine. Want to see it?"

Livermore seemed to ponder the offer, then decided against it. "Do you own a .32 revolver?"

"No."

Burrows continued, "You didn't like Tony Caswell, did you?"

"Couldn't stand the little bastard."

"Did you kill him?"

Before she could answer, Burrows added, "You had a motive. He said your affair with Stern had been going on for weeks before his wife was killed. That you asked about his prenup and wanted to move to France if Diana was out of the way."

"And you believed that crap? He was a liar, who lived in a fantasy land of his own making." She stayed riveted to Burrows. "After hearing what really happened, you can't still think Michael hired Marrs."

Burrows switched off the recorder. "No forcible entry. No alarm. He's in Colorado. He's got Marrs's parole file. Marrs has his cash."

391

"I'm through with Stern, but I do know he wouldn't—*couldn't*—have done *anything* to let Sarah get hurt."

Livermore muttered, "He resolved the custody fight and got rich too."

"You're only going to focus on that and not the other possibilities that actually make some sense? Haven't you thought somebody tried to frame Michael?"

"Got a candidate?"

"Let me nominate your former, now dead, star witness. He had access to Michael's office. It would be easy to lift a few bills."

"Motive?"

"Revenge, jealousy, among other things."

Livermore smirked. "And your nominee buys the farm while Marrs is locked up."

"I want a statement from your sister," Burrows demanded.

Kristen tried to redirect the discussion. "What does Mesquite know about Caswell's death?"

"We ask the questions."

"Yeah, but you don't listen to the answers."

Livermore snorted obvious derision as he got up. "We saw the tussle on your porch with Stern. Decided you couldn't trust him?"

"Good decision," Burrows added.

She couldn't forge a response.

Livermore stomped away and jerked open her front door, the baby-faced cop in tow.

Burrows lingered, then whispered, "You know how to tell the whole truth, no matter who it hurts. You should try it now."

It took her a second to realize he was talking about home—Trenton, New Jersey.

She felt her face redden in anger. How the hell did he find out?

The goddamn transcripts.

She felt the urge to tell him Michael had stabbed Diana himself.

CHAPTER 48

BURROWS FLASHED HIS badge at Stern's maid as she stood behind her screen door. He reintroduced himself and asked if he could come in.

Rita grasped the silver cross hanging in front of her white T-shirt. "I am citizen." She didn't make a move to open the door.

Burrows barely heard her over the blaring television. "I know that, but I need to know if you told Kristen Kerry about shooting—"

"I know nothing."

Her kids started yelling back at the TV, making the din worse.

Burrows shouted, "Could you turn that down?"

The maid glared, not moving.

He decided not to press the noise issue, but wondered why she was now so uncooperative, as opposed to when she'd found Diana. "Did a man try to steal your car? The man you shot?"

"I know nothing."

"I have to verify Kristen's story about—"

"I already tell you, I—"

"Yeah. I got it, you know nothing." Burrows hollered, "Without your help, I can't find Mrs. Stern's killer. Would you please let me in?"

"I know nothing about shooting."

"Did you talk to Kristen Kerry?"

Burrows noticed neighbors on both sides of Rita's old stucco bungalow poking their heads out their doors.

"There may be more people involved," he added.

"I know nothing."

Burrows cursed. Dragging her to a grand jury would be pointless, and no judge would give him a search warrant based on Kristen's wild tale. So much for finding the gun used to shoot Marrs last summer. Latinas could often be intimidated, especially if there were immigration issues, but this one was born in Texas and had picked up some savvy while working in Highland Park.

* * *

Marrs studied the little sister's ex-boyfriend in the murky light of the GitAway Club. Will Fett's paint-stained thumb and forefinger rolled his dying cigarette back and forth. He smoked like a man who longed to quit. From the copper color of his nails, Marrs figured he painted landscapes. From the size of his ass, he must sell enough to cram lots of potato chips into his fat mouth, but not enough to afford razors.

A few feet away, rough-looking guys in ball caps plugged more quarters into the undersized, uneven pool table. One was the cop who'd followed him out of the court building. Marrs turned his back to the spies and continued the sales pitch over the guitar-pickin' music. Although he had convinced Lottie Lewis of his utter innocence, and she'd volunteered to help for a slice of the pie, Will might be more likely to get him inside the Kerry girls' place.

Marrs used his salesman's charm. "The fifty grand is chicken feed. I've got a letter they'll pay a million for."

After listening to Marrs schmooze for another minute in a near stupor, Will shook his head. "Kristen was involved in this murder?"

Marrs pushed the two *Morning News* clippings closer to the tubby boy. "The police couldn't prove she and this Stern bigwig were involved before he killed his wife. He threw a big case for her, part of their plot to get out of town before Mrs. Stern died."

Will peered at the paper without picking it up. "This story says they were in Vail."

Marrs couldn't hide his frustration. This guy was dumber than the rocks he painted. "You think that's just coincidence? That they bumped into each other and decided to party the weekend his wife gets slashed?"

Will crushed his stub on the Bud logo in the ashtray. "So what'll they pay a million for?"

"A love letter promising Kristen she'd be wealthy after he got rid of Diana." Before Will could ask, Marrs added, "One of his law partners found it and is cooperating."

"I *am* surprised about Kristen. Didn't think she had any sexual impulse either way. But how does that prove they killed his wife?"

Marrs pulled out the letter written on Stern's stationery that he'd found in the study, and had hidden at Lottie's. "Read it."

Will leaned closer, but treated the document like it was contaminated. "Rich enough to live in Provence with Diana gone? How do I know he wrote it?"

"I've had the writing analyzed."

"Why are you bringing me in?"

"You can get us a meeting through Kristen's sister for a simple trade. The free market working."

Will jammed another cigarette in his mouth and lit up. "I would like Tina one more time. Best tail I ever had."

* * *

Burrows navigated the mess of boxes in Stern's study and sat by the fireplace.

Stern looked thoroughly drained.

Burrows figured this would be the last time the pseudo-patrician would talk to him. So far, Stern's ego thought he could handle a bedroom community detective on his own, but more heat would chase Stern into the embrace of a criminal defense lawyer. He'd get the best, who would immediately insist Stern quit talking to cops.

"We found Marrs's number on a message Janet took," Burrows said.

Stern clasped his manicured fingers together. "I get lots of messages."

"How come Marrs had hundred-dollar bills with your prints on them?"

"Christ, Burrows—he stole money from this room."

"You keep that kind of cash here?"

"I heard my old firm turned down that drunk, Livermore, for a job. Is that what's driving this?"

Burrows wondered if Stern had a mole in the DA's office. Probably, just like they had Caswell. Stern's confidence was eroding Burrows's nerves, but he decided to bring out his heavy artillery, now that he had Kristen's confession.

"So, how did Kristen find Sarah?"

Stern blinked. His mouth hung open for several seconds before snapping shut.

"What?"

Burrows scoffed. "When exactly did you tell her where Sarah was?"

"I . . . assumed it was Marrs's girlfriend who rescued Sarah. Lottie what's-her-name. She didn't ask for the reward so she wouldn't implicate him." Stern covered his eyes. "Kristen. Kristen fought that awful killer? Oh my God."

Burrows watched Stern carefully. The act was pretty good, but the guy was a professional phony. "How'd she know where to look? If you didn't tell her?"

Stern stood and paced, running his fingers through his hair. "I have no idea."

"How do you explain Marrs's parole file in your office?"

Stern clenched his fists in frustration. "I found it on my wife's printer upstairs. I thought she had some bizarre interest in the guy, so I copied the file. She was looking it over, but now I suspect she'd seen him hanging around. Stalking her."

"So you admit you copied it?"

Stern shrugged. "I'm sure you found my prints on the copies and Janet's as well."

Burrows smiled.

Stern leaned forward with the smirk of a poker player, calling with a full house. "Detective, let's quit jacking around. If you think you got enough to convict me, get your indictment, and let's boogie. I'm tired of this cat-and-mouse bullshit."

Burrows was in too deep to give up and decided to use his last reserve ammo. "Do you know where Kristen was the night Caswell was killed?"

Stern's eyes stared. Behind them, it looked like the dots were being connected. Like he now realized Kristen had a motive to shoot Caswell.

"Burrows, I'm busy." Stern got up and opened the library door.

Confidence returning, Burrows couldn't resist a parting chuckle. "Too bad she dumped your ass. Bet you're worried you don't know what she'll tell us."

* * *

Saturday

Sleepless in Jim's rental dump, Marrs felt pressure building. His parole hearing was on for the day after Christmas. He'd gotten a few more days, since it was hard to round up board members the week before Christmas. He dressed, angry with himself for not having a solid plan. Even with two potential assistants recruited—Lottie and Will—he wasn't sure how to proceed. So far, he hadn't been out of surveillance long enough to piss in private. He decided to risk a look.

He lifted a dusty blind and eyed the dark street. Zelner's personal minivan sat across from his house. If today's schedule was the same as yesterday's, the real cops would arrive soon to take over for the Boy Scout, who was willing to spend the night sipping coffee from a thermos. Didn't he have a pretty little wife to snuggle with on a Saturday morning? And where was his pal, the storm trooper with the gigantic oozing zit?

He couldn't check, but figured the cops had stuck a tracking device on Jimmy's Cherokee, which explained why his half brother had been only too glad to let him keep it until the parole hearing.

Time to gamble. He could hardly steal a police car. He stood on a rickety chair and jerked the bolt back on the deer rifle he'd dug up from the meth-head neighbor's yard. From behind the window, he aimed at Zelner. Hopefully, he was angling down enough for the damn thing to fire.

Marrs squeezed the trigger. An explosion erupted through the house, the van window shattered, and Zelner disappeared. Marrs dashed out the front door toward the van. The driver's window glass sported a hole and spiderweb of cracked glass. Half of Zelner's head had gone AWOL. Marrs looked around. No natives darted out of their huts. It was now or never.

He opened the door and shoved Zelner's carcass across the seat. He had maybe a couple of hours and would need help getting into Kristen's place. Fett seemed like the better option. If he couldn't get in, Lottie could play the *We need to visit, I've got evidence* card. They might be eager to talk to her. He wouldn't be driving his brother's car, so until Zelner was missed, he was free.

Marrs sped to Lottie's. In the dark nobody noticed the gore splashed on the windshield. Despite the time, she was already getting ready for work when he arrived. He had no trouble charming her into letting him borrow her Honda and a small revolver, allowing him to abandon Zelner's van. He dropped her off at the truck stop, promising nobody would get hurt and he'd keep her informed of his progress without furnishing any details.

Marrs drove to the motel where Will was staying, woke him up, and suggested he spruce himself up a little. Half an hour later, they headed to Kristen's place.

The sun was coming up when they parked three townhouses down from hers. Marrs knew he was running out of time, but hesitated, unsure what to do.

The places surrounding Kristen's were lit with an array of shining Christmas lights despite the dawn. Fake Christmas trees could be seen in two picture windows. Light frost coated the small, neat yards. Perfectly shaped birch trees fronted each unit. The street's charm made Marrs hate Kristen even more.

Will bitched and yawned between slurps of coffee. If he hadn't needed him, Marrs would've sliced the irritating artist. By eight, no plan had come to mind, other than sending Will to the front door, which he wasn't very eager to do. Will whined that if Kristen answered, she would beat him up. Based on personal experience, Marrs knew Kristen could beat Will to a pulp in two seconds.

Papers in the courtyard had not been picked up. Thankfully, everyone seemed to be sleeping in on Saturday. They had a fifty-fifty chance. If Tina answered the door, Will might get in without any fuss. If Wonder Woman appeared, he'd have to improvise.

"Fuck this shit. I wanna get some breakfast," Will muttered as he lit up again.

Just as he was going to throttle Will, a BMW backed out of Kristen's garage.

"Get down!"

Marrs peeked above the dash and spotted Kristen leaving the cul-de-sac. She turned onto Northwest Highway. They'd gotten a break.

Hopefully little sis hadn't had a hot date sleep over. Marrs shoved the fat boy toward the passenger door. "Go."

The guy was so slow, Marrs beat him to Kristen's front door on a bad leg.

Marrs pressed himself against the brick next to the door, making himself invisible, as Will tapped Kristen Kerry's doorbell.

Nothing.

Will pressed the button again, rocking back and forth, like he had the shits.

The door opened, but the glass storm remained closed.

Will flapped, "Tina, honey, I was in town and brought some of your—"

She slammed the door.

Will was as useless as Viagra in a lesbian bar. All the schemes Marrs cooked up came down to this dweeb getting in, and he couldn't get the door open.

Marrs looked around the courtyard, saw nobody, elbowed Will in the ribs, and mouthed, *Come on.*

Will rang again.

The door cracked again. "Get out!"

"Don't you want your silver jewelry?" Will managed to sound like he was returning her lost puppy that was going to be put to sleep if she didn't take it.

Tina pushed on the glass enough to stick out her hand. It was all they needed. Will jerked the door open. Marrs shoved the fat boy inside, then followed him through the door.

The sister stood frozen, then started to scream, so Marrs punched her in the belly, stunning and silencing her. He shoved Tina onto the nearest chair, pulled a roll of duct tape from his pocket, and ordered Will to tie her up.

Will grimaced. "I didn't want her to get hurt."

"This way she won't." Marrs cased the place, keeping Lottie's cheap little revolver ready. The townhome smelled of fresh coffee and furniture polish. Precious little antique knickknacks were everywhere. Ritzy prints adorned the walls. He wished he had cow shit on his boots.

Marrs tiptoed up the stairs, gun ready, listening at the top. He checked both bedrooms, finding no sign of anyone else.

Downstairs, Marrs motioned Will out of the way. He'd done a pitiful job. A kindergartener with polio could get out of that. Marrs jerked Tina's socks off and stuffed one in her mouth so he wouldn't have to listen to her sobbing. He re-taped her bare ankles, then wrapped half the roll around her and the chair to be safe. As he brushed his fingertips over her nice tits, his cock stiffened.

Will collapsed into a chair, chewing remnants of his nails. "I don't know about this."

Marrs glared at the blubbering idiot, sitting under a picture of disgusting little brats playing in a fountain, painted by some French fuck.

"She'll live."

* * *

Kristen tossed Sarah the basketball. They'd made it to the gym early enough on Saturday to get their own hoop and still let Sarah make winter batting practice. "Take your first shot from the top of the key. Follow your misses and shoot from where you rebound. I'll feed your goals."

Sarah nodded, dribbled a couple of times, and shot, bumping the ball off the front rim. She hustled after the ball and shot again.

"Use your left hand. Don't watch the ball while you dribble."

Kristen gave her fifteen minutes of solo work. The kid's knee seemed better.

"Good."

Sarah pursed her lips. "You mean, good for not having played in two years."

"No, I mean *good*."

"Okay, Coach."

They shot and passed for half an hour. Kristen occasionally offered suggestions, but knew not to overcoach. Sarah was tall for her age and very athletic, even on a gimpy leg. When she drained a three, Kristen said, "Nice. Water time."

"Think I've got potential?"

"Start violin lessons," Kristen deadpanned.

Sarah scrunched her face in exaggerated anger and fired the ball at Kristen. She ducked, and they laughed like they'd been friends for years.

After a drink, Sarah hung her head and spoke into her sweatshirt, "Wish I'd taken violin instead of playing that soccer tournament."

"Anybody can have a bad day."

She shook her head. "Every day's bad. My friends act weird."

"They don't know what to say."

Sarah picked at her warm-ups. "Dad wants to sell our house. I'd like to move to another country. I'm tired of taking pills the doctors give me."

"I had a bad time in high school. Everybody made me feel like I had leprosy."

"What happened?"

"Long story. My parents were nutty as a Snickers. I'll tell you sometime."

"I think of all the times I popped off to my mom. All the stupid arguments I started." She sniffed, rubbing her eyes. "Wish I could tell her I'm sorry. That I'm really sorry I was so bad to her."

Kristen squeezed Sarah's shoulder. "I don't believe you were bad."

She pulled Sarah closer as the kid sobbed. In a minute, Sarah was struggling to catch her breath. Kristen stroked her short blond hair. "I understand. It's okay."

Sarah asked between breaths, "Can you come skiing with us next week? Dad really wants you to."

"No, I can't."

Sarah sniffed hard and shook her head, as if to clear it. "Are you still mad at him?"

Kristen decided not to fib. "Yes." Their eyes locked, searching each other. "You and I can still be friends."

"He's crazy about you."

"I know."

"He can be a little embarrassing sometimes, acts kind of old. But he's a cool dad. Even my friends think so."

Kristen kept her tone neutral. "Uh-huh."

The last thing the girl needed was doubt about Michael's wonderful qualities.

A minute passed as Sarah studied Kristen. Kristen guessed what was coming and got ready.

"It was you, wasn't it? In the closet. At the hospital?"

"Yes."

Sarah's voice cracked, tears flowing again. "I'll never forget you."

"Same here." Remembering the near rape and the fight, Kristen's eyes blurred. It took awhile to regain any composure. She was glad the gym was still empty. Sarah cried with her.

They hugged again. Kristen wondered if she could adopt Sarah without having to marry her dad.

Kristen let go an instant after Sarah did.

"How about a game of horse. I'll give you two steps every shot. Bet you a stack of pancakes."

"You're on." Sarah picked up the ball. "I hope I can play something in college. Like you did."

"Lots of late-night bus trips, make-up tests. No sorority parties."

Sarah dribbled, then fired from the line, the ball kissing off the board. "I know, but I'd have a real college jersey and ring. Anybody can buy fakes. And my best friends are the girls I play with."

Kristen retrieved the ball, stepped behind the free throw line, and popped the net. "I'm impressed with anybody who can play fast-pitch. I couldn't hit a lick."

Sarah trotted to the ball. "Maybe I could give *you* a lesson sometime."

Kristen smiled. "I've got a drawer full of old practice jerseys with sweat stains, and a bunch of shooting videos. You're welcome to any of it."

"Wow! Thanks."

"We'll swing by my house on the way back."

CHAPTER 49

MARRS HELD HIS KNIFE in one hand and slapped the little sister. "I'm gonna take the tape off, and you're gonna tell me when Kristen's coming back, or I'll cut off your pretty nose."

Will paced across Kristen's carpet, sending pitiful glances toward his former girlfriend. "Don't hurt her!"

"Shut up." Marrs hit Tina again, then held her head still and slipped the tip of his stiletto into one nostril. Blood dribbled toward her nice lips. He ripped the tape from her mouth, risking a scream a neighbor might hear.

She answered between staccato breaths, "I . . . don't . . . know . . . I . . . haven't . . . seen . . . her . . . She got up . . . before I did . . . and left . . . Last night . . . she said she was . . . going to shoot baskets."

Marrs jammed the sock back into her mouth. She wasn't as tough as her big sis and probably told the truth. Where the hell had Kristen gone this early on a Saturday?

He considered calling Lottie and asking her to do a drive-by at Stern's, but remembered he had her car. Blood flowed to his dick, as much from fear as excitement. Soon the cops would miss Zelner and this place would be on their list to look. Maybe not the first place, so he might have some time.

"I didn't think anybody would get hurt," the big fat pussy said.

Marrs pointed a gloved finger at Will. "I said watch the street."

"What if Stern won't buy the letter? What if he calls the cops?"

Marrs sneered at the human grease trap. "Go to the fucking window."

After a minute, looking like he'd been hypnotized, Will complied.

Marrs decided to do a more thorough search, hoping to find an answer to where Kristen had gone. He limped back up the stairs. In the bigger bedroom, he found Kristen's 9 mm Browning in a vinyl case under the canopy bed. The beautiful black piece with its wide clip smelled of gun oil. He stuffed the big automatic in his pants and headed back downstairs.

Will held the curtain aside, kissing the glass. As Marrs approached, he turned. Marrs aimed Lottie's .22 at the fat boy, whose anxious expression morphed into wide-eyed terror.

Marrs fired. Will Fett had served his purpose.

Will's hands clamped over the crimson stain on his white shirt.

Marrs stepped closer. The next bullet drilled a hole in Will's forehead. Mr. Artsy of Santa Fe farted, then flopped to the floor like a sack of dog food.

The little sister squirmed and moaned like she suddenly decided she liked the dumbass. Marrs looked at her and shook his head like he was so sorry.

A modified plan hatched in his head. He ambled away from the stench, over to Tina. He spun the chair, so that her secured hand faced the dead boyfriend. Marrs clamped the revolver against her palm and fired toward Will. Powder residue would look like she'd shot the shithead.

He jerked the gun away and knelt beside her. "Aren't you a doll?"

He ran his hands under her sweatshirt and squeezed her firm little tits. Tugging her nipples, he felt the old intensity in his groin.

"No brassiere? What bad manners with company here."

Marrs unsnapped her jeans. He jammed his hand down and

fingered her while chuckling in her face. Playing around helped reduce his fear. She was smart enough not to squirm.

Her vagina dampened. Marrs figured she actually enjoyed it and wondered if he could make her come. He probed back and forth, making her wetter. Her wax job further excited him. His thumb stroked her clit. Her breathing quickened, but he figured she was faking for the audience.

He pulled his hand out of her pants and wiped his fingers on her shirt. Hitting her would be more fun. Marrs pulled her sweatshirt up and punched her tight stomach, not hard at first, but with more force each time, then around the kidneys with all his strength. Enough of this and she'd be pissing blood. Marrs learned this trick in prison.

She gagged, her tongue pushing at the sock in her mouth. Giggling, he moved to her tits. Welts rose on her breasts. Tears ran over her cheeks. Aroused now, Marrs used his blade to rip open her underwear. He returned to her crotch, warming up for Kristen.

He lost track of time.

Jesus H. Christ, she's cute. No wonder Will thought she was fine.

The garage door rattled up, interrupting the fun. Marrs pulled away.

He positioned himself behind the kitchen door, hearing two female voices yakking away, happy as larks.

Two?

The door opened. Kristen and the Stern kid strolled in. Their shoes stuck to the tile, pie holes gaping.

His lucky day. He'd hit the daily double. Now he didn't have to worry about hurting Stern's jock girlfriend before getting paid. The kid was worth far more. Stern could always get a new babe, but not a daughter.

All Marrs had to worry about was how much time he had here in Disneyland.

* * *

Sitting in Tammy Robberson's living room Detective Burrows checked his recorder again, making sure it would capture every word. Point by point, he was exposing that Kristen's tale was just as bogus as the Loch Ness Monster. Soon, he'd hand Livermore enough to round up the whole herd of conspirators, even without Caswell to back it up. He would make the front page of the paper, hauling Stern and the Kerry girls to the hoosegow.

The former Adventist insurance adjuster, dressed in a robe and thick socks, plopped her big feet on her coffee table. "I don't know a thing about any patient list," she said.

"Nothing?"

Tammy shrugged. "It'd be illegal as hell."

"But it could be done?" Burrows asked.

"I s'pose, if one wanted to risk going to jail, but why would I do her any favors after she got me in trouble?"

"Didn't she support you in the disciplinary hearing?"

"She told the truth. For once. She sure never told me she was involved with Stern, though I suspected it when she wouldn't do what Pete and I told her."

"Let me make this clear. Did Kristen Kerry ever ask you for help locating any person treated in emergency—"

"I wouldn't piss on that bitch if she was on fire." Tammy's lips turned down for an instant before she added, "You know, it's sad."

"What?"

"I warned Kristen to stay away from Stern, that he would kill his own mother."

* * *

After dropping Sarah at the gym for her basketball session and returning home, Stern poured himself more coffee. It hadn't been hard to sell Sarah on asking Kristen for a basketball lesson. Sarah wanted to play on the school team with her classmates and admired anybody who played college ball. Sarah had called Kristen herself, giving him plausible deniability. When he'd dropped Sarah off, he hadn't walked her in, so he could avoid Kristen.

Stern had been surprised Kristen had agreed to the tutoring, giving him a shred of hope he might be able to repair the damage he'd done. Perhaps his daughter could bring them back together. He craved Kristen's legs around him, her taut belly, her hair hanging freshly washed. But mostly, he yearned for her forgiveness.

Then, last night, Burrows dropped his bombshell. Stern castigated himself for his stupidity, not realizing Kristen had been the one who saved his daughter. By delivering his princess, she'd shown him more loyalty and love than he deserved.

Spiriting Sarah from those cutthroats would've taken amazing guts and smarts. No wonder she'd looked like she wanted to rip his balls off that day in the library. He guessed she hadn't told him because she worried that he'd only want her out of obligation.

He'd mined his brain half the night, trying to retrace Kristen's steps without success. Setting his mug aside, he stacked the stories on Diana's death on his desk and studied them again. He knew that if Kristen had first denied finding Sarah, then confessed under pressure, Burrows would think he'd turned an unassisted double play.

While sorting through the articles, he cursed his folly in hanging onto the transcripts. His curiosity and Kristen's mistrust of him could get them charged with murder. Had she announced herself in the ER and explained then how she'd found Sarah, the cops' conspiracy theory would've been buried like a dry hole in a depleted Texas oilfield.

He sipped hot coffee. For the first time since Diana was killed, he was scared. Dallas County was notorious for sending innocent men to prison. In front of a typical jury, he'd have zero appeal as the rich Highland Park lawyer. Hitler would have a better chance. He pictured himself in prison, away from his princess. He'd rather leave Sarah with Diana's sister and shoot himself.

Stern found a story on Marrs, recounting that the bastard had previously been shot, supposedly protecting some unknown woman. The tone suggested the tale told by Marrs was nonsense. Perhaps the prior shooting was Kristen's clue.

Tammy Robberson could get Kristen the identity of a shooting victim by supplying a date or hospital, or both. And Kristen had protected Tammy at Proctor's kangaroo court. Two months ago, Kristen would have sent her former client to death row, given the chance.

But how would Kristen know somebody tied to Diana's murder had once been shot? She must have been tipped off by whoever plugged him, someone who didn't want police involvement, but might tell a charming private detective.

He smiled. She was a better cop than the slobs with badges.

His smile disappeared as he realized Tammy was also extremely dangerous. Burrows, trying to prove his conspiracy, would attempt to demolish Kristen's story. If he was right that hospital treatment led Kristen to Marrs, Tammy wouldn't admit to hacking patient records. It'd be a HIPAA violation, a crime punishable by ten years in the federal country club.

Stern gulped the last of the coffee, grabbed a jacket, and darted out the back door. If he could get to Tammy before Burrows, he had enough dirt on her to force her to 'fess up.

He drove out of the garage and through the archway, making no attempt to avoid his assigned tail. Stern waved at the cop as he passed.

Trailed all the way, Stern drove to the swank Palomar Hotel on Mockingbird and parked near the entrance. He checked his mirror and noticed the officer use his radio, giving his location, probably requesting instructions.

Stern got out, strolled across the marble lobby, went into the restaurant, and ordered breakfast. He killed another minute sipping coffee. Not seeing the tail, he figured the patrolman had been told to wait outside, until their hot suspect reemerged. His expense account probably couldn't handle breakfast in this joint.

Stern rose and ducked into the restroom in the lobby. The john attendant happily took a hundred to cover the meal and get the bellman to send a cab to the back delivery door.

Twenty minutes later, the taxi stopped in front of Tammy's two-story near Las Colinas, a place way too plush for an insurance supervisor's salary. He guessed it had been bought with kickbacks from settlements and fees. Not that he'd ever paid any. Servicing her had been enough to get a Purple Heart. As he got out, he recognized the big four-door parked across the street. *Too late.*

Stern trotted up the walk. Before he reached Tammy's porch, Burrows shuffled out, closing the door behind him. The detective craned his neck, looking for the tailing cop car. Shock spread across his fat face. "What're you doin' here?"

Every time he saw Burrows in his green jacket, Stern wanted to ask him when he won the fucking Masters, but settled for, "What did Tammy tell you?"

Burrows stuck a finger in Stern's chest. "You're interfering in an investigation."

Stern slapped the hand away. "You ought to ask your *witness* how Layne could've croaked from a gut bug in his lungs."

"Get outta here!"

"Galway got religion. Going to do public service with Indian Health in Arizona. Told me Layne died because somebody swabbed his throat with shit."

Burrows snarled, "I don't give a goddamn about your case." Burrows strode past Stern.

Stern grabbed the cop's sleeve. "Tammy's lying, and you're not smart enough or interested enough to listen. You're believing a murderer."

Burrows jerked his arm free. "And I'm seein' one now."

"I only need five minutes with that liar, and you'll get the truth."

"One more word and you're under arrest."

The teenage boys next door, who had been chatting and shooting baskets in their driveway when Stern arrived, stood mute in shock while their ball rolled into the street.

Stern pointed at the cop. "Thanks to you and the DA, nobody in town can sleep without worrying about getting their throat sliced."

"Okay, Stern." Burrows jerked open the passenger door of his car, flipped down the glove box, and pulled out a pair of cuffs. "I should've clamped you at the airport."

Stern thrust his fists out. "Go ahead. And get ready for my lawsuit."

Burrows's face turned purple. He slapped the cuffs on Stern's outstretched wrists, then tugged open the car's back door. "Get in!"

Stern felt more anger than fear. "Why don't you pick up Kristen and Tina, too? Charge them with unauthorized rescue. For doing *your* fucking job."

Burrows slammed his palms into Stern, spinning him toward the backseat. "You're about to get hurt, resisting arrest."

Stern let the Doughboy have the last word. The cop might well shoot him without a moment's thought. Stern ducked, plopping down behind the wire cage separating the backseat from the front.

Burrows piled in and slammed the door, shaking the car. Stern noticed the back doors had no handles.

The cop swiveled around, grinning at Stern. "Got news for you, Counselor. The witness to Caswell's killing is now sure the shooter was a woman, tall, maybe five-ten. Let's get your girlfriend in for a lineup and a search warrant since her story done came unraveled."

Stern's gut clenched.

Was Kristen capable of cold-blooded murder? Nobody deserved to be wasted more than Caswell, but could she kill Caswell to protect both of them? Fighting the idiotic plot Burrows dreamed up was one thing.

Beating a murder rap with an eyewitness was another.

Or was Burrows bluffing? Hoping to bait him into a mistake?

Burrows must have noticed Stern's anxiety. "Too bad they don't allow conjugal visits between prisoners. I bet she's a real fine piece of ass."

For once Stern was too scared for a comeback.

* * *

A stench slapped Kristen. Her eyes locked onto Tina, who was tied to her Chippendale chair, her hands and ankles taped, her mouth gagged with a sock, her shirt up to her breasts, her jeans open. Nasty welts everywhere. Kristen's nose directed her to the front window. Will lay against the wall, lifeless eyes open.

Will?

"Freeze."

She spun around and saw Marrs leveling a small revolver at her. Her heart bounced off the inside of her chest.

Mother of God.

"You can eat a bullet, like cuntface there, or you can cooperate. This heater ain't very loud, so I'll be happy to use it again."

A rat raced through her brain. He was a good five steps away. She had no option but to raise her hands.

Sarah backed toward the door, tears streaming down her cheeks.

Kristen grabbed Sarah's shoulder and managed a throaty whisper. "Hold it, sugar. We'll be okay. Your dad's coming."

Marrs flung a roll of duct tape at Kristen. "You wish. Wrap up the kid."

Sarah struggled to pull away. Kristen, afraid Marrs would shoot if Sarah ran, tightened her grip on Sarah's sweatshirt. The kid was strong. Kristen had to tug her back hard, practically tackling her, corralling her until she could figure out something.

Sarah started wailing, her legs unsteady. "It's him!"

Kristen held Sarah, praying she would settle down so she could think.

What had he done to Tina, and what the hell was Will doing here? *Dead.*

Grabbing the tape, she debated whether to fling it at his face and dive into the bastard. There could be a better chance later, but she'd only get one.

He must have read her mind. "Don't even think about it. I just want the kid out of the way." He curled his nose. "She ain't my type."

Her heart pounded so loud, the monster had to hear it. She needed Sarah to calm down, so she could think.

"It's okay, honey."

"Wrap it tight, dollface."

"It's him, it's him," Sarah screamed.

Marrs shook the pistol. "Shut her up!"

Kristen cupped Sarah's mouth. "Sarah, it'll be all right."

Sarah sank to the floor, choking on her own saliva.

Kristen knelt and unrolled a strand of tape. She wrapped Sarah's wrists together, then her ankles. "We're going to be okay." Kristen didn't believe her own words.

"Good. Now, we're going to deal with those feet of yours. Tape your ankles."

Her own breathing came in a staccato of gulps, but she managed to spit out, "The police will eventually come here. You could take my car and ATM card. Make the border in five hours."

"Better yet, drop those britches." He laughed. "Works better on bare skin. Slow."

She began unlacing her Reeboks. "Why?"

"I figured Stern would pay for your sweet ass, but now I hit the mother lode."

"He can't spit without the cops on him." She tugged off her shoes.

"How can he pay—"

"He'll find a way." He jerked the gun, his voice more agitated. Sweat beaded over his lip. "Get 'em off."

Kristen knew she had to keep him calm. She methodically untied her warm-ups and pushed them to the floor. A sea of goose bumps covered her skin. She felt like she was naked in Texas Stadium on Thanksgiving. She pulled off her socks. Sweat flooded from every pore.

Hail Mary, full of Grace.

Kristen slowly taped her own ankles together. "What makes you do this?"

Marrs's stare crawled to her crotch. "Tighter. We're gonna have some fun."

Kristen did another loop, tore, and placed the roll of tape down. "Was it childhood abuse? I know about—"

"Shut the fuck up! I'll do your hands. If there's any shit, the girl dies."

That had been a mistake. How long would it be before Michael wondered where Sarah was? Probably too long. The only way to buy time might be to let him do with her what he wanted, but the thought of his hands on her made her guts start to dissolve. Unless she came up with something fast, she would die. After killing Will, Marrs had no reason to let her or Tina live.

"You can claim self-defense with that killing," Kristen said. "He was a vicious prick." Kristen nodded at Will's corpse, even managing something resembling a come-hither smile that didn't seem to register.

"Quiet, bitch! Your yappin' is going to make everything hurt more." He slid closer. "Hands together, behind your back. But, first, put this over your head." He tossed what must have been Will's coat. "If I see a fuckin' flinch, the kid gets shot."

Screw your courage to the sticking place.

Kristen pulled the coat over her head, becoming blind.

Imitate the tiger.

She pressed her wrists together behind her back and listened for his footsteps, knowing this would be her only chance.

* * *

Burrows squealed his unmarked Crown Vic to a stop in the courtyard in front of Kristen's townhouse. He twisted toward Stern in the backseat. "You want your girlfriend arrested? You got it."

"You don't have shit."

Burrows smirked at Stern, who now didn't sound quite so cocky. "Save it."

After locking Stern in the car, Burrows stormed up the brick sidewalk.

His cell rang. "What?"

A Park officer blubbered in his ear, "Boss, we got a trace from the State Department on that bank account number in Costa Rica. It's a conduit to another numbered account in Switzerland."

"I don't give a damn."

"Feds leaned on the Swiss. They said it's registered to Caswell's father."

Burrows barely heard, focusing on Stern, snickering in the backseat. The pompous shit could do his lawyering from a corner cell. Burrows barked into his phone, "I got Stern and his girlfriend nailed. Get me a backup from DPD at her condo."

Burrows hung up. He should wait for help and get a warrant, but he wanted Stern to see his girlfriend and her sister frog-marched out, wanted to see them sharing the backseat of *his* car. Paperwork could be sorted out later. Even if a judge called the pinch invalid, they could take the mess to the grand jury and redo everything without prejudicing a conviction.

Burrows pressed the doorbell.

No answer.

He pressed his ear to the door and listened.

Curtains in the picture window fluttered.

Burrows flung open the storm door and pounded. "Open up. Police!"

No answer. He banged harder. "This is Detective Burrows. You're under arrest! Both of you!" The veins in his neck swelled. His blood pressure likely hit 180.

He kicked the door, shaking it. Rearing back, he kicked again, blasting the bolt out of the jamb.

Burrows put his hand on his revolver, but didn't draw it, thinking the two women wouldn't put up any resistance.

Stepping in, the scene took his labored breath away. The Stern kid lay tied up, her eyes as big as flashlights. A body to his left, some fat guy he'd never seen before, was very dead. His cholesterol-lined heart pumped. Burrows had never used his gun in thirty years as a cop.

As he pulled out his Colt Detective Special, he heard shots and felt sharp pain through his belly and chest. His legs gave out. The last thing he saw were the pavers on the entryway.

* * *

While Marrs fired, Kristen threw off the jacket, then ripped the tape from her ankles.

Marrs booted the front door closed. Springing to her feet, she charged him.

Before she could tear out his eyeballs, he fired.

Kristen's right leg buckled, taking her to her knees. Her thigh felt like a hot rivet had been driven through it.

She tried to stand, but teetered back to the floor, her leg unable to support any weight. The bullet may have nicked bone, but the femoral artery wasn't severed, or blood would be squirting across the room instead of just streaming down.

She clamped a palm over the hole and guessed she wouldn't bleed to death right away.

Marrs giggled. His tight jeans bulged in front as he aimed the revolver at her other leg. "No more kicking out of you."

Kristen held up her clean hand. "I'm not worth anything dead."

Marrs nodded at Sarah. "Got all the goodies I need."

He stepped nearer and pulled the trigger, but the hammer dropped with only a click.

The breath she'd been holding gushed out.

While Marrs flipped the cylinder out, checking for ammo, she pushed herself to her bare feet, her balance precarious. Pain sharpened with each step.

As she neared him, Marrs pulled a big automatic pistol from behind his waistband. It looked like her own 9 mm Browning. He pointed it at her good leg.

Kristen grabbed the closest thing she could get her hands on, her nineteenth-century serving tray from the coffee table.

Marrs clucked, wagged a finger, and shook his head, as if she were a naughty little tyke. He worked the slide back, ejecting a round, apparently unfamiliar with a double-action weapon. He pointed the pistol at her unwounded leg.

"Come on, bitch."

She drew the tray back, weight on her good leg, unsure whether to throw it or get closer.

Before she could decide, Marrs squeezed the trigger.

No sound. He stepped back, worked the slide once more, and ejected another round. He pulled the trigger again. Still nothing happened.

She tottered toward him. *Hurry!*

Marrs stared, perplexed, then spotted the safety prongs on each side of the pistol's hammer.

Before he could flip the safety, Kristen swung the antique, slashing like one of Tennyson's Hussars, catching his hand square on. The Browning sailed almost all the way to the kitchen, the tray not as far. She jabbed into Marrs's solar plexus, the blow pathetic without balance behind it. No point kicking with only one good leg.

She punched at his throat, but he blocked her, sidestepped, and booted her unwounded leg out from under her, sending her crashing to the carpet.

Fire surged through her thigh. As she struggled to stand again, Marrs planted his shoe in her ribs.

Christ, it hurt, but she spun away.

He kicked her again and again, following her. Each blow into her torso sucked more air from her lungs. Tissue crunched and snapped. She prayed he wouldn't strike her head.

The last kick likely cracked a rib, doubling her agony. It was painful to inhale. Her strength ebbed. Almost out of time.

She reached the wall and attempted to stand against it, but he drove his foot into her bleeding wound.

Pain came in a tsunami. She yelled, praying somebody would hear. Foul bile filled her mouth.

Giggling like a kindergartner hunting candy Easter eggs, he stepped back to strike her again. It gave her enough room to twist away and grab his ankle, but he jerked free.

She cursed her growing weakness. She should have been able to hold him. He wasn't that big.

Marrs glanced to his left and saw her Browning on the floor, near the kitchen table, where it had landed a few feet from Sarah. He scurried toward it.

Tina struggled against her bindings, but hadn't made any progress. She looked terrified. If only Tina could get loose, they'd have a chance.

Kristen pushed herself onto her good leg and limped as fast as she could after Marrs, leaving a maroon trail on the alabaster Berber carpet. Seconds seemed like days as she followed the killer.

A movie flashed through her mind: basketball, Gina and her siblings, Michael's beautiful hands on her breasts.

Pray for us sinners. Now and at the hour of our death.

But before Marrs reached the pistol, Sarah rolled herself over it.

Way to go, girl!

"Move, you little cunt!"

Marrs stooped to shove her off, but the young athlete braced her feet against the baseboard and held fast. He kicked her, but Sarah stayed rooted on the pistol, shrieking behind the tape, absorbing the blow. Somehow Sarah's strength held.

Picking up the tray and plodding after him, Kristen finally reached Marrs. She swung the tray at his head, but he ducked.

Fuck! He was too quick for her.

Marrs reached into his back pocket. Seeing the flash of steel, Kristen bear-hugged him before he could draw the blade. They teetered together for a second, Kristen able to smell his awful sour sweat. Or maybe it was hers.

Keeping a grip on Marrs as tight as she could with her remaining strength, Kristen shoved off with her good leg.

For a moment, maybe a lifetime, they teetered before they toppled over Sarah.

Sarah became part of the tangle, uncovering the Browning.

Marrs stretched for the automatic pistol, but Kristen landed closer. She grabbed it, lunged away, and flipped the safety, revealing the red dots on each side of the hammer.

Before Kristen could shoot, Marrs jerked Sarah up on her bound feet and crouched behind her, using her as a shield. He was only a couple of inches taller than the kid. He edged toward the kitchen door, taking Sarah with him. Holding her with one arm, his other hand pressed a stiletto to Sarah's neck.

"I'll slice her throat, bitch."

Kristen aimed at them, unsure what to do, too scared to fire.

"I'll toss the pistol if you let her go."

"You're gonna lose it soon anyway. You're bleeding like a stuck pig."

Half a minute passed. Kristen blinked, pretending to grow feeble. Not a hard act. Blood now flowed freely down her calf. She lowered the gun to her waist and stared at the floor, like she was about to land on it.

Sarah seemed to understand, twisted, and dropped to a knee.

Burning her last store of energy, Kristen whipped her weapon back up and, with two hands on the pistol, fired over Sarah before Marrs could reclaim his shield. Marrs rocketed back into the wall, his palm vaulting to his wounded shoulder. Blood soaked his shirt.

Sarah rolled away.

Kristen's ears rang from the thunder of the big automatic. A 9 mm pistol fired in a closed room sounded like a ton of TNT. She was damn glad she had gone to the firing range last summer.

As Sarah rolled to her, Kristen lowered her aim and fired.

Squealing like a little girl, Marrs crumpled to the floor.

Keeping the cocked Browning poised to inflict more destruction, Kristen smiled. "I've got nine rounds left. The next is for your balls. Who gave you the key? How'd you get into the Stern house?"

Blood coated his shirt. Marrs dropped the blade to the floor. "Don't shoot. This guy came to my place, but I never saw him." Marrs loosed a ripping cough. "I got the key in the mail with the alarm code . . ."

"Who?"

"Please . . ."

"I said who was it!"

"Never saw him . . . young lawyer I think. Talked funny. Odd accent."

Kristen's vision clouded. She blinked several times, unable to see clearly.

Marrs changed to the misshapen monster chasing her in her dreams. She fired as fast as she could pull the trigger, the sound almost a continuous roar. The hulk in her nightmares, standing in for her father. Marrs died long before her magazine emptied.

Tina groaned something that sounded like *Way to go.*

Kristen knelt, threw the pistol aside, and tried deep breaths to clear her head. Finding determination from Lord knew where, she scooped up her sweats, wrapped them on her leg, and tied a hard knot over the hole. She crawled over to Sarah and tugged tape from the girl's mouth.

Sarah said she was okay; she seemed more concerned about Kristen. Kristen's shaking hands just managed to tear the tape on Sarah's wrists.

Kristen crawled to Burrows. She found a faint pulse, heard shallow breath sounds, and pressed hard against the chest wound, but she sensed herself fading.

Sarah limped to the phone and dialed 911, then began helping Tina.

Kristen had enough consciousness left to feel the cold tile she collapsed on before everything went dark.

CHAPTER 50

Tuesday, December 30

FOR THE FIRST TIME IN fifteen years, Kristen walked up the center aisle of a Catholic church. She focused on the crucifix, the symbol of suffering and sacrifice, knowing she had to confront her anger. Anger at God for letting a pretty good kid be abused.

Sarah Stern didn't deserve to be kidnapped, and maybe she was alive because the Blessed Mother heard Kristen's prayers. Perhaps everything served a purpose. The nightmares had diminished. She'd learned she could love and be loved, though the guy was flawed. She could even leave him, heart more or less intact. People could think of her what they wanted, but no one could call her a coward.

Her wound still tender, she half-genuflected, crossed herself, and dropped into a pew. She felt like she had found the innocent child within her, the kid who'd received First Communion in second grade, wearing white, who hadn't yet been afraid to sleep.

She knelt, weight on the uninjured leg. Clasping her hands, she prayed for Sarah and Michael. She did the same for her constantly afraid and drugged-up mom. Gathering her resolve, she prayed that her father find solace from his addictions, and that she receive the grace to forgive him.

After confession and Mass, she left Holy Trinity Church, resolved to fly to Jersey, see her baby sister, and confront her mother. When she returned, she'd meet Michael. She'd asked Tina to keep him away, despite the avalanche of flowers, Christmas presents, and catered steak dinners in her hospital room, as well as him paying for new carpet and paint in her townhouse. He deserved a decent good-bye.

* * *

Saturday, February 10th.

Sinking low in her car so as not to be seen, Janet Wharton watched Michael walk toward Kristen. Buds on the trees looked ready to burst, but she felt no anticipation of spring. Agonizing loneliness mingled with cold guilt. If she'd had the energy, she would've hated Kristen.

Kristen's gorgeous hair, which should be outlawed, hung loose, as if it had just been washed and brushed. Despite the chill, she wore knee-length shorts showing off long shapely legs. Her V-neck sweater showed tight skin—bronzed, flawless, passable for a coed's.

As he neared her, Michael's expression carried a buoyancy tinged with anxiety. It was the anxiety of a man who'd spent a lifetime searching for a holy relic, had found it, but now couldn't get the grail home.

By a pixie statue in Prather Park, Kristen slouched on a bench, hands in her windbreaker, watching him. Every time Janet talked to Michael, the conversation always drifted back to Kristen. *Had Janet heard anything? Where was she? What did she think Kristen might be thinking?*

She recalled Michael's affairs, how painful it had been to cover for him. If only it could have been her, just once, to fix his breakfast, straighten his tie, and kiss him good-bye.

Kristen was everything Michael ever desired, but wasn't the least intimidated by him. He loved her all the more for it. Kristen rescued Sarah. Twice. She could bop him when he needed it. Michael would never get over Kristen, even if she told him to shove off.

Janet was no competition to Kristen Kerry. All she had to offer was loyalty, loyalty barely acknowledged. And love, unrequited.

Time to get out of town while the getting was good, before the Mesquite police came around again. Michael would figure out the cryptic note she had left. He might even be grateful and remember her forever. That would make what she'd done worth it.

Janet Wharton eased her car away, a U-Haul trailing with every useful possession.

She couldn't resist another glance, but didn't let it linger. Start over, find a new town with a new dream lover.

Michael would never be hers, though she had killed a man for him.

* * *

Sitting on a big metal turtle next to the steel pixie, Kristen spotted Stern, striding across the yellow-flowered spring weeds.

She stood, goose bumps rising on her skin. She attributed her reaction to the breeze, in denial that there remained any attraction. She reminded herself to be firm. Let him go, no matter what he said.

He gave her a shy smile. He slowed his steps, seeming uncertain how to greet her. Kristen folded her arms, warding him off.

He stopped a yard away.

After an awkward moment, he asked, "How was Jersey?"

She realized the old hustler, God's gift to women, was as nervous as an acne-covered boy on his first date. Might as well talk about the weather.

"Good. I spent time with Beth, talked about drugs and losers. I think she listened. Took her and Tina to Aruba. Beth's coming out here for college in the fall."

"And your mom?" He was going through the motions, but at least he remembered them.

"We argued, but didn't yell. She was actually sober. Most of the time."

He glanced down. "And Tina?"

"She's enrolled at UT Dallas and has a job that requires clothes."

He smiled. "And your leg?"

"Full recovery. Thanks for the orthopedic referral. I got a queen's treatment."

He eyed the ground a second, perhaps unsure what to say next. It took him a minute, but he finally said, "I heard they still don't have anything on Caswell's murder."

She realized he suspected *she* had shot Caswell. She wasn't sure whether to deny it or take credit. She shook her head. "Too bad, so sad."

He kept eye contact a moment, as if trying to read her mind. "I'm glad the bar only gave you a reprimand."

She shrugged. "They thought it would look bad to disbar me, but didn't want to condone burglary and privacy violations. The feds agreed to a misdemeanor with probation." She smiled. "I heard you dodged the perjury rap."

"Honestly, I didn't know." He drew a deep breath. "Can we go somewhere?"

"We can talk here."

He seemed to deflate, then gather resolve. "Will you give us another chance?"

Her response was well rehearsed. "My mind's made up."

"Kristen . . . I love you with all my heart. I've changed. You know that."

"We've both changed."

"I've got plenty of faults, but Burrows's theory was nonsense. He's retired on disability. I had nothing to do with Diana's death. That was crazy. Livermore quit. They discovered Caswell used his dad's overseas account for the ransom drop."

She remembered Marrs's last words. Was the *he* Marrs mentioned—was it Caswell? Tony was certainly capable of such a hideous plot.

Marrs had said, "accent."

She shook her head. "I don't think you killed anybody."

Kristen locked her jaw, deciding to let him have it one more time.

"But you broke a sealed court order that was there to protect an innocent kid from gossiping assholes. I was a minor when I testified!" She planted her palms against her hips and leaned closer. "Don't you know how much that hurt? I never wanted another living soul to know what happened. Even the stupid cops and DA found out."

His eyes moistened. He held his hands up in surrender. "How many times do I have to ask you to forgive me? Don't you Catholics allow for penance? Can't I do *something* to atone?"

"I have forgiven you. I saw a priest, who said I should. But it doesn't mean I want to get involved with you again. The pain was too much. Somebody I cared about really hurt me."

He stared at his shoes, running his fingers through hair grayer than last summer. He was even thinner than the last time she saw him. She felt an odd motherly instinct to ask if he was eating.

"I would cut off a hand to undo what I did." He stopped, sniffed. "Sarah and I owe you so much. I wish you'd let me show you how grateful we are, how much I love you. *We* love you."

Love. That word carried so much danger. She'd never used that word with a man and wondered if she ever would. "Sarah needs all your energy, all your time," she said.

"Sarah's pretty crazy about you. If she'd known I was meeting you, she would've insisted on coming, too."

Kristen felt a gush of emotion. Though they'd exchanged texts about basketball, Kristen was damn glad Sarah wasn't here. She would have melted, would have caved in a second. She told herself to get a grip, that she didn't come here to be stampeded into his arms.

Despite her self-lecturing, she blurted, "I'll never forget that girl." She paused. "Or Vail."

He started to speak, but his voice broke. He turned his face.

She, too, had to look away.

The statues of darling children in the park tugged her heart even more, so she spun back. Her hand, as if under its own volition, left her jacket pocket and took his. She remembered laughing on the trail, the hot tub, the shampoo, and the dreamless nights.

A glance at his broad shoulders sent a tremor through her. She felt his body heat even a yard away and remembered the first time he'd entered her, how she'd pulled him in deeper, and how she hadn't wanted him to finish.

If not for the huge emotional risks, she could drag him to the backseat of her car, which was parked a few yards away.

Looking back at the pixies, she wondered what their kids might look like. His strong nose? Blue eyes and tall? Tall for sure. Would she get to coach her own daughters? Could she give him a son—a beautiful baby boy for Sarah to dote over?

He moved nearer, his lips a foot away.

She retreated a step, shook her head . . . and then asked herself what the point was of seeking forgiveness, without forgiving another in return? She knew she'd never love anyone, except maybe her own children, like she did Michael and Sarah.

The lawyer in her took over. "I have an offer for you, Counselor."

He cocked his head, perplexed.

"It won't be easy," she warned.

He frowned, looking confused.

"We had a fabulous weekend, a great Thanksgiving, but not enough time to know whether it will last."

"Sometimes you live more in a day than a year."

"Maybe so, but I've still got issues. Your plate is crammed full."

"We can work through—"

"And you don't owe me a thing. Don't love me for saving Sarah. Please."

"Baby, I—"

Her forefinger stopped him.

"Here's the deal."

She paused, holding his gaze, letting him suffer a little.

"Yes?" He spoke like the word had four syllables.

"You're on *probation*."

Kristen let that sink in.

"Be a hell of a dad. Stay out of bars and stay home with your daughter. I won't miss many of Sarah's games or the ice cream after. I'll see how the three of us get along, and make sure I don't remind her of the trauma." She used her power voice. "And we're not sleeping together until I know it's going to work, and I know I can trust you. So no foot rubs."

He blinked. "Baby—"

"You do that, and it goes okay with Sarah . . . I mean better than *okay*." She took a long breath. "You probably haven't yet seen how difficult it'll be for her. Kids will ask questions . . . about us." She sniffed, rubbed her nose. "*If* it all works—"

"Yes?"

She paused and pictured his gorgeous body stepping into the hot tub. She had to temper a lascivious grin. "I'll get a place at Vail on the Fourth. Arrange for Sarah to visit her cousins . . . if you still want me."

"Of course I—"

"And haven't found anyone else."

"There's no—"

"Those are the terms." She let go of his hand and wagged a finger again. "They are unconditional. And I want to go back to Lake Whitney, so you've got some time to get in shape. And start eating. I don't want to have to carry your ass down the mountain."

She brushed her lips against his, like she'd done the night in the parking garage. This time he responded, pulling her tight against his chest.

Kristen hoped *she* wouldn't break the probation.

ABOUT THE AUTHOR

STEVE CLARK PRACTICES medical law in Oklahoma City. He has attended the Book Passage Mystery Writers Conference in Marin County and taken writing classes at U.C.O. and Rose State College. He and his wife, Jane have five children. He received his BA in History and English and his J.D. at the University of Oklahoma. Kristen's adventures will continue in *Justice Is for the Deserving*, coming soon.